We In Pieces

Tales from Arctic Alaska

Elizaveta Ristrova

We In Pieces

This is a work of fiction. Any resemblance to actual persons, living or dead, is purely coincidental.

ISBN 13: 978-0-9846517-5-7

Library of Congress Control Number: 2011938169

Cover design by All Things That Matter Press and Elizaveta Ristrova
Published in 2011 by All Things That Matter Press

Thanks to Kate and Jim for the edits and suggestions!

Prologue- The Way It Was

"Tell me again the way it was before they came."

"We are here for thousands of years. We are always the People, the *Iñupiat*. We are one with everything around us. Land and sky, life and death is a continuing heartbeat ... the same sound as the steady boom of our drums ... the same motion as our arms turning slow in dance. We pass it down through generations just the way it is. *Aarigaa*—good! Then *they* come, and they turn our dance into little lines on white sheets."

Larry knew what his grandfather would say about the introduction of writing and money and everything else. But he liked to ask every so often, just to be sure.

More than fifty years later, when he's the Director of the Community Development Department of the largest and northernmost municipality in America, he wishes his grandfather were still here to tell him the way it was.

Larry Atkoot and the rest of us know without having to ask what happened after *they* came. It's all in writing, starting with their search for the Northwest Passage some 1800 years after the birth of Jesus. The *tanik*, the white man, came again fifty years later. The demand for oil—whale oil back then—drove them into the attic of the American territory, into Iñupiat land.

Then came the Alaska purchase in 1867, and *tanik* whaling swelled like rotting walrus. Even after the market for whale oil dried up, the price of baleen made *tanik* whaling worthwhile.

With *tanik* whaling came the *tanik* disease. In 1900 and 1902, flu and measles took out half the population of Iñupiat Eskimos on the Arctic coast. Then, just a few years later, *tanik* whaling was gone.

The religion that came with the whalers has stayed on. Who needs the *anatqut*—the shamans—and all the complicated taboos when praying to Jesus brings earthly blessings, missionary charity, and eternal life? It's easy to believe missionaries when they say the old ways are from the devil.

In the 1930s the last masked dances were performed. Then the masks became crafts to sell, and the *anatqut* who'd worn them had to disappear.

Christianity took root so deeply that even the American convention of separating church and state bows before it. It's one of the first things Vik Alcazar notices when she arrives from the Lower 48 at the end of 2007.

Vik thinks she's going to save the Arctic with her environmental lawyering skills. She marches thigh deep in the post-blizzard snow and darkness, wearing an inadequate coat and waiting for her own brand of salvation to kick in.

The sun rises in January to reveal a glistening desert of snow. Somehow, even in this desert, more and more snow falls. It stands in frozen mounds along the streets, between houses—anywhere it can fit. By April the ground is pregnant with seven months of snow. In May, when the continuous daylight shines through the snow crystals, they begin to melt or just vaporize into the desert air. Then the temperature rises, and the snow melts until the tundra becomes an endless wetland. In June, the tundra grass grows tall where no one walks. Birds arrive from across the continent to nest in it. Duty done, the sun goes behind the clouds and rarely shows itself for the rest of the summer. The last week in August is autumn. The grass turned red, and then the color of straw. In September, the snow starts to stick.

Vik has many disappointments in 2008 besides the lack of sun and the realization that winter will come back. The houses here aren't igloos or heat-efficient sod artifacts—they're just jumbles of wooden planks that look like they might blow away any minute. Huskies are alive and well, untied from their harnesses and retied to aimless, immobile lives in front of the plank houses. Only a couple of white people, the ones who make igloos in their backyards for fun, still use dogsleds for novelty's sake. Melting snow reveals rusted-out cars and appliances and other relics of Western junk. High fructose corn syrup rivals alcohol for the Western element most incompatible with the Iñupiat Eskimo civilization. The former is cheap and consumed to the point of diabetes. The latter is sold at bootleg prices but consumed past the state of oblivion. Gas is consumed as much as it is anywhere else in America, even though a gallon here cost three times more than one in the Lower 48.

But the Iñupiat civilization goes on, in spite of what the *taniks* may have done to it and what the *taniks* are saying about it now. There's no room for romanticizing in the Arctic.

Chapter 1- The Gift of the Whale

The large skulls parked in front of public buildings on the Arctic Slope of Alaska are more than just the remnants of previous feasts. They are symbols of the bowhead whale, which is the symbol of Iñupiat Eskimo identity.

The whaling civilization emerged on the Arctic Slope some 5,000 years ago. Why did it occur to a man standing on the shore, seeing the occasional blow or flip of a tail, that these creatures could be eaten? Who figured out that a single whale, at 50 tons, could save a village from starvation during the long winter? Who was the first to convince a group of men to go out on a boat and chase after the whale, and how many boats were lost before someone figured out how to kill the whale and bring it to shore?

There is a scattering of stories linking the modern whalers to the past, irretrievably bound up in the Iñupiaq language. Much of the collective memory has been lost. But one memory burns hotter than any other: what happened in 1977, when we found out that whaling was banned.

President Carter can take credit for that. He was the one who told the International Whalers Council that the Eskimos didn't need to go whaling anymore. But what did he know about the Iñupiat people, who might not be starving to death anymore, but who were watching the death of their identity?

The *tanik* anthropologists wrote about the Iñupiat: "Vigilant adaptation is the mark of a culture living in an environment with narrow margins of error." The whalers adapted, creating what the Americans called a "non-profit group." The Alaska Eskimo Whalers Council would fight the ban, organize the whaling communities, and hire lobbyists to go to Washington and shame the president.

The result: the quota.

Larry was 28 when the whalers signed a management agreement with the federal government, and Harow got its first quota of five whales. That fall, the whalers struck five whales but didn't land any of them. They could strike no more. Larry's dad paddled out with his sons, looking for the struck whales, but didn't find them.

Without whale, there could be no feast and no *maktak*—the top layer of whale blubber and the bottom layer of skin—to keep them warm in the winter. Larry remembered going without whale as a child in a Lower 48 Indian school. The food there was never filling, and he got skinny and pale. He foresaw a town of skinny and pale Iñupiat.

The outsiders who had imposed the quota didn't understand the Iñupiaq whaling traditions. It wasn't the Iñupiaq way to hunt with the intention of landing a set number of whales. It would be arrogant for a whaler to put a number on what he would get. Every whaler knows that the whale chooses to give itself to the *umialik*—the whaling captain—who deserves it, in honor of the captain's wife. And that if the whale's body is treated well, used to nourish the people, then its soul will return to the sea and become a new whale.

The quota was colonialism. The proud whaling captains strapped with the quota couldn't look their own people in the eyes. They asked themselves if this was what it meant to be American.

Yet most of the whalers obeyed the quota, lest the federal government ban whaling altogether. The first fall that the quota was in place, just as the last crew was coming in, an unstruck bowhead came up to the side of the boat to give itself up. The whalers let it go.

The Iñupiat Community of the Arctic, an umbrella tribal government for the Arctic Slope that had formed a few years before the Alaska Eskimo Whalers Council, sensed its displacement. Luther Ericsen, the leader of the tribal government, announced that he had no intention of obeying the quota. When he heard about the whale that got away, he went out in his boat to look for it.

Luther wasn't a member of the Alaska Eskimo Whalers Council, which meant he wasn't authorized by federal law to hunt for whales. He told the obedient whalers, "Any 15-year old who ever goes whaling has more scientific knowledge about the bowhead than those scientists who make up the quota. What's the point of your council anyway? You sign the management agreement with the federal government like they were holding a gun to your heads. You agree to impose a $10,000 penalty on yourself for violating the agreement. But there's no gun. The Iñupiat never give up their right to whaling before, and until you did, the U.S. laws couldn't affect us."

It was late in the spring whaling season already, and Luther couldn't find the willing whale. When he got back, he sent a telegram to President Carter advising him that Luther's tribe had passed a resolution to allow the hunt to continue. The telegram explained, "All government officials coming to monitor the hunt will have to confront themselves to our tribal government."

When the president didn't respond to the telegram after a week, Luther sent him another telegram, with copies to the United Nations, the Soviet Embassy in Washington, the Secretary of State, the Secretary of the Interior, the Alaska Governor, and the Alaska Eskimo Whalers Council.

"The quota was set by white fascist pigs like you," the telegram said. "If the U.S. will enforce the quota, then you have 3 days to evacuate your

U.S. citizens from the Arctic Slope. If I as an Iñupiaq *umialik* cannot meet my people's nutritional needs, then you leave us no choice but starvation. I already notify the USSR for détente."

Luther later had to explain to the skeptical Arctic Slope community that calling the U.S. president a white fascist pig was the only way to get anybody's attention about the whalers' situation. He hadn't really asked the Soviets to get ready for détente.

The Alaska Eskimo Whalers Council ignored Luther. Its members had taken a chance in heeding the quota, hoping that their obedience would boost their negotiating power. They would stick to it.

The whalers felt somewhat vindicated when the *tanik* scientists agreed to work with the Iñupiat to do a recount of the whales the next spring. The Iñupiat would show the *taniks* that their numbers were wrong.

What Luther had said about the scientists' lack of knowledge was true. The *taniks* didn't know that the slightest bit of noise would send the whales away. They didn't understand the way the whales traveled, and how the lead whales set the path for the others. And they couldn't tell the difference between male and female whales, like the oldest whaling captains could.

When the continuous daylight arrived in the spring of 1979, a group of Iñupiat men were sitting on the ice in 12-hour shifts to count. They would sit here for the next 10 springs, showing the *tanik* biologists how to count whales. They did it for their grandchildren and great-grandchildren and great-great-grandchildren, so these future generations would have the same chance as this generation of whalers. So their identity would not die.

The recounts paid off. The bowhead quota for Harow went up to 32 strikes, and would stay in the thirties until 2011.

The Iñupiat whalers shared seven of their allotted strikes with the Siberian Yupik Eskimos, who had forgotten how to whale but were amenable to being re-taught by their Alaskan cousins.

In the 1990s, the whalers made three mission trips to give the Siberian Eskimos back the knowledge the Soviet Union had taken away from them. Gill Whitehead, the Iñupiaq grandson of Harow's first white settler, went on each trip. The Siberian Eskimos' story was almost sad enough to make him proud to be an American.

The Siberia Eskimos had been hauled off their native islands in the 1950s and relocated to settlements on the mainland. One Japanese boat operated by white Russians caught all of the 169 gray whales allotted in the Siberian Eskimos' quota and delivered the carcasses to each settlement. Like their Alaskan cousins, the Siberian Eskimos greeted the whales with the traditional welcoming drink of water. But then the whales were fed to blue foxes at breeding farms the Soviets had set up. The blubber was rendered down in huge vats and shipped back to Moscow to be used as machine lubricant. The Eskimos ate meat imported from Vladivostok.

In 1991, the Soviet Union crashed and the Eskimos were left with nothing. There was only one elder in Chukotka, Russia who still remembered when the Siberian Eskimos lived on the islands and whaled. The old man cried when he understood that Gill had come to rekindle the extinguished flame. Gill gave the man a $1,000 darting gun, and the man gave Gill a solid ivory antique harpoon that Gill would later sell to the Iñupiat museum in Harow for $3,000.

The Alaska whalers donated motor boats and a forklift to the Siberian Eskimos.

"What do we do when this breaks?" the old man asked Gill. "There's no one here who can fix it, and no money to buy more."

Gill didn't know how to answer. Alaska's Iñupiat Eskimos have been blessed with oil money. The Siberian Eskimos have not.

Gill is far more used to answering the questions of *tanik* Outsiders, who don't think Eskimos should be using modern technology to hunt whales. He likes to respond, "Did you go out and shoot your hamburger with a bow and arrow?"

The Iñupiat abandoned bows and arrows and ivory harpoons a century ago for *tanik* weapons. If *tanik* weapons can kill more gently and quickly than the old harpoons, wouldn't it offend the whales to deliver anything less than a fatal gunshot?

When Gill got on the plane to leave Chukotka for the last time, all he could think about was the blank, hungry look of the Siberian Eskimos, and how the women, even the ones who were part *tanik,* were not beautiful the way he'd imagined Russian women to be. He was glad when his plane touched down in Harow.

Gill's maternal grandfather, who was Larry Atkoot's paternal grandfather, was a young man when the *tanik* whalers first came to Harow in the late 1800s. He was one of the few Eskimos willing to work with the *tanik* whaling crews in exchange for American goods. He watched the *taniks* break up the half-ton of baleen that came out of each whale. Who would have thought that people down below would pay nearly five dollars for a pound of it, or that women would use it in their dresses?

Gill's grandfather said nothing when the other men chastised him. He knew it was the beginning of the end, no matter what he did. He watched in silence while the Iñupiat around him got sick with tuberculosis, measles, and flu. And he watched the *taniks* take the Iñupiat women for their wives.

A century later, Gill is one of the few in his generation who speak fluent Iñupiaq. He explains that it's because his father, the son of the first white settler and an Iñupiaq woman, kept him at home when all the other kids were being sent off to the Indian boarding schools.

Gill learned early how to hunt, and shot his first seal when he was six. It was incredible to him that one minute the animal could be barking up a storm and the next minute it was just a piece of meat. He laughed, but his father told him not to. That would offend the seal, his father explained. The seals didn't have to give themselves up—they chose to, just like the whales. One day they might get tired of men and slip under the sea ice forever.

Gill had to give his first seal to the oldest woman in the family to get her blessing. Otherwise, his father explained, he'd have a hard time catching anything else. The old woman let Gill have the seal skin on top of her blessing, and his mother made him a vest out of it. He wore it on the day he went with his older brothers to the airport, to send them back to the Indian school. They were seven, nine, ten, and twelve, but none had shot a seal yet. It occurred to Gill that his brothers might never shoot a seal. There would be more seals, then, ready to give themselves to Gill.

Gill was the only boy for four years of spring whaling, and he took on all the grunt work the whaling captains could give him. His first job was to help put the *umiaq*—the skin boat for whaling—and gear on the sled so the dogs could pull it.

Other whaling captains had skidoos, but Gill's father had scoffed at the idea. "When a skidoo runs out of fuel, that's it. But a dog keeps running until we catch something ... it knows that otherwise it don't eat."

The dogs would struggle down the trail that the whaling captains had cut through the ice. Gill ran alongside to steady the *umiaq* over the rough parts. Gill ran back and forth between the whalers, who were waiting near the open water for the first sight of a whale, and the tent where his mom was cooking. He brought the whalers donuts and Sailor Boy crackers. He plucked the feathers from the birds they shot. He chipped ice from the snow to make coffee.

Gill learned the hard way not to use the snow just outside the tent where the men slept at night. When the men tasted their own urine in the coffee, they tossed it at Gill.

In the spring that Gill was 10, the wind was stronger and the ice more brittle than anyone had seen in years. No one could catch a bird, and the whalers subsisted on nothing but Sailor Boy crackers and the donuts Gill's mother made. It was fortunate that, after watching the *tanik* whalers, the Iñupiat abandoned their belief that cooking on the ice would bring bad luck.

By the time the first whale finally came, a number of the crew members had gone back home. Gill's father gave him a paddle and told him he was going out with the crew to meet the whale. Gill took the paddle with relish and slid into the *umiaq*.

The crew drew closer to the spouting whale in absolute silence. Gill's father stood mutely at the bow, holding his weapon. It was a six-foot wooden shaft that would release a metal harpoon. Attached to the harpoon were a float with a long line, which would be used to keep track of the whale, and a darting gun, which would release a black powder bomb within the whale.

When the *umiaq* hit the whale's back, he thrust the weapon in with all his might. Almost instantly, the darting gun released its bomb. The whale shuddered, and its 20-foot tail sliced through the air like a giant helicopter blade.

Predictably, the whale dived, along with the harpoon. The whalers waited silently, praying and keeping their eyes on the float. After an hour, the water began to bubble and seethe, and the black form of the whale rose up again. The whalers rowed onto its back and thrust another harpoon into the flesh. When the bomb went off, the boat was still on the whale's back. The whale rolled. The *umiaq* rocked back into the water, tilting as if it might go all the way under. The whalers jumped back and forth to straighten it out, while the whale thrashed in every direction. They were all soaked, and the *umiaq* was filling up with water.

Gill's father released a final harpoon into the whale. The water turned red with blood, and the whale slowly released its soul.

There would not be any cheering just yet. The men prayed and fastened a harpoon to the tail. Two other boats joined them, and together they towed the whale to a butchering spot near the spit. Then the flippers—twice as tall as Gill—were cut off and hauled up onto the ice. All of the men heaved forward with the rope to drag the rest of the carcass onto land. Each time it was almost on the ice, it managed to slip back down into the bloody water. Finally the whalers butchered the animal from the water, pulling up chunks of flesh with giant hooks and dragging them messily onto the ice. In the end, they were able to haul the bony remains onto the ice and cut off every part.

The crew followed the traditional rules to distribute each piece of the whale to each whaler, in order of their participation. A properly divided whale would tell the other whales of the good treatment it received, and encourage these whales to give themselves to the same crew in the future.

Gill's father got the heart, most of the baleen, part of a kidney, and the *uati*—the circular cut from the navel to the genitals—since he was the first to strike the whale. Most of the back bone went to one of the artists for carving. Gill was allowed to have the giant blowhole, since no one else wanted it.

So many things have changed since then. There's no longer a sacred order to dividing up the parts of a whale. The whales caught in the spring are smaller than ever—small whales are easier to haul up onto the thin ice we have now. Motors do almost everything that human muscles used to do. The whale makes its final journey to the butchering spot on a forklift.

But when we gather together at holidays and festivals to share the whale, there is no less joy and triumph.

Chapter 2- The Birth of a Borough

History doesn't talk about how the Iñupiat discovered Arctic oil. Except for the archeologists and former tribe president Luther Ericsen, who asserts that the Iñupiaq collective memory goes back three ice ages, no one can explain how the Iñupiat had used oil seeps for fuel long before the *taniks* started drilling.

The *taniks* learned about Arctic petroleum just after they brought the source of whale oil to the brink of extinction. In 1923, the federal government declared Harow and its surroundings to be the "Naval Petroleum Reserve No. 4," an emergency oil supply for military purposes. The military dabbled in drilling over the years, but never found anything worth taking out of the ground. Then in 1968, nine years after Alaska became a state, massive reserves were found to the east at Prudhoe Bay. The State of Alaska and the federal government were poised to get the oil to market at all costs.

But piping oil over the frozen tundra meant wading through a morass of native land issues. Alaska Natives claimed the rights to all of Alaska. How, at the end of the morally enlightened twentieth century, could the "native occupation problem" be solved?

Congress came up with the Alaska Native Claims Settlement Act in 1971, a Little Mermaid sort of a bargain that allowed the Natives to get legs in the American capitalist society in exchange for all of their aboriginal land rights. The act created regional and village corporations out of tribes, threw bundles of cash at them, and let them pick 40 million acres from the land that hadn't already been taken by Alaska and the federal government.

People like Luther thought that Alaska Natives were crazy for going along with the act. He would say, "They want to give us their leftovers when we already got claim to the whole state and the sea ice beyond?" But most felt like they had little control over the *tanik* Congress 4,000 miles away.

The Iñupiat divide over the act would replay itself every time American Progress marched across the Arctic Slope. Should we acknowledge the "progress" and try to get something out of it, or refuse to acknowledge it and take nothing at all?

In the meantime, with aboriginal rights out of the way, work on the pipeline took off. In the spirit of taking *something* rather than nothing, Iñupiat leaders decided to create a municipality that could tax the oil. Led by Harow native Evan Hooper, they created the Arctic Slope Borough—a municipality the size of Minnesota covering all the land north of Alaska's Brooks Mountain Range.

As the first elected mayor, Evan Hooper pledged that the Iñupiat would no longer have to carry their wastes to village tank trucks or hunt for blocks of blue ice to melt for drinking water. People would be able to take off their parkas in their houses and still be warm. There would be well-paying cash jobs for everyone who wanted them. And the subsistence harvest would thrive.

Hooper died in 1980, leaving behind a few new public works and a number of museum icons. Ernie Whitehead, the 33-year-old graduate of an Indian school and first cousin of Gill Whitehead, assumed the role of mayor. It would be up to him to take Harow from the Stone Age to the space age as fast as possible. He knew that getting there would require lots more public works, which would raise the Borough's debt from $435 million to $1.2 billion in three years. But Ernie Whitehead was bringing Evan Hooper's dream of universal toilets to life.

Installing flushable toilets in the middle of the frozen tundra required constructing the "Utilador," a masterpiece among public works. The rock-saw, basically a giant chainsaw on a bulldozer, brought in to make the Utilador was one of only seven in the world. Ten-by-ten-foot sections of permafrost were cut out of the ground, leaving behind a six-by-six foot tunnel that would carry Harow's sewage, drinking water, phone lines, cables, and electricity.

Sandwiched between the tunnel and the permafrost were layers of PCP-coated wood, insulation, and gravel. The Public Works director had figured that the wood needed to be covered with PCP so it wouldn't mess up the insulation. He had gotten it on the cheap from Portland, Oregon, where PCP coatings had been banned.

The reason for the ban became apparent when workers installing the wood found themselves covered with rashes.

When Luther Ericsen got wind of the rashes, he came out for a firsthand look.

The workers showed him the label that came with the wood. It was some sort of "Materials Safety Data Sheet" saying that the wood was treated with chemicals, and should be handled with protective clothing and dust masks or respirators and goggles. The label also said that exposed areas of the skin should be thoroughly washed. The workers, dressed only in jeans and sweatshirts, looked at each other. "Nobody ever tell us that," one of them said.

Luther was indignant. He was well aware that the federal government had exposed the Iñupiat to radiation, but he never thought that a Borough formed by Evan Hooper would expose the Iñupiat to PCP. Not that he was one of those mindless devotees to the Borough, like so many in Harow seemed to be. It worried Luther that all the tax revenue from the oil was going only to the Borough, and not to his tribal government. The Borough controlled everything—schools, jobs, and housing. There was no way for a village or a tribe to "opt out" of the Borough. To Luther, the Borough was undermining Native sovereignty.

Luther went to the director of Public Works the next day to ball him out. The director wasn't there, so Luther left a message telling him to get rid of the PCP or else.

A week later, Luther came back to the site to make sure Public Works had complied with his directive. But the same wood was still there.

"They just take the labels away, but leave the wood," one of the workers explained. "*Aaqqaa*—it stinks."

It took a rousing meeting between Luther and the Public Works director to get the workers protective clothing, and a plea to the Borough Assembly to have the wood scraps hauled away, instead of burned onsite.

Mayor Ernie Whitehead was a bit annoyed by Luther's antics. The Borough Assembly had already invited up an expert to test the PCP coating, and the expert had explained that it was only a 5% PCP solution, insoluble in water, and virtually harmless.

Luther's tribal government hired a different expert, who tested the water near the Utilador and told Luther that small quantities of PCP had leached into it.

"Those PCPs will kill people, for sure," Luther said to anyone who would listen. "And I don't think the elders want to see their grandchildren deformed."

Luther didn't mention the other thing the expert had said, that PCP couldn't dissolve into the water unless it somehow combined with diesel or caught on fire.

A week later, fire broke out at the Utilador. Mayor Whitehead and the Public Works director rushed to the scene, but appropriately masked Borough firefighters were already putting the fire out. To confirm his own hypothesis that PCP was safe, Mayor Whitehead climbed down into the Utilador and took off the mask he'd been given. He came out with no apparent injury.

"See?" he said to the Luther later. "I'm still alive."

"Yeah, but wait. You might get deformed grandkids."

Undaunted by the tribal government's lack of jurisdiction over anything but tribal affairs, Luther directed the tribe's board to pass a resolution banning PCP from the Arctic Slope. To increase the likelihood that the ban would take effect, Luther presented the Assembly with a similar resolution. But the Assembly didn't see the need to do anything more. It had already hired the *tanik* expert, who said everything was fine.

A man from the state labor agency did come out and interview the workers, but nobody ever heard anything from him after that. Mayor Whitehead concluded that there must not have been any problems.

The tribal government started to have its own problems. The federal Bureau of Indian Affairs, which funded the tribal government, decided that something funny was going on with the hundreds of contracts and social service programs that the tribal government ran. The Bureau yanked the tribe's funding and demanded to see a paper trail. But the loss of funds meant that the tribe couldn't afford an accountant, and the Bureau didn't want to pay for one. So the Bureau ended up handling most of the tribal government services out of its office in Fairbanks. This was one of many examples we would see of Outsiders making decisions for the Iñupiat.

Luther retired from the tribal government in disgust. He didn't know a heck of a lot about contracts, but he was pretty sure the feds were trying to wipe out his tribe, at least administratively.

Sometime after the installation of the Utilador and Luther's retirement, the Public Works Director, Mayor Ernie Whitehead, and everyone else who had contributed to the Borough's billions in debt were indicted for income tax evasion, wire fraud and extortion.

No one in Harow blamed Mayor Whitehead. The vulture lobbyists, left over from Evan Hooper's administration, were the ones picking the Borough's treasury clean. The lobbyists-cum-mayoral advisors got salaries three times bigger than the mayor's, and the companies they owned made obscene profits off Borough contracts. We didn't know back then that the lobbyists also paid for Ernie Whitehead's new house, his boat, and his groceries.

The best years for Ernie Whitehead and maybe the Borough ended in 1989 with an eight-month trial, the longest in Alaska's history. Ernie Whitehead, seeking cover in his image as a naive young Iñupiaq, cooperated with prosecutors in return for a 30-day jail sentence and a $5,000 fine. The lobbyists were hit with seven years in prison and $11 million in collective fines.

Later, one of the lobbyists secretly tape-recorded Ernie Whitehead admitting that he gave false testimony after the prosecutor had threatened to publish nude photos of Ernie's wife. The photos showed her before and after a lobbyist-sponsored plastic surgery. Armed with this confession, the lobbyists appealed. But the convictions stuck, and Ernie and his plastic wife both went on to serve many terms as Borough Assembly members.

After Mayor Ernie Whitehead went to jail, we elected James Ahgak five times in a row. He won on a platform of cutting off the rich *tanik* Outsiders who came to Harow to suck up the Borough's fortunes. Mayor

Ahgak had worked on and off for the oil industry, and he wasn't opposed to development, but that didn't mean he had to like the people it brought to the Arctic Slope.

Once, he came reeling down the stairs of the Borough building just after Shant Oil Co. representatives had left, taking large whiffs of the air and laughing.

"Smells like *taniks*," he announced.

"Maybe you smell me," one of the receptionists said. "I'm part-white."

Now that it's 2008, who in Harow isn't part-white? The Whitehead clan is white enough to have freckles and to burn in the summertime. Their first *tanik* ancestor, the grandfather of Gill and Ernie Whitehead, was one of five commercial whalers who had rolled onto Harow's shores in the 1870s. Since then, many more *taniks* have come, contributed to the gene pool of the Whiteheads and all of Harow, and pulled in massive Borough salaries.

Taniks aren't the only Outsiders to come to Harow, looking to get a piece of the oil money. With its slew of Asians, islanders, *taniks*, and everything in between, Harow is the least Iñupiaq settlement on the Arctic Slope. The Asians and islanders are behind every check-out counter and the wheel of every taxi. They rake in the good wages for as long as they can stand it, and then go back to Thailand, Tonga, or wherever they came from.

Every now and then, being steeped in so much diversity makes Larry Atkoot a little nervous. Many of the Outsiders have dominating attitudes that can make Eskimos feel insecure. Even so, the urge to follow the dominant force is strong. Larry remembers the first time he saw a flush toilet at an Indian school. It would be twenty years before he was finally able to build his own house with flush toilets. Just after that, microwaves came out. Two years later, he and his wife bought one, and they ate nothing but microwavable foods for months.

Borough Assemblyman Chuck Lovett does what he can to keep the Iñupiat identity strong. In 1997, he led the Assembly to enact an employment preference law for qualified Native Alaskans. In 1998, the Assembly extended the ordinance to unqualified Native Alaskans who might be able to get qualified after being hired. These laws lasted until 2003, when the Borough's Housing Department rejected an application from a Filipino plumber in favor of an Eskimo who was planning on going to school to be a plumber one day. The Filipino sued and won.

The Assembly had to repeal its laws on preferential hiring, but it allowed the Housing Department to break off from the Borough and incorporate as a Tribal Housing Authority that was free to engage in preferential hiring and housing.

In 2004, the federal government opened up Arctic waters to oil and gas leasing, and opposition to offshore drilling became a much better platform than racism. That was the year Charlie Kitok beat James Ahgak in the mayoral election. Instead of taking a sixth term as mayor, James Ahgak went off to work for Shant Oil Co.

Mayor Kitok was the one who promoted Larry Atkoot from a field inspector to the director of the Borough's Community Development Department. In appointing his old friend, Mayor Kitok had to overlook the five years Larry spent in jail for an alleged sex assault. Of course, Mayor Kitok knew that Larry had never done it. Larry might drink every now and then and go off with someone who wasn't his wife—hell, the mayor might do the same—but Larry was no pervert.

As the director, Larry is entrusted with regulating all the oil industry from the Brooks Mountain Range to three miles offshore. Larry is uneasy with this power, although he won't burden the rest of us with his doubts.

If Larry is ever bothered about something, no one's going to know about it—maybe not even him. When his garage burned down while his wife was away, he rebuilt it without ever telling her what happened. When his mother died, he didn't cry. When he walked in on his brother and another man, he just closed the door and never mentioned it. We see Larry only with only two expressions. One is stoic and unreadable. The other is a half smile he puts on for difficult conversations, especially with white Outsiders.

Larry has one of the bigger offices at the Community Development Department, which is fortunate, since it holds stacks and stacks of paper. People in the Borough talk about going electronic and getting rid of all the paper. But Larry hasn't even come to terms with the stacks of paper, let alone their electronic versions. Sometimes, when digging though the stacks for a lost permit application, he's tempted to just push them over and walk out of the office. When did we get so dependent on all these white sheets with lines etched on them?

Mayor Kitok was also responsible for appointing Bertie Bowman as the director of the Borough's Law Department. Bertie is one of the only black people in Harow and the longest-serving lawyer in town. Unlike Larry, she embraces the modernizing vision of the Borough's first mayor, Evan Hooper. She thinks, why shouldn't these people have a swimming pool and functioning cars in addition to their traditional ways? When Assistant Borough Attorney Vik Alcazar tells Bertie there's no way Iñupiat people can live in both their traditional world and the modern world, Bertie asks her sharply why not.

"This modern western way of life is just unsustainable," Vik explains. "It works out all right if you can just go around colonizing the world and messing up other people's homes, but if you expect to stay put in your own backyard and still consume all that food and oil and make all that crap, it's not going to work."

"Anyway," Vik says, "it's not like all this oil money is solving all the problems here." She takes the liberty to paraphrase some wisdom she got from an Eskimo elder at a recent oil company meeting. The man shouted at the oil company representative like an angry Job yelling at God, "You have given me light, you've given me nice clothes, but you haven't even worried one bit about my health. What are you? I can't get like you. I can't get mad at you. I don't have the power to tell you to stop, but at least recognize the fact that you're dirty. You're filthy! And we gotta pay for it, and here it is again."

Bertie sighs, realizing that Vik probably won't be working here for too long.

Nelson Cowen, the Borough's lieutenant mayor, likewise doubts that Vik will last more than a year. In his time with the Borough, he's seen a lot of people come and go. They like the money and the power, but they can't take the darkness and the Outsider scorn. The ones who stay the shortest are usually the Bohemian environmentalists bent on saving whales. Vik seems to fall into this category.

Nelson has been with the Borough for most of the past three decades, ever since he came up from Anchorage to work for Mayor Ernie Brown. If he's not working for a mayor or heading the Law Department, then he's down in Anchorage doing consulting work for one of the departments. Mayors call on Nelson because he seems to know how everything works, regardless of whether he really cares about us.

Nelson and his wife, who runs the Borough's government affairs office out of Anchorage, make sure that the mayor has a script for everything he says in public. Nelson knows how easy to get off topic it is for a well-meaning Iñupiaq mayor, especially one that goes off on occasional drinking binges.

Back in the 1980s, Nelson served as the head of the Law Department under Mayor Ernie Whitehead. He was the only Whitehead appointee to escape indictment, and only because he wrote daily memos on everything he encountered and mailed them to himself. During Mayor Whitehead's trial in 1989, Nelson came to court with the unopened envelopes and a contemptuous smile for everyone there.

A journalist who used to live in Harow before he relocated to Iowa is in charge of writing all of the mayor's press releases. No one in the press knows about him—that way no one can call him up and pester him with questions. Nelson knows that once the Borough starts talking to the journalists, they'll twist everything around, and we'll all come out looking like blood-thirsty savage whale-killers.

Nelson is even careful about what he says to people in the Borough. The lawyer Vik replaced—a young guy fresh out of law school—quit when he learned about the outside counsel Nelson kept on hand for sensitive matters. Nelson tried to explain that the Borough has to deal with a lot of issues that aren't well suited for the Law Department staff. Harow's a cozy town, and anything he sends to the Law Department is bound to get passed on to someone who shouldn't be hearing about it, especially with the turnover rate being so high.

"But you're using the same law firm who represents Shant Oil in the law suit we brought against Shant's offshore Arctic drilling," the young lawyer pointed out.

Nelson clicked his tongue, sympathetic to the idealism of youth.

"You know the rules of professional conduct as well as any lawyer," Nelson said. "As long as the firm keeps a firewall between the lawyer working for us and the lawyer working for Shant, there's no violation of the rules. That's the way it works in the real world. We have to take what we can get."

The lawsuit against drilling in the Beaufort Sea, just north of the Borough, was the product of a shaky alliance the Borough has with the tribal government, known as the Iñupiat Community of the Arctic Slope, the Alaska Eskimo Whalers Council, and environmentalists. The tribal government and the whalers worry that drilling noise would drive whales out of the hunting range, and that an oil spill would ensure that the whales would never return. The environmentalists can live with a few dead whales at the hands of the Iñupiat, as long as it cuts down on the whales killed by the oil industry and the chances of a massive oil spill.

The environmentalists do their best to convince the Iñupiat that they care about subsistence. We know they don't, but it doesn't matter. What matters is the environmentalists' money and lawyering ability, combined with the compelling story of a small group of natives whose garden is the ocean. The result of this combination was that in 2007, the court blocked Shant Oil Co.'s Arctic offshore drilling plans. The court said that inadequate consideration had been given to the impacts the drilling would have on the Iñupiat whalers.

Most of the environmentalists are happy to give the glory to the Iñupiat whalers. Without the alliance, theirs would be the proverbial lone voice in the wilderness. And Big Oil might buy off the Iñupiat, like it did with minority communities everywhere else.

Vik, who hails from a state that was completely bought off by the petrochemical industry years ago, doesn't think that the values of the Borough or the Iñupiat are immune from being rerouted by Big Oil Money. As much as the Borough harangues about offshore drilling, it's quite happy to allow drilling in areas that it can tax. Ninety percent of the

Borough's revenue comes from the spider web of pipelines and wells extending across the Slope and three miles into the sea, where the Borough's taxing authority ends.

Yet even with an annual tax revenue of $13 billion, a fifth of the Borough's 5,000 or so Iñupiat residents live below the poverty level. Fifty years ago, not having money wouldn't have been such a big deal. But today, everything costs money, even subsistence. Hunters need snowmachines and gas to travel from static villages through the hundreds of miles of ever-shifting subsistence areas. A hunter could spend a month's salary on a hunting trip, only to come home empty-handed.

Fifty years ago, whaling cost nothing in dollars, only in labor. By the late 1970s, a couple of weeks of whaling in the fall cost a community $2,000. These days, between the fancy humane weapons, tracking equipment, grub, gas, etc., one whaling captain can spend $20,000 each season.

Of course, there's something to be gained from all of this money. Hunting and whaling have become much safer, and fewer lives are lost. A snowmachine can be started in an instant, whereas a pack of sled dogs might take an hour to harness. It no longer takes an entire community pulling desperately on a rope to harvest a whale. We're warm, and no one's starving.

We often hear people say, "We can't go back," although it might be just as true to say, "We can't go forward." We aren't going to get off oil any time soon.

Chapter 3- Iñupiaq Face

Bertie is a sucker for Native art. She lingers at the entrance to the Harow grocery store, where local artists sit waiting for tourists or enlightened *tanik* residents to buy their art. Most of the art is made out of whalebone, baleen, or ivory. Items can go for $300, depending on the enlightenment of the buyer. Each year, Bertie drops at least $700 on Native art, usually from the peddlers who show up weekly at the Law Department. There's no prohibition on soliciting at Borough offices.

Bertie's desk and shelves are covered with Native art—animals and little demons with jade eyes who should probably be covered or turned the other way at night. Bertie doesn't know when she'll leave Harow, but when the time comes, she wants to have something worth taking.

Bertie dusts her art and vacuums her office twice a year. She doesn't want to waste too much time cleaning up. Cleaning is too much like exercise, which she hates. She could have the department hire a janitor, but she's decided against it. The idea of someone coming in at night, pilfering through the files, makes her nervous. And people who worry too much about appearances and propriety make her nervous. She cut off her afro years ago, leaving behind a controlled crop of graying hair. Since she doesn't bother with hair, clothes, makeup, or jewelry, getting ready for work takes amazingly little time.

Bertie feels a bit removed from the whites who huddle together at wine and cheese parties as if they were ex-pats, or colonists. She knows what it means to be a suppressed race, and she welcomes the chance to expose the racism of the people who come here just for the oil money.

Back when she first got here in the late 1980s, she heard whites say things about the Iñupiat like, "We just give 'em a few bucks and take their land, and they don't even see it coming." She also heard the Iñupiat complain, "We're tired of being treated like Indians!"

Bertie sometimes wonders if it's wrong for her to be leading the Law Department. Is she taking a job that should belong to an Iñupiaq? But then, she only knows of three Iñupiat who've gone to law school, and none of them came back to the Arctic Slope.

Former tribe president Luther Ericsen, now an elder with nothing to stop him from saying exactly what he thinks, likes to explain the "Outsider Problem" to anyone in the Borough who'll listen.

Luther sidelines Bertie and Vik after an Assembly meeting and declares, "The problem with the Assembly is they're starting to get Outsiders elected. And you know what happens when Outsiders start trying to run the place. Next thing you know, you got a *tanik* mayor and alcohol comes in and you stop praying in public and forget the Iñupiat values and it all just goes to hell."

Bertie tends to avoid Luther because he's so confrontational. When Luther lumbers into the Law Department, she usually picks up her phone and pretends to be talking to someone. Vik relishes Luther's appearances, mostly because he provides interesting commentary at public meetings and has the kind of voice that's good for yelling at dogs.

"You know that only half the population on the Slope right now are Iñupiat?" Luther says. "But thank the Lord, for voting purposes we got 74 percent. Because the *tanik* oil workers at Prudhoe Bay don't want to stay on the Slope more than two weeks at a time."

"So what do you do about all the people who are part Native and part white?" Vik asks, as Bertie slips off into the restroom. "I've heard some people say that the Whiteheads are too white too be Iñupiaq anymore. But then I've heard other people say that anyone with a drop of Iñupiaq blood who practices the Iñupiaq values is Iñupiaq. Which one is it?"

The old man doesn't acknowledge Vik. He continues talking to the space where Bertie stood. "You should see those *tanik* oilfield workers when they get on the plane to go back to Anchorage. It don't matter what time of day it is, he got a can of beer in one hand and a shot of tequila in the other. Can't even wait 'til he get home."

Vik tries again, "So how come local people aren't hired to do the work?"

Luther appears to look in Vik's direction. He's only got one good eye, and sometimes he wears a patch over the bad eye. Today he's not wearing the patch and Vik can't remember which one is the bad eye. She leans in, going back and forth between both eyes.

Vik has a way of standing too close to people and staring at them too long. There's something a little too sharp about her pointed nose and too unnerving about her large white teeth. Luther takes a step back before bellowing, "They won't use local workers! I know. I got hired to work over there in 1969. All of us got a trade—electricians, administrators, warehousemen, carpenters. But they only use the *tanik* Outsiders for the good jobs. I got to train to drive a truck so I can keep my job. I stay two years already, but they never hire me for the office job as an administrator. So I quit and start the Iñupiat Community of the Arctic."

Vik tilts her head and sort of nods. She watched as Bertie emerges from the restroom, only to be followed by Luther back to the Law Department.

Just by looking at Luther, Vik can't tell that he's Iñupiaq. He's almost as white as Gill Whitehead, and Vik thought Gill was white when she first got to town. She didn't figure it out until she asked Community

Development Department Director Larry Atkoot if Gill, a manager in the Community Development Department, ever did any subsistence like the Iñupiat.

Seemingly not bothered by Vik's ignorance, Larry gives Vik a half smile. "You know," he said, "my dad's an *umialik*, and my mom used to say, 'You can make a *tanik* Iñupiaq if you let him work with you.' She had a *tanik* brother-in-law that joined my dad's crew, and he learned everything, from when the ice is safe to all the names of the cuts."

"But can you turn an Eskimo into a, uh, *tanik*?" Vik asked.

Larry looked at her strangely and then laughed roughly. "Sure, send him to Indian school, make him forget the Iñupiaq language, and put him in an office 40 hours a week."

Larry was shipped off to one of many schools set up in the 1940s by the Bureau of Indian Affairs to educate the Eskimos and Indians in American English. The compulsory-school law cemented the bonds of civilization, requiring the Iñupiat to settle down in one place so the kids could go to school there. Entire communities uprooted themselves and moved to cities with schools, deciding to abandon their homes rather than their children.

Harow stayed in place, and its winters became long, childless winters. The kids returned like migratory birds in the summer, with new minds.

"It was like a lobotomy of our native identity," Larry would tell his nephews, when they complained about having to go to Harow High School.

Larry went to the Chemtok Indian School in Oregon, which had the honor of being the oldest continuously operating boarding school in the United States. He'd been sort of excited about going, since the recruiter told his parents he would make lots of Indian friends, and there would be real toilets and other American luxuries.

Larry learned that one of the luxuries was booze. The kids drank even though the punishment was being handcuffed to a chair. As for his fellow natives, only the Iñupiat were his friends. All the tribes beat each other up—it was their only defense against becoming assimilated.

The impacts of the Indian schools lingered long after they were closed. Indian-school students didn't speak Iñupiaq to their children. They wanted life to be easier for the next generation. And it was.

The children of the Indian-school students learned English on TV, went to school in cars, and came home to houses that were never cold. They grew up and some got office jobs. They shivered in their jeans and T-shirts during the run from the car to the office.

Now, it's up to the children of these children to relearn the Iñupiaq language. The Borough School Board has invested $5 million in language teaching technology just for this purpose. Each student at Harow High

School gets a laptop complete with a microphone, headset, and a disc containing Iñupiaq sounds that the student is supposed to imitate. The *tanik* kids actually catch on pretty well, but of course, the whole education system was created by the *taniks*.

The School Board has known for years that something must be done to get past the Western ways of teaching that denigrate the Iñupiaq culture. Most of the School Board members grew up going to Indian schools themselves, where they were taught that their only hope was to get an education and move to the big cities. The teachers didn't have to say it directly—each action reinforced the concept that the Iñupiat were stupid and hopeless.

In 2005, the School Board declared a no-homework policy for elementary and middle school students. The idea was that Iñupiat kids should be Iñupiat kids—they should get to play in the evening, and they should have time to learn more traditional skills from their elders. The Board also tried to hire more Alaska Native teachers, but this proved to be almost as difficult as it was for the Borough to hire Native lawyers.

So the School Board decided to focus on retention. In 2006, it raised annual teacher salaries to $50,000, and offered $7,000 in performance bonuses to teachers deemed effective. Troublemakers who wanted to change the Iñupiaq culture under the guise of raising standards wouldn't be deemed effective. The School Board President said that the Outside teachers would need to realize that the school and its kids had more to teach the teachers than the teachers had to teach them.

In 2007, the middle and elementary schools started teaching Western science for the first time. The eighth graders couldn't stand their teacher—a bird-like *tanik* who tried to tell them about things like pollution and decomposition.

"This is your chance to learn about science before you go off into the world and get a job!" the *tanik* teacher would howl. The kids rolled their eyes. They were perfectly capable of learning and reading at home—school was for hanging out.

And what does science have to do with a job? Most students have no more than one parent employed, usually with a Borough or a native corporation office job. Aside from these employers, just about the only jobs on the Arctic Slope are with the oil industry and the federal government. Two generations of Eskimos struggled against these very entities, and for many students, the idea of going to work for one of them is out of the question.

The *tanik* science teacher grew up in a world where nuns beat her with a stick when she talked in class. She didn't know what to do with kids who talked back to her. When one of the kids called her a bitch, she couldn't understand it.

"He's not even Iñupiaq," she told her husband. "He's a smart Filipino kid who used to make really good grades, but then he started acting just like everyone else. I don't know if he's just trying to fit in, or if he wants the same vacation every other kid is taking from any kind of discipline."

She told the superintendent she was quitting.

"Why?" he asked, not really wanting to know the response.

"The kids don't respect me. They don't even respect you. They don't listen to anyone."

The superintendent, a sympathetic white man, smiled gently and said, "We can't fix every problem that goes on at home. All we can do is try to inspire kids to do their best. If you can't accept that challenge, then you're better off in Anchorage."

"And," the teacher continued, "I only have a $600 budget for a whole year's worth of labs. I'm taking money out of my own pocket just to buy the materials we need. Meanwhile, you spend a couple hundred thousand on the football team each year."

The superintendent shrugged. A science teacher couldn't be expected to understand the reasoning behind the school budget. It was worth spending $180,000 a year on football if it lowered dropout rates and increased attendance. And oil companies were inspired to donate $500,000 towards the installation of a blue artificial turf field, which is free of snow three months a year.

Money started getting tight at the end of 2007, and the superintendent decided to resign before anyone accused him of mismanaging or even embezzling school funds.

The School Board still can't find anyone to take over the job. It keeps the superintendent on with a month-to-month contract until somebody else can be convinced to take the job for half the current pay. It holds out hope that an Iñupiaq superintendent can be found, or at least someone with Iñupiat values.

By now, everyone on the Arctic Slope should be able to list the Iñupiat values, even if not everyone practices them. They were popularized back in the 1980s, at the height of *tanik* excesses. An Iñupiaq Spirit Committee, formed by concerned citizens, identified fifteen Iñupiaq values: Sharing, Family, Knowledge of Language, Hunting Traditions, Respect for Nature, Humility, Compassion, Avoidance of Conflict, Love and Respect for Elders, Cooperation, Spirituality, Humor, Knowledge of Family Tree, Domestic Skills, and Hard Work.

At some point the last three values were weeded out, leaving the more biblical number of twelve. In 2006, the School Board contracted an artist to develop posters depicting each of the twelve values. Many would feature the former mayor Evan Hooper, who had told his people that native corporations and land wouldn't be enough to hold the Iñupiat together. Only Iñupiaq values could do that.

The School Board and the Assembly drafted a joint resolution to declare Evan Hooper's birthday as Iñupiat Day, and the School Board decided to launch the finished product on Iñupiat Day of 2007. A poster-hanging ceremony was held in the gym at Harow High School. Assemblyman Chuck gave a little speech about Iñupiat history and values for the students, and each member of the Assembly hung a poster on the wall.

Afterwards, a curvaceous high school girl in tight jeans and a belt supporting two cell phones came up to him and said, "This is awesome. I didn't know our lifestyle was that awesome."

Chuck smiled, smoothed back his hair quickly, and shook her hand. "What's your name?"

"I'm Gloria Whitehead, Ernie Whitehead's granddaughter." She nodded towards her grandfather, who was serving his third term in a row as the President of the Assembly.

Chuck nodded, although a trace of a scowl darkened his large pasty face. He couldn't stand Ernie Whitehead and Mayor Kitok, precisely because they had lost sight of the Iñupiat values. The mayor had surrounded himself with *taniks*. And Ernie was a Whitehead with a family history of taking advantage of the Iñupiat.

But Gloria Whitehead seemed to understand something that the rest of her family didn't. Chuck put his hand on her shoulder and struggled to say something that might inspire her.

"Don't forget your values," he finally mumbled.

"Right on," Gloria said, popping her gum.

Chapter 4- All Around the Borough

We sometimes say that Harow is the only place in America with two mayors. There's the mayor of the Arctic Slope Borough, Mayor Kitok. And then there's the mayor of Harow, one of Harow's many Whiteheads. The other settlements on the Arctic Slope also have their own mayor and "city" council.

The city government is one of three entities in charge of each village. The second entity is the Native Village, the tribal government, which has its own council but no land. Congress gave the land to the third entity, the Native Village Corporation, when it passed the Alaska Native Claims Settlement Act in 1971. The act also set up regional native corporations, which got a few patches of land outside of the villages.

Some of the native corporations sputtered and died. Others caught on to capitalism so well, they outdid their *tanik* competitors. These are the corporations that now own everything in the villages that's not owned by the Borough, including the grocery stores that sell milk for $10 a gallon. They say the money goes back to the shareholders. The corporations have subsidiaries all over the world, run by *taniks*, taking advantage of the U.S. Department of Defense's preferential contracting program for native corporations and small businesses.

The Northern Slope Regional Co., the Native Regional Corporation that owns land across the Arctic Slope, is Alaska's most profitable corporation, year after year. Oil companies rely on the Regional Co. not only for its land, but also for its equipment, technical assistance, and public relations with the Iñupiat people. At public meetings, representatives of the corporation appear alongside the oil companies, testifying that air pollution and subsistence impacts won't be a big deal.

The spills are hard to overlook, though. We can count on a big crude oil spill at least once a year. BX Petro's Alaska record is 201,000 gallons at Prudhoe Bay in 2006. In 2007, Cacoco Oil left a 4,000-gallon oily Christmas present on the tundra near its Alpine site. In 2008, it was 25,000-gallons from BX's Middle Point oil field northwest of Prudhoe Bay. But the vast majority of oil spills are tiny—the oil companies tell us the tundra can eat them up with no trouble.

Sometimes we believe them. Sometimes we don't. Sometimes the Regional Co. representatives don't even believe their own rhetoric, and stand up at the meetings to testify against what their oil company colleagues just said. We never knew who's on whose side. Maybe we don't know what sides we're on ourselves.

When the Regional Co. first formed, its directors were the same as the Borough's Assembly members, and all were whalers. All were unified in their opposition to offshore drilling. But by the 21st century, when offshore drilling began to seem inevitable, the Regional Co. and other native corporations prepared themselves to make the most of it.

The president of the native village corporation for the village of Winters is working on a deal with Shant Oil Co. to provide a supply base for offshore operations. Vik is amazed to learn that this is the same man who led the only Winters crew to catch a whale in 2007. But then, Vik doesn't understand whaling in the first place, or the reverence wrapped around whaling captains. Anyone who's a whaling captain always introduces himself to a white person as such. Luther Ericsen starts every speech at every meeting with the words, "I'm Luther Ericsen, an *umialik*, a whaling captain." It's the very foundation of his identity.

Being a whaling captain isn't something you retire from. Season after season, whaling captains sit in their *umiat*—their whaling boats—like Queen Elizabeth II refusing to get off the throne. Most of the whaling captains are so old that their mouths tremble involuntarily at public meetings. Vik can't imagine how they manage to go on living in the same place and doing the same thing year after year, century after century.

But even the sacred aspects of whaling are changing. Vik overhears a conversation in the Community Development Department about the new crop of whaling captains.

"They don't share like they used to. It used to be when somebody strike a whale, all the other crews stop and help. Not anymore. Last spring, only four whales got struck, and only two landed up on the ice."

"That's 'cause those crews are full of cowboys. Everybody knows you can't get a 40-foot whale in the spring—how you're going to pull that thing up on that thin ice? They just want to show off."

"And then the other whale rotted already because they don't cut it up soon enough. *Ikkii*—yuck!"

Most of us know that the body heat of the whale is enough to cook it from the inside if it isn't opened up right after the crew takes its picture with the whale.

"Anyhow, the whaling captains who don't help, they're not sharing their knowledge, either. Their crews gonna die out because they don't teach anyone new."

"It's a shame. Not sharing the knowledge, it's like not sharing the meat."

Larry sees Vik and nods at her. The others look at her skeptically. Vik has no idea what the politically appropriate thing to say is here. She sure doesn't want to keep talking about whale meat. She decides to diss white people by talking about a movie she's seen called "Ending Jim Crowe in Alaska." Everyone can rally around this.

"Would you believe there used to be signs in Juneau restaurants that said, 'No dogs or Natives allowed?'" Vik asks. Everyone is quiet, and Vik realizes that there were no whites there to fill the silence with nervous laughter.

"That's the *tanik* for you," one of the men finally mutters, wondering back to his desk.

"Yep, pretty embarrassing," Vik announces. Vik never feels embarrassed for herself, because she has a vague sense of superiority over everyone else regardless of their race.

A superiority complex is not an asset for the Borough's new Outside employees, who typically spend years kowtowing to their superiors and local leaders before they get any respect. Vik has known this since her job interview, when Bertie asked her, "What does the chain of command mean to you?" Once she was hired, Bertie told Vik to never speak directly to the mayor. Any communication from Vik would have to go first through Bertie, and then up to Nelson, the lieutenant mayor.

It's obvious that Nelson makes Bertie nervous. She calls him "her boss" even though she hasn't worked directly under him since he was the Borough Attorney three years ago. But Nelson makes a lot of people nervous. He's 6'4", white-haired, and smarter than everyone else.

Vik realizes this the first time she talks to him. She actually feels her own superiority complex waiver as he picks apart a legal memo she's written. After that, she avoids talking to him about anything work-related. She learns that he's a recovering Catholic, still suffering from a heavy dose of sexual repression and vacuous guilt. She puts Nelson on the defensive by quizzing him as to what Jesus would have done to address various Borough problems.

Nelson, aware that the duty of holding the Borough together has been placed squarely on his shoulders, works 12-hour days. He keeps his sanity with regular workouts at the high school pool, which the Borough had paid for in the interest of community health. They used to let him come in before the general swim time, so he could have the pool all to himself. But these days something is always breaking or going wrong at the pool, and the School Board doesn't want the liability of letting a lawyer poke around a place that's supposed to be closed.

Now when Nelson swims, it's during regular hours, through swarms of nameless kids. Nelson doesn't have any kids, and this is the only time he ever has to deal with them. The kids don't have a care in the world. They swim backwards without looking and run into him, or they jump in the pool, cannonball style, and almost land on top of him.

Nelson likes teachable moments, so he usually takes the opportunity to explain to the children that their careless behavior could result in an accident. He watches them get out of the pool without even acknowledging him, leaving behind their towels or even the clothes they came in. He sighs helplessly sometimes, telling himself he's doing the best he can for the Iñupiat people.

Chapter 5- Lord Over Harow

Larry's grandfather was an *anatquq*—a shaman—and traditional healer from the village of Point Courage, the oldest settlement still standing in the Western hemisphere. He never converted to Christianity and wouldn't let go of the old teachings. He told Larry that the world hadn't always been so stuck in time and space, and one could move from the physical world to that of the spirits, or from the form of man to an animal.

"Why you don't turn into a bird now?" Larry once asked his grandfather.

His grandfather shook his head furiously, and said, "*Naagga*—no, the door is closed. The only way to do it is go back in time, and this is also lost." Larry's grandfather had heard the tales of whole villages renouncing Christianity and returning to shamanism, but it would not happen here.

"Why?" Larry asked.

"You think there's answers to everything. They already teach you that."

Larry's grandfather had taught Larry to hunt. He took him out to *Tuungaqagvik,* the Place of Devils, and the other spots where most Eskimos were scared to hunt.

"You got to remember that animals decide to let human hunters take him," Larry's grandfather said. "Moose, caribou, and wolves are faster than you, they got better eyesight."

When they were out hunting together, Larry's grandfather would sing the song for the animals. They always came, especially the seals. They even looked at his grandfather, with soft brown eyes that could have been human. It was as if they didn't mind being taken by him.

Larry's grandfather said that in the old days, seals could take off their seal coats and walk on the shore like humans. There was a story of a man who hid one of the seal coats, so the lady whose coat it was couldn't go back to sea. The man said he would give back the coat in seven years if she married him, and she agreed. They had a child. At the end of the seven years, she asked for her coat back so she could return to the sea. By then, her skin was drying up and her flesh was wasting away. But the husband was heartbroken, and wouldn't let go of the coat. The lady picked up the child, ran out to the end of the shorefast ice, and plunged both of them into the icy water. The husband never knew whether she died or just turned into a seal again.

"What happened to the boy?" Larry asked.

"I think they both come back as seals," Larry's grandfather said.

"And the man?"

"His people turn away from him. They know he took too much."

"Where'd the man go?"

"He goes away and never come back." Larry's grandfather said with a sigh.

Larry didn't realize until he grew up that his grandfather, like the man in the story, was an outcast. He was the only one in his village who didn't believe the missionaries, and wouldn't come with his wife and children to the church. People stopped going to him for healing—they waited until a traveling *tanik* nurse from the main mission came into town.

Larry's mother, the only daughter of the *anatquq*, saw lots of her friends die waiting for the nurse to come. After she grew up and moved to Harow, she joined the Fresh Start church, because its people had the power to heal through God, simply by laying their hands on the sick. It was the closest thing to the teachings of her father.

Even with the Lord working through the people, too many Eskimos died before their time. They fell through ice, were shot or shot themselves, or got lost in the snow and never came back.

When the Second World War came, the Eskimos joined the National Guard and offered themselves up as soldiers. Now, in 2008, they're doing it again, this time for Iraq and Afghanistan. A month ago, Larry's 19-year-old cousin came home from the war in a coffin. The boy never actually made it to the battlefield—a tractor-trailer slammed into the back of his Humvee during training at a Mississippi base. The boy's aunt waited at the airport all morning for Polar Cargo to bring his body up on the flight from Anchorage.

Everyone with no excuse for missing it had to show up at the funeral and say something. None of us could understand why the wars were going so badly that the military had to scrape up a few hundred Eskimos and send them to a foreign desert.

The boy's friends had spent the day at the new graveyard behind the airport, digging a grave through the permafrost with a backhoe borrowed from the Borough. They put a nice wooden cross on top.

The boy with the wooden cross was luckier than the lawyer that Vik's predecessor had replaced. That lawyer died in the middle of winter without any family in the Lower 48 asking to have him shipped home. He was such an unlikeable guy that there was really no one in Harow who wanted to go out in the winter and dig a grave for him. The body stayed in the morgue until the May thaw. When the Public Works staff dug his grave, they dug a few extra. Most Harow residents wouldn't want a pre-dug grave, but they might as well have spare graves in case another unlikeable person died in the winter.

Back when Larry's grandfather died in Harow, the family decided not to take his body home to Point Courage for burial. Larry and his brothers dug the grave in Harow over three days using augers. Larry's son was born just after his grandfather died. The child was given the same Eskimo name as the deceased, in the Iñupiaq tradition of naming a child after the last person in the family to die. Only, the son would have a Christian name, too. And they would all go to the Fresh Start church on Sundays.

Larry isn't quite convinced that Jesus came to a foreign desert in the Middle East out of love for the Eskimos. He isn't sure Jesus came at all. But he thinks it's better to be safe than end up in Hell.

Vik disagrees. She says it's better to have self-respect and strong convictions than to wager on a deified Santa Claus. It takes her some time to realize how deeply religious her new community is.

Before coming to this realization, Vik asks the local high school biology teacher if she teaches evolution.

"I'm open to any *theory*." The teacher spits out the word "theory" like it's a fad, and evolution might be the equivalent of goldfish-swallowing. "I mean, there's micro-evolution and then there's macro-evolution. We're all Christian. I stand behind the Christian faith." She explains that Christianity has brought good to the people to counteract the forces of shamanism.

"It's kind of sad, isn't it," Vik asks, "That part of the culture is gone?"

The biology teacher bristles at the question, and explains, "Some people confuse culture with religion."

It's easy to do, Vik thinks, and just as easy to confuse culture with race. And it can get confusing when an Anchorage-born Iñupiaq who's never been to Harow gets his annual dividend from the Harow Native Corporation, while nothing goes to the Filipino who's grown up in Harow and speaks the same ten words of Iñupiaq as his neighbors.

But Filipinos don't concern themselves much with Iñupiaq issues. They have their colonial Catholicism that's a far cry from the free-spirited Eskimo evangelicalism. Vik knows the Filipino world view well, having married a Filipino while living on a tropical island. Since Vik's husband had never been anywhere else in America, Vik was able to convince him that Harow would be a great place for him. And it's not all bad. He manages to get a job at the Iñupiat Housing Authority a year after applying for it.

"They have to try to keep the jobs here open for Eskimos," the Filipina receptionist at the housing authority had explained. "But they don't apply."

Harow is home to 400 Filipinos who spend as little time outside as possible and remain steadfastly focused on the day that they will have accumulated enough money to justify moving away.

The Filipino cable man who installs cable for free at all Filipino homes lives in a house he made out of a garage fourteen years ago. His wife decorated the inside with pictures of the previous family home in Las Vegas. The pictures reveal an all-American affair with spacious rooms, a glassy bar, fake indoor palm trees, and a giant Hummer in the driveway.

Vik gets stuck looking at the pictures when she accompanies her husband to see about getting free cable. She listens impatiently to the wife's mournful description of the life they left behind in Las Vegas, interrupting to ask about the dried pellets hanging from the light fixture.

"Oh, those are grapes we hung up for New Year's. You know, Filipinos have the Christian decorations, like the wreaths and Santa Claus, and then the Chinese ones, like hanging fruit for good luck. See, there's exactly eight pieces of fruit."

"What do you think of all these pagan rituals?" Vik asks the cable man. He stops sucking on his soda bottle but continues to watch his cable TV.

"Whatever brings good luck," he mumbles.

Relying on luck is a bit foreign to the white Americans, who are used to controlling everything. It does take the pressure off, though. The Arctic Slope city governments earn get more revenue from their weekly bingo nights than they do from taxes.

"What do you do for fun here?" Vik asks the cable man and his wife. "Bingo?"

"Nothing," the wife sighs.

"What about church?" Vik asks. "I know there's no Catholic church in town, but there's always Fresh Start for people who can't go without Jesus. They let anybody come. Even Filipinos get to do that healing-with-the-hands stuff."

"I'm too tired on Sundays."

"You could take some college courses," Vik suggests.

"When I come home from work I just want to stay inside."

"But what do you do?"

"Help my girls with homework and then watch the Filipino channel on the Internet. My husband stays in here and watches cable. There's nothing to do here." She sighs dejectedly.

"Think you'll move back to the house in Las Vegas ever?" Vik asks.

"No, the pay's not good enough."

It's true. The minimum wage in Harow is $10. If you eat nothing but canned food and have free cable, you can save a lot. Fresh food, on the other hand, goes for up to $10 a pound.

A group of *taniks* who don't want to pay more than $8 a pound for fresh food start a club that has organic vegetables shipped up from the Lower 48 once a week. Vik refuses to participate on grounds that flying in produce from thousands of miles away leaves too big of a carbon footprint. She says that if she weren't a vegetarian, she would eat locally. But in Harow, the only local food is caribou, fish, and marine mammals. So Vik sticks to buying outdated half-off food from the grocery store.

Vik imagines that Larry Atkoot lives without anything Western in his kitchen except a jar of mayonnaise and some Sailor Boy crackers. Having heard him talk about the camp where his family goes fishing and hunting for caribou, she'd love to get an invitation to go out to the camp and see a real Eskimo family subsisting off the land. She makes blunt efforts to endear herself to Larry, taking every opportunity to give him legal advice, even on his criminal background. She's confirmed the rumors by finding his name, Larry P. Atkoot, on Alaska's sex offender list.

Vik catches Larry in the lobby one day after a meeting and whispers a little too loudly, "Hey, I could help you get that offender thing removed from your record."

He looks at her blankly. For a minute, Vik thinks she's got the wrong Larry P. Atkoot. She's said before that people in Harow are as inbred as southerners, and now she considers the possibility that there could be three Larry P. Atkoots in this town.

Then Larry mutters through a half smile, "You got my Borough cell phone number, you can call me." He goes back to his office and leaves her to wonder if she's been socially inappropriate.

Back in the Law Department, Vik thumbs through a cultural guidance booklet that Shant Oil Co. had prepared for its employees and submitted to the Borough as proof of its cultural intelligence. For the benefit of both races, the book explains each one's perspective on the other.

Tanik: "They won't respond to the question, or they just change the subject!"

Iñupiaq: "They talk too much. They always brag about themselves."

Tanik: "They just walk away without saying goodbye!"

Iñupiaq: "They insist on making a big goodbye even when they can see you're leaving."

Tanik: "They're not really Christians, in the traditional sense."

Iñupiaq: "They don't talk to Jesus like we do."

The booklet advises white people to look down, leave lots of pauses in the conversation, and not object to the long prayers that accompany every public meeting.

Vik remembers that Lieutenant Mayor Nelson Cowen, who's been with the Borough at least thirty years, seems unable to make eye contact and spends a lot of time with a quiet little smile on his face. Even though he knows better than anyone the constitutional principle of separating church and state, he never objects to the public prayers. Before, Vik attributed these habits to Nelson's Catholic disorder and inability to relate to anyone. But maybe he's on to something. She vows to spend more time looking at the floor, particularly during prayer time.

Chapter 6- Fishing, Dancing and Oil

Lisa Luckie, a native woman with a big smile, wide eyes, and a hug for everyone, works in the Borough's Law Department as a secretary. She's lived in Harow all her life. The oldest of four sisters, she grew up in a family where no one talked about things like sex. She didn't know what it was, and when her boyfriend got her pregnant at age sixteen, she had no idea what was wrong with her. Lisa's first taste of motherhood was short-lived. Her boyfriend was killed in a car accident just before the baby was born, and a cousin convinced her to give the child up.

Following the Iñupiaq tradition, Lisa gave the baby the same Eskimo name as his dead father, and the Christian name of Tommy. But Lisa's cousin, who was married to a *tanik,* dropped the Eskimo name and changed the Christian name to William. Later, Lisa's cousin moved to Anchorage with the boy. Lisa never saw her son except when her cousin was visiting in Harow, and even then it would be by chance. A couple times Lisa saw them at the grocery store, where she struggled to remember the boy's new name.

Lisa ended up with a lanky old Eskimo dancer, a man who was most comfortable sitting quietly in front of the TV with a beer. He said he didn't believe in marriage but agreed to live with her and maybe have kids. Lisa didn't mind having a permanent boyfriend instead of a husband, as long as they'd have kids. She introduced him to her family as "my honey," and eventually, everyone just called him "Lisa's honey."

At 29, Lisa put his and her beer aside, and said they would have the baby she should have had years ago. As if to make up for the lost child, God gave Lisa twins, a boy and a girl. Lisa swore she'd never let them out of her site if she could help it. And since they were born, she's gone no further from them than the Law Department and the grocery store. Going away for vacations is out of the question—the best vacation is at home with the twins.

Home is a two-bedroom apartment in a housing complex subsidized by the Iñupiat Housing Authority, for whom Lisa's honey sometimes works as a laborer. The building is solid and the heat is good—so good the windows have to be kept open. Vik lives in one of the unsubsidized units in the same building and comes over every so often to borrow something she's too cheap to buy.

Lisa's apartment is like any other Eskimo's, filled with hand-carved Eskimo art, jumbles of plastic that might be toys or nothing at all, and a plasma TV. The nine-year old twins crawl over the junk on the floor, playing with whichever children happen to be visiting. Lisa's honey, in his late fifties but still skinny and still a dancer, is out of work these days. He sits quietly in front of the TV while listening to the VHF radio and his yowling children.

Lisa's honey isn't much of a hunter anymore. He got enough of it as a child. Most of his long periods of unemployment are spent with a six-pack and a basketball game. As the kids get older, Lisa wonders who will take them hunting. She's especially concerned about her son. At nine, he's lanky and buck-teethed, with thick glasses and uncombed hair. Lisa thinks that if he doesn't get out and shoot a seal soon, he'll fall into the low-self-esteem-beer-drinking trap of his dad.

The problem is that Jimmy has zero interest in hunting. It's Britney, his twin sister, who's destined to be a hunter. She's skinny, restless, and has decent aim with a BB gun. She went hunting a few times with Lisa's brother before he moved away. So far, she's shot two non-endangered eiders ducks, a fox, and a number of inedible lemmings—just for practice. If Jimmy ever takes up hunting, it'll be because of Britney's influence.

Britney has no trouble telling her twin what to do. She's the older twin, she always reminds him. She figured out how to drive the four-wheeler when they were seven, and the snowmachine that same winter. There's a 10:00 p.m. curfew for kids set by the city of Harow, but no one pays any attention to it. In the summer, Britney is out on the four-wheeler any time of day, usually with Jimmy sitting on the back. In the winter, she lets him ride on a sled tied to the snowmachine, so he can look up at the Northern Lights.

Lisa often stands by the living room window, craning her head to catch a glimpse of the twins riding by. She smiles with relief when she sees them. Her honey tells her she should stop worrying so much. When he was nine, he says, his parents sent him and his brother miles upriver to look for fish. He never got lost, and he never got anything worse than a little frostbite.

Those were the times when the Iñupiat made camps right next to their fishing spots. A place to stay was a place where there was something fresh to eat. Before electric freezers and snowmachines that could pull heavy loads, his family saved fish in an ice house made out of blocks of ice cut from the river or lake. His brothers fished in rowboats even after motor boats came out, because they knew that noise—even footsteps on the frozen river—would scare the fish away.

Lisa's honey remembers when the Navy started doing seismic testing near his family's fishing area. One fall, just after the rivers had frozen, a couple of guys came around blasting dynamite on the ice. The next spring, when the ice broke up and the Arctic Slope turned into a series of interconnected lakes and rivers, the dead fish rose up to the surface. Piles of them lined the banks. The family smoked and dried as many as they could, and it was practically all they ate that winter.

The spring after that, there were no fish. By fall, the family had only caught a handful, and that winter someone had to sit out by the ice hole almost 24-7.

Lisa, almost twenty years younger than her honey, is part of the first generation that doesn't have to worry about whether there'll be enough to eat. She's fat in the comfortable sense of an American with an office job. She knows she has it easy. When her twins don't want to eat the breaded fish sticks she's heated up in the microwave, Lisa reminds them of what their grandparents went through.

"Your grandma used to tell me about the winter when the pickled walrus and whale from the year before was all they have to eat. Because nobody never catch a whale that fall. And grandma's sisters died of botulism, because the pickled walrus was too old."

"Gross," Britney declares unsympathetically. "Almost as gross as fish sticks."

"You don't like subsistence food, and you don't like American food," Lisa sighs, "except for junk."

"She liked McDonald's that time we went to Anchorage," Jimmy says, dutifully relieving Britney's plate of its remaining fish sticks.

"We got rivers full of fish up here but we eat frozen fish sticks," Lisa's honey mumbles into his beer. "She's right, *ikkii*—gross."

"Honey, you already sold all those fish you got last month, remember?" Lisa reminds him.

They both remember that he exchanged four ice chests of fish he'd caught for the case of beer he's finishing off now.

"There's gonna be more next summer," he mumbles about the fish. "I got enough ice fishing already, I'm not gonna do it."

Lisa's honey isn't the only one who doesn't fish much these days. Most of us aren't willing to sit around an ice hole waiting to catch a fish. Many have stopped going out to their camps for spring and fall fishing, because the mush and melting ice don't work well with snowmachines and four-wheelers. That leaves only summer fishing, unless one has time to snowmachine out to the camp before the spring ice-break-up and stay there until after fall freeze-up.

The drought we've been having the last few years hasn't helped the situation. The rivers are so shallow in the summer that a lot of hunters can't get to their camps by boat—they have to make the whole trip by four-wheelers.

Back in the 1980s, the Borough or oil companies would bring people out to their camps on prop planes. Every camp had its own little runway.

But then the economy went down, and these days it's rare that someone can get a free flight out to a camp.

Since oil companies have quit helping hunters get to their camps, some hunters have started speaking up about how much the oil companies interfere with hunting. Hunters come to the Borough's Community Development Department to complain about noise from drilling and helicopters keeping the caribou away.

It's up to Larry Atkoot to address these concerns through the Community Development Department's permitting process. When Charlie Kitok was elected mayor, he declared an end to the days when Big Oil could march into the mayor's office and get permission to drill without a permit. Kitok said that the Community Development Director would be the gatekeeper to the Arctic Slope's oil, shepherding anyone who wants to drill through a thorough permitting process.

BX Petro is aware of the permitting requirements, and is prepared to treat them with the seriousness that someone might regard a child's announcement that henceforth permits would be needed to enter his room. BX was the first oil company to drill in the Arctic waters off the coast of the Arctic Slope, but it had assured the Borough that the Iñupiat whaling traditions would come first. It built an island within the reach of the Borough's taxing authority, but far away from the whales. From there, it drilled wells in all directions.

BX's latest plans are to construct the longest-ever "extended reach" drilling wells out to a new oil reservoir. That way, the BX representative explains to the Borough Assembly during a dazzling PowerPoint presentation, BX won't have to build a new island in the whale path. The wells will stretch eight miles from the original island through the subsurface of the seafloor, arriving finally at the sweet spot where the whales pass above and the oil flows below. The BX representative explains how many extra millions of dollars BX will incur to preserve the Iñupiat whaling traditions.

BX further humors the Borough by agreeing to sign an oil spill mitigation agreement. The agreement is the Borough's standard plan for addressing the impacts an oil spill could have on whaling, and it's pulled out every time an oil company wants to start a new drilling project in or near the ocean. The agreement requires the oil company to put up a $25 million dollar bond that the Borough can draw on, no questions asked, if ever there's a spill. Twenty-five million is the cost, as calculated by a Borough accountant, of transporting whalers out to untarnished waters, transporting the whalers and their whales back home, and giving every affected hunter a couple barrels of fuel and maybe a snowmachine so he can hunt caribou inland.

Vik says that the oil companies go along with the agreement only because of the unlikelihood that the Borough would be able to enforce it against them. She doesn't see anything altruistic in BX's willingness to sign the agreement, or in BX's enthusiasm to undertake the longest horizontal drilling project ever.

"It's part of a bigger plan that will save them money later," Vik informs Larry. "They're looking ahead, but not so far ahead that they want to get out of the oil business in time to save the planet from global-warming-induced collapse."

Larry doesn't say much about global warming. He isn't one to make quick judgments, and anyway, his mind is on spring whaling. His crew didn't land any whales last year, and it'll be pretty embarrassing if they come home empty handed this spring.

Vik, whose mission appears to be vilifying oil companies, continues to fill Larry's ear with reasons why the Borough shouldn't give BX any permits.

"Okay, so they have directional drilling, and they promise—cross their hearts—not to spill. The fact is, if they do spill, they don't have the capacity to clean it up." Vik has plowed through BX's entire spill prevention plan, and decided that there's no way BX could get its equipment and experts from Texas to the Arctic Slope in time to stop barrels and barrels from leaking into the sea. Triumphant that she's caught BX in a lie, Vik shows Larry the part of the plan talking about the twelve-hour deployment of the Texas cleanup crew.

"Larry, even if a plane could make it from Houston to Harow in twelve hours, it's not going to work. All that cleanup equipment is so big, it's gotta be brought in on ships or roligons. You've got to make BX fix this plan before you give out any more permits."

Larry sighs. "I'm gonna talk to the mayor about it whenever he gets back from his meeting in Seattle."

"When's that going to be?"

"Next week, maybe. But he's probably gonna be busy getting ready for spring whaling then."

Vik taps her fingers impatiently on the table in Larry's office. She thinks that things move way too slowly up here, except when it comes to oil companies rutting up the earth. She stands up and attempts to ask a polite question about the spring whale hunt.

"If you get a whale this spring, how big do you think it'll be? I heard they're getting smaller."

"I don't know," Larry mumbles. He likes Vik all right, but he feels a little funny talking to a vegetarian *tanik* about a sacred Iñupiaq tradition.

"Huh," Vik grunts. "Hey, do you always eat the whale meat raw, or do you ever cook it?"

Vik's attempts at conversation are overheard by Gill Whitehead, the Community Development Department's permits manager, whose office is next door to Larry's. Gill laughs out loud and hollers, "Why do *taniks* always say we eat raw meat?"

"I thought that was what Eskimo meant in another Native American language," Vik says. "Raw meat-eaters, or something."

Larry lets out a sedated laugh and explains that Eskimos do not eat raw meat. "If we don't cook the meat, then we put it in the ice cellar to freeze. We don't eat it until months later, when it's cured."

"Oh, like ham and cheese," Vik says ignorantly. "But I thought that some people eat the whale right after they drag it onshore, before rigor mortis sets in."

"Are you crazy?" Gill guffaws from his desk. "That's gonna make you sick!" He sticks his head in Larry's office to explain the science of it.

"Especially with the polar bear liver," Gill says. "If you even have a cut on your hand and you get the raw liver juice in it, you're gonna turn white. It's the vitamins in it or something. And even your eyes, they're gonna be pink."

"Uh, so you mean there's a troop of albinos roaming around town, who've all come into contact with polar bear liver?" Vik asks.

Gill scratches his chin. "There was Sam Kitok, but he passed away."

"Oh," Vik says. "Well." She feels as if her skin is prickling with whiteness. It's time for her to go back to the Law Department.

A month after Vik's talk with Larry about BX's oil spill plan and polar bear blood, she reads an article in the paper about BX's drilling plans. The article says that the Borough has given approval for BX to start its seismic surveys.

Vik feverishly calls Larry to ask what happened. "Weren't we supposed to have a meeting with BX to talk about changing their oil spill plan before they can get any new permits?"

"They went to the mayor's office and said they would build a new island in the middle of the whale migration path if the Borough tries to roadblock them with a bunch of new requirements," Larry says stoically. "The mayor called me and said to go ahead and get the permits going."

"But I didn't even get to check over them!" Vik wails.

"That's the way it is around here," Larry concludes.

"I thought nobody got a pass to walk into the mayor's office anymore, and everybody had to go through the Community Development Department's normal permitting process," Vik says.

Larry is silent. Vik wonders what he's thinking. "Well," she finally says. "Let me know if I can do anything else."

"Okay," Larry says. He hangs up and goes outside to smoke. He finishes one cigarette and smokes two more, not wanting to go back to his office.

Other than Bertie, the head of the Law Department, few people on the Arctic Slope have ever given up smoking. It's only in the last few years that Harow has banned smoking from office buildings. It's still allowed out in the villages. But the climate isn't kind to smokers. Most people can't smoke a cigarette in the freezing air without coughing their way through it.

Bertie pestered Larry to quit smoking, and he told her he'd quit for his New Year's resolution. He never did. When she asks why he's still smoking, he shrugs and says, "Pray for me." He knows that none of the Borough lawyers believe in Jesus.

Bertie gives him a wry smile. "Honestly it's not that great to quit smoking. I gained forty pounds and I'm anxious all the time. They say it'll make me live longer, but sometimes I wonder if it's worth it."

Larry nods. For *taniks* and Outsiders, living longer doesn't seem like it would be much of a prize. Whereas with the Iñupiat, respect for elders is one of the most binding values. Elders speak first at any meeting and are served first at any meal. They get a discount on their utility bills and at the grocery store. The Borough repairs elders' homes for free. Elders are the living relics of a time that's long gone—so much so that sometimes we can't understand them.

Larry sees himself as far from achieving the status of an elder. It alarms him that he might die without ever becoming one. His younger brother, a 45-year-old grandfather, has already had his first heart attack. It came on mid-song while he was leading the choir at the Fresh Start church service. Not stopping to consider the religious significance of being struck down in the middle of the service, an off-duty nurse went for the defibrillator. Fortunately Fresh Start is a 21st-century church, equipped with an amplified drum set, plasma TV screens, and a defibrillator. The nurse did CPR until a helicopter came and medevacked him off to Anchorage.

Larry's brother came back a month later, fifty pounds lighter, with strict orders not to eat hamburgers or go out hunting. He got a desk job in Larry's department, where he reminisces about his hunting days.

As a result of his felony conviction, Larry isn't supposed to hunt either. It seems crazy to him that all the felons on the Arctic Slope can no longer provide for themselves and their families because of Alaska's felony-arms rule. Larry is one of the few who makes a pretext of following it, since he is, after all, the head of the Borough's Community Development Department. He keeps his guns in the hull of one of his boats and only pulls them out at his camp. He isn't going to completely give up his right to arms and his part in a culture that has hunted for millennia.

At eighty, Larry's father has yet to give up hunting. He's still the captain of the Atkoot's whaling crew, and he'll probably remain so for as long as he lives. He's also one of the few who knows how to perform all the traditional dances, including the one for the yellow-billed loon. He's made three of the four original yellow-billed loon masks in Harow.

New masks can only be made when there are enough feathers, and since the federal government has listed the yellow-billed loon as threatened, feathers are hard to come by. The Iñupiat are allowed to take the birds only when they accidentally get caught in fishing nets. But we all know what happened last summer when an agent from the U.S. Fish and Wildlife Service found a loon in Gill Whitehead's net—she cut up the net to set the bird free. And Gill never got paid back for his net.

Larry knows most of the dances that his father does, but he isn't one for dancing in public. He prefers watching his dad take the stage during the Christmas Eskimo dances and *Kigvik*.

Kigvik is the tri-annual festival where Eskimos from the Arctic Slope, Western Alaska, and sometimes other Arctic countries congregate in one place to sing and dance. *Kigvik* 2008 is held in Harow with the sponsorship of oil companies and the Borough. Every company that gives at least $25,000 gets to have its own banner hung up next to all the tribal banners.

The festivities kick off in early March with a parade through the high school gym. Members of each tribe dress in matching *atiklut*—hooded jackets made out of cotton print and braided trim—or just hooded sweatshirts and jeans. They sing together without harmony to the accompaniment of skin drums, which are tapped with the steadiness of a human heartbeat.

Vik sits restlessly in the bleachers, holding onto her large polythene coat, complete with fake leopard trim that her husband added for warmth. She reads the *Kigvik* brochure about the importance of preserving the language, and listens to the announcer rattle off Iñupiaq phrases that are largely unintelligible to most of the crowd. He's supposed to announce the winners of the *Kigvik* race, but the run was called off on account of the cold. He calls the names of the would-have-been participants and declares them all to be in first place.

"This is like watching an arthritic obese ex-football player reminisce about the winning touchdown he made back in high school," Vik whispers to Bertie.

Bertie ignores Vik. Bertie and the other non-Iñupiat Borough employees are much more enthusiastic. They say to each other that *Kigvik* is the cultural event of the year. Of the next three years, even. Vik later tells her husband, "You know what these Borough people are like? A bunch of white Americans eating sushi and pretending it's filling."

Lisa Luckie, the Law Department's secretary, comes to *Kigvik* each night with her kids so they can watch their father dance. For a man who spends most of his time seated in front of a TV, he has some incredible moves. He gets to do three solo performances, each one telling the story of a different animal.

Assemblyman Chuck sits in the crowd with his arms crossed, shaking his head every so often.

Lisa ventures to put her arm around him and ask how he is. They aren't related or even close, but they share a half-brother.

"It's not the same," he grunts. "It's supposed to be the elders up there dancing. But they're not here."

"Didn't you see the one elder get out of her wheelchair and dance?" Lisa asks him.

"Yeah, but except for Old Man Atkoot, the Harow elders aren't here."

"Well," Lisa says. "I guess a lot of them passed on."

She stops talking to watch a solo dance by Mayor Kitok, who is slowly sliding into elder status.

"Maybe you'll be one of the elders leading the dance one day," Lisa says optimistically. Chuck is quiet. He doesn't really know any of the dances.

Lisa thinks about the dancing elders the following weekend, when she finds herself in a decorated gymnasium full of immobile middle school students. She's been duped into chaperoning.

School dances in Harow are even more awkward than they are in the Lower 48. Kids listen to the hip-hop and teen-angst music that gets played at dances, but they don't *dance* to it.

After two hours, someone has the sense to turn on the AM radio nightly broadcast of Iñupiaq music. Lisa feels the heartbeat rhythm and gets up from her chair. She raises her arms in the circles that are the female part of the Eskimo dance. Another chaperone puts down his whiskey-filled Pepsi can and joins Lisa. The male dancers have the fun part—the half-squat stomping and tapping. The whiskey-drinking chaperone can hold the position better than any American aerobics instructor. An enormous old man struggles to get out of his chair, and then he, too, moves in time with the music.

The kids uncross their arms and, for a moment, forget about appearing cool. All of them, even the Asian kids and *taniks,* suddenly know how to dance. Arms waive and feet stomp, and for another hour, several generations find unexpected joy in a middle school dance.

Chapter 7- Cold Brew

Bad weather makes the Alaska news almost every day in the winter of 2007-2008. In Anchorage, temperatures drop so low that the winter skiing contests have to be cancelled. But the next week, it's 35 above and raining. In Harow, the shoreline ice cracks in January—months ahead of schedule—and slips out into the Chukchi Sea. This, when last fall the Bering Sea froze up faster than it had in 30 years, and the fuel barges couldn't get to the Arctic Slope.

The remote villages bear the brunt of the bad weather. Vik reads a letter to the editor from residents of a village at the western edge of the Borough:

Our families got to choose between buying heating fuel and food. Last week the governor sent a commission out here to see what can be done, but they don't do nothing. We got back a letter from the governor saying our situation don't meet the state requirements for declaring economic disaster. What are we suppose to do now? Move to Anchorage and live in a shelter? The government refusing to declare economic disaster is just a green light for cultural genocide. We're asking all the oil companies to help us—send $100,000 to our village tribal council so we can buy food and fuel.

Vik pauses on the dollar figure. She knows that oil companies don't give out more than $50,000 at a time in good will money, and that's only when they're buying people off for a specific oil project. She's surprised the village hasn't asked the Borough for help. But then, most of the villages are so anti-Borough.

The City of Harow takes up a canned food drive for the village, but with fuel costs so high, we here in Harow are hurting too. The Community Development Department huddles and decides to send Gill out to the village to figure out how the Borough can best help.

Back in the Law Department, Bertie is scrambling to make sure that the Borough isn't giving any handouts to the village church. Not that anyone would make a stink about it, but, hell, there is a constitution to follow. She can't stop the praying that opens all public meetings, although she's had a few small successes. One was advising the secretary, Lisa, that she couldn't sing religious Christmas carols during the Borough's Christmas party. Another was getting the Borough Clerk to take that "Yea though I walk through the shadow of the valley of death" slogan out of her standard email closing.

Bertie calls Gill, who's out in the village, and confirms that the author of the letter to the editor—as opposed to a church—is the one receiving all the food from the canned food drive. His house has become a distribution center for donations, with people coming at all hours to carry away fuel and boxes of cans.

"There's booze over here, too," Gill tells her, "even though it's supposed to be a dry town!"

Bertie sighs. "The Borough doesn't enforce the no-alcohol laws, Gill. That's something enacted by each village through referendum. It's up to their councils and the State Troopers to deal with that."

"Hmmmm," Gill mumbles. "Do you think this guy ought to be getting a permit to be running a food distribution center? Or would it qualify as an emergency?"

"What's that noise in the background?" Bertie asks him, ignoring the permit question. Gill thinks that every human activity—aside from subsistence—requires a permit from his department, and that any and all activity can be done as long as a permit is in place.

"Oh, it's a Sing-spiration, you know, a prayer-singing session for the starving villagers," Gill explains.

"Fine, as long as the Borough isn't leading it," Bertie mutters, and hangs up.

Bertie's been in a foul mood since last week, when she took her first and last trip to Harow's swimming pool. In all the years that she's been in Harow, she's managed to avoid slipping on the ice. But as soon as she stepped into the locker room at the pool, she slipped on a puddle and put her back out. She's mad at herself for having slipped, and mad at Nelson for having suggested swimming to ease her nerves. What does Nelson know about nerves, anyway? Ever since Bertie took on the job of Law Department Director, Nelson no longer has to deal with legal matters. He simply manages the mayor and gets to go on a lot of trips to Anchorage.

Bertie has a lot to worry about at the Law Department. It's full of lawyers who wouldn't make it in the real world, including Vik, who was canned from her previous law firm job for being a communist; a former teen-drug dealer; a functioning alcoholic; and a belligerent atheist who has a hard time completing a sentence without saying "goddamn."

New lawyers come and go all the time, and the turnover rate of the locally hired support staff is just as high. Lisa quit her secretary position a few months after Vik started, saying she needed to spend more time with her kids. Lisa's replacement loses files and knits at her desk. Bertie hasn't had time to fire her.

Bertie looks up and sees that Assemblyman Chuck is marching past the knitting secretary, right towards Bertie's office. He's waving around his latest proposed resolution for the Assembly.

"How's it going, Chuck?" Bertie says with resignation.

"I got a resolution to ban alcohol from Harow."

Bertie raises an eyebrow. She's seen Chuck drunk in Assembly meetings, trying to work in references to the Second Coming and Nostradamus.

Chuck looks around nervously and closes Bertie's office door.

"Okay, I'll tell you what this is all about," Chuck says. "Some people in this town, I mean, my uncle, my sister-in-law—maybe people you know, too—need to quit drinking. And I figure, the best way to do it is to just ban alcohol all together."

"Well, let's think this through," Bertie says, trying to sound civil. "It's actually up to each city—not the Borough—to decide this. You'd need to go through a number of steps to—"

Chuck's cell phone rings, and he picks it up. "Oh hi, Gloria," he says. He puts the resolution on Bertie's desk, mouths the words "thank you," and marches out before Bertie can explain to him the petition and referendum process for banning alcohol.

Bertie is well aware of the Arctic Slope's history with alcohol, which goes all the way back to the turn of the twentieth century. Eskimos had bought a large quantity of liquor from a trader and, while under the influence, neglected to hunt for the winter. A number of them starved. The elders asked the traders and whalers to never bring alcohol to them again.

Contact with missionaries brought in more of the outside world, including alcohol. In the 1930s a missionary nurse and a group of concerned Iñupiat mothers started the Mothers' Club. The mothers patrolled the community regularly, making sure we were all well fed and alcohol-free.

The Mothers' Club lasted until the 1960s, when regular air service led to regular alcohol delivery. The *taniks* who were starting to move to Harow called it the "Booze Bomber." But the boozing *taniks* mostly stayed out by the Naval Arctic Research Lab—two miles from Harow proper—which had its own bar. When an Eskimo did go out there and got drunk, everybody back in Harow knew about it.

At that time, all alcohol was sold at a single store operated as a non-profit by a group of village leaders, who didn't touch the stuff themselves. The sales revenue was enough to allow Harow to open up a library in 1964. A year later, Harow banned alcohol, and the library closed. Alcohol consumption went underground, and alcoholism replaced tuberculosis as the number one disease of Arctic Slope natives. As long as there was money to buy alcohol, it was going to be bought and sold.

In 1967, the Bureau of Indian Affairs stepped in with an all-Native Alcoholic Anonymous program. The Bureau knew that segregation was starting to become unfashionable, but it also knew that the natives weren't going to talk if the whites were talking. Even if a native had a good grasp of English, it would be hard to talk about alcoholism.

After oil was discovered at Prudhoe Bay in 1968, and oil workers were coming and going daily, the alcohol problem flared up like never before. Harow was on fire, with Iñupiat women and children fleeing their alcoholic men for safety in the homes of the teetotalers. There was no women's shelter back then, and sometimes the floor space of the "safe homes" would be completely filled at all hours of the night with children seeking refuge.

In the late 1970s, Harow controlled drinking by jailing drunks for seven or eight hours until they sobered up. Half the population spent time at the jail, and the former distribution center was turned into a makeshift drunk tank.

By then the Borough was revving up, and had a good deal of oil money to throw at the problem. A Blue Ribbon Panel established by the Borough hired a group of white sociologists to come up to Harow, assess the situation, and recommend a solution.

The researchers came out with a report called "Alcohol, Economics, and the Iñupiat on the Alaskan Arctic Slope." The event merited a press release, which was picked up by the New York Times and turned into a front page story entitled "Alcohol Plagues Eskimos." The article explained that the Eskimos were practically committing suicide by mass alcoholism. With the alcoholism rate at 72%, violence was becoming the most frequent cause of death. The researchers predicted that offshore oil development would peak in 2010 or 2015, and they didn't see the Eskimos surviving until then.

"This is not a collection of individual alcoholics," the researchers said, "but rather a society which is alcoholic, and thus facing extinction." The researchers attributed the Iñupiat's rate of alcoholism—which is still higher than that of every other group in America—not to their unique physiology, but to oil. Money and alcohol were flowing in as fast as oil was coming out of Prudhoe Bay, they said, and the solution was to slow down the cash flow. "Eskimos are like the endangered snail darter fish," the researchers concluded, "a victim of America's unquenchable thirst for energy."

The Iñupiat realized that the white sociologists they had hired to solve their problem had simply profited from describing their problem. Going back to a cashless economy was not the solution.

The white sociologists would not be the last to breeze through the Arctic Slope, reaping the benefits of oil money and pushing aside Iñupiat values. As the Borough grew more bloated with oil money, it created more and more highly skilled positions that it filled with Outsiders. Many of them lived in Harow just for the salary and were only interested in themselves. They thought that drinking alcohol was a right that shouldn't be denied just because it might be bad for the community or run counter to the culture that surrounded them. They were the ones who had incorporated the City of Harow—a separate municipality within the Borough—and voted to make alcohol legal within the city limits. Then they left the community a few years later when the battle to live in the Arctic no longer seemed worth their big salaries.

By then, a State law was in place allowing villages and cities to vote themselves dry, wet, or damp, and providing for State Troopers to enforce the chosen status. Harow changed its status every couple of years, and each election resulted in community upheaval. The *taniks* were not in the majority, but they spoke the loudest. Ads on the radio and around town proclaimed, "This is America! We have the freedom to do whatever we want!"

The elders said the elections weren't fair, since the ballot language was confusing and the people running the elections weren't translating correctly. Some wondered if the *taniks* were recruiting drinkers from outside of Harow just to come in and vote the town wet. A succession of Harow mayors, who really had no say over the status, were elected, driven out of office, or sued based on their alcohol stance.

In the late 1990s, Harow finally rested on a damp status. The Freedom Committee, formed by *taniks* who'd been in Harow long enough not to say anything too racist, convinced the city to resurrect the old distribution center. All the alcohol would arrive there, and the police could monitor who was picking up what and how much. Anyone who wanted to import alcohol would have to get a license, which would cost $200 a year and would require a clean criminal record. No one would be able to get more than five cases of beer a month. Licenses couldn't be denied to pregnant women, but at least they would be under the public eye if they wanted to buy booze.

Vik goes to the Distribution Center once a month to pick up beer for her functioning alcoholic co-worker, who paid for Vik's license to double his own monthly beer quota. Vik relishes the trips. A man whose import license had been suspended for three months after a drunk driving arrest might be picking up his first post-suspension load and talking about how he was quitting any day now. A woman drunk on vanilla extract might be trying to convince the attendant that she's not too drunk to pick up her beer, and that the beer would be healthier than vanilla anyway.

But for those of us on the wagon, the distribution center is an ugly symbol of the ruin caused by alcohol.

In March 2008, the State tells the City of Harow that the distribution center will need to be relocated from its current location at the state-owned airport, so the State can use the building for airport purposes. The City of Harow finds a new location for the distribution center some 500 feet south of the airport, and goes to the Community Development Department to get a permit for the relocation. As the director of the Community Development Department, Larry decides that the controversy would be best handled by the Borough's Development Planning Commission.

The commission's meeting on the relocation has an enormous turnout.

"The place where they want to move the distribution center is already really unsafe," a grizzled older resident testifies, "because of the hotel parking across the street. You practically have to go to the middle of the intersection to see sometimes because there are vehicles parked there at the hotel."

The discussion focuses on parking requirements for some time before another resident announces that the real concern is that the new location is just three blocks from the high school, and students using the road are going to be exposed to the Distribution Center.

"And the place they want to put the Distribution Center looks just like a house," a comfortably overweight woman declares. "It's gonna send a mixed message to our youth that home is a place to pick up alcohol."

Gill Whitehead suggests putting the distribution center somewhere outside of town, so people would have a longer ride home and a greater chance of getting arrested for drinking in their cars.

An elder stands up to say that she's lost two sons-in-law because of booze. "I don't want to see more people losing their life, going over to the Distribution Center to pick up booze. The government's supposed to be protecting our community, not ruining it. So why do they allow a Distribution Center?"

The white president of the commission reminds us all that Harow voted to be damp, and that without a distribution center there would be no regulation of the incoming alcohol. He suggests putting up a barricade to block off the view. "There is nothing that we can do to eliminate alcohol on the Arctic Slope unless we get rid of Western society," he concludes.

And we all know that's not going to happen.

Chapter 8- Safe and Warm

Whaling has always been risky business. Winds and currents mash the ice together and then pull it apart. At any time, the ice beneath the whalers' feet could collapse or break off and head out to sea. A whaler who falls in the icy water has little chance of emerging alive.

Whaling is risky even in the 21st century. The weather is unpredictable—gone are the days when whalers could look up at the clouds and predict the movements of the ice. There is less solid ice, and the Beaufort is turning as violent as the Chukchi, its sister sea to the west.

Larry remembers spring whaling in the 1970s, when there were six to eight weeks of good whale hunting on solid ice. Spring whaling in 2008 lasts only five days, and the Harow crews only land four whales.

Larry's crew is among the lucky ones. The whalers get the last whale just before the ice gets too thin for anyone to risk walking on it.

As the whalers are butchering the whale, they experience another impact of the warming trend—more spectators. A man with a camera saunters right up to them, narrating what he thinks he can turn into a National Geographic special. He whoops and hollers as Larry separates the whale into pieces for each whaler and each upcoming festival.

Larry lets out a cry when he sees the tourist. Gill Whitehead, who's helping Larry's crew, pulls the tourist away and tells him he can't film without a Borough permit.

No one wants whaling to be filmed. It's almost sure to get in the hands of Greenpeace and be used to reduce the Iñupiat whaling quota.

More and more tourists like the would-be National Geographic cameramen are coming each year. Many of them are benign—they just want to have their pictures taken in front of a clean whale skull and the Welcome to Harow sign, and then go home. Other tourists come to disgust themselves with the sight of litter-strewn streets, flimsy houses, drunk Eskimos, frigid gray summers, and large dead mammals.

More development is coming, too. The summer season is longer now, and there's a buzz of vessel traffic and construction by the oil companies. The whalers say that development is pushing the whales further out to sea, forcing the crews to travel further out into the stormy sea than ever before. And the whales are acting strange—they're skittish and easily spooked. Whales are said to have thrown icebergs out of the water in an effort to get away from the whalers, or even drag *umiat*—whaling boats—under water with their tails.

Larry knows the changing times aren't all bad. He remembers the days before the Borough had its own search and rescue squad, when whalers could get stranded out on an ice floe with no hope of surviving. Those were the days when every whaling captain's wife hung her husband's mukluks on a line stretched across the house. If the boots moved together or stayed put, her husband was alive. If they moved to opposite sides, he was dead and that was that.

Now that the Borough has its own search and rescue squad, all we have to do is radio for help and wait for the helicopter to come. We've come to expect the Borough to provide a remedy for almost everything, from roof repairs to health care to domestic squabbles.

The Borough's domestic violence management system is one of the best in Alaska. All a woman has to do is call the hotline. A Borough social worker and a fleet of cops will come to her rescue, and the Law Department will help with the paper work for a domestic violence protection order. She can stay at the women's shelter as long as she likes. And the shelter workers will look the other way if she wants to slip out at night to visit her perpetrator.

Assemblyman Chuck's wife ditched him for the women's shelter a year ago. He'd never hit her—she weighed twice as much as he did—but his drinking and deep thoughts scared her. Chuck's wife was one of the few women who wouldn't forgive her man and come back home. Once Chuck realized she was truly gone, he became the only conservative who wouldn't carry the torch for family values.

In early 2008, Chuck leads the Assembly in passing an anti-nepotism ordinance. He says he doesn't have a problem with Native people hiring their family members, since every native in Harow is related somehow. The problem, he says, is the white police chief's son who was hired to be a drug cop. This cop knows nothing of Iñupiaq values, and his hard-line, anti-Iñupiaq methods are destroying community trust. Chuck explains that his ordinance will remedy the problem by prohibiting Borough directors from hiring any of their relatives unless there's specific Assembly approval for the hiring. Chuck knows, as we all know, that almost every department director is a *tanik* Outsider.

Chuck is also the source of an ordinance requiring any sales contract between the Borough and any Borough employee to get specific approval from the Assembly. He doesn't like to see some imported *tanik* entrepreneur making a buck off the Borough. The ordinance is tested for the first time when an employee with a helicopter business offers the Borough a cut-rate deal on helicopter services. The offer comes when the search and rescue squad is down to a single helicopter, since the other one is being repaired.

The employee comes before the Assembly to get special permission for the contract. The manager of the search and rescue squad testifies that he was the one who initiated the contract, not the employee. But Chuck advises his fellow Assemblymen to nix the deal. He says there are plenty of four-wheelers and snowmachines around in case somebody needs rescuing. Looking at the Assembly President Ernie Whitehead, Chuck adds, "Everyone knows what happened when our former mayor got involved in side deals—the Borough became shrouded in corruption."

Gill Whitehead, the permits manager at the Community Development Department and Ernie Whitehead's first cousin, speaks in favor of the contract. He reminds the Assembly of the good old days in the 1980s, which coincided with Ernie Whitehead's mayorship, when Arctic Slope residents could catch rides to their camps in helicopters.

"But now, in the summer when the river dries out and we can't get out in boats, we're stuck here in Harow. In fact, last summer we had bears breaking into people's camps, and the Borough should have been helicoptering people out to their camps to shoot the nuisance bears and bring back subsistence food for those stuck in Harow."

Gill knows how to appeal to Chuck's sense of Iñupiat values. "Remember, the Borough was founded on preserving the Iñupiat subsistence lifestyle. We really need these helicopter services not just for the search and rescue squad, but also to assist people in getting to their subsistence camps."

Chuck relents, and the Assembly unanimously passes a resolution allowing the Borough to purchase private helicopter services from its employee for both subsistence and rescue purposes.

Gill is glad for the free helicopter rides, although he's not going to be dependent on them. Gill knows the changing climate better than anyone, and he's got all the equipment he needs to travel and hunt safely. Each fall, when the weather gets clear and cold and a steady wind comes from the north—the elders call it *nanuq* or polar bear wind—and most people are staying inside, Gill likes to go out alone on the sea ice.

Last fall, on one of the final days of sun before the winter, Gill found one of the unfortunates who lacked his aptitude.

There was an overturned snowmachine close to the young ice, and Gill went to investigate. The body of the driver, a *tanik* teen who'd grown up in Harow, was just below the ice. Gill broke through the ice with the pole he used for testing hardness. He pulled the body to the safety of the thicker ice and radioed the search and rescue squad with the GPS location. Someone would be there soon, they told him.

Gill crouched down by the body, trying to guess how long the kid had been under the ice.

It certainly wasn't the first frozen body he'd found. A few years ago, when his father hadn't come back to Harow in time for the mayor's election, Gill and his brothers went out on a search. Gill didn't want his father's body brought back on a search and rescue squad helicopter.

They found their father's snowmachine sunk into a pond of ice two miles from the family's cabin. The old man must have crashed through the ice, but he'd managed to pull himself out of the water and keep going. His frozen body was found almost within sight of the cabin. Gill put the body in front of him on the snowmachine and carried it sixty miles home.

The officer that came out for the *tanik* teen's body wrote down the serial number of the snowmachine, and observed that it was Borough property.

"Which department's missing a snowmachine?" he wondered out loud. "And how far away was the body?"

Gill pointed over to the young ice. "A hundred yards over that way."

The rest of the details unravel later in a lawsuit by the *tanik* teen's mother against the Borough. The teen had stolen the snowmachine—just for a joyride—from the Borough's search and rescue squad. But the machine was improperly maintained, and it failed once it got over fifty miles per hour. The teen was thrown off the machine and through the ice, where he'd drowned in a state of shock. A *tanik* lawyer from Fairbanks who heard the story from a friend of a friend contacted the teen's mother and convinced her to sue the Borough for failing to maintain its equipment.

Bertie passes the lawsuit on to one of the Borough's outside law firms. She doesn't like for the Borough's Law Department to get tangled up in the kind of lawsuit that requires arguing against local residents. And the Law Department is too busy handling the daily minutia of all of the Borough's departments, boards, and commissions to actually litigate.

Vik doesn't even hear about the lawsuit until it comes up at a Development Planning Commission meeting dedicated to safety issues. The commission hadn't planned to dedicate an entire meeting to safety issues, but there was nothing else on the agenda, and the commissioners wanted to make sure a full length meeting was held so they could get their honorarium for attending.

Gill is instrumental in raising safety concerns. After talk of the need to better maintain Borough snowmachines trails off, Gill says, "I think the bull rails the Borough has around the fire hydrants are a problem. I know they put them up to keep people from running into the fire hydrants, but then people just run into the bullrails. We've had two fatalities in the past year."

"Are you saying that people have actually died from crashing into the pipes around the fire hydrants?" Vik pipes up. Vik attends all Development Planning Commission meetings, mainly for purposes of gathering writing material.

"What about the orange plastic barricades that the Public Works Department put up all around the bull rails?" a commissioner asks. "I thought those were supposed to cushion the blow."

"Geez," Gill says, "I don't know about those, but I think we can all agree that it's better to lose a fire hydrant than a life."

The commissioners make noises of agreement.

"Definitely there are already too many fatalities like that this year," Gill continues. "We gotta be more proactive."

Fresh on everyone's mind is the death of two four-year-old girls who went sledding over and through the not-yet-frozen lagoon. No one was around to notice that they had fallen through, and by the time they were medevacked to Anchorage they were a lost cause.

"Gill's right," declares a large-headed, humorless commissioner whose cell phone goes off every twenty minutes or so. "I'm thinking about the lagoons around here ... I'm thinking we can put up a hurricane fence around all the lagoons, maybe with entrances every 300 feet and signs to remind people the ice might be thin in the fall. We can't let those deaths go in vain."

"But someone going really fast on a snowmachine could end up going right through the hurricane fence and still crash into the lagoon," another commissioner points out.

Vik takes a spare microphone and suggests with due seriousness, "Maybe we could put bull rails around all the lagoons? And, ah, orange plastic barricades in front of the bullrails?"

A few commissioners nod, and one describes the fence that the nearby village of Atkuq put up around a lake after a kid drowned there.

"On the other hand, maybe we could just do a better job of teaching safety and common sense?" Vik suggests. "I actually had someone brag to me that he could get up to seventy miles an hour on the lagoon in front of the hospital, as long as he's drunk."

Gill takes the microphone away from Vik and steers the conversation back toward fire hydrants. Vik remembers that the mother of the 70-mph-snowmachiner is one of the commissioners, so maybe it's just as well that they stick to fire hydrants. She decides she better keep quiet for the rest of the meeting. The commission, unburdened by Vik's commentary, passes a resolution that the Borough should relocate all fire hydrants at least twenty feet back from any streets and snowmachine corridors.

Larry sits silently in the back of the room for the duration of the meeting. He's remembering the death of his own son from a car wreck.

The flimsy Asian car skidded on the ice and rolled into the semi-frozen lagoon. His son was twenty years old. He might have been drunk, or he might have been sober—it didn't matter either way. He was dead, and he had left behind childless parents and an unborn child. The expectant mother was his son's sixteen-year-old girlfriend, Lisa Luckie.

Larry had known about the pregnancy, but he hadn't told his wife. He thought he would tell her after the baby was born, but then Lisa gave the baby to her cousin, and things got awkward. He went to visit the baby once, but the adopted *tanik* father hovered over Larry the whole time as if Larry might try to steal or molest the baby.

Larry never tried to visit again. No one told him out loud that he couldn't come, but he understood this. Larry saw the boy every so often in the grocery store with his adopted mother, an abrasive Athabascan woman with few friends in the Iñupiat community. If the boy knew who his grandfather was, he didn't acknowledge it. Neither did the boy's adopted mother.

Larry kept the secret from his wife—he was sure it would break her heart.

Larry's wife Mandy is a dumpling of a woman with a happy smile and a heart of gold. She works at the Community Development Department doing a mindless job that keeps her on the payroll but mostly out of sight.

Vik doesn't even know the wife exists when, on a trip to Anchorage for an oil and gas convention, she asks Larry if he wants to go out to a bar.

"My wife is flying in this afternoon," Larry replies, looking at the floor. "Maybe we can all go to dinner together."

"Actually, I was just going to graze at the Cacoco Oil meet-and-greet party," she says. "It's free, you know. Why don't you all come to that?"

Larry nods in reluctant agreement. He doesn't do so well at parties, but he understands the importance of Western chit-chat and handshaking.

At the party, he braces himself against a column while one Cacoco Oil person after another comes over to shake his hand. Mandy stays back by the food table, smiling good-naturedly to no one in particular. Canned indigenous music screeches through the speakers, and Vik asks Mandy if she and Larry ever dance.

"Oh! Not me. But Larry can do all the Eskimo dances when he's stoned."

"I'd like to see that," Vik says.

Vik politely admires Mandy's parka, made out of cloth-covered sheepskin fringed with giant wolverine pelts and decorated with tiny beads.

"I do the sewing myself," Mandy says. "I get the hides from Larry, and send them to a tannery in Idaho. I made Larry a sealskin vest, but he never wears it."

A sealskin vests is the Eskimo equivalent of a Western suit.

"Larry's too humble," Vik suggests.

Later, when Vik gets some embroidery beads as a door prize from a public meeting, she passes them off to Larry for his wife.

Unduly appreciative, Larry says he's about to go to Hawaii on vacation and asks what he should bring back for her.

"How about a bottle of cheap wine?" Vik asks.

Two weeks later, on a Friday night, Larry knocks on Vik's door to deliver the bottle of cheap wine. Vik is dressed in a swimsuit and a fake hula skirt for a spring solstice party that her functioning alcoholic co-worker is hosting. She considers not opening the door, but sees that it's Larry with her wine.

"Aloha," she says. "I'd offer to invite you in, but I'm kind of underdressed."

Larry declines the non-invitation and leaves without ever making eye contact. Vik puts on her polythene coat and a burkha, which keeps the wind off her face, and heads to the party. Since she's invested in the coat and a set of burkhas, she's been walking everywhere in every kind of weather.

On Monday morning, just after she's gotten to work and taken off her coat, she gets a phone call from Larry's wife.

"Do you have time to meet me out in my car for a few minutes?" Mandy asks.

"Uh, sure," Vik says, wondering if Mandy is going to give her a bible lesson about not tempting married men.

Vik walks out of the Borough building, and finds Mandy standing next to her SUV, shaking out an Eskimo parka. It's the full shebang, with a sheepskin interior, fur trimming, and a wolverine ruff—paws and claws intact—wrapped around the hood. Vik has seen similar parkas sell for $1,000.

"Try this on," Mandy says with a big smile. "I'm tired of seeing you walk around without warm clothes."

Vik is an animal rights activist. She puts the parka on gingerly, not letting the wolverine claws touch her neck. She's not sure what the appropriate protocol is—should she refuse it? Offer to pay? Take it and give it to the battered women's shelter?

She opts for a big hug instead of words, and tells herself she'll keep it in her office to wear whenever she has meetings with Eskimos. She tries it out on the way home that day, and finds it so warm that she doesn't even need her burkha.

A car horn sounds behind her. It's one of the Community Development Department vans, which Gill uses liberally.

"Want a ride?" Gill asks, pulling over.

Normally, Vik declines ride offers so she can maintain her sense of superiority over gasoline users. But a van ride with Gill is too good to pass up. She's compiled a heap of gossip about him, mostly regarding the Russian bride he ordered from some website. Vik never got to meet the woman—apparently she didn't waste much time in Harow before moving on to the Lower 48. Undaunted, Gill took up with a gangly elementary school teacher who shared his love for frozen uncooked fish. They had two kids while it lasted.

Putting aside his omnipresent fishy smell, Gill is the romanticized version of the modern Eskimo. He's big, long-nosed, and laughs heartily about anything and nothing. He can hunt as well as he can text and email, and he tells wonderful stories in both Iñupiaq and English. Every time the oil companies come to meet with the Community Development Department, Gill is sure to go off on a tangent about fighting with a polar bear or being whacked by a whale's tail. The oil people are intrigued, or at least pretend to be.

Vik hops into the front seat of the van and pushes back her wolverine hood.

"Oh, I didn't know it was you," Gill says. He doesn't get back on the road, apparently giving Vik a chance to abandon the ride.

"Yeah, I just got this coat from Larry's wife."

Gill touches the wolverine hood in disbelief and slowly pulls back onto the road. Vik is debating whether to try and buckle the apparently broken seatbelt when a bump sends them skidding into a snowdrift.

Vik pushes her door open cautiously. The van has no problem taking a beating. The engine and all the lights are still on. The source of the bump—a snow machine—hasn't fared as well. The track and the riders have come off and are lying in a jumble by the side of the road. Vik sees that it's Assemblyman Chuck and Gloria Whitehead. Chuck smells like a pitcher of beer that's been left on the counter for a week.

Gill looked at Chuck incredulously. "Were you driving drunk?" he asks.

"Maybe someone should call 911," Vik says. She's concerned enough to suggest it, but not concerned enough to go and find a phone. Gloria, who usually carries two cell phones, has already picked herself up and exited the scene.

Voyeurs are approaching the scene, and someone with a cell phone calls 911.

"I'm fine, I'm fine," Chuck says, trying to stand up. His glasses are lost in the snow, and without them he looks beady-eyed and dense.

"I don't think you should stand up," Gill advises. "What happened to Gloria?" he asks, looking around. "And what was she doing with you?"

An ambulance pulls up, and a group of paramedics get out.

"You know about Nostradamus?" Chuck asks Vik.

"You better tell me," Vik says.

"He predicted that the Savior would come back, only to fall to a great machine." Chuck nods dizzily at the Community Development Department van.

"So does that mean you're the savior?" Vik asks.

Chuck falls back dramatically into the paramedics' stretcher without answering.

The police arrive, and Gill explains to them what happened. No one's paying attention to Vik. She resumes her walk home, a block closer than she was before Gill pulled over. She's actually glad to have the wolverine coat that day, since it's dropped to forty below with the wind chill.

It's the end of March, and there are only two more months of snow.

Chapter 9- Nukes and Birds

When the Cold War was center-stage, the Arctic Slope was the first line of defense. The federal government, which already owned and ran just about everything up here, got busy setting up "Distant Early Warning" stations with satellites and military stockpiles along the coastline. We were never really sure what purpose these stations served, although the government did let Eskimos work there. Maybe that's where they kept nukes. But it wasn't the only place.

In the 1950s, the federal Atomic Energy Commission came up with the "Plowshare Program" to show that nukes had peaceful uses in addition to protecting us from the communists. Part of the program involved creating an Arctic harbor through a huge atomic blast near Cape Thompson, on the Chukchi Sea. All the coal in northwestern Alaska could then be dug up and easily exported. The Commission dubbed this "Project Chariot."

To the government, Cape Thompson was a coast in the middle of nowhere. To the Iñupiat, it was rich hunting land—Iñupiat land.

The inventor of the H-bomb toured the territory of Alaska in the summer of 1958 to promote Project Chariot. He told the people that the Atomic Energy Commission could dig a harbor in the shape of a polar bear, if they wanted. Everyone living nearby could watch the blast before being temporarily relocated to another part of the state. Residents would then be relocated again—not back to their original homes, which would no longer exist, but to modern dwellings near the brand new harbor.

The Iñupiat wouldn't have it, though, so the government changed its plan. It decided to bury several thousand pounds of spent nukes in a dozen pits between the Chukchi Sea villages of Point Courage and Point Latch. The government would dig it all up in a few decades and show that no damage had been done. This would teach the Iñupiat that radioactivity was less harmful in frigid conditions, so maybe one day Project Chariot could go forward after all. In the meantime, the government didn't tell Iñupiat anything about the plan.

Leaving radioactive material in pits wasn't the government's only science experiment on the Arctic Slope. In 1956 and 1957, Air Force doctors decided to do a study on how the Eskimos' thyroids helped them handle the cold. The idea was to give Iñupiat volunteers various levels of radioactive iodine, and then compare their thyroid function with that of a small group of similarly dosed American servicemen.

Except none of the volunteers knew what they were volunteering for, or that the testing would violate the Nuremburg Code on medical experimentation that America had adopted just ten years before. Most of the Eskimos couldn't really speak English back then. They were impressed by X-ray pictures the scientists took of their heads and trusted that the experiments were being done for their benefit.

The scientists concluded that thyroids didn't play a significant role in human acclimatization to cold, but it would be years before we understood all the implications of the experiment.

In the 1960s, the Atomic Energy Commission came back to the Arctic Slope with yet another idea—to test nuclear explosives underground near Point Latch. A scientist from the Commission said that there had already been 200 tests in the Aleutian Islands, and they were perfectly safe. If, by chance, some of the radioactive gas were to escape, only the iodine vapor would get into the food supply. Heavier elements would filter out. The Commission had determined that there wasn't much wildlife in the testing area, but just to be safe, testing would be done only when there were no caribou around.

The governor of Alaska thought the testing was a great idea. When someone told him about the major caribou fawning area surrounding Point Latch, he suggested that the testing site could be moved just outside the fawning area, and a permanent road could be built from the site to Point Latch. It would be a great way to employ the natives, he said.

Even the Iñupiat leader Evan Hooper dismissed his people's fear of nuclear testing. He said that the Eskimos' knee jerk reaction to the testing was damaging their highly patriotic reputation, and that Eskimos ought to read up on the matter before they made up their minds. By isolating themselves in the face of a national security crisis, he said, Eskimos were treading on thin ice.

The Iñupiat managed to fight off nuclear testing without their leader.

Sometime later, radiologists from Lower 48 universities came to Alaska to measure radiation levels in villages where caribou and reindeer were the main source of food. The results, published in 1965, suggested that an Alaska Native who ate caribou or reindeer had a radiation body burden 22 times higher than the average Lower 48 resident.

The government blamed the radiation levels not on its own waste-burying activities, but on the Soviets, who were dumping their nuclear waste in the sea and didn't know how to conduct atomic tests safely. At any rate, the government said, radiation levels in Alaska villages didn't exceed the guidance recommendations set by the Federal Radiation Council.

In 1966, four families from the Arctic Slope village of Ankvut—considered the hottest spot in the world for radiation—undertook their own scientific experiment to see if the *tanik* diet would reduce their radiation levels. Eating caribou had never caused them any trouble before, and they couldn't be sure that it was harming them now. But the radiation count in their bodies had been building up ever since America started experimenting with atomic bombs. Radioactive fallout was all over the world. It wasn't that caribou were magnets for radiation, but the lichen they ate could soak up fallout like blotting paper.

The Eskimos didn't come up with the *tanik* diet plan on their own. A *tanik* scientist had flown in from a laboratory in the Lower 48 to suggest it. He brought the experimental subjects a month's worth of T-bone steaks, pork chops, ribs, vegetables, milk, bread, hamburgers, hotdogs, and apple pie. The meat alone was worth $4,000 in 1966 dollars.

Tanik food was a tasty novelty at first. Then the caribou started coming through on their fall migration. The dieting men helped the others hunt but watched, mouths watering, while the others ate. The steaks became like dirt in the dieters' mouths. They could stand the *tanik* meat only when it was made into a soup. The dieting elders complained bitterly about the taste of steak—all they wanted was to bite into the fat on a caribou rib.

When the month was over, the *tanik* scientist measured the families' radiation levels and said they'd dropped. But after the *tanik* scientist went back to the Lower 48, the families returned to their caribou. Even if they could stand the taste of *tanik* food, there was none to be bought in the remote village of Ankvut. And there was hardly any of it elsewhere on the Arctic Slope, at least not until the oil workers came—just endless fields of caribou and occasional pockets of American excrement.

By the late 1970s, the worst of the Cold War seemed to have passed, and the Distant Early Warning sites suddenly seemed ridiculous. The different branches of the federal government started trading the sites with each other—surely some use could be made of them. But no use was found, and by the 1990s, the sites had dwindled into slabs of cracked pavement and dumps that were crumbling into the ocean. When federal government agents finally came up to inspect the land, they found toxic wastes in the dumps.

The government agreed to dig up the dumps and ship the toxic waste to secure landfills in the Lower 48. But when it found out this would cost $5 million, it decided to just move the dumps inland a quarter-mile. Agents assured us that the new sites would be lined, so the toxic wastes wouldn't leach into the surrounding wetlands and get into the food chain.

Around the time the government was digging through the dumps, we finally learned the truth about the spent nukes that had been buried between the villages of Point Latch and Point Courage back in the 1950s.

The Borough threatened to sue the feds unless they tested the soil above the nukes and agreed to pay for any damage caused.

The government tested the soil and reported that radiation levels were not above average. The spent nukes would be left in place, the agents said. The Borough protested, pointing out that cancer rates on the Arctic Slope were far above average. The feds said that the Eskimos' problem was too much alcohol, sugar, and smoking.

"People from Hiroshima and Nagasaki never came down with lung cancer," one of them said.

The federal government also denied responsibility for any harm caused by its radioactive iodine experiments on Iñupiat thyroids. In 1996, Air Force representatives came to the Arctic Slope to announce that the Air Force was apologizing even though it had nothing to be sorry for, since the experiments hadn't really hurt anyone. They said the research was typical of the times, and the important thing was to move forward rather than assigning any blame.

The English-speaking children and grandchildren of the iodine guinea pigs came forward with a different story. One told of his grandmother, whose thyroid became so numb she could no longer talk. Another told of a father that ended up with a hole in his thyroid. Others lost their vision. A living survivor who had since learned English described the tests: "We spent a week in a little room lined with lead foil, where we got the iodine. We stood naked with all our openings wired—ear, mouth, underarms, and so forth, and we shivered from dropping temperatures."

The Borough sued the feds on behalf of everyone subjected to the tests. In 2001, Congress passed a bill authorizing a $7 million settlement in favor of the Borough. The Borough had won, but this didn't mean any of us would forget what the feds had done.

The federal government's adventures with radioactivity weren't their only sins against the Iñupiat. Before the government tried to end whaling, it tried to ax subsistence bird hunting.

Back in the days when colonialism was still in vogue, America and the rest of the world used to shoot migratory birds for fun and for feathers to put in ladies' hats. In the 1930s, long before the environmental movement that would bring America the Endangered Species Act and the Marine Mammals Protection Act, someone realized that the birds were dying out. America signed treaties with Mexico, Canada, Russia, and Japan to end all spring and summer hunting.

The treaties and the American acts regulating bird hunts left no room for the traditional Iñupiat spring bird hunt. Still, the spring hunt continued as it had for thousands of years among an isolated and forgotten Arctic population.

But in 1961, the U.S. Fish and Wildlife Service decided to educate the forgotten Iñupiat on the rules of migratory bird hunting. Agents came north of the Brooks Mountain Range for the first time and informed the people of the Arctic Slope that migratory bird hunting was closed.

The Iñupiat revolted. Led by future mayor Evan Hooper, everyone of shooting age in Harow showed up at the post office with a dead duck. Instead of a sit-in, it was the *Duck-in.*

"*Kiita*—let's go! Take us to jail," the hunters said to the Fish and Wildlife agent waiting for them.

The Fish and Wildlife agent lined up all the offenders in the local meeting hall. He wrote down their names and confessions and sent the confessions and a pile of dead ducks to a federal prosecutor in Fairbanks. But the government lost in court because it couldn't match each dead duck in the pile with a particular hunter.

The Fish and Wildlife agents stayed away for a few decades, during which the Borough managed to get the laws and treaties amended to legalize the Iñupiat spring bird hunt. The new laws allowed all indigenous residents of Alaska to participate in the spring hunt, as long as they followed certain rules and bought licenses and duck stamps.

In the 2000s, the agents started coming back to the Arctic Slope see if our hunters were following the new laws. While they were here, they would also make sure we were following the Endangered Species Act, the Marine Mammals Protection Act, and any other law that related to hunting.

Chuck had his run-in with the Fish and Wildlife Service the first and only time he ever set fishing nets in Ikpuq River. In retrospect, he realized he'd gone about it all wrong. He'd never set nets before, and that was an embarrassment in itself. He'd wanted to run for a seat on the Assembly, and he was worried that people would think he wasn't Iñupiat enough. It was true that his diet consisted mostly of Styrofoam-tray meat and sweet rolls from the grocery store. All the subsistence food he'd ever eaten had been given to him by his Iñupiat uncles.

Instead of deftly setting the nets and moving on to take care of other business, Chuck clumsily dropped his nets in the water and sat on the bank to watch them. He was hoping someone else would pass by and notice his participation in the subsistence lifestyle. After several hours of seeing neither people nor fish, he went home to eat.

At that point, a Fish and Wildlife agent came along and spotted the nets, which, being poorly anchored, had floated to the surface. The agent shook his head in disbelief that someone had failed to comprehend the federal regulations prohibiting fishing nets within 500 feet of a river mouth. Feeling almost sorry for the foolish owner, the agent went over to the grocery store to ask if anyone there knew the owner of the nets.

No one would talk to the agent.

When Chuck went back to check his nets the next day, they were gone. A note tied to a stick in the ground explained that the Fish and Wildlife agent had been forced to seize the nets because they violated federal law. The note said that the agent had left town, but could be reached in Fairbanks by phone.

Chuck was furious enough to fly down to Fairbanks in search of the officer who had treaded upon his sovereign Iñupiaq right to fish. At the Fish and Wildlife office, the agent on duty explained the 500-feet rule to Chuck in slow, loud English, and added that the agent could have cited Chuck for failing to mark his name on all his fishing gear. That was a violation, too.

"Why don't you send someone to Harow to meet with our tribal leaders and the public to explain these rules to us?" Chuck railed helplessly. "And bring promotional materials, you know, people like to have T-shirts and mugs."

The agent said he would send the suggestions to Juneau, but that he didn't think they could spare the men and resources to do it. "If we sent all our men up there," he said, "who would take care of the rest of the state?"

The agent handed Chuck the seized nets, which had been cut for easy handling, wadded up, and stuffed wet into a plastic bag. They were in the early stages of rotting, and Chuck had no idea how to go about fixing them anyway. He left the dripping bag at the agent's feet. He'd lost his nets but gained complaining rights.

When Chuck got back to Harow, he went over to the Law Department to ask if the Borough could sue the Fish and Wildlife Service for destroying his nets.

"Unfortunately, I think this would be more of a personal action that you'd have to bring yourself," Bertie said.

Chuck frowned. "But maybe the Fish and Wildlife people could be targeting us as a whole because of our Iñupiaq culture and values." Remembering a line from one of many speeches made by his Uncle Luther, Chuck added, "Maybe the feds are retaliating against us because we oppose offshore oil."

"Hmmm, do you think the U.S. Fish and Wildlife Service has an interest in oil drilling?" Bertie asked dryly. "Seems like it would interfere with endangered animals."

"You bet they care about oil. They're *the feds*."

Regardless of their interests and motives, someone at the U.S. Fish and Wildlife Service decided it would be worth taking the time to educate us about the federal law. Agents started holding public meetings to explain to hunters that they couldn't just go out and shoot a duck.

They'd have to get a duck stamp, and limit themselves to a certain number in a certain area in a certain season, and shoot in certain places at certain times using certain bullets. The agents figured the rules for hunting shouldn't have been any more trouble than the rules for driving.

Bertie knew it was going to be a hell of a lot of trouble. She had been to only one meeting on hunting rules, during which the director of the Borough's Wildlife and Subsistence Department broke into tears and shouted, "There's no way me and my kids are gonna drive down to the post office to get stamps to practice our aboriginal rights!"

When Vik came on board, Bertie decided to task her with all migratory bird issues.

In March 2008, Vik goes to a public meeting hosted by Fish and Wildlife agents, and takes notes on public concerns. She watches an unhappy Fish and Wildlife biologist with a sagging face sigh and take the microphone. He's already made two mistakes, Vik observes. First, he didn't open the meeting with a prayer. Second, he didn't have an Iñupiaq translator.

Most of the elders can speak English, but don't if they have a choice. Outsiders who subject elders to public meetings are expected to pay someone in the community to be a translator.

The Fish and Wildlife biologist would have liked to be friendly with the Arctic Slope residents, since he's gone to so much trouble to save their birds. But he knows by the angry looks he's getting that this is not going to happen. He braces himself for the first question, which is about how the Fish and Wildlife Service's own research is impacting migratory birds.

The biologist exhales into the microphone, ready to disabuse the locals once again of their notion that birds abandon nests that have been touched by humans.

"Actually, we've done studies on this very question," he says. He attempts to explain the concept of a control group of nests that weren't touched, and an experimental group of touched nests. He says that the number of birds who abandoned their nests were the same in each group.

The audience doesn't buy it. "I'm sure the birds in the control group sensed the stress of the others," one woman in an enormous jogging suit says, "and that's why they left, too. It's the same thing with us—if we know something bad is happening with our neighbors, we're going to be stressed, just like them."

Another woman says it's not fair that Fish and Wildlife biologists don't get citations for birds hurt by their research. "I understand what you're doing," she says. "You're trying to study them to death. Try knocking off the science for a couple of years."

The concern shifts from the birds' welfare to the welfare of the ecosystem. "You shouldn't play God," announces a reformed alcoholic. "That's what you're doing if you try to increase the eider population with all your studies."

The agents move on to the more earthly topic of using steel shot instead of lead shot. But the rules on what kinds of shot can be used are almost as complicated as the rules for medical marijuana. Vik sees the agents floundering, and takes the task of deciphering the rules on herself. She stands up and adopts a voice like John Travolta in *Pulp Fiction*.

"Okay, it breaks down like this. It's legal to sell it. It's legal to buy it. It's legal to POSSESS it, but not when—" she finds herself forced back into her normal legalese "—not when you have the objective appearance to the reasonable person of being out in the field with the intention of hunting ducks."

The woman in the enormous jogging suit stands up and began a series of what-ifs.

"What if there's no steel shot around? Or what if there is steel shot, but I don't have enough money to afford it? What if my children are hungry, and I gotta go out in the field with lead shot to get them some food?"

The speech would have been more compelling if the Borough's Wildlife and Subsistence Department hadn't just announced that anyone with lead shot could exchange it for free steel shot at the department's office.

The audience turns toward more constructive solutions. The Fish and Wildlife agents in Washington could step outside their office, march next door to Congress, tell them to make lead shot illegal. That way no one would try to trick people into buying it. And the Fish and Wildlife agents could do more than just breeze in and out of town for meetings—they should come to the local whaling celebrations or Thanksgiving so we can see what kind of people they really are.

We know who the Iñupiat are. The Iñupiat have hunted migratory birds for thousands of years. Until now, the Iñupiat have never had a federal agent hovering over them, saying that the duck-hunting rules apply to everyone, not just the *tanik* sport hunters. The reformed alcoholic points to her head. "This is my license right here," he says. "I'm Iñupiaq."

A man who heard that Fish and Wildlife agents were testing for avian flu asks, "Why is the government testing our birds for flu when it never tests anything else around here to see if it's healthy? No one's testing the caribou meat to see if it's contaminated with radiation or toxic chemicals. And then the government expects us to bring it all home whether it's contaminated or not!"

The biologist casts a puzzled look around the room. Vik takes the microphone and clears her throat.

"I think the gentleman is referring to the state law prohibiting waste of caribou meat. The law requires, um, at least the legs and the back, I think, of the caribou to be brought home, regardless of the health of the animal before it died."

The audience has started talking over Vik. Someone yells, "Our people have hunted since time immemorial and we know our own animals and we know if one is sick. Take your biologists and go home!"

The Fish and Wildlife agents sit frozen in their chairs behind the table that separates them from the audience. A few people push over their chairs in disgust and march out. The rest of the audience follows, along with Vik, who doesn't want to be left alone with the Fish and Wildlife agents. She's already been mistaken for one at the beginning of the meeting, and wonders if this was why no one wanted to listen to her. Or maybe it's just plainly obvious to everyone that Vik has never once held a gun, and couldn't possibly have anything to offer on the subject of bird hunting.

Chapter 10- Junk

We know it's springtime in Arctic Alaska when the mounds of snow begin to subside. Some of the snow sublimates strait into the dry air. Some of it melts from the sunlight shining through the crystals of snow and ice, even though the temperature is still below zero.

In April, every rooftop and ceiling on the Arctic Slope begins to drip. In May, the first patches of barren dirt emerge. The land becomes soft, and then slushy, and there's hope that something green will come up eventually.

With the melting snow comes a burst of activity—it's a time for new life and a time for new oil and gas projects. For the Borough's Community Development Department, it's a time for fieldtrips to inspect whatever might need inspecting.

Gill is good at finding ways to go on fieldtrips, and generous about letting others, even *taniks,* come along. When he realizes that Vik has never been to a real village, he asks if she wants to come and examine the gravel airstrip in the village of Atkuq.

"Why?" Vik asks. She has a hard enough time living in Harow, and fears being stranded in an even smaller village. She's heard about people getting stuck in remote villages for days when storms keep the planes from flying.

"They got a grant to expand their airstrip a couple of years ago but never did any work on it. The Borough's gonna take the grant over, but, you know, we want to inspect the area first. I heard somebody drilled some wells near the airstrip a long time ago without a permit and then left a bunch of trash around."

"Oh," Vik says. "Maybe you could sue somebody to clean it all up."

"If it wasn't the Borough or the village who did the damage. We'll see."

On a Tuesday afternoon in early May, Vik finds herself trudging behind Gill through the slushy tundra just past the airstrip near the village of Atkuq. A weather-beaten man in the village who says he knows the where-abouts of the junk pile accompanies them.

"It's right near my camp," he says. "I want to take you out on my four-wheeler, but it got stalled yesterday from all the mush. Give it a few more weeks and this is gonna be one big pond—you're gonna see all kinds of fish flopping around in the middle of the tundra."

"We're just on a day trip," Vik says, concerned about catching the evening flight.

"The junk starts right about here," the man says, ignoring Vik. "Here you got some old bones and old skid frames, then over there's the mud buckets, then the springs and pipe wrenches and glass soda bottles. Finally you got the whole big junk pile over there, more than a hundred 55-gallon drums."

The drums are arranged in groups of four and covered with gashes. Whatever was inside has long since joined the greater tundra environment. But there's nothing that looks like an abandoned well, at least. Gill and Vik can hope that the damage is only surface-deep.

"What do you think was in there?" Vik asks the man.

"I don't know about that, but I do know our city council passed a resolution saying you guys gotta clean the mess up."

"You mean the Borough, or white people in general?" Vik asks.

"But your lieutenant mayor, the big *tanik* with the glasses, says the Borough won't clean up a mess that the U.S. military made. Except the military don't want to clean it up either. They probably done it back in the 40s or 50s, when they called this whole area of our land the Naval Petroleum Reserve. Now they say the military don't control it anymore."

"Probably because the National Petroleum Reserve–Alaska is now under the jurisdiction of the Bureau of Land Management," Vik explains.

"Anyway, you wanna see my camp?" the man asks.

"What kinda grub you got?" Gill asks, rubbing his stomach.

"Whatever the bears didn't get," the man responds, and he and Gill chuckle. They walk in the direction of the camp, and, out of a mixture of social obligation and curiosity, Vik follows.

The camp is a shed and a generator that the man had hauled out to the tundra with his snowmachine. The man's grub is a sampling of everything available at the local store, which is the size of Vik's office and mostly sells outdated products whose first ingredient is corn syrup. The man turns on the generator to fire up the space heater and play a Christian music CD recorded by his cousin in Anchorage. Vik eats a Sailor Boy cracker and waits for the experience to be over.

Gill finally checks his watch and reckons they should get back to make the evening flight. But when Gill and Vik get to town, they learn that the plane came and went early to medevac someone to Fairbanks. If they're lucky, it'll come back this evening. Otherwise, they'll have to stay in the village health clinic, since there's no hotel in this town of 224 souls.

The village liaison, who is hired by the Borough to sit in the Borough's Atkuq office all day and answer the phone, offers to take Gill and Vik on a driving tour of the village.

Vik protests, "Uh, since Atkuq's only three blocks long, couldn't we just walk?" Gill and the liaison climb into the Borough's Atkuq office truck, ignoring Vik, and Vik scrambles in after them.

"There's actually a city council meeting going on tonight," the liaison says a few minutes later, when the tour ends. "You should go while you're waiting for the plane."

"Yeah," Gill says noncommittally.

"You can explain when the Borough's gonna clean up that junk pile—isn't that what you're out here to do?"

"Maybe we should go and explain that it's the liability of the federal Bureau of Land Management, not the Borough," Vik suggests. "We could just sort of educate them on how the different federal agencies work. I've noticed that people around here like to lump all the government agencies together into what they call 'the feds.'"

It turns out that no one on the city council is interested in the inner mechanisms of the feds. Of much greater importance is the Atkuq Salvation Church's request for an $8,000 donation from the city council.

"What is this money supposed to be for?" asks one of the councilmen apologetically. The church leader explains that it's for whatever the church might need, from hymnals to sponsoring Sing-spirations to traveling to other villages for their celebrations.

"Kusoq invited us to their village's 35th anniversary and we had to miss it because we didn't have the money," the church leader explains.

Eight thousand dollars would be just enough to cover the plane tickets for twelve church members to travel the two hundred miles between Atkuq and Kusoq.

The apologetic councilman explains that the city is also obliged to make donations to the Food Bank and the search and rescue squad, and usually donations are only given after a group has made some effort to raise its own funds. The other councilmen nod.

"We probably couldn't give any more than $5,000," the apologetic councilman says.

Vik opens her mouth to say something about the separation of church and state but closes it. This is not her beat.

The church leader says that $5,000 would be okay, and the council votes unanimously to approve the donation. The village liaison stands up and applauds, and everyone else in the room follows suit.

The applause is drowned out by the sound of the plane landing. Vik stands up nervously.

"I'll give you a ride to the airstrip," the village liaison offers.

At the airstrip one block over, Gill and Vik wait while the plane is unloaded.

"There's the new cop," the village liaison points. "She just started last month. Comes in every month for a two-week shift."

"What happened to the old cop?" Vik asks.

The village liaison shakes her head. "They finally got rid of him. But not before he took away our kids."

"What do you mean?" Vik asks.

"'Cause he said the parents were drunk. They took my grandkids, who I was raising, and I wasn't even drunk. Now they're adopted in Harow, and they got a different last name."

"Wouldn't someone have to take you to court before they could take your kids away?" Vik asks. "It's pretty hard to take someone's kids, actually. It ought to be easier."

The village liaison shrugs and says she gave up. "Nobody can never afford a lawyer around here. Except the Borough."

The pilot waves at Vik and Gill to get on the plane or be left behind, and Vik runs to claim her spot. After takeoff, Vik watches the village, airstrip, and junk pile melt into the massive tundra.

"What a mess," she says.

Gill, assuming she's referring to the junk pile, says, "The feds left all kinds of junk on our land. Just go northeast from Harow five miles to Point Lonely, if you want to see more."

"Yep. I guess it's kind of ironic that environmentalists in the Lower 48 don't want to open up the Arctic National Wildlife Refuge for drilling, because they think everything up here is so pristine."

Gill pauses. He's not sure what Vik is trying to say with the word "pristine." But he's pretty sure that Vik is actually one of those environmentalist opposed to drilling everywhere, while he and most everyone else in the Borough support onshore drilling. As long as the oil companies get permits from him, and the permits have stipulations to protect the Iñupiat's subsistence hunting, he doesn't see any reason to oppose development.

Vik changes the subject. "Does your family have any allotments around here?" She knows that the Whiteheads have allotments all over the place. The 1906 Native Allotment Act allowed any native to apply for up to 160 acres of land, but it was left completely up to the natives to decipher the law into the vernacular. It was no surprise that less than one percent of the Iñupiat had managed to get allotments, and that most of the one percent were from the half-*tanik* Whitehead family.

The Act was repealed in 1972, and any last applications were to be submitted by 1973. Every member of the extended Whitehead family applied for and received an allotment, except for Gill's older brother, who was in Vietnam. Gill and his other siblings picked out spots next to where their father had discovered oil seeps. They knew that one day the oil companies would be knocking at their door, ready to pay all kinds of rent to get at the oil. They're still waiting, but the oil companies are bound to come some day.

"I think Ernie Whitehead's got an allotment somewhere around here," Gill said absently.

"Ernie Whitehead the ex-mayor/Assembly president?"

"Uh huh."

"Did you know there's another Ernie Whitehead in town?"

"Uh ..." Gill can't keep up with how many kids and grandkids each of his first cousins have by now. He has a hard enough time keeping up with his own kids. One's in Eugene, Oregon, where Gill goes for conferences. The one from the Tovak girl already has kids of her own. Then there are two from the elementary school teacher, and one more from his current girlfriend.

"Yep. There's a Filipino family who had their last name changed in court." Vik knows because she ran Ernie Whitehead's name through a legal search engine to check out his criminal conviction. "They had a kid named Ernie, and the court granted their petition, so I guess the kid's name is Ernie Whitehead now."

"*Arraa*—no way!" Gill says. "I wonder what the real Ernie Whitehead would say about that."

"Who knows. Anyhow, there're so many Filipinos around here now that some of them are starting to marry Eskimos. Look at Luther Ericsen, the old president of the Iñupiat Community of the Arctic Slope—he's got half-Filipino grandkids now."

"We-ell," Gill drawls. Gill only knows one half-Filipino in Harow, and that one is gay. Not that Gill's homophobic. As Gill can tell you, no one in Harow is really homophobic because no one in Harow is gay, aside from a few Filipinos.

Gill looks out the window and is relieved to see that they're already flying over Point Harow—the end of a 10-mile spit that starts just outside of Harow. Being alone with Vik for too long makes him nervous, and he's ready to get out and go shoot something with his son.

Gill and his brothers like to take their sons out to the "Duck Camp" near Point Harow for target practice, even though the Whiteheads have much nicer places to hunt at their allotments. In the days before four-wheelers, Gill's father and many others built shacks at Duck Camp. They'd stay out there hunting ducks for days at a time, instead of going back and forth to their homes in Harow.

The shacks were pretty much abandoned once everyone got four-wheelers. Their only use now is by teenage couples who want a little privacy. And even with the convenience of four-wheelers, some hunters have stopped going all the way out to Duck Camp. Gill's seen more than one hunter stop his truck where the gravel road ends, open the truck door, crouch behind it, and wait for a flock of ducks to shoot at. Today's guns are so fast and good that a hunter has to resist the temptation to take out the whole flock.

When they were at Duck Camp last year, Gill's seven-year-old son managed to shoot half of a flock before it scattered. The rest fell down in various states of mortality, some in the water, and some on the land. Gill's son must have used up forty bullets in the process. Gill laughed and told his son, "You're going to have a lot of duck to eat, 'cause I'm not going to eat nothing with that much lead in it!"

Gill usually lets the ducks that fall in the water go unless he has his lab to retrieve them. He'll wait a bit until the landed ducks are dead and then wring their necks if for some reason they're still alive.

Of course Gill wasn't really going to make his son eat something that was shot up too badly, or even something that was shot the wrong way. That would be contrary to custom and common sense. Gill has told his son many times how lucky the boy is—the Filipinos and Koreans who've started hunting ducks as of late never had the benefit of learning the Iñupiat hunting values. With all these different people hunting at Duck Camp, things aren't like they used to be.

A few days after Gill's Atkuq trip, a Coast Guard officer calls to ask if it'll be possible for the Coast Guard to practice their aerial target shooting out near Duck Camp. They won't be right over Duck Camp, they'll just be aiming at the nearby landfill.

"I don't know, I think you gotta get a conditional use permit for that," Gill says. "The Development Planning Commission has to approve that, and it takes a few months. My staff can only approve the minor stuff. Like with the Fish and Wildlife agents, I had them come in and get a permit to drive their four-wheelers off the road out there, but it was just an administrative permit."

The officer pauses. "Actually, uh, some of our guys will be up there next week, maybe we could just show you what we plan to do. We're not going to be hitting anything too explosive."

"We-ell," Gill pauses to think. "We could have a pre-application meeting out at the proposed shooting site, and then we could always do an after-the-fact permit if you have to start right away." He doesn't want to stand in the way of development, even target practice, just because he's not the one authorized to give out a permit.

On the appointed pre-application meeting day, Gill parks the Community Development Department van by the landfill and waits for the Coast Guard. The Coast Guard officers stiffly emerge from their unmarked car and look with wrinkled noses at the heaps of junk around them.

On the spectrum of landfills, running from sanitary to dumpy, the Harow landfill is at the dumpy end. It sits just a short distance from the ocean, waiting to be dragged in by a storm.

The Coast Guard officials shake hands firmly with Gill and try to make small talk about the landfill.

"So what's that stuff in those piles?" one of them asks Gill, pointing to a pair of ten-foot mounds near the entrance.

"Oh, those are just the leftover eider ducks," Gill said.

The Coast Guard officials look alarmed.

"It's not like any kind of endangered species," Gill assures them. "Just common and king eiders."

One of the officials pokes the pile with his combat boot, sending a cascade of snow down the side. The smell of rot seeps through the cold air.

"Usually we have special dumpsters for them," Gill says, "but Public Works hasn't had time to set them up this year."

The officials stare at Gill in disbelief.

"What's the big deal?" Gill asks. "You never clean out your freezer in the spring? That's all this is. It just so happened we had a pretty good whale harvest this spring, so folks had to make space in their ice cellars."

In the end, the Coast Guard officers are okay with dropping targets on dead ducks, and Gill's okay with it too as long as they have some sort of permit.

Chapter 11- Officer Shoak on the Prowl

In May 2008, Gill decides he's going to build a greenhouse in his backyard. It will be the second greenhouse on the Arctic Slope—his mother built the first when they were kids, and raised them with potatoes and cabbage.

Getting a Borough permit for the greenhouse is easy, since Gill's in charge of the Community Development Department's permitting division. All he has to do is type up the permit and get Larry to sign it. Then it's time to get out there and dig. And there's nothing like swinging into the ground with a pickaxe!

He hasn't gotten very far when he strikes a bone. It shouldn't have been a surprise. When the *taniks* brought the flu in the early 1900s, dozens of bodies had been buried right outside of people's homes. Even the Borough's Iñupiat museum was built on top of a gravesite.

Gill knows he's supposed to stop digging right then and there and call the police, even though he drafted his permit to exclude this standard requirement. He leans over and smoothes the dusty soil over the bone. It's a dry year—the snow started sublimating into vapor in early April. The dirt's like cement.

Gill moves two feet over and takes another swing into the ground. A few more swings reveal another bone. He puts the pickaxe down and looks around the yard for another spot for the greenhouse. But if the archeologists come out here to investigate, they'll probably dig up his whole yard. There'll be no way to get a greenhouse in for the summer growing season.

Gill reluctantly calls the police, and the chief agrees to send someone out the next morning.

Gill forgets to tell his girlfriend about the police coming, and she answers the door just after putting out her morning joint.

Officer Gray Shoak is waiting at the door with his tight little mustache and bullet-proof vest. He stares at Gill's girlfriend, clears his throat, and addresses her breasts: "Police. Can I come in?"

In theory, Gill's girlfriend doesn't have anything to worry about. Anyone in Alaska can have up to four ounces of weed or 25 live plants in the house. It's guaranteed in the Alaska constitution.

Dealing with Officer Shoak is another story. He's a recovering alcoholic with violent tendencies exacerbated by sobriety. Last year, he beat up his girlfriend after she threw out all his booze. The police chief had to arrest him. He didn't get fired, though, until he threatened to use his sniper skills to take out every cop in Harow. The Police Department ended up rehiring him out of desperation a few months later, since it was woefully understaffed. The chief took his guns away and left him with a billy club. Officer Shoak swore off alcohol for good, and made himself into a rescuer of drunk women at parties needing a ride home.

Gill's girlfriend pulls her robe over as much of her cleavage as it can cover.

"What do you want?" she asks.

Officer Shoak likes to get people talking. If the words are slurry, there's a good chance he's found an alcoholic. He'll make a note to hang out near the house in a patrol car and catch her driving drunk. If the words are too fast, then she might be on meth.

"How are we?" Officer Shoak tries to put people at ease by using the first person plural.

"Who's we?"

"You been smoking weed?" he asks.

"Yeah," she says. "But I know my rights."

"You dealing?"

"No."

Gill comes out of the kitchen and stares at his half-naked stoned girlfriend and the officer dressed in a bullet proof vest with a billy club.

"What the heck are you doing? Somebody was supposed to be here looking at the bones in my backyard."

Officer Shoak gives up the ghost and goes out to the back of the house to look at the bones. But he doesn't know any more about bones than Gill does. He pokes at one of the exposed bones with his billy club.

"Don't look recent," he says.

"It sure don't," Gill agrees.

"Well, I think we're not looking at a crime scene, so you could go ahead and call an archeologist." He brushes nonexistent dust off his hands and heads up the steps to the back door.

"You don't have to go through the house to get out of here, you know," Gill informs him. He pointed the way out with his pickaxe.

Officer Shoak starts to reach for his billy club, but an alert comes over his VHF radio about a stolen car a few streets over.

"10-4," Officer Shoak says into the radio. He jumps into his police SUV and activates the siren. There are so few times when a Harow officer can justify activating the siren, and Officer Shoak makes sure he takes full advantage of each one.

The perpetrator is rounding the block, in no particular hurry, when Officer Shoak stops her. It's the high school daughter of one of his neighbors.

"How are we today?" he asks politely.

"Okay," the girl says, glancing nervously at Officer Shoak's billy club.

"Headed anywhere in particular or just for a joyride?"

"It's my cousin's car. I was just taking it home from the store 'cause I didn't have money for a taxi, and it's still way cold."

It's a common story. No one locks their car doors in Harow. To keep things from freezing up, car owners will leave their keys in the ignition with the engine running. An owner's best friend or cousin or neighbor or distant relative might "borrow" the car and might bring it back some time later on. Or not.

The police chief has a policy of reporting back to the victim and allowing him/her to decide whether to arrest the carnapper. The victim almost never wants to be responsible for an arrest—he or she just wants the carnapper to put gas in the car before bringing it back.

When Officer Shoak gets the girl's cousin on the line, the cousin just requests that the car be brought back sometime before tomorrow with a full tank. Turning off the siren but leaving on the flashing lights, Officer Shoak follows the girl to the gas station. He waits while she uses her parents' credit card to fill up the tank.

"If taxis would just accept credit cards, I wouldn't a-had to borrow my cousin's car," the girl says. Officer Shoak follows the girl to the cousin's house, where she leaves the car.

"Want a ride back to your house?" Officer Shoak asks, observing the girls nipples showing through her shirt. "You seem to have lost your coat. And I'm feeling nice today."

The girl shrugs her shoulders and climbs into the front seat of the police SUV. She's silent except for popping her gum.

"You're Ernie Whitehead's granddaughter, aren't you?"

"Yeah? So?"

"What's your name?"

"Gloria."

"Well, Gloria, you should be glad we didn't have to arrest you today," he says, envisioning how she would look in handcuffs.

When they get to her house, he pats her knee and tells her to behave herself. She slams the door so hard that the window comes open.

Officer Shoak touches the handcuffs he keeps on his belt. It's rare that he gets to use them on anyone, actually. Usually, arrestees are handcuffed only when traveling by plane with the State Marshal to the Anchorage prison. The convicts go out, while alcohol—often the basis of the convicts' crime—comes in on pallet after pallet.

In the past, the airline let Officer Shoak search bags for illegal alcohol before they went to the baggage claim area. Then someone raised a fuss about unconstitutional searches, and the officers were left with the sole option of securing a warrant based on probable cause that alcohol would be in a particular bag.

Given the near impossibility of securing this kind of warrant, Officer Shoak went to the Law Department to see if there was any way he could get around the Constitution.

"I could just go out on the runway and stop the whole plane, couldn't I?" he asked Vik. "I mean, it's pretty probable that someone on that plane's bootlegging something."

"I don't think you can seize the plane," Vik said. "But I'll do some research and get back to you."

Since then, Vik has never flown into Harow without a suitcase full of booze. Officer Shoak resorted to standing near the airport exit looking menacing, but Vik knew he couldn't do any more than that.

Vik had worked on Officer Shoak's discharge and reinstatement in 2007, and had read through his lengthy personnel file. She found out that he'd been fired three years before for brewing peach whiskey moonshine. A news article in the file said he sold it in white plastic trash bags for $50 a gallon to as many as ten people a day. The state trooper who busted him found more than nineteen gallons of homebrew—topped with rehydrated dried peaches for flavor—in a large trash can in Officer Shoak's closet. Office Shoak had apparently resigned before he could be fired. The file said only that he left the job because he was "unable to follow the policies of his employer."

Fourteen months later, Officer Shoak was rehired. A job ad had been out for the entire time, and no one but Officer Shoak applied for the position. Eskimos in Harow didn't want to be affiliated with the police, so it was near-impossible to hire locally. And it was almost as hard to lure someone from Anchorage to do time in Harow on a police officer's salary.

Officer Shoak isn't Iñupiaq or even Eskimo. He's half Athabascan, the tribe from Alaska's interior, and half *tanik*. He shares a *tanik* father from Mississippi with Assemblyman Chuck, who's lucky enough to have an Iñupiaq mother. After a teenage identity crisis, Chuck decided that he was Iñupiaq, and that he had to preserve his family's Iñupiaq heritage.

In his early twenties, Chuck didn't have much going for him in the Iñupiaq culture department. He couldn't do the Eskimo dances and didn't know how to hunt. His teenage crisis had kept him from going whaling, and he figured it was too late to learn. He could speak no more Iñupiaq than a *tanik*.

At age 25, Chuck decided to bolster his Iñupiaqness by making himself the announcer for all Iñupiaq events that had never before needed an announcer, like the Spring Games or the Christmas dance. He overcame his shyness with the help of a little meth. This was back in the days before the Alaska public radio stations aired anti-meth commercials every hour, and when Sudafed was put out on the grocery shelves for the taking.

Chuck got himself elected to the School Board on a platform of bringing the Iñupiaq language back to the schools. It became a fifty-minute class, held twice a week, until it was done in by the frenzy to meet the standards of the No Child Left Behind Act. He moved on to the Assembly with fiery rhetoric about Oriental people taking over all the Arctic Slope jobs. He took a brief hiatus to go to rehab for his meth problem, and then came back full of proposed resolutions and ordinances to better Iñupiat society.

The rehab wasn't really voluntary. Officer Shoak had found Chuck running around naked in the snow drifts around his car, screaming about the Apocalypse. The meth was right there in the ashtray. Since Chuck was technically his brother, Officer Shoak decided that the right thing to do would be to bring Chuck back to his house and leave him in a quiet storage closet until the trip was over. Officer Shoak offered to refrain from arresting Chuck if he could get the Assembly to pass a resolution raising the police officer's salary. The resolution got voted down, though, and in a moment of panic, Chuck flew to Anchorage and checked himself into rehab.

It amazes Officer Shoak that people like Chuck are allowed to be in positions of power.

Chapter 12 - Meeting Again

Going to public meetings on the Arctic Slope is like an unpaid part-time job. Almost every weeknight, some outfit from Anchorage swoops down on Harow or a village and explains the important changes that are about to take place all around. The meeting might be the one and only chance to comment.

The oil companies have learned how to make a few concessions for all the hours of PowerPoint presentations they put us through. They offer hors d'oeuvres and door prizes, and they let an Iñupiaq elder kick off the meeting with a prayer.

The federal government put on no such façade—it's all business. Agents come in, ask questions, and record hours of local knowledge that will be stored in boxes on shelves set aside for Arctic Slope meeting records. The following year, different agents will come back, ask the same questions, and put the same answers on the same shelves. The proposed agency actions always go forward, unhindered by any of our concerns.

Vik limits herself to one meeting a week in Harow, and sometimes she gets sent out to monitor village meetings. She actually prefers the meetings put on by federal agencies—they're shorter since fewer people show up.

At a meeting in one of the villages with five federal agents and only three residents, one young woman takes pains to set the agency straight.

"You gotta bring door prizes, or nobody's gonna show up. That's the way it is."

An agent in overly tight pants explains to the young woman that the agency has a public trust responsibility to avoid wasting taxpayer money.

"Our offices don't even provide coffee for us," he says. "All the employees have to chip in and get it themselves."

"Well, there's a Cacoco Oil meeting going on at the high school across the street," the young woman says, "and they're giving out door prizes."

"And it's Wednesday," says a woman with freckles, who could be one of the Whiteheads. "You aren't supposed to have meetings on Wednesday. It's our church night."

The agent in tight pants looks defeated. He's also given up his church night to come to the meeting.

"We'll come back, then," he says. "How about next week, on a different night?"

The supervisor of the agent in tight pants looks at him in wonder. Even if only two agents come, the plane tickets alone will cost $2,000.

But the agents do come back on a Thursday night. With nothing but free mouse pads to offer, they manage to draw a crowd of 32 residents.

The agent from the last meeting, who's wearing a different pair of tight pants, takes the microphone and introduces himself. He adds, "Before we do anything, we are going to say a prayer to steer us hopefully in the right direction." He figures he might as well violate the First Amendment principle of separation of church and state, since he's already violating the public trust doctrine with the mouse pad giveaway.

The theme of the meeting is the government's plan to lease the Chukchi Sea to the highest-bidding oil companies. The audience sits through the government's PowerPoint presentation with clenched jaws. We tell them again and again that we don't want offshore development, and it just gets lost of the noise of Sarah Palin's "Drill, Baby, Drill."

The young woman who came to the last meeting is back, trying to explain to the agents that the ocean is the Iñupiat garden.

"Go drill by the North Pole if you have to, but leave our garden alone. I mean, we all depend on it, and you want to make it into a toilet."

The agency has brought a translator from Nome, with the wrong Iñupiaq dialect, to translate the elders' testimonies. She sits mute while the elders testify in mournful chants, as if praying. They tell their life histories, from the days with no electricity to these days of Twittering. The translator reduces each history to a simple paragraph in English, in part to save time and in part to avoid criticism from audience members who understand Iñupiaq well enough to shout out corrections, but not well enough to do simultaneous translations.

One elder ventures a testimony in English, to make sure the feds understand her.

"I know the old times my grandfather tell me about. There is more than one Iñupiat—the coast people and the mountain people. They are both independent, but they got a communication system to trade merchandise and to keep each other supplies with goods. The inland people are the ones that move at all times, depends mostly on the location of the *tuttu*—the caribou—and fish. But when there is no *tuttu*, we starve. Sometimes got to leave new born babies and elders on the way. The elders just request a little shelter and tell their sons and grandchildren goodbye, he die to save them. That's how life goes."

The elder pauses to catch her breath. The room is silent except for a group of kids chasing each other in the hallway. The elder continues, "Many now living say the oil rigs on the Arctic Slope stand where his grandfathers fought and starved to keep the land."

She heaves and shudders, and then sits down. The resident *tanik* pastor puts an arm around her and asks if she wants to keep going. She shakes her head.

The pastor takes the microphone and tells the audience he's been shepherding the village for a year and a half now. "But I've already had 27 funerals in my congregation. And when you look at the cause of death, you will see a lot of suicide. And if you want to know why there is suicide, let me tell you something. These Elders taught the people, you know, how to live, how to be proud. Taught us how to hunt. And then when these children of ours get big enough to go do that, what do they run into? State law that says no, federal law that says no, oil development that's destroyed the land. This is the reason for suicide amongst our young kids, something that should have never happened. We can't stop it. All we can do is try to teach them how to be proud of who they are."

The room sags with the weight of the last two testimonies. A man with a double chin takes the microphone to liven things up.

"I'm an *umialik*, a whaling captain, and I'm telling you first thing, you need to stop leasing out there for a while. We just got done suing you, and you send us some environmental assessment saying it's okay to lease more of our garden in violation of your own laws. I think you guys don't learn very fast."

"Are you referring to the lawsuit that the Arctic Slope Borough, the Iñupiat Community of the Arctic, and the Alaska Eskimo Whalers Council brought against the Department of the Interior for approving oil and gas lease sales of the Beaufort Sea? Because that's a different agency from the one I represent."

The man with the double chin looks angry. "You think I'm stupid? Let me tell you, we are educated. We went to your schools. We can even speak your language just as good as you. I mean, what gives?"

The man sits down, not expecting an answer. The agents nervously whisper to each other, and an older woman with a weather-beaten face gets up to take his place.

"In the past few years, I harvested two sick animals in the ocean, a walrus and a bearded seal. I had them tested by the Borough's wildlife people, and they came back with malignant cancer. I'm sorry but how does a seal in the ocean come up with cancer? You know, it has to be from what it's eating, the food chain. You can tell when an animal is sick. I had an eight-foot bearded seal that had absolutely, absolutely no meat on—on its rear end. When I asked the wildlife people why—if they could come over and check, they told me that I put that animal out of its misery."

The Borough biologist who ran the tests also said that there was a background incidence of cancer in any animal population, and that the animals found with cancer were nothing out of the norm. The woman testifying didn't believe it.

"It's in the food chain," she says again, "and you're just gonna make it worse."

The man with the double chin comes back for another round.

"You know, if that oil spills, the traditional way of hunting walrus, bearded seal, and polar bears gonna be gone forever. I am a believer of traditional beliefs that a whale deliberately give itself up to a whaling crew."

The elders and whaling captains in the room nod.

"The whale knows this when he begins his journey from the breeding grounds. The whale don't give up until it's successfully struck. It's the same with the other animals. All animals great and small are treated with respect, and I don't want this ritual to get lost by some oil spill or all that noise in our ocean.

"I'm telling you what happened in the seventies when you people told my father—a whaling captain—that he couldn't hunt whale no more 'cause the population was too low. It drove him to drinking."

The other agent, the one without tight pants, giggles and becomes the recipient of 32 cold stares.

"I'm sorry," he promptly apologizes, "I'm not laughing at your father. It's just a figurative American expression, what you said about being driven to drinking. I'm sorry."

The testimony continues.

"My dad's a whaling captain, and that's what I am now since he died. And being a whaling captain is not cheap. Early in the season, a captain can spend maybe twenty grand getting the whale hunt ready for this community. A captain, everybody knows he's a highly-respected provider. And we don't get anything out of it, what we spend. We do it because we are Iñupiat and this is our tradition."

A white teacher who considers herself part of the community takes the microphone next and says softly, "I want you to know that I respect the way the Iñupiaqs respect their tradition and live in the modern era at the same time." She clears her throat, and the audience looks at her skeptically. *Iñupiaq* with a "q" refers to the language or one person. *Iñupiat* with a "t" refers to the people. There's no such word as *Iñupiaqs*.

"All those animal rights activists crying over the fact that today's whale hunters use modern equipment is ridiculous. This is coming from people that do their hunting/gathering at Costless and Giga-Mart! This is coming from people whose idea of traditional food is hot dogs on July Fourth, people who wouldn't dream of plowing their field with oxen."

The audience claps politely. The woman beams and sits down, taking off the huge fur parka she had been wearing up until then.

The audience has already started to thin out, and the remainders shuffle home with mouse pads and a vague sense of déjà-vu. There's an

Ethon Gas Co. meeting in two days, and they'll have to gather their strength and go through this all over again.

Chapter 13- Iñupiaq Bones

Iñupiaq was not a written language until 1944, when a white linguist helped an Iñupiaq preacher translate the New Testament into Iñupiaq. Spellings were a point of debate between the different Iñupiat settlements, with each wanting to spell according to its own distinct pronunciations. In 2008, there are still no standardized spellings and only a handful of Iñupiat elders that can't speak English. They speak their native language softly in public, as if in a hangover from the days when speaking the vernacular was as suspect as practicing communism.

Most of the elders agree that their knowledge should be passed down orally in Iñupiaq. Write it down, the thinking goes, and it'll be snatched up by *taniks* from the Outside and misused. All of the secret hunting places, trails, and locations of oil seeps will be discovered and eviscerated.

The Iñupiat History, Language, and Culture Commission has been in place since the formation of the Borough, to guard against the constant creep of *tanik* civilization. The commission, composed of mayor-appointed, bearded old men who speak English only when they have to, meet four times a year to conduct official business.

The commission isn't totally opposed to working with *tanik* professionals to refine the collective body of traditional knowledge. It endorsed a project where *tanik* biologists worked with elders to put together a booklet about fishing practices on the Arctic Slope. But the commission voted against publishing the booklet. A single copy is kept in the Borough's Iñupiat museum and checked out once a year by a visiting anthropologist.

No one on the commission is a professional archeologist, anthropologist, or historian in the Western/university sense. This means that the commission is disqualified from getting state or federal funding unless it keeps a "professional" on staff or under contract. Recognizing the benefits of government money, the commission retains a local *tanik* elementary school teacher with a degree in archeology.

The commission pays the teacher to supervise the archeological expeditions that take place along Harow's coastline. Every summer, a slew of Outsider archeologists flock to the sites of pre- and early Iñupiat civilization, hoping to find a few more relics before the sites completely erode into the ocean. The teacher's job is to make sure that nobody hauls to the Lower 48 what belongs to the Iñupiat.

Since the teacher's been on the beat, no one's tried to make off with an Iñupiaq relic. The archeologists bring whatever they find to the Borough's Iñupiat museum, and then sign agreements allowing their Lower 48 universities to borrow the relic for the next decade. Chances are that the Iñupiat museum will lose the paperwork.

Gill calls the elementary-school-teacher-cum-archeologist a few days after finding bones in his backyard and asks if she can take a look. She joins Gill in his backyard and quickly determines that the bones are at least 100 years old.

At the next Iñupiat History, Language, and Culture Commission meeting, the archeologist presents a report on the bones and asks how the commission would like the matter to be handled. The commissioners decide that the bones should be excavated and then immediately reburied in a proper grave, just like any member of the community would be treated.

The State Historic Preservation Office agrees to fund the excavation only if it's allowed to analyze the bones and postpone burial if they're found to be archeologically significant. But the commission votes not to have the analysis take place, since it would disrespect the deceased. So the bones stay put, and Gill's backyard becomes one of many gravesites in Harow.

Gill isn't bothered by the commission's decision. He's already given up on having a greenhouse there, anyway. He's applied for and granted himself a permit amendment allowing the greenhouse to be built on a lot he owns just outside of Harow.

The commission has one more important decision to make this year, regarding how the Iñupiaq language will be taught in the Borough's schools. In a gesture designed to say, "We care about your culture," Shant Oil Co. has offered to pay for a program to create software for teaching the Iñupiaq language. Or at least, Shant has offered to put up a record amount of $100,000 toward the project.

The software company representative who comes to the commission meeting says that $100,000 will cover the cost of the software, but the Borough can expect to run up four times this amount in service fees.

"Still, it's worth the money," the representative says. "We did a similar program for a near-extinct tribe in Florida, so even if the tribe dies out, at least there's a record of the language. Besides, this software is the way of the future. Kids just want to click a button to learn these days, nobody wants to read language textbooks or crunch through grammar exercises."

The commissioners are skeptical. If the point of language is to talk to each other and learn from one another, what good will computers do?

Besides, the software company will only allow a single spelling and dialect of Iñupiaq, and no one can agree which one to use.

Like the bones in Gill's backyard, the language software project hangs in limbo. Iñupiaq continues to be taught the same way English was taught at the Indian schools, with textbooks, grammar exercises, and no bling. The Iñupiaq teachers, many of them *taniks*, stand in front of their classes reading from books and writing on boards. The kids mindlessly fill out worksheets.

Lisa's daughter Britney is in the same boat as a lot of her friends. She's about as bilingual as any white kid in the Lower 48 suffering through a high school Spanish class—all she knows are the conversational basics and the curse words. She thinks sitting through Iñupiaq lessons is boring, and she shouldn't have to learn it from *taniks*. Truth be told, Britney has a hard time finding enough ways to be Iñupiaq. She likes to hunt, but she doesn't really like to eat subsistence food. She wants to learn Eskimo dancing from her dad, but he's too busy watching TV to teach her. Her mom can't speak Iñupiaq, and her dad doesn't feel like speaking anything at all.

A *tanik* history teacher burdened with white guilt had assigned Britney's class a project about family culture and history. The students are supposed to interview their parents and grandparents about what life was like back in the old days of Harow and write a report.

Britney sits down next to her dad while he's watching a ballgame and asks if she can interview him. He opens a beer without looking at her and says, "Not now."

Since he's not even looking at her, Britney decides she might as well pull a beer off of his six-pack and have a sip. She manages to pop it open before her dad smacks the beer out of her hands.

"No beer, Britney," he says.

Britney picks up the can that's foaming onto the carpet and carries it to the kitchen sink. With her back to the living room, she takes a long drink. Then she throws the can away, goes back to the living room, and avoiding the spilled beer spot, sits down again next to her silent father.

She looks at him out of the corner of her eyes. His eyes are two slits, barely open enough to see the ballgame. He doesn't look good. She wonders if he's sick. What if he has cancer? Or worse, what if he decides to kill himself?

Three years before, someone in the apartment next door killed himself. No one ever talked about it, and it might as well not have happened.

"Jimmy, you remember a few years ago when that guy shot himself in the apartment behind us?" Britney asks her brother that night, after

Lisa has turned off the lights and video games and sentenced the twins to bed.

"Not really," Jimmy says, though he remembers it all too well.

"It was just on the other side of this wall, you know," she says, pointing to the wall closest to Jimmy's bed. "I wonder if there's any little bits of meat and bone trapped in that wall."

Jimmy doesn't say anything. He wants to believe that the guy's soul went to heaven and everything turned out okay. He can't bear to think of any alternative.

"What's the matter, you scared of bones? Bones are everywhere here, live with it!" She points to the owl carving on Jimmy's nightstand, which looks like lava rock but is actually whale bone. Then there's the walrus skull with the uneven tusks, hanging on the living room wall next to the plasma T.V., and the caribou skull that their dad made into a miniature sled.

"Hey, you know what I saw at the Whiteheads' house the other day?" she asks.

"No."

"What's-his-name, that Whitehead kid in our class, his dad was building a greenhouse in the back, and he found a human skeleton."

"So?"

"So it's really old! It could be our ancestor from thousands of years ago! Anyway, Mr. Whitehead's hardly ever home, so we're thinking we can go dig it up some time."

"What are you gonna do if you can dig it up? Anyway, I don't know how you can get it out of the ground—it's too cold."

"Hot water, dummy. We'll just pour it on there. It's not frozen anymore, it'll be easy. Are you coming with us?"

Jimmy says "no," but he knows he'll have to come anyway. Britney always gets what she wants. He'll regret it either way, whether he goes along with the dig or stays at home and has to hear about the fun he missed.

A few days later, after the bones have been torn clumsily out of the soil and placed to rest in a plastic grocery bag, Jimmy decides that the regret for having gone along is probably more than the regret he would have had from staying behind. Watching Britney and the Whitehead kid jump on the dirt they dug up to pack it down, he begins to feel sick.

The Whitehead kid doesn't look so well either. He doesn't want to keep any of the bones, so Britney takes the whole plastic bagful back home. She puts it on a shelf in the back of the twins' closet and makes Jimmy swear he'll never tell.

Sometime later, Gill notices that the exposed bones have been removed from his back yard. But by then, he's already finished putting up the greenhouse on the new lot, and he's started building a new home there. He's gotten a permit for everything he's done, and followed all the instructions on the permits, so he figures he's got nothing to worry about.

Chapter 14- Polar Bears and Parties

Before the 1972 Marine Mammals Protection Act, whalers could find whole polar bears lying out on the ice, completely skinned by trophy hunters. The meat was delicious when boiled, even if it had been sitting out there a month. If they weren't so focused on whaling, they could have gone on a search for polar bear carcasses.

All the trophy hunters knew the Act was coming, and there was a fever to take out the biggest bears in the Arctic before it was too late. Hunters in private airplanes chased the bears until they collapsed on the pack ice. The hunters even risked crossing into Soviet airspace to find the perfect bear. The liberal New York Times compared the practice to machine-gunning a cow.

The Act meant that only Alaska Natives could hunt polar bears, and then only for subsistence and handicrafts. Over time, many Iñupiat lost their taste for the bears, although the fur still made great parka trim. The bears were not so much actively hunted as they were shot for being in the way of whaling crews.

Environmentalists are okay with the Iñupiat shooting birds and caribou, but there's something unsettling about the idea of a polar bear—the poster child for global warming—being shot for its fur. In 2008, the environmentalists petition the federal government to have the bear listed as a threatened species under the Endangered Species Act. And they don't ask the Iñupiat for permission. Maybe they figure they have no time to waste. Melting Arctic sea ice is leaving the bears stranded a hundred miles out, wondering whether to head north for the ice they need to hunt seals, or swim all the way back to shore and scrounge. Some just drown. The ones who make it to shore collapse on the beach, unable to move.

The environmentalists win their case, but the listing sets off waves of alarm across Alaska. Mostly, Alaskans don't want the feds and their polar bears getting in the way of oil drilling. On the Arctic Slope, some of the Iñupiat worry that the feds will impose a polar bear quota on the Eskimos like the whaling quota. Luther Ericsen leads the charge against the feds, telling whoever will listen that polar bears are as capable as the Iñupiat at adapting to whatever trouble the *taniks* cause.

He explains his reasoning to Vik, working his way through a bag of peanuts as he talks. Flecks of peanut shells and peelings occasionally spill onto his shirt and then onto Vik's desk.

"It's one thing to sue the feds for leasing the Arctic to oil companies without no review of what that's gonna do to the whales. It's something else when they start suing to put each one of our subsistence foods on the endangered species list. There isn't another food source that protects the Iñupiat people from the cold like marine mammal oil and *maktak*. You take away parts of the food chain, of any food chain, the food chain is altered and eventually, you know, it dies. And the Iñupiat, which are part of that same food chain, will—"

"I guess I don't get why you're so concerned," Vik interrupts. "Alaska Natives are exempt from the Endangered Species Act, unless the species population would get so low that even subsistence hunting would be unsustainable."

"That's what you don't understand," Luther says. "The feds are going to put all their agents up here, poking into our hunting, and then all the sudden we're going to hear that we're not allowed to hunt anymore."

"Are you trying to say that it's easier for the feds to measure hunting mortality than it is to measure mortalities from global warming?" Vik asks, flicking a peanut shell off her arm. "In that case I could maybe see your point."

Luther exhales a gaping "Ha!" along with a mouthful of peanuts. "And the environmentalists are suing to get seals and walruses listed, too. You can be sure I'm gonna do my best to get the Iñupiat to fight that lawsuit. I hunt these animals and I more than understand that they can survive without the ice."

"So you're saying you don't believe in global warming?" Vik interjects.

Luther continues without answering. "We as the Iñupiat people never got asked what we think of this action. We just recently learned to work with the environmentalist and now they're gonna throw our support away?"

Vik shrugs. She's planning on applying for a job with some kind of treehugger outfit when she finishes her contract with the Borough.

"Anyway," Luther says, wiping his mouth with his sleeve, "The mayor agrees with me."

"You mean he really believes that marine mammals are going to survive just fine even if all the ice melts?"

"Absolutely."

"I wonder if he, uh, talked to any of the biologists in the Borough's Wildlife and Subsistence Department."

"Ha," Luther expels again. "The biologists are just a bunch of *tanik* Outsiders who are going to go get a job with Greenpeace as soon as they finish taking all the Borough's money. You know that some other *tanik* scientists already decide that the *nanuq*—polar bear—'evolved' from a grizzly?"

Vik, anxious to have a conversation about evolution, leans closer in time to get a fleck of Luther's spit in her eye. "What are you getting at?" she asks.

"Now the grizzlies are moving up here again. I seen one last summer fighting with a *nanuq* over a whale carcass. The grizzlies are figuring out how to go out on the ice and hunt seals just as sure as they're figuring out how to break into our cabins out on the Chiliq River."

"But it would take millennia for the grizzlies to evolve, and the polar bear could be wiped out in the next century," Vik says.

"Well, in that case, you can tell your federal government to just take every *nanuq* out of the zoos in the Lower 48 and bring them here. It should be illegal to keep 'em in zoos, with the zookeepers being all *tanik* and the law saying we're the only ones allowed to take them."

"I'll talk to George Bush about it," Vik says with a smile.

Luther curses in Iñupiaq and leaves Vik with a pile of peanut shells on her desk. Vik scrapes the shells into the trashcan, still smiling. A good conversation with Luther is worth at least a pile of peanut shells.

It turns out that the mayor does agree with Luther on the perils of the listing, but for a different reason. A press release put out by the mayor—actually, by his public relations man in Iowa—says,

Our culture is not something preserved under a bell jar, nor is it simply a matter of continuing subsistence hunting and crafts. The existence of native culture and villages cannot be severed from the economic benefits of development. Listing the polar bear threatens our onshore oil and gas production. And without oil and gas, there are fewer tax revenues for our villages, meaning no schools, no medical services, and no jobs. This could well destroy us.

Unaware of the brouhaha they're causing, polar bears continue to wash up on the shores of Harow. Some people in Harow—especially the *taniks*—like to drive up and down the beach looking for them.

Britney is no different. On a dry and windy afternoon in late June, when almost all the snow is gone, she tells her twin Jimmy that they should take the four-wheeler out to Duck Camp and look for polar bears. She gets a couple of guns from their father's closet, and they head down the spit towards Duck Camp and Point Harow.

Jimmy sits on the rack behind Britney, holding one of the guns. Britney's got her earbuds in and can't hear him, so he jumps off the back without Britney noticing. He wants to take some practice shots without Britney hovering over him. It's not that Jimmy really wants to be a hunter, but sometimes all the teasing about his sister being more of a man than her twin gets to him.

He pulls the trigger.

POW! The bullet soars in an arch over the ocean and lands in the water with an anticlimactic "plop." He shoots off a few more before Britney comes back, indignant that Jimmy is shooting without her.

"You're not doing it right," she says, picking up the gun and showing Jimmy how to hold it. A sea gull bravely approaches the four-wheeler and is shot before it can land.

"That's how you do it," she says. She fires a few more, just for fun, and then they sit on the four-wheeler rack and look out on the ocean.

Something moves on the horizon. They watch it come closer and closer until it takes the shape of a polar bear.

"I think we should go back," Jimmy says.

"No way," Britney says. "We're going to catch it and eat it."

"You're not gonna eat that," Jimmy points out. "You don't like subsistence food."

Britney shushes Jimmy. He sits paralyzed while Britney positions herself behind the four-wheeler with the biggest gun. The bear is almost to shore, but moving slowly.

"I think there's something wrong with him," Jimmy says. "I think his arm is bleeding."

"Then we really gotta shoot it," Britney says. "Otherwise it's gonna just lie on the shore and bleed to death."

Britney's uncle taught her the basics—always assume the gun is loaded, don't put your finger on the trigger until you're ready, and never point at something you don't want to shoot. But he moved away before they got to any techniques on shooting large mammals. Britney has no idea how far away she should stand, where to aim, or when the bear might charge. None of this is cause for concern, though.

The bear flops onto the shore, just twenty feet away them. Jimmy's right—its front leg is already wounded. It licks the wound, oblivious to the pile of sooty sand coloring its underside gray.

BAM! Britney aims for the mouth and hits the collarbone.

If the bear weren't already wounded, it might have easily charged toward the four-wheeler and torn Britney's face off. Instead it hesitates, turning to Britney, and then turning to the ocean. It manages to get a few feet into the water before Britney shoots again. The bullet hits the windpipe, leaving the bear gasping and trying to come back to the beach.

Jimmy lets out all the curse words he knows. "Look what you did!" he screams.

Britney is pale, hardly breathing. "He's drowning," she says, her voice breaking. "Now I really have to kill it." The bear seems to be looking at her, asking her why she did it.

BAM! This one goes into the forehead. Its brain put to rest, the bear gives in to the warm red water. A large wave pushes its body halfway back onto the beach. Britney falls over the four wheeler, sobbing. She didn't know death would be so ugly and personal.

"Oh man," Jimmy says. "We gotta go."

Britney is howling.

"Come on," Jimmy says, pushing her shoulder, "You gotta get up and drive the four-wheeler back. I don't know how."

Jimmy waits for her to get up and snap out of it, but Britney can't be moved. The bear isn't moving either. It's still lying halfway in the water, with the occasional wave washing away the blood from the sand.

They're only a half mile from home, and Jimmy runs back to get his mother.

Lisa comes out with her honey and Jimmy, all squeezed onto another four-wheeler. Britney is still doubled over the four-wheeler, and the two guns she took without asking are lying on the ground. Lisa wails and grabs Britney. She holds both of the twins together, all of them crying.

Lisa's honey is not one to overreact. There's a harvested bear on the beach, and it needs to be butchered and eaten. These days people aren't catching them like they used to, maybe since younger folks don't like the taste as much. His was the last generation to really savor the taste of polar bears, especially those fat ones who'd just eaten a bunch of seal meat. Lisa's honey radios friends with trucks and gear to come and help him with the carcass. It's too sandy to do any butchering here. He'll put some tarps in front of his apartment building and do it there. He'll give most of the meat to his parents—they'll be grateful. And there should be just enough fur to trim new parkas for both of the twins.

Officer Shoak is cruising aimlessly around Harow, flipping through the VHF radio channels, when he hears Lisa's honey. He heads toward Lisa's apartment and circles it until the polar bear butchering crew shows up. Lisa's honey and a few men drag the bloody carcass off a trailer and onto a tarp. A bunch of kids wander over. They're squeamish at first, then drawn in by the beauty of the *ulu*—Iñupiaq knife—making clean cuts through the layers of bear.

For a minute, Officer Shoak is nostalgic, thinking of the time his Athabascan uncle showed him how to butcher a moose. Then Lisa's honey notices the police SUV and gestures violently with his *ulu* for Officer Shoak to go away. Officer Shoak reaches for his billy club and prepares to confront Lisa's honey, but then changes his mind. The party he's been invited to is about to start, and he doesn't want to miss it on account of having to arrest Lisa's honey.

It's the first time Officer Shoak has ever been invited to a party. Usually he goes to parties on his own accord, to bust them up. But now he's got an actual invitation from the Police Department's new secretary.

"This is Gray Shoak, everyone," the secretary says when Officer Shoak arrives. "Go put all your police crap in the bedroom, Gray."

Officer Shoak obligingly undoes his weapons belt, which only contains a billy club and a VHF radio, and puts it on the secretary's bed. Then he positions himself behind a group of girls playing drinking games. He can learn from this.

The party is as ethnically mixed as any Harow party is ever going to get. That's because no one but Officer Shoak is older than 25. The mixed lot of Filipino-Eskimos, *tanik*-Eskimos, and one black-Eskimo have gone to high school together in Harow and bonded through alcohol and snowmachine racing. The plain *taniks* are imports—teachers and nurses who want to be ethnically sensitive.

Officer Shoak's eyes shift around nervously when people start to take off their clothes. It's been a long time since he last played strip poker. He wants to cut loose and join in, but still be alert and ready to arrest someone if it comes to that.

He leans on the wall next to a particularly pale Eskimo who's been picking up all the finished bottles and cans to suck the last drops out of them. "I didn't bring my own, and I don't want to get started on somebody else's bottle," the pale Eskimo explains. Later, unable to get drunk, the pale Eskimo announces that he's bringing his truck home and coming back with his snowmachine and a case of beer. "So I won't be driving drunk," he says to Officer Shoak.

Many of us share his logic—licenses aren't required for snowmachines, so there's no reason to drive them sober.

After the pale Eskimo leaves, Officer Shoak observes that there are only two other males in the room and nine females. His chances of getting a hook-up are looking pretty good. He wanders over to the island in the kitchen, which has been converted into a card table, and grabs at the closest piece of ass. It's the secretary's, and it's too bony and flat to have merited the gesture.

The secretary, unperturbed, giggles. "Gray wants his own hand of cards!" she howls, and guides Officer Shoak by his belt loops to a spot at the card table. The dealer, who is also the public defender, ignores him.

Officer Shoak doesn't remember the rules for poker anyway, so he goes back to leaning against the wall. An obviously gay Filipino-Eskimo patronizes him by asking about his work.

Outside, a band of snowmachines rev their engines in harmony, climaxing in front of the secretary's apartment. It's the pale Eskimo, who's back with several cases of beer and a couple of people to share it with. Officer Shoak is about to ask if they have licenses to import all that alcohol, when the secretary leans against the wall next to him.

"This party's about to get real funky," she says matter-of-factly. "You might even want to put your belt back on." The Eskimos see Officer Shoak, stiffen, tip-toe into the secretary's bedroom, and close the door. Officer Shoak gets suspicious. He steps into the *qanichaq*—the Arctic entry—pulls out his cell phone, and calls for back-up. Within five minutes, there are three more cops at the secretary's apartment. They burst into the secretary's bedroom and come upon five Eskimos smoking weed.

Even if private weed smoking is protected by the Alaska constitution, Officer Shoak feels duty-bound to search the Eskimos for evidence of a large stash and lots of bills, which might suggest dealing. He finds nothing but a couple more joints.

The public defender comes in shaking her head. "You know you just made a totally unconstitutional search, right?" she says to Officer Shoak.

Thinking quickly, Officer Shoak puts on his weapons belt and hollers, "I think we have a disturbance of the peace here, and this party's going to have to shut down, or some of us may wind up in 'cuffs."

The secretary cackles drunkly and waves her guests towards the door.

A slow migration to the next party begins. People want to take the rest of their alcohol with them, but don't want Officer Shoak to see them driving away with open containers. Officer Shoak is torn between monitoring vehicles for alcohol and making the most of his opportunity to be alone with the secretary and a lot of liquor. He opts for the latter.

The secretary's cell phone rings and she goes into the bedroom to talk. It's the public defender, calling to tell her to where the next party is.

"I have to go, Gray," the secretary says. "Sorry to be kicking you out so soon."

"Maybe you need an escort," Officer Shoak says, walking towards her. "Looks like we had a bit to drink."

The secretary looks at him out of the corner of her eye. There's something about his buzz cut that's just a little too sharp. And the way he's clutching the billy club is kind of freaky.

"Probably not," she says, putting on her jacket. She goes out the front door and around to the back of the building before Officer Shoak can think of anything to say. He doesn't know that the public defender's apartment is on the other side of the secretary's.

Officer Shoak surveys the living room. There are various pieces of clothing that people didn't bother to put back on. He considers taking off his underwear and leaving it there as a sort of calling card, but decides that the tight white briefs he has on wouldn't do much for his cause. The secretary wouldn't even know whose underwear it was. He shrugs and goes back to the police SUV. He can probably catch somebody drunk driving later on.

Chapter 15- Summer

Fifty years ago, there were no cars on the Arctic Slope and hardly any *taniks*. An Eskimo could step outside and in one breath know the day's weather and in which direction he should go hunting.

These days, hardly any Eskimo walks anywhere. Some say that walking is dangerous because of the lost polar bears who wander into town looking for food. We all know the story of the guy who was killed in broad daylight near the gas station—a polar bear broke through his windshield to get him.

But some *taniks* aren't worried. Luther sees the *tanik* lawyer for the Borough Law Department walking to work every day, wearing some sort of plasticky space suit with fake fur on it. Once he asks her what she would do if she came across a polar bear, since she's not Iñupiaq and has no clue how to handle them.

"According to Greenpeace," Vik retorts, "only one person has been killed by a polar bear in the U.S. in the past 30 years."

"Dumb as a tourist," Luther says to himself, walking away.

Since his retirement from the tribal government, Luther's made a business out of taking dumb tourists to Point Harow in his Hummer. They'll pay eighty bucks each just for the chance of seeing a bear, but only in the summer when the bears are least likely to come.

Or that's the way it used to be. The past few summers have seen a number of half-drowned bears washing up on the beach. The tourists swarm around the bears with their cameras, while somebody from the Borough's Wildlife and Subsistence Department with a bullhorn shouts at them to step back. Last year Luther shot a sickly looking bear to put it out of its misery. The tourists went crazy screaming and taking pictures, but everybody calmed down when Luther butchered the animal and offered the meat to anyone who wanted in. The *tanik* spectators wouldn't take any of the meat, although one of them had the nerve to ask Luther for the hide.

Luther doesn't mind the tourists doing touristy things, but it makes him a little uncomfortable the way more and more are showing up these days as spectators at *nalukatat*, the summer celebrations of whaling.

Nalukataq—held to appease the spirits of the deceased whale and ensure the success of future hunting seasons—is one of the most joyful Iñupiat traditions. Even Christianity couldn't stop it. *Nalukatat* are held in early summer by each crew that caught a whale during spring whaling.

In Harow, they're held at a big grassy area near the ocean that has enough parking space for everyone in town.

There's food all day, starting with goose soup. The whale meat is brought out next, starting with the *quaq*, frozen cubes of whale muscle. Then comes the *avarraq*, the flukes of the whale cut into thin strips. Then comes the *maktak*, the best part, especially when the whale was young. And then there's the blanket toss. We all get a chance to jump on the blanket, which is made out of tightly stretched walrus hides with heavy rope threaded around the edges. Forty or 50 people pull up and down on the rope, tossing the person on the blanket high into the air. Each pull is like a beat, and the blanket beats steadily late into the evening.

Lots of tourists come to the Whitehead crew's *nalukataq* in June 2008. Whiteheads of all ages and skin tones sit on folding chairs and blankets in a giant circle, waiting for the whale to be served. It's drizzling, and they brush the water off their coats with a few curses. It hardly ever rained on the Arctic Slope until the late twentieth century. Before, the only thing to get in the way of a *nalukataq* was a snow storm.

Most of the *tanik* tourists sit on hotel towels eating cheeseburgers from one of the Korean restaurants. We look at them with a combination of annoyance and a desire to be seen as good hosts. Those of us who are tired of waiting for whale wouldn't mind having our own cheeseburgers right now.

The Coast Guard happens to be in Harow at this time. To show good will, Coast Guard officers are building a half of a basketball court, which will be the only cemented area in town aside from the airport. The officers invite themselves to the *nalukataq* and pass out plastic Frisbees with the Coast Guard logo. The appreciative participants turn them over and use them as plates.

Chuck comes to every *nalukataq*, as do many in Harow, regardless of whether he gets along with the crew members. He knows his appearance at the Whitehead's *nalukataq* might not be as well received as it is at others, but this doesn't bother him. If anyone has something to say about him dating the young Gloria Whitehead, they can say it to him in person.

Chuck approaches the tourists first, shaking hands and asking where they're from. "Did you bring enough cheeseburgers to share?" he asks. The tourists laugh, thinking Chuck is just joking.

"Sharing is an Iñupiaq value, you know," Chuck says. The tourists stop laughing and one holds out the last quarter of his ketchup-soaked burger. Then Chuck laughs, slaps the guy on the back, and explains that humor is an Iñupiaq value, too.

The servers come around offering *akutuq*, "Eskimo ice cream" made out of caribou fat. Chuck takes a bite-sized morsel and hands it to an attractive teen. "Here," he says. "Try it!"

The teen, sensing her family's and race's dignity are at stake, pops the whole piece in her mouth. It looked like fudge but turns out not to be. She chews. And chews. And finally hides behind a parked car to spit out the chewed-up remnants.

"A little caribou fat can do you a world of good," Chuck says with a grin.

The teen's mother smiles as best as she can, and whispers to her husband that it's time to go on to the next activity. The couple collects their towels and retching teen and marches back to their hotel in the rain.

"There you go, there you go!" Chuck hears his Uncle Luther's booming gravelly voice, and feels the old man's hand on his shoulder. "They're probably going to go join the Polar Bear Club next." The Polar Bear Club was the invention of the *tanik* owner of Harow's Mexican restaurant, who's been profiting from Harow's tourists for the last 20 years. To join, a tourist has to pay $30 and completely submerse herself in the Arctic waters of the Chukchi Sea. The $30 covers the van ride, fresh towels, and a certificate of membership.

Chuck continues to stand in place and grin. Since none of the Whiteheads aside from Gloria have acknowledged him, he figures he'll be standing around entertaining his uncle for the duration of the event.

As much as Chuck champions Iñupiaq traditions, he has to admit that a *nalukataq* can be a bit boring. They happen in exactly the same way each time, and the entire focus is on the victorious whalers. Since Chuck isn't on a whaling crew, he's never been the object of the celebration. His chance to be in the spotlight really comes during the Fourth of July.

The Fourth isn't the patriotic celebration it is in the Lower 48, since many of us up here would just as soon be independent from America. But it's a holiday from work, and the weather's usually good, so everyone trots out to celebrate. In past years, the Borough or the City of Harow organized a couple of days of Eskimo games. But in recent years, the event is just a collection of fried food booths with nothing traditional except for Eskimo donuts.

Since he's been on the Assembly, Chuck has taken on the role as Harow's one and only auctioneer. All of the Iñupiat artists whose items have sat unsold for months on folding tables outside the local grocery store are invited to bring their art to Chuck. On the Fourth, Chuck plants himself in the middle of the food booths with a bullhorn and auctions off the art to the highest bidders.

Bertie has taken a rare holiday from the Law Department in an effort to spend more time with the community she represents. She managed to miss every *nalukataq* this year, and the mayor teased her about being locked up in the office all the time.

She looks around and sees no one familiar besides Chuck and Larry Atkoot's wife, whose name she can't remember. Bertie buys a Samoan donut from one of the booths and stands next to Larry's wife.

"Isn't he a hoot?" Bertie says, nodding towards Chuck, who's just sold a long handcrafted knife to the lieutenant mayor for $170.

"Um," Larry's wife Mandy says, torn between wanting to say something nice and wanting to warn Bertie about Chuck's deviance. "He's got a bit of a reputation."

"A reputation?" Bertie asks, torn between wanting to be in the know about community ongoings and not wanting to appear gossipy.

Mandy sighs. "The rumor is he's fooling around with Ernie Whitehead's 17-year-old granddaughter Gloria."

"Goodness," Bertie says. She looks down at her feet, not sure how to further contribute to the conversation.

"My oldest brother Luther is related to him by marriage. Luther's wife is Chuck's aunt," Mandy says. "He tries to help Chuck out, but, you see how it goes ..." She trails off, and they watch Gloria Whitehead shuffle over to where Chuck is standing. She had on a lot of makeup and a giant new parka with polar bear trim.

"Well," Bertie says. "Isn't your family related to the Whiteheads?"

"Sort of," Mandy says, "The first Whitehead to come over here, you know, the Yankee whaler, he was my father's stepfather. He stole my father's mother from her Eskimo husband, who was my grandfather. So I'm half-first cousins with Gill and Ernie Whitehead."

"Oh god, how awful," Bertie says, trying to be sensitive, and corrects herself. "I mean, not about being related to the Whiteheads, I mean about the, uh, Yankee whaler stealing your grandmother."

Mandy shrugs. "Well, my grandmother wasn't too upset about it. Anyway, you know I'm an Ericsen, and my Ericsen grandfather from Norway did the same thing—took my other Eskimo grandmother from her Eskimo husband."

"Oh," Bertie says. She wishes she had a Harow family tree. It would have saved her from a lot of *faux pas*. "Where's Larry today?" she asks, hoping it's a safe subject.

"He don't like these Fourth of July things," Mandy says. "Anyway, he's been kinda stressed out, keeping to himself these days."

"Why?" Bertie asks. "I mean, if you don't mind me asking."

"He's kinda upset with the mayor. You know the mayor ran on this platform of opposing offshore oil development, and now it looks like he's changing his mind. The rumor is that after his term is over, he's gonna get a job with Shant Oil, just like the last mayor, Ahgak."

"I haven't heard that," Bertie says stiffly.

"Well, Mayor Kitok was gonna sue the federal government for approving Shant's plan to start drilling offshore in the Chukchi Sea, like he did for the Beaufort Sea, but then he changed his mind."

"As far as I know," Bertie says, wondering if she really knows anything at all, "The Borough is still opposed to offshore, but the position is a bit nuanced."

"Uh, what you mean, nuanced?"

"There's some talk that the federal government might be willing to share revenue with the State of Alaska and the Borough, the way it does with offshore drilling in the Gulf of Mexico. So there would be money available to mitigate some of the damage. And another thing, BX's not going to be doing its ultra reach drilling project anymore, so the Borough is going to lose out on a big revenue source."

Mandy sighs. "It's all about money, huh?"

"Well," Bertie says, "I guess from the mayor's vantage, it would be about opportunity for the Iñupiat people. I know some of the local native corporations and Northern Slope Regional Co. have plans to work with Shant to provide infrastructure."

Bertie wonders if she's taken the conversation in the wrong direction. She stops talking and finishes off her donut. The two women watch as Chuck auctions off what appears to be a birthday cake for $80.

"I hate to say it," Mandy says, "but I got to agree with my brother Luther here. That law that created the native corporations was the idea of *tanik* American corporations to undermine tribal integrity."

"What do you mean?" Bertie asks.

"Everywhere else in the U.S., tribes have their own government, their own land, and their own money."

"They have a monopoly on casinos, you mean," Bertie says cautiously.

"Whatever it is. Our tribes in Alaska don't have nothing. It's the native corporations who have all the land and the money, and they're the ones making decisions."

"But don't you think they're making decisions in the best interests of their shareholders, the native people?"

"They're just making money for their shareholders like any other corporation," Mandy says.

"And they hire *taniks* in Anchorage offices to carry out their business. They don't care about whether people up here are taking their dividends and drinking them away. I hate to say it, but I got to agree with Luther. It's a long, slow genocide, all done under the corporations' laws."

"Well," Bertie says, relieved to not be white. She waves obligatorily to Lieutenant Mayor Nelson Cowen, who's walking toward them with a bag full of donuts.

"You're going to eat all that?" she says incredulously, as he pulls out a donut and begins gnawing on it.

Nelson's diabetes has never stopped him from eating gobs of sugar. When he was her boss in the Law Department, he kept all kinds of sweets in the office. Bertie credits Nelson for helping her quit smoking, but blames him for letting her get as fat as she is now.

Nelson ignores Bertie's question. Bertie can tell from his glazed look that he's high on insulin. Mandy takes a cautious step back from him.

"Look what I got in the auction," he says, dangerously waving around the long, handcrafted knife. "An Eskimo machete! Cool, huh?"

"'Cool,'" Mandy says.

Chapter 16 - Money and Justice for All

We know there's a line between accepting money for damage mitigation and accepting blood money. The Iñupiat have had to dance over this line ever since the government and the oil companies took an interest in the Arctic Slope.

When he led the Iñupiat Community of the Arctic, Luther always tried to keep the tribe far away from anything that smacked of blood money. Getting grants from the Bureau of Indian Affairs was as close as he could bring himself. His successors were the first to take money from the Arctic Slope Borough, a government that Luther mistrusted almost as much as the State of Alaska.

The Alaska Eskimo Whalers Council was different. It had little federal money to rely on, and received millions each year from the Borough. When it became apparent that this was still not enough, the council's president—then-Mayor Ahgak's wife and Gill Whitehead's sister—started the practice of accepting cash from oil companies. It was part of a "conflict avoidance agreement" that oil companies were supposed to sign onto each year to avoid interfering with whaling season.

At first the payments were just administrative fees to cover the council's costs for monitoring and enforcing the agreement. Later, after Mayor Ahgak lost the election and went to work for Shant Oil, the payments grew by hundreds of thousands of dollars. We never knew exactly how much they were, since they were kept out of the record books and neither the Borough nor the federal government saw fit to audit the council.

When Nelson—then the head of the Borough's Law Department—made rumblings about an audit, Ahgak's wife moved the council's headquarters down to Anchorage. She bought a half-million dollar house in a new subdivision and a Hummer before resigning from her position.

Nelson later backed off from talk about an audit, realizing that the Borough needed the Iñupiat Community of the Arctic and the Alaska Eskimo Whalers Council as much as they needed the Borough. Aside from the Borough's dependants and the moderate environmentalists, the Borough doesn't have many friends. The Alaska governor ridiculed the Borough's role in anti-offshore oil lawsuits. Alaska urbanites carped on the Borough's search and rescue helicopters and lavish public facilities, reminding the Borough that it was the oil companies' money that kept everyone in the Borough "living like sheiks."

Neither the State nor the Borough can draw revenue from most offshore drilling, since their taxing authority stops three miles from the coast line. But the State is more likely than the Borough to benefit from it, since the oil companies will have offices in State's big cities and create jobs there. And the State doesn't care a jot about whaling.

Vik claims that if the federal law changed to allow the Borough to get tax money from offshore drilling, the Borough would be just as eager as the State for drilling to begin. She's sure the mayor would concede the inevitability of offshore drilling, and gracefully accept the money "To mitigate the impacts."

Maybe that would be the right thing to do. If the drilling can't be stopped, why not benefit from it?

The Borough would be glad to see some benefits from the oil buried under the Arctic National Wildlife Refuge, which covers a fifth of the Borough's taxing territory. And the Borough isn't the only one. Except for a few environmentalists, most Alaskans are disgusted with Congress's prohibition against drilling in a piece of their state. These Alaskans see it as another example of the U.S. treating Alaska like a colony—allowing liberals in Washington to make decisions about land they'll never set foot on.

Of the few people who have set foot in the Refuge, most are Iñupiat. The Iñupiat village of Tovak is entirely contained within the refuge. Its residents live with all the restrictions of being in a national wildlife refuge, including restrictions on new construction and four-wheelers, and an airport that's often under water. The Borough Assemblyman from Tovak says it's high time that drilling starts in the Refuge, so maybe some decent infrastructure could get built around his village.

Every few years, Alaska's delegation to Congress, along with other Congressmen elected by oil money, trot out a bill to open up the Refuge to drilling.When a new bill surfaces in the summer of 2008, Assemblyman Chuck and the Assemblyman from Tovak present the Assembly with a resolution in support of the bill.

"When Congress passed the Alaska Native Claims Settlement Act, they told us to build a future for our culture based in our land and natural resources," Chuck says, reading a speech that he partially lifted from the mayor's press release on the polar bear listing. "Now, after our hard work to come so far, we see that future at risk by Outsiders who don't understand our way of life. Our culture is now in the 21st century, built on traditional activities united with contemporary economic enterprises. It can't be separated from the economic solutions established by the settlement act."

The Assemblyman from Tovak adds, "This past winter, Tovak got down to 60 below one time. We need oil and gas money to heat our homes and help put food on the table. Without it, many of our people got to abandon their ancestral homes to get the work and the basic services that oil and gas money make possible."

The resolution in support of opening up the Refuge passes unanimously, as does almost everything that's put before the Assembly.

Luther Ericsen, Chuck's uncle, is furious when he finds out about the resolution the next day. He's talked to the real hunters from Tovak, and he knows the last thing they need is a bunch of pipelines driving the caribou even further away.

When Chuck doesn't answer his phone, Luther marches over to Mayor Kitok's office to brief him on the folly of the resolution. The mayor's secretary informs Luther that the mayor is in a meeting.

"I'll wait," Luther says. He pulls out a handful of sunflower seeds from his pocket, cracks them open with his teeth, and deposits the husks on the secretary's desk. The secretary stands up and knocks on the mayor's door.

The door opens, and Luther squeezes his way in and sits down in the mayor's armchair. "Good morning to you, Mayor Kitok," Luther says.

"Good morning," the mayor says reluctantly, looking at the sunflower husks on the side of Luther's face and hoping they won't find their way onto his chair.

"Well, I'll get to the point," Luther says. "That resolution your Assembly passed last night supporting the drilling in the Arctic National Wildlife Refuge is a true embarrassment. It don't represent what the Iñupiat really believe. I am related to 82 out of every 100 Iñupiat in the whole Arctic Slope within the third cousin degree, so I do know what I'm talking about."

The mayor knows Luther well enough to wait quietly until the whole speech is over.

Luther goes on, "Apparently, you didn't attempt to talk with the people of Kusoq, who now have to travel over thirty miles and more to get their *tuttu*—caribou. Why? 'Cause the *tuttu* migration got altered by the development of Prudhoe Bay and the connected oil fields. Let me tell you, you open up the Refuge and you open up the Beaufort Sea for offshore drilling. There can't be offshore drilling without a land base and that land base is the Refuge. And your Assembly is opposed to offshore drilling."

The mayor starts to explain that he's not the Assembly and wasn't able to vote on the matter, but decides to say nothing. He would have voted the same way as the Assembly. Nelson has shown him how much tax the Borough could get from oil and gas in the Refuge. With the Borough's budget slowly shrinking as the oil at Prudhoe Bay declines, oil revenue will have to come from somewhere else in the Borough. Or his people will end up leaving.

"We're both whaling captains, Luther," the mayor says. "We both have to live with the decisions we make for our people."

"Well," Luther says, "I got a degree in geology and petroleum engineering, and I can tell you that the amount of oil and gas in that refuge isn't going to pay for taking it out of the ground and building a pipeline to Prudhoe Bay. They just want to drill out to sea, and you know the Borough won't get any money from offshore. I tell you what, I know the people of Tovak complain sometimes about having to be in a refuge run by the feds, but I'd rather have the government on my ass than oil and gas developers."

The secretary steps into the mayor's office to see if he needs any assistance. The mayor gives her a special nod, which means for her to go find Nelson. The mayor always relies on Nelson to handle difficult visitors.

Nelson comes into the mayor's office with a vague smile and says, "Luther, we missed you at the Assembly meeting last night. Lots happened while you weren't there."

"Yeah, I had to go out hunting to feed my family." Luther coughs and a stray sunflower seed falls from his breast to the floor. "I've got to get back on home, now. I have three grandchildren I'm taking care of these days."

Nelson nods. The mayor sits behind his desk and looks out the window.

"You know, it's that time of year to go hunting for *nigliq*—goose," Luther says to Nelson. No one says anything more to Luther. He shuffles out of the office and makes his way home.

We aren't surprised that Congress's bill to open up the Arctic National Wildlife Refuge doesn't go anywhere in 2008. Congress certainly isn't going to listen to the Arctic Slope Borough Assembly, the people of Tovak, or even Luther Ericsen. It will open the Refuge as soon as drilling there makes economic sense. In the meantime, the Borough and its villages will have to take revenue wherever it can be found.

The year before, the Borough negotiated a cash settlement with Cacoco Oil to mitigate subsistence impacts from the latest oil development near the village of Kusoq. Cacoco agreed to the settlement in lieu of having to conduct a study on the impacts of its drilling on subsistence and human health. Now, for as long as the development is in place, Kusoq residents will get annual checks. With these, they can buy extra fuel and camping supplies, allowing them to go forth and hunt in untrammeled areas. Or they can buy hotdogs and cigarettes—it's their choice.

There was just a handful of Kusoq residents who'd wanted a health impact assessment rather than annual checks. One of them was a nurse, another an elder, and the other, a *tanik* school teacher.

Just after the first annual check is issued, Vik asks Bertie to let her put on an environmental justice workshop in Kusoq.

"I think by now people are probably realizing that the checks aren't worth all that much," she says. "Maybe they'll be open to a discussion about what their rights are regarding development."

"You mean so they can negotiate more money next time?" Bertie asks with a raised eyebrow.

"No, I mean their tribal rights to government consultation and that sort of thing."

Bertie nods. She's a proponent of Native Rights, after all. She agrees to let Vik put on the workshop, and even proposes to have the Law Department cover the costs of food for all.

"The only thing is," Vik says apologetically, "we might need to have door prizes, too, if we actually want anyone to come." She's been to enough meetings on the Arctic Slope to know the way the system works.

"Hmmm," Bertie says. Funding environmental justice is one thing, but door prizes rub her the wrong way. Then she looks at the piece of Native art she bought last week—a giant doorstop carved from whale bone that its creator might have intended to be a walrus. A pair of toothpicks protrudes from the bulbous end that resembles a head. The artist had apologized for not using real ivory on the "tusks," saying that once he sold this piece he'd be able to buy some.

Bertie points at the doorstop, "You can use that."

Vik nods, and Bertie says, "But you'll have to bring along some local people from the Community Development Department to help you with the workshop. No one's going to pay any attention if it's just you."

Vik acknowledges that Bertie's right. People here have a way of looking straight through her. She asks Gill and Larry to come, telling them it'll be good for community relations. Kusoq residents are always mad at the Borough about something, and some have even threatened to secede and form their own borough.

Vik schedules the workshop in the middle of the workweek, since she doesn't want to spend her weekend in Kusoq. Anyway, she figures, most people in the villages don't have regular jobs. They'll show up as long as there's a chance of winning something, even if it's a rhino carved from whale bone.

Flights come in and out of Kusoq only once a day, so there's no avoiding an overnight stay. Kusoq has only two places to stay, and both are designed for transient oil field workers. One is the 60-room Big Man Camp, open during the winter drilling season. The other is the Little Man

Camp, which is open from May to September while the Big Man Camp is closed. The Little Man Camp consists of six rooms, each with two beds. A single bathroom with two toilets and a cardboard handwritten sign that said, "Women in hear, don't enter" serves all of the rooms. Women are told to tack the sign on the door when they enter and take it down when they leave.

A haggard-looking cook from the Big Man Camp is the sole employee at the Little Man Camp. When Vik, Gill, and Larry arrive, he asks, "Where's the other woman?"

"There's only three of us," Vik says, puzzled.

"The Borough ought to know the policy by now," he says, throwing his hands up. "You have to bring an even number of men and women so—so it'll only be women rooming with women."

"It doesn't bother me," Vik says, shrugging. "If there's no open room, I'll just share with one of these guys, okay?"

Larry blushes, and Gill picks at the dirt under his fingernails. The cook shakes his head slowly. "Or, I'll just ask, uh, some of the other ladies here, if there are any, if I can stay in their room, and I'll sleep on the floor."

"There aren't any other women."

"Then I'm quite happy to sleep on the couch in this, uh, lobby," Vik says. This seems to settle the matter.

The lobby consists of a single couch with the stuffing coming out, a wooden crate that serves as a coffee table, and a large plasma T.V. that stays on at all times. Gill and Larry sit on the couch and speak to each other in Iñupiaq.

"You guys mind if I use your room to change?" Vik asks.

"Uh, no," Larry says.

Vik goes into the room with her bags and emerges a few minutes later in a tank top and shorts. She plops down on the couch between Larry and Gill, waiting for them to feel uncomfortable and leave so she can figure out how to turn off the T.V.

"Well, I guess I'm gonna get to bed early," Gill says during the next commercial break, getting up and leaving Larry and Vik on the couch.

Vik wonders whether she's supposed to scoot over and sit where Gill was sitting, to put a respectable distance between her and Larry. Or would that seem rude? She tries to remember if there was anything about seating arrangements in the cultural guidance booklet Bertie gave her.

Vik decides to stay put. She thinks there's something attractive about Larry, even though he must be pushing sixty and his nose is slightly off kilter. She puts her head on the back of the couch and lets it fall slowly toward Larry's shoulder.

She wakes up just in time to avoid drooling on Larry's shirt.

"Sorry," she mumbles. Larry puts his arm around her, kisses the top of her head, and goes off to his room without saying anything.

The next morning, Vik wakes up to the sound of the T.V. She gets up and goes straight to the community center where the workshop will be, not wanting to run into Larry in the bathroom.

The community center consists of a large meeting room, a recreation center for teens, a kitchen, bathrooms, and offices—all constructed with a grant Kusoq received from the state to address community impacts from oil and gas. The Borough ended up taking over the grant when it appeared the Kusoq couldn't manage on its own—another reason Kusoq residents have to mistrust the Borough.

Vik lays out Law Department-funded junk food on a sagging table and starts arranging all her props. She's prepared some kitschy posters with questions for people to consider, like "How important is my homeland?"

At 9:00, when the workshop is scheduled to begin, no one but Vik is there. Larry and Gill shuffle in twenty minutes later, followed by the three Kusoq residents who'd wanted a health impact assessment rather than annual checks. Vik asks one of them, the nurse, if she wouldn't mind calling some other residents so they could at least get enough people to eat all the junk food.

"I don't want to take that stuff back home with me," Vik says.

The nurse shrugs. "Someone will eat it. Any junk you people bring to the villages always gets eaten."

The nurse does call her kids, and Gill calls all the Whiteheads in Kusoq. Within an hour, there's a crowd of 20 or so and a significant dent in the junk food. Vik waves around a roll of door prize tickets, and eager hands reach out for them.

The rest of the morning goes mostly according to schedule, with pauses every five minutes for Gill to translate a summary to the elders. For lunch, Vik brings out day-old sandwiches, more junk food, and the biodegradable paperware she convinced Bertie to order for the Law Department.

The *tanik* school teacher excuses herself, telling Vik she has an appointment. As she makes her way out of the room, three people ask if they can have her door prize ticket.

"I forget to get one," she apologizes.

The afternoon session is supposed to empower Kusoq residents to participate in the decision-making process about offshore drilling. Vik isn't sure if it's having the right effect. To the Kusoq residents, it probably seems like she's holding a long meeting just to convince them to participate in other long meetings with federal government officials where there won't be any food or door prizes.

Vik asks the elders if they'd like to talk about how the ocean has always been their garden, so she can tell them how offshore drilling is about to ruin it.

A couple of elders stand up and deliver speeches in Iñupiaq. Vik waits impatiently for the translations, but understands little more of Gill's rambling in English than what was said in Iñupiaq. It sounds like the elders are just reminiscing about their childhood.

Vik cuts Gill off. "We're facing a huge threat from a project the federal government is now considering for the Beaufort Sea—"

"Who's we?" someone interrupts.

As long as you have a drop of Iñupiaq blood, even if you look completely white, you can say "we" without having the rest of us raise our eyebrows. Everyone knows Vik doesn't have a drop of Iñupiaq blood and has been on the Arctic Slope all of eight months.

Vik, who doesn't realize the significance of having said "we," turns to look at the speaker and says matter-of-factly, "Everyone who lives here and anyone who cares about life in the Arctic."

One of the elders mutters something in Iñupiaq, and Gill translates, "We—in pieces."

"What does that mean?" Vik asks. The elder rattles off something else in Iñupiaq.

"She said that the Iñupiaq people aren't one anymore," Gill translates, "That they've been divided by *taniks* and money."

Vik shrugs. "Can't argue with that."

A heated discussion arises among some of the residents, and to cool things down, Vik announces that it's time for the door prize drawing. The residents all reach for their tickets and sit quietly.

One of the elders wins, and Vik hands over Bertie's door stop to the elder's son. The elder has extensive commentary on the artwork, but no one translates. The others residents have wandered towards the food table, where they're making to-go plates. The already degrading paperware appears to be scattered around the room, and Styrofoam-ware has been produced from the kitchen.

By 3:00, only Vik, Gill, Larry, and the nurse are left. The nurse thanks them for coming to Kusoq and leaves without making a to-go plate. Gill and Larry wander outside to smoke, and Vik starts on what will be a long cleanup.

Chapter 17- Shooting

In August 2008, after a tense public meeting on the need for residents to buy duck stamps if they want to hunt, a U.S. Fish and Wildlife Service agent decides to drive out to Duck Camp. The meeting was full of people who declared they'd never buy a duck stamp, no matter what. He figures the chances of catching someone shooting without the required stamps are pretty good tonight.

It's after 10 p.m., but far from dark. Around this time of year, a lot of hunters are out all night. But tonight, no one's around. Maybe the forecast of rain is keeping them away.

The sign that says "Do not hunt the threatened Steller's eider" catches his eye. Beneath the sign is a pile of bird carcasses. He gasps, slams on the brakes, and gets out of his truck. The carcasses are Steller's eiders—a mother and six ducklings.

The agent turns in a circle, staring out at the endless tundra, but there's no one in sight. He walks further out into the tall, dry grass and finds another Steller's eider mother, shot dead on her nest. The first drops of rain begin falling. The agent photographs all the eiders and puts them in a plastic bag in the back of his truck.

"Those people are just crazy," the agent tells his supervisor a week later, after finding five more dead Steller's eiders with no culprit in sight, and no sign of anyone coming forward to accept responsibility. "We're going to have to do something big. We could close their hunt, you know. We could shut it down altogether."

The supervisor isn't sure she can do this. Anyway, by now, most of the Steller's eiders have flown to their winter home in southwest Alaska. And the supervisor knows the story of the *Duck-In* all too well. She isn't about to give the Eskimos a chance to start another revolution and appear as martyrs for Native American hunting rights.

"Send the photos you took to one of those environmentalist groups," she says to the agent. "Let them do the damage. As for us, we'll just have to double the number of agents up there next year. We ought to start now, in fact. Who knows what else they're doing."

Even as the summer hunting season is closing, new Fish and Wildlife agents arrive on the Arctic Slope. They station themselves at the popular hunting areas and stand behind any Eskimo with a gun. If an Eskimo goes out in the middle of a pond to get away from the agents, they watch him through binoculars. They set up a check-point on the spit to verify that hunters returning from Duck Camp aren't making off with any threatened eiders.

No one ever owns up to the shootings. The only success enjoyed by Fish and Wildlife is when agents pull two Steller's eiders out from under the tarp of a suspicious-looking man with a truck. The man says he found them dead on the road and was bringing them home to eat. The agents write him a $450 ticket, $225 for each bird.

When the man doesn't pay the fine and doesn't show up for his court date in Fairbanks, a bench warrant for his arrest goes out. Agents find him in Harow two weeks later and take him down to Anchorage in handcuffs.

Most of us here have a hard time making sense of all the hunting rules. The government encourages the killing of some animals, but there are some we aren't even allowed to touch. These days, bears and wolves are a government target, since the government listens to *tanik* hunters who want more "predator control." The *tanik* hunters say that wolves are killing too many caribou, and sometimes just for sport. They say they've found caribou left dead in the field, some with only the tongues eaten.

The government comes up with a predator control plan that involves setting snares for bears and wolves and gassing wolf pups in their dens. Citizens are allowed to shoot bears and wolves wherever they find them, and those with private helicopters are encouraged to shoot from the air.

The government says that all this shooting is not just for the benefit of sport hunters—it will help the subsistence hunters who depend on caribou and moose. The government says that the 124 wolves aerially eliminated in 2008 translates to 1,488 moose or 2,976 caribou saved.

The government has no problem with wasting bear and wolf meat, but wasting caribou meat is out of the question. When apparently wasted caribou are found near Point Courage just a month after the Steller's eider shooting, it ignites all the passions of sport hunters versus subsistence hunters, the urban government versus the rural governed, and *taniks* versus natives.

The "Caribou Massacre," as many in Alaska call it, begins with State Troopers responding to a *tanik* teacher's report of 120 slaughtered caribou rotting along a 40-mile tundra trail. The teacher has put together a photo album of severed caribou heads, whole, unbutchered carcasses, stranded calves still trying to suckle milk from their decomposing mothers, and a few soda cans and gum wrappers.

The troopers arrive in the village of Point Courage with a cameraman from Animal Planet. They find the *tanik* school teacher and head down the trail towards the scene of the Caribou Massacre. The group comes back with 20 pictures of seven caribou, shot from different angles. No one knows what was really found, since the troopers cordoned off the site.

Word of the Caribou Massacre gets back to the Borough, and Gill is sent by helicopter to investigate the site. He reports back to the mayor that he only saw seven carcasses. He also calls up the Northern Slope Regional Co., who owns the land around the site.

"You know somebody from Animal Planet was going on your land with a camera?" Gill asks the corporation's land manager after telling him what happened. "I don't think he got a permit from us or from you to do all that filming."

Meanwhile, the troopers have taken their investigation into the village, but find no one there willing to cooperate with them. The village elders say they want to work out the problem themselves.

The troopers call a Point Courage local charged with illegally importing alcohol and offer him a reduced sentence if he can get statements from the hunters involved. The bootlegger calls up all his friends and acquaintances to ask how their hunting's been. He manages to get an admission from a 17-year-old kid, who says he left some sick caribou out in the field.

The State charges the 17-year-old kid with indiscriminately gunning down dozens of caribou on the Arctic tundra. The kid rats out seven other hunters. Two of them come voluntarily to the Point Courage station with their grandfather and agree to be questioned.

"Well, well," the questioning trooper announces. "A village elder who's going to cooperate. Your people should follow your example."

The elder says nothing. He's hard of hearing and seeing. He's also hard of speaking English.

One of the hunters tries to explain that while he was dressing his kill, he nicked the animal's stomach. "All the guts spilled onto the meat so I can't eat it no more. And another *tuttu* got hit in the back, and nobody takes a *tuttu* that's hit in the back."

The other hunter swallows nervously and gives his own defense. "The one I shot had lumps in its liver," he says. "And there's two more with cuts on their legs, and they're all messy."

Now the elder speaks up. "When I was young, it don't happen much, killing sick *tuttu*. If it happen, we cut off the head and point it toward the village. So the *tuttu* return. But it don't happen much."

One of the young hunters adds, "It's part of our custom, to leave the sick meat behind. We don't have no federal agency to check our meat and make sure it's safe. We got to use the sense the good Lord gave us."

The elder continues, "It don't happen much because we know the *tuttu* come to us. We have to wait. Sometimes five days before the *tuttu* come. The sick *tuttu* sometimes come, but we don't shoot him, we wait."

The other young hunter looks annoyed with the elder. "We were out there all day. It's not like the *tanik* who can just walk in the store and get what he want in five minutes. We don't have that kind of money."

"We wait, and the good animals come," the elder is saying.

The trooper asks the elder, "Who taught your grandchildren how to hunt?"

"We don't hardly know them now. We don't know how he hunt. They go away on the snow-go or to Harow or Anchorage. And when he stay here," he coughs heavily, "he drink alcohol."

The young hunters look at their grandfather strangely. They've hardly gotten drunk at all since last year, when their inebriated uncle landed his snowmachine upside-down and broke his neck.

The elder turns to the trooper, "You brought us the guns and the snow-gos and the Good Lord Jesus, but you brought us the devil, too. Now with the alcohol we're all sick"—he coughs and his cough turns into a sob.

The trooper gives up the questioning. He already has enough evidence for the record.

Back in her office, Vik reads the report that the trooper released to the media. Bertie has asked her to follow the investigation in case the mayor decides that the Borough should intervene.

Vik's not happy with this task. To her, the Caribou Massacre is even grislier than the Steller's eider shootings. We often hear Vik proudly professing that she's never shot a gun in her life.

When she says this to Larry, he nods silently. But alarm bells are going off in his head. How is Vik the Vegetarian going to defend the subsistence way of life? He asks his wife what she thinks about it.

"Why don't you invite her to come to our camp next time?" Mandy suggests.

"Maybe," he says. Naive and white as Vik is, Larry finds himself slightly attracted to her. The idea of having her there in his one-room cabin with his wife and family all in their pajamas is a little unnerving.

"I'll invite her," Mandy says.

"Okay."

Vik gets a call from Mandy at 3:30 on a Wednesday afternoon. "Hey, do you want to come out to our camp?"

"Oh god, I'd love to," Vik says gleefully. She's always looking for an anthropological expedition. Going camping with an Eskimo family fits the bill.

"When are you going, this weekend?" she asks.

"Right now," Mandy says. "We go by boat and we gotta go while the water's high."

"Oh," Vik says. "I don't think I can just take off and leave work without giving Bertie advanced notice. So I don't know if I can make it ... are you going to go again anytime soon?"

"Sure, we'll call you then!"

The next time Mandy calls, it's 4:30 on Friday. "Can you come right now?" she asks. "The wind's supposed to get bad later on."

"Uh, yeah," Vik says, desperately trying to control her type-A need to have everything planned out. "I'll just go home and pack and meet you at your house."

In her rush to get out the door, Vik doesn't have time to grab any of her meds or sleeping pills. She gets to Larry's just as the last ice chest is being loaded on the largest of the four Atkoot boats.

"I think the water's finally high enough to use the big boat," Mandy says, "So it's only gonna take four hours to get there. Last time the river dried up before we got there, and we left the boat and carried all our stuff for two hours. I hope that don't happen this time, with the babies coming along."

"The babies?" Vik asks.

"My niece is coming," Mandy says, "and she got her two-year old and two-month old."

They drive out to the boat launch, where they are met by a pale skinny teen with blue eyes and a giant parka. She climbs onto the boat awkwardly, clutching with one arm at the two-month-old zipped inside her parka. The two-year-old, jealous of any attention to the two-month old, hangs off her mother's shoulders. A half-blind dog jumps on after them, followed by its owner, Larry's nephew.

The Atkoots' camp is 70 miles into the National Petroleum Reserve-Alaska, through a lagoon and then the narrow Chiliq River. Various hunters have built a total of 13 camps on the Chiliq River, each identified by a number. The Atkoots'— Chiliq 2—is built on an Ericsen family allotment.

Mandy is an Ericsen. Her father had the sense to apply for the allotment before the timeline ran out. We all know that the land was really the hunting grounds of Wesley Nutak, but then, there's nothing to stop Wesley from coming and hunting on the place even now.

Four hours later, the boat pulls up at a sandy bluff. Vik can see the outline of a one-room cabin in the twilight. They begin the slow process of dragging all the food and supplies out of the boat. Vik counts three ice chests and five grub boxes. The wind is picking up, and a few paper plates fly out of an open box. Vik watches helplessly as they disappear into the night.

Larry pulls out a hammer and begins prying off the plywood he nailed on the door frame last year to keep bears out.

"People still come in and trash the place," Mandy explains. "But not as much as they used to. Anyway, the bears are the worse. They bite right through the canned goods and make a mess."

"The good thing is that our camp's on the river instead of the ocean," Larry says. He's known people who chose allotments along the coast, only to lose large chunks of the land to the intruding sea.

Vik goes off with a roll of toilet paper in search of a little seclusion. She observes that the bluffs along the river and the relative lack of litter are the only things that set the landscape apart from what surrounds Harow. Otherwise, it's just endless tundra under cold gray skies.

When Vik comes back, the younger baby is screaming and everyone else is eating the breaded chicken patties that Mandy heated up on the Coleman stove. "I think he's got colic," the niece says.

Vik discretely puts in her earplugs, which she carries in her backpack everywhere she goes, and curls up on a mat in the corner to sleep. When she wakes up, she notices a large pair of exposed feet next to hers. The niece's boyfriend came in during the night with his cousin and another dog. Larry mumbles passive-aggressively for the rest of the trip about proper etiquette requiring young men to travel with their own tents, but no one gets it. Anyway, no one's going to sleep outside when the wind's blowing 30 miles an hour. The campers spend most of their time inside the little cabin, filling it with the exhaust of Coleman stove-cooked bacon, sausage, and steak.

"Are you, uh, going to hunt while you're here?" Vik asks Larry during one of the rare moments when the niece and her entourage have gone outside. She's a little alarmed to see Larry eating so much Western food.

"I don't do that so much anymore," Larry says. "Not since I've been working fulltime with the Community Development Department, you know."

"Oh. Well, maybe you can show me how to shoot a gun," Vik says.

Larry stands up without saying anything, opens one of the ice chests by the door way, and pulls out a case of beer.

Larry's wife rolls her eyes. "He gets it from a bootlegger in town. He can't get a license to have it imported to the Distribution Center because of his conviction."

Larry pops open a beer and says into the can, "That fucking conviction ruined everything."

"You, uh, don't have to—if it's personal—" Vik stammers, wondering how obvious it is that she really wants to hear the story.

Larry takes a long swig and says, "No, I'm going to tell you about it. Because you're a lawyer and you understand about rights and what happened to mine." He takes another swig, and Mandy puts the case back in the ice chest.

"A girl was raped in one of those shacks out by Duck Camp. She was drunk, and when the cops got her statement, she just said, 'It was Larry.'"

Larry finishes his beer in another gulp and looks up at Vik. "You know how many 'Larrys' there are in town?"

"I can think of at least three Larrys," Vik volunteers. "I wouldn't be surprised if there were more than one Larry Atkoot ..." She almost says, "what with everyone being so related and there being so few last names."

"Well, I can tell you it wasn't this Larry," he says, getting up to grab another beer. "And everyone in Harow knew it wasn't me."

"I knew it wasn't him," Mandy whispers. "We were dating already. You know, we got married while Larry was in jail. I had to wait two years after that until he got out ..."

"Wait," Vik interrupts. "I don't see how he could've gotten convicted. Didn't you have a jury trial? How could anyone from here find you guilty if they knew you didn't do it?"

"I had a lawyer, and he was actually okay," Larry says. "But the jury was made up of a bunch of *taniks* from the Freedom Committee. They were pissed at me because I supported the Harow mayor when he was running on a dry campaign. Can you imagine?" he asks, holding up his beer. "I used to be opposed to drinking." He laughs bitterly.

Mandy sighs. "Those were bad times. But they're over."

"They're not over!" Larry says. It's the closest Vik has ever heard him come to raising his voice. "I'm a convicted felon. I'm not even supposed to have a gun!"

Vik mumbles, "I'm sorry, I shouldn't have asked you to show me how to shoot—"

"And it's not just me," Larry goes on. "You know how many native men aren't allowed to hunt and provide for their families and communities because of a felony conviction? You know how many more can't leave town to hunt because of being on probation? It's one thing for them to take away my right to hunt, but subsistence is a group right. You tell a man he can't hunt, and you're telling him he can't provide for his elders no more."

"We're lucky we both have jobs," Mandy says.

"But hey, I can teach you how to shoot." Larry laughs a bit too loudly and finishes his beer. "There's no cops out here, just you and me and the wild."

"And your wife," Vik says to herself.

A couple days later, after the wind dies down, Larry picks a gun from the pile next to the door. It has a scope on top that does very little to help focus the bullets, as Larry finds out when he sets up a practice target.

Vik attempts to shoot the target but instead shoots into the Chiliq River, 30 feet away from the target. "I think I'm deaf now," she shouts. "I think that's enough for me."

"Let me just calibrate the gun, then you can try again," Larry says. Vik and the two-year-old pick berries around the cabin while Larry takes shots at the target. Despite Larry's good aim, the bullets land at least five feet from the target for 20 shots in a row.

"Maybe we should try one of the other guns?" Vik asks.

"They're not good for caribou," Larry explains.

The sun comes out, and Larry decides they should all go hunting in spite of the lack of good guns. Adults, babies, and dogs pile into the little motor boat Larry keeps at the camp. They tool down the river looking for caribou up on the bluffs. Finally Larry sees something worth shooting at and turns off the motor. The caribou stares stupidly at the would-be hunters while the boat drifts towards it.

"Hold the dogs," Larry says. He jumps onto the river bank and creeps up the bluffs toward the caribou. There's a loud thud and then another, but neither has any more success than the 21 bullets that were fired earlier.

On the way back, Larry suggests that they visit Mandy's brother Luther, who spends a good part of the year in the old cabin that their parents built.

"Luther's a man who really lives off the land," Larry says. "And that's the reason I took you out here—to show you what the subsistence lifestyle is all about, so you'll know what people are talking about when they say they're going camping. So you can represent us better."

It occurs to Vik that the only subsistence activity that has taken place other than the failed caribou mission was her and the two-year-old's berry picking.

"You may see people with all those cell phones and nice things in town," Larry continues, "but a lot of people are too poor to buy groceries. Milk is $9 a gallon. People like Luther depend on subsistence."

Luther hears the motor boat and comes out to see who's there. "Good Lord," he says with a smile. "Never thought I see a *tanik* out here! Come on in!"

The tiny cabin is decorated with 40-year-old prayer calendars, and heated by an antique wood stove that Luther has filled with charcoal. The floor is covered with boxes of chips, bread, and poptarts.

"I left them with my brother last time we were here," Mandy explains, "So the bears won't try to break into our camp and get 'em."

"They're great for bear bait," Luther says with a grin, opening a poptart wrapper with his teeth. With a mouthful of poptart, he asks, "Did you catch anything since you've been out here?"

Larry scrapes the floor with his foot. He doesn't want to admit to Luther that he hasn't. Nor does he want to give any credit to his niece's boyfriend, who, using Larry's boat and bullets, went further upriver and brought back three caribou.

One of the niece's babies begins wailing, and the niece quiets him with a piece of a poptart that Luther dropped. "My boyfriend got some caribou," she says.

"Well, well," Luther says. "How's your daddy these days?" The niece's father is Luther's youngest brother and the president of the Harow Native Corporation.

"Go-od," the niece smiles, revealing a row of braces. Her father's business trips accrue enough frequent flyer miles for her to go to Anchorage once a month and have her braces tightened.

"Didn't see him in a while," Luther says. "You either, Larry."

"I can't get out much with my job these days," Larry mumbles.

"Huh. Too bad," Luther says. "Director of Community Development for the Borough, is it? What about your deputy, one of the Whitehead sons? He manages to get to his camp out here all the time."

"Gill Whitehead?" Larry asks, shrugging. "He does what he wants. He's just an employee. I got to work directly with the mayor. It's a lot of stress, dealing with all these oil companies."

The niece's iPhone rings, and she goes outside to answer it. The two-year old swipes at Luther's poptart.

"I'm really glad I got to come out here and—and see what it's all about," Vik stammers.

"Well, we'll be seeing you," Mandy says to her brother. She herds the flock back into the boat, and then back to the cabin for a dinner of Coleman stove-cooked hamburgers. Vik eats the berries she picked, mixed with soy powder.

The wind begins to pick up again the next day, and Larry decides they should head back before the water gets too choppy. The niece's boyfriend discovers that his boat has run out of gas, and, for reasons unclear to Vik, decides to tie his boat to the top of Larry's boat. Adults, babies, and dogs pile into Larry's boat with the three caribou carcasses. Vik opts to sit on the deck with the caribou to avoid the wailing of the babies in the boat cabin.

Larry comes out and looks at the caribou with what could be a smile. "I let my wife drive," he says. He sits between two carcasses and stares out at the water all the way home to Harow.

Another homecoming takes place the same day—Lisa's brother moves back to Harow after three years of working in Anchorage. He's got one thing on his mind, fall whaling. He's missed five whaling seasons already with his family's crew.

He goes over to Lisa's to see if Jimmy has started helping with the crew yet. But Lisa's honey hasn't even taken his son on a bird hunt. The boy has no clue what it means to be a whaler.

"What's happening to you?" he asks Lisa in disgust. "Or should I say, what's happening to us?"

Britney, who's listening, giggles and says, "Jimmy don't even have Iñupiat friends. Just some funny Oriental."

Lisa's brother ignores Britney. "Lisa, if nobody else is gonna teach this kid what to do, then I'm taking him out with our crew this fall."

Britney jumps up and down, hollering, "I wanna go! I wanna go!"

Lisa's brother smiles gently and says, "There's plenty of work to get done. You can help make the donuts."

"I wanna kill the whale," Britney says, and Lisa's brother laughs.

"Whoever says that is never gonna get a whale. You gotta show respect. The whale's gonna come to you, but only if you show respect."

Without looking up from his video game, Jimmy announces, "Well, I DON'T want to kill a whale, so there."

"You're gonna learn, you're gonna learn," Lisa's brother says, stroking Jimmy's hair. Jimmy shudders. He doesn't like going out in the cold, unless Britney's driving him on the four-wheeler or snowmachine.

But lessons begin that weekend. Lisa's brother takes Jimmy to the beach out by Duck Camp, while his wife takes Britney into the kitchen for baking lessons.

Britney knows she won't last long in the kitchen. Cooking is bad enough, but waiting around for the men to come home is even worse. At least in the spring, the women get to cook out on the shorefast ice. In the fall, there's no ice to camp on, and the women wait at home to feed the crew during breaks. Britney's aunt has no satellite T.V., making the waiting all the harder.

Jimmy would love to be at home watching T.V., but realizes how disappointed his uncle will be if he gives up the first day. He'll have to stick it out at least until next weekend.

"We got the shoulder gun as backup," Lisa's brother tells Jimmy, "but you gotta learn how to use the harpoon with the darting gun on it, 'cause it always comes first. It's got the float and line attached." He hands Jimmy the heavy weapon and the boy shakes.

"Raise it up and get used to the feel!"

Jimmy stands immobile.

"You never even been hunting before, huh," Lisa's brother mumbles to himself, taking the weapon away from Jimmy. "Maybe I better teach you how to shoot first."

He roots through the back of his SUV for the lightest rifle he can find, hands the gun to Jimmy, and points to a washed out cereal box on the ground 10 yards away.

"That's our target," he says. "See if you can hit it."

Jimmy squints and shakes.

"You gotta open your eyes and keep your arms steady, son," Lisa's brother says.

Jimmy opens his eyes and holds his breath, then fires a bullet within inches of the box.

"Not bad, not bad," Lisa's brother says. "Try that soda bottle right next to the water."

The bullet grazes the bottle, which rolls toward the ocean.

"All right, bring that bottle over here and try again," Lisa's brother says.

"It's already in the water," says.

Lisa's brother shrugs. "It don't matter much about the bottle, but you can't be afraid of getting wet, son."

Jimmy meekly steps into the icy water and retrieves the bottle. Shivering, he brings it back to his uncle.

They practice the rest of the day, until Jimmy is shivering so much he can't hold the gun straight.

Back at home, Britney refuses to speak to Jimmy. "It's not fair that he gets to go whaling and I don't," she hisses to her mother after Jimmy has resumed his spot in front of the video game concourse.

Lisa sighs. "I'm not the one making these decisions," she says. "You should be grateful that your aunt wants to take the time to show you something." She looks at her honey out of the corner of her eye. He's fallen asleep in his chair.

"I don't wanna make donuts for a bunch of men!" Britney howls.

"Well, you don't have to if you don't want to, but you should be grateful to learn traditional cooking. One day you might get tired of potato chips."

"No way!" says Britney, getting a new bag out of the pantry and opening it. She sits down next to her sleeping father and watches Jimmy lose his video game.

Lisa doesn't want the kids to miss school for fall whaling, so she only lets Jimmy go out with the crew on weekends. Britney refuses to go back to her aunt's kitchen. When Jimmy's gone, she takes off alone on the four-wheeler.

One Saturday she rides out to the old airport. Once a landing strip for the U.S. Navy, it's now the place where successful crews cut up their whales.

Someone's caught a whale, and the town has come out to celebrate. Kids are standing on the whale taking pictures before it gets butchered. People are already on the other side of the whale making the first cuts.

"Hey, come over here and help," someone yells at Britney. It's her nineteen-year-old cousin, whose father took Jimmy whaling.

"Is that your crew's whale?" Britney asks.

"Yeah, and if you can believe it, your brother was the one to kill it."

Britney gasps and turns around to see Jimmy wearing a blood-covered white jacket. He smiles with the sheepishness of beginner's luck. The cousin is divided between enjoying the afterglow of a successful catch and resenting the ten-year-old star of the show, who'd only been training for a few days.

"I was lucky," Jimmy says. "The whale was hardly moving, and I got the harpoon just at the back of the head. And the bomb went off right away."

"It was an ideal shot," Lisa's brother says proudly. "That's how you dispatch a whale immediately. I called over at your mom's place to tell her to come out here, but no one answered. You heard about it on the VHF?"

Britney wrinkles her nose. Just because her father leaves the VHF radio on all day doesn't mean she has to listen to it. She gets all her news from Twitter and Facebook.

"Just dumb luck that I came out here," she says, shouting the word "luck" and glaring at Jimmy.

"This kind of thing sure don't happen too often," Lisa's brother continues. "Jimmy's the youngest guy ever in my crew to get a whale. My son's the one who seen it first, and we followed it for twenty minutes. I harpooned the whale first with the darting gun, but the whale wasn't ready to give up. My son used the shoulder gun to launch another bomb, but it didn't go off. That's when I told Jimmy I wanted him to go up front and put the harpoon right into the whale. Put one last bomb in. That's what he did, tough little guy." He rubs Jimmy's hair with his blood stained fingers, and Jimmy grins.

Britney and her cousin scowl.

Chapter- 18 More Meetings

A Borough Assembly meeting can easily rise to the level of a Baptist wedding. There's no booze and no dancing, but a sense of absolute solemnity, a rented camera man poised to immortalize every pose of the participants, and teary-eyed speeches with two standing ovations per speaker. The most applauded speeches are in Iñupiaq. *Taniks* listen with smiles plastered on their faces, letting go a polite laugh when cued by the laughter of the people who understand.

Every good speech goes back to Evan Hooper, the George Washington of the Iñupiat. His bodiless head looks down on the Assembly Room from a huge mural, lest we forget him.

"What would Evan Hooper do now?" thunders the voice of a 73-year-old *tanik* lawyer at one meeting. The Assembly has presented him with a Friend of the Borough award for serving the Borough back in the 1970s, and he's capitalizing on his acceptance speech to lobby for a current client.

The client is one of the eight Point Courage hunters that the State of Alaska has charged with wanton waste of caribou meat in the "Caribou Massacre." The lawyer explains what really happened: "A group of young hunters went out and killed some caribou and left them there. Maybe the meat was bad, maybe the hunters didn't know what they were doing. They were practically children, those hunters. They left the caribou there and a school teacher found out about it, then got the word back to the state police. And the troopers didn't care about the childhood joy of hunting, or whether the meat was contaminated. They wanted to use this as an opportunity to attack subsistence hunting. They found a man from Point Courage who'd been arrested for booze and put a wire on him. They told the wired man to call everyone he knew in the village and ask if they'd gone hunting lately and how many caribou they got."

The lawyer starts to shake. The photographer snaps pictures.

"We have a strong hunting tradition, and part of that tradition is that we don't touch contaminated caribou meat. We leave it there. And what do the cops do? They find every man who's left behind a caribou carcass and arrest him!"

A few of the Assemblymen raise their eyebrows. Although the lawyer is a Friend of the Borough, he's not part of the collective Iñupiat "we." The lawyer seems to remember this suddenly, and explains, "When I say 'we' I just mean that I'm so lucky to have the privilege to defend this great tradition."

Everyone claps, and the lawyer continues, "If Evan Hooper were here he'd go right to the governor and do something about this caribou mess. And you, Mayor Kitok, that's what you need to do."

The mayor seems divided between informing the shouting *tanik* that he's out of order and applauding the plug for subsistence. Everyone remains still except the camera man. One of Evan Hooper's grandsons rescues the moment by announcing that the Hooper family has a gift for the lawyer, and trading the gift for the microphone.

As the lawyer peels away the wrapping paper, the audience members crane their necks to see the gift. It's an owl carved from ivory, only the neck is slightly too long, and the owl's head looks like the weight on a miniature dumbbell. The audience rises automatically and applauds.

Perhaps having anticipated the gift, the lawyer is prepared to offer his own. He hands the Hooper grandson a large picture wrapped in brown paper, and manages to take back the microphone in the process.

"Yesterday's struggle for the bowhead whale is today's fight for the right to hunt caribou," the lawyer hollers hoarsely. "The gift of the whale. In 1972 the federal government brought a bunch of children in red T-shirts to put up big tents on the ice and count the whales. Based on that 'count, which really just scared the whales away, they wanted to reduce our quota. The feds and all those activists who talked about shooting whales with machine guns wanted to take away the gift of the whale!"

Meanwhile, the Hooper grandson has ripped open the brown paper to expose a 1980 photograph of Evan Hooper sitting next to the lawyer at a table covered with whale meat. The lawyer's mouth is open and poised to accept a large piece of *maktak*.

The lawyer is still talking but the audience drowns him out with a standing ovation. The mayor seizes the moment to grab the microphone, and the lawyer, acknowledging that his moment has passed, makes his way to his seat. He pauses in front of the Evan Hooper mural and gestures wildly. The ivory owl still in his left hand smashes into the back of a vacant chair, and the decapitated head rolls beneath it. The lawyer quickly grabs the head and shoves both parts of the owl into his coat pocket. Failing to notice the decapitation, the audience continues its mechanical clapping. The mayor rubs his hands and calls for a 15-minute break.

A week later, the mayor sends a $5,000 check from the Borough to each of the eight defendants. When angry letters from non-Natives start pouring into the office, the mayor's press agent from Iowa releases a statement quoting the mayor:

Our traditional subsistence hunt shouldn't be criminalized. It's our way of life. The trophy hunting laws shouldn't be applied to our subsistence hunters, especially when they are protecting their family by leaving contaminated meat out in the field. We don't have the Food and Drug Administration to regulate our caribou meat.

Assemblyman Chuck is pissed. At the next Assembly meeting he stands up and says, "I just want to thank the mayor for giving every non-Native another reason to hate Natives. I don't know any Iñupiaq in Harow who doesn't think that leaving all that caribou on the tundra was wanton waste. Even whalers can't hunt mother whales and leave behind baby calves. I don't care what you're taught or what you think your tradition is ..."

For perhaps the only time in his adult life, Chuck harkens to his Mississippi blood, "But my ancestors had a tradition of brewing moonshine. That's how they supported the family during the Great Depression, and they passed on the tradition to my mom. So if I respect the family tradition and bootleg up here, is it okay to break the law?"

The assemblyman from the village of Kusoq frowns. "I support the mayor and those defendants who did what they had to do. We got to go further and further out to catch caribou these days, 'cause their route change. 'Cause of all the seismic testing, helicopters, small aircraft scare the caribou. So we go way way out. But what happens when the belt breaks on your snow machine when you're out there? I walked ten hours home once. And when you got to go far out it takes so long, if you got a job you can't get the time off. The weekend's not enough time so people just don't even go."

The assemblyman from the village of Ankvut clears his throat and says, "We got a caribou problem, too, that we need help with. We know all our caribou shoulda come through Ankvut already this fall but they're nowhere around. Meanwhile the trophy hunters is coming in on planes, taking the antlers of our caribou, and leaving the bodies to rot."

The mayor looks nervously at the Ankvut assemblyman. "What is it you want the Borough to do?"

The assemblyman continues. "Our village wants to charter a float plane with a few hunters to go out and hunt for the community, and bring back all the caribou. We got to do it now and we need your help. You know, like my uncle says back during the *Duck-in*, 'Hunger is not bound by law.'"

The audience stands and claps, and the mayor mumbles that he'll take the suggestion into consideration. Lieutenant Mayor Nelson smiles blankly and, looking at no one, confirms that the matter will be looked into.

The assemblyman from Ankvut frowned. He knows that the mayor's *tanik* sidekick has no intention of chartering a plane for the Iñupiat hunters. They'd be lucky to get a shipment of free dog food from him.

After the Assembly meeting, the mayor asks Nelson, "Didn't we send a charter to Ankvut back in the 1980s when they were having trouble getting caribou?"

"That was under the Ernie Whitehead administration, in the same era when the Borough provided free washeterias for all Borough residents and a Christmas present for every child. The advice of the Law Department, which I headed at the time, was not taken."

The next day, Nelson produces his Law Department memo from the 1980s saying that federal law would make the charter hunting plan near-impossible. He's also got an email from the Borough biologist who put tracking collars on the herd of caribou the Ankvut hunt. The email says the caribou passed just south of Ankvut in late summer, but no one bothered to go out and hunt them.

The mayor sighs. "No matter how you look at it, the routes have changed. I don't know if it's global warming or what. We were always told not to shoot the first group that comes through. Any disturbance to the first group, whether it's trophy hunting or seismic, and they go the other way. And now they're not coming to us no more."

Nelson tries to bring the mayor down to earth without being critical. "The thing to do is let one of the churches take care of it. Let them have a canned food drive or something. We can even funnel the church some money if we do it through a grant for faith-based charitable initiatives."

"I don't really know what to do ..." the mayor says. "I'll call the native corporation over there and see if they can't help the people out with fuel, so they could at least go out in four-wheelers ..."

"Well," Nelson sighs. "I do feel for the people. I'm tempted to make a charitable donation to them, even. But then, you know, Mayor, people have to learn to live with the consequences of their actions. And once you start giving money to one group for one thing, everyone's going to be asking for it."

"It's not always about money, Nelson, but what do I know ..." The mayor gives Nelson a twisted smile and goes out for a smoke break. If Nelson didn't know the mayor better, he'd sense a trace of pity.

While Nelson and the mayor are sorting out caribou conundrums, Shant Oil's "Social Performance Coordinator" is planning the oil company's next Arctic Slope meeting.

The Social Performance Coordinator was hired two years ago, after Shant representatives made the mistake of showing up in a village for a meeting without having the community's permission to be there. She soon learned that the villages wanted more than just notice—they wanted to be fed and entertained. She tells her boss that it's a huge cost to put on meetings with all the bells and whistles that people expect, but it would be much more expensive in the long run to have anti-Shant communities.

The lawsuit the Borough and others brought to void Shant's offshore drilling leases hasn't made things easier. The court decision lets Shant keep its leases, but Shant's going to have to change its plans a bit. The Social Performance Coordinator suggests to her boss that Shant take a repentant approach, telling the Borough that Shant has heard the people's concerns and changed its ways. She says most people won't guess that it was the court decision that forced the changes.

"It's still not going to be easy to get them to play ball," her boss says. "Eskimos are about as scared of offshore as all those Outsider environmentalists. The one time I went up there, they all kept saying, 'The ocean is our garden' and 'we've been here since time immemorial.'"

"Don't I know it," the Social Performance Coordinator says. "I was hoping some of the hysteria would die down after BX Petro decided to pick up its toys out of the Eskimos' garden and move to Brazil. But it's the same as ever."

The Social Performance Coordinator and her boss come up with a new format for meetings—something like a county fair with a bunch of flashy exhibits. There'll be a marine mammal booth showing how whales and oil drilling are really compatible. Another booth will show how, despite what the environmentalists say, oil really can be cleaned up from icy water. There'll even be a hands-on kiddie exhibit showing how blown-out wells can be capped. To top all this off and to keep conversation to a minimum, the Harowtiks, Harow's only band, will play live music throughout the meeting.

The Social Performance Coordinator spends two weeks arranging for the next meeting. She spends a day in Harow setting up the exhibits. Then she waits nervously as the appointed hour for the meeting comes and goes.

Twenty minutes later, Harow residents trickle in. After another twenty minutes, all of the residents are still by the food table, and only one Harowtik has shown up. It takes another hour before the full band starts playing. By then, residents are meandering around the booths, looking at the shiny graphics with a mixture of curiosity and distrust.

"You know," one resident shouts over the din to the Social Performance Coordinator, "There's just a lot of development going on these days, and people are tired of going to meetings. It's having an effect on the community. It takes people away from what they normally do."

The Social Performance Coordinator nods and tries to look sympathetic. "That's why we tried to do something different today!" she says cheerily. She waves at a familiar face before remembering it's Luther

Ericsen, the man who kills every meeting by moaning about how the world is out to get the Eskimos.

Luther smiles and waves back. Then he goes over to the Harowtiks and asks them to stop playing for a minute. The lead singer obligingly stops and hands Luther the microphone.

"I got something to say," Luther's gravelly voice booms through the speakers.

"First of all I want to welcome Shant to Harow and thank them for the food and all the door prizes. But it's not going to change my mind about oil. My grandfather discovered oil at Prudhoe Bay forty years before you all started drilling in 1968. And I was right there in 1968 when the oil companies came, I help them get going. I know how you work. I seen with my own eyes how they let those drilling fluids loose on the tundra. There's caustic soda and lead ore in the drilling fluids. And, what else ... Dust was a problem on the roads, so they just put crude oil right on the road."

The Social Performance Coordinator frantically looks around the room for the president of one of the village native corporations, who was supposed to come and talk about how local business is going to benefit from offshore drilling and how Shant's going to contract with his company. He's not here.

The crowd is putting down their plates and clapping for Luther. The Social Performance Coordinator figures there's nothing to do but wait for him to run out of steam or break into a coughing fit. She's decided that Luther, like many older Iñupiat, must have smoked for years and is probably well on his way to lung disease.

After ten minutes, the audience's attention span begins to wane. Luther decides to wrap up his speech with a raised fist and his favorite rallying cry, "We can live without petroleum, but we cannot live without the whale!" He steps heavily off the Harowtiks' makeshift stage. The audience claps, and the Harowtiks break into the only song they composed themselves, "Keep on Whalin'."

The Social Performance Coordinator doesn't know a thing about whaling, except that she's been instructed to ask us how whaling season is going and congratulate us any time someone gets a whale. Last year when she came in June, she was obliged to go to the Whiteheads' *nalukataq* and force down a piece of whale blubber. She's planned carefully ever since then to avoid coming in June.

The Social Performance Coordinator isn't opposed to subsistence, but she doesn't understand why people have to go out on boats and harpoon whales when they could just go to the grocery store. She watches the plates of pizza and noodles that the meeting attendees are helping themselves to on the way out the door, and concludes they must like store-bought food. And why stand in the cold, waiting for an animal to come by, when there's a chance of getting arrested for improperly harvesting the meat?

She's read the news about the Arctic Slope Borough donating money to the defendants in the Point Courage caribou case. The online Anchorage news site is still clogged with comments on the story from angry urban Alaskans who think subsistence rights have gone too far.

Back at the Community Development Department, Larry is also reading the comments. He laughs out loud at a comment criticizing Mayor Kitok for wasting taxpayer money on "people who broke the law." He writes his own comment, "Isn't that what jail is all about?" But he doesn't click on the "send" button. It's not worth throwing himself into the controversy.

Soon enough, the comments shift to the same old saw about how traditional native culture is dying in the wake of outboard motors, central heating, pickup trucks, snowmachines and polio vaccines. Larry stops reading them. He wonders why Outsiders think that "traditional" Iñupiat culture belongs in a museum or in a scrapheap along with every other culture America has swallowed up in the past few centuries.

Once the American majority starts dismantling cultures, it's hard to tell what to keep and what to throw out. Should we be allowed to shoot migratory birds if there's already a nice supply of chicken nuggets in the grocery store freezers? Is it okay to use central heating at traditional Eskimo dance festivals? On the other hand, should we get rid of the rusty relics of American culture? Does anyone actually like the Star Spangled Banner?

Gill interrupts Larry's thoughts by bursting into the office with news of a loose Korean out on the tundra. "He's been roaming around, living off the land. Somebody saw him a few years ago near Kusoq, and just now Chuck called to tell me that he's somewhere near Harow."

"Hmm," Larry mutters, envying the loose Korean.

"Can he legally do that without a permit?" Gill asks.

"Uh," Larry says, "Subsistence doesn't require a permit. Or else we'd have to get one every time we go out hunting."

Gill sighs. "I don't even know where we'd send the notice of violation to."

Larry thinks about Gill's words when he boats out to his camp that weekend. Larry built his cabin five years before, without a thought as to whether it would need a permit. The cabin is for subsistence. If Larry's harming the land there, he'll be the one who has to live with it.

By the time he gets to the camp, it's totally dark. Taking only a gun and the supplies he needs for the night, he climbs out of the boat and up on the bluff. He can barely see the cabin but knows exactly where it is. It's more home to him than the house he shares with his wife back in Harow.

Larry feels for the plywood around the doorframe and realizes that it's gone. Someone must have pulled it off to take shelter there. He hopes whoever it was cleaned up after himself.

He's left the flashlight in the boat and can't find the one on the shelf. But he doesn't really need it. It's already 11 p.m. He just needs to roll out the bedding in the corner and go to sleep.

In the morning when the light streams in through the open doorway, Larry sees the brown bear on the floor by the stove. He bristles. His gun is by the door on the other side of the bear. And it's no good for shooting bears, anyway.

Larry sits quietly, listening and waiting. The bear also seems to be waiting, not wanting to look at Larry. The bear is motionless except for its fur, which ruffles with the wind blowing in through the doorway.

Larry stands up silently and inches toward the door. The bear doesn't move, and it occurs to Larry that the bear might be dead. But when he pulls on one of the limbs, it's not stiff.

The bear groans softly. Larry looks around to see what the bear's gotten into—maybe it's poisoned itself with kerosene. But the food and supply shelves are bare. Someone cleaned out everything in the cabin except the bedding and the furniture.

Larry waits to see if the bear will get up and leave. Ten minutes pass, then twenty. The bear stays put. Maybe it's starving to death—it's definitely skinny. Larry decides he's going to have to shoot it. He can't just leave it suffering here in his cabin.

Larry wonders if he can drag the bear outside first to avoid a mess. As he starts to tug on a limb, he remembers a story his grandfather told him about turning into a bear and back into a man. Feeling dizzy, he drops the limb and walks outside. He decides he'll just get in his boat and go back to Harow. Anyway, he didn't tell his wife he was coming out here.

Larry gets in the boat and starts the engine, but remembers that he left his gun in the cabin. He leaves the engine running and goes back inside. The gun is leaning against the wall, but the bear is gone. Larry rubs his eyes and wonders if he dreamed the whole thing. Maybe he'll stay, after all, and see if the bear comes back. He goes back out to turn off the boat engine.

But back in the boat, he changes his mind again. For a moment, at least, the world of permits and online news seems to make more sense than the strange events at his camp. And he's got a meeting with the mayor in the afternoon. He pulls the anchor up and tugs his body and soul back to Harow.

Chapter 19- From the Night Sky

We hardly notice the nights when they first start to fall at the end of the summer. Then in September, they come earlier and earlier, and by October, we are left with just a few rays of sunlight in the afternoon.

It's early October, just before the snowmachines replace four-wheelers for the winter, when Jimmy sets off for his first ever camping trip. It's not Lisa's brother who's invited him, but a Korean kid, the only person who shows any interest in Jimmy besides his family. The two boys head inland on the twins' four-wheeler, with the Korean kid driving, since Jimmy still doesn't know how.

It's the first time Jimmy's gone anywhere without someone in his family. Part of him is grateful to the Korean kid, and the other part wonders if he were invited only because of his four-wheeler.

The Korean kid was born in Harow to parents who barely spoke English. His older sister married an Eskimo, who occasionally let the kid tag along on family camping trips. The kid has learned how to pitch a tent and how to start a fire from the scruffy willow bushes that grow along the inland river bluffs.

The Korean kid stops the four-wheeler in a spot that looks to Jimmy like any other, sets up the tent in the dark, and goes to sleep right away. Jimmy sits outside on the four-wheeler for a while, perhaps because it's the only thing in the entire landscape that's familiar to him. Finally, he crawls into the tent and tries to make himself comfortable in the sleeping bag that the Korean kid put there for him. But he stays awake for what seem like hours, listening to the night sounds. They're far enough inland that there might be grizzly bears. Even the idea of caribou scares him. A herd could easily trample the tent.

Jimmy has to pee. He tries to forget about it and fall asleep, but it's useless. When he can't take it anymore, he ventures out of the tent. He's just started when he happens to look up at the sky and see the red and green lights. They're not the Northern Lights, which ebb and flow like his computer screensaver. These lights are more like a beacon, radiating from a single spot in the east. The lights moves once, twice, and then they're gone. Jimmy stares at them the whole time before realizing he's peed on his feet. He crawls back into the tent and decides not to tell anyone about them.

He sees the lights again a few weeks later, when Britney is pulling him on a sled attached to her snowmachine. This time the lights are much closer. Jimmy sees that they're coming from what looks like a satellite or a rocket.

He figures he better tell his mom about the lights.

Lisa gasps when she hears about the lights. Her boyfriend, the one that died when he was twenty, had also seen a UFO. That was just before he died. She squeezes Jimmy tightly, worrying that a UFO sighting at a young age must be a bad omen.

"What is it, Mom?" Jimmy asks.

"It means you have to stay inside. You can't go out camping with your friend or do all those crazy things Britney does. You stay here, with me."

A month later, Vik, Bertie and Gill are walking out of a workshop on oil spill control technology, when Gill looks up says, "What the heck ..."

Vik looks at him and frowns, and then follows his gaze. The sun is already gone for the year, and she can clearly see a light or maybe a disc in the sky that changes colors from pink-red to orange. It hovers over the video store and then moves out of sight. Bertie is starting up the car and doesn't see anything.

"Hmm," Vik says. "Maybe it's a satellite out of orbit. I'll call the Federal Aviation Administration when we get back to the office and ask about it. I have to call them today, anyway."

Vik jokingly mentions the lights to a Federal Aviation Administration agent, who takes her seriously. He comes up to Harow the next week and has the Public Works Department shut off the city lights so he can look around for the UFO.

Of course he doesn't see anything. The UFO and the Federal Aviation Administration agent become the office joke in the Borough's Law Department.

But not in the Community Development Department.

"I don't know what's the big deal about them, anyway," Gill says. "They're like anything else. Some are good, some are bad. I seen a lot of them. The last one I seen was all lit up so much that I couldn't hardly see it. It was too early for stars, and if it was a plane I woulda heard it, so I knew it was a UFO. The weird thing was, it suddenly came down, close to the land, and all the lights went off except for the kind of lights you see on a snow machine. Then it was there, going just above the land for a while, and then suddenly it went back up."

One of the other employees says, "When I used to work in the search and rescue squad we got a few calls to go out and do a rescue, but they were really UFOs."

"How did you know?" Larry asks.

"'Cause they just kept moving further away, the closer we got to them. All the sudden we realized we were way out over the Chukchi, and there was no way anyone could be that far out. So we turned around and gave up."

"They can block you off if they want to," Gill says matter-of-factly. "When my dad and I saw 'em once when we were out hunting by *Tuungaqagvik*, the Place of Devils. They wouldn't let us get by—we had to turn around and hunt somewheres else. We didn't catch nothing that day."

"Maybe it was just a satellite operated by Greenpeace, trying to keep you from hunting," someone says, and they all laugh.

Gill suggests they get the Federal Aviation Administration man to come back some other time to make sure there really is a UFO, and not someone trying to do research without a proper permit.

But the holidays are already upon us, and not much will get done until mid-January.

Thanksgiving kicks off what Vik likes to call the Eating Season. Each of the departments in the Borough has its own Thanksgiving dinner on a different day of Thanksgiving week, so we can go to them all. The Mayor's Office holds its dinner on Wednesday, and everyone in Harow is invited. The department directors are constrained to act as food servers.

On Wednesday, Bertie stoically puts on the required shower-cap-hair-net and plastic gloves and parks herself behind the desert table. Her job is to make sure that each person only gets one slice of pie at a time. But within 15 minutes, every slice of pie is carted away. Bertie stands back, not daring to reprimand the people who make off with four-plate stacks of desert. It's Thanksgiving, after all.

Thanksgiving is to the fall as *nalukataq* is to the summer—a time to share the season's whale harvest. Whaling captains donate boxes upon boxes of pre-cut whale to their churches, and church leaders cook up all the other delicacies that go with *nalukataq*. On Thanksgiving proper, every family picks a church to sit at all day and receive the blessings of the whale.

Christmas parties start just after Thanksgiving, with the Borough's official Christmas dinner on December 1st. The mayor has put Bertie in charge of managing the dinner this year, and she's determined to avoid the Thanksgiving stampede. She holds the event in the Borough building's lobby, which is already so full of Christmas decorations that there's no room for running children and no clear path to the food.

Bertie would have liked to buy subsistence food for the event, but of course it's illegal to buy and sell marine mammals. She gets one of Harow's six Korean restaurants to cater the event, and orders steak, king crab, vegetables, and cheesecake. The food turns out so bad that Vik, who's normally a food hoarder, doesn't even get a to-go plate. Bertie is left with gallons of overcooked canned peas and half raw steak, which she donates to the food bank. There's so much grumbling about the food that Bertie ends up bumming a cigarette, just to calm herself down. She stands outside smoking and watching the snow fall, staring out at all the houses lit up with Christmas lights and neon crosses.

But as Christmas Day comes closer, Harow becomes a lonely place. Most of the *taniks* go back to wherever they came from, and the Eskimos with Borough salaries go to Anchorage or Hawaii. Bertie's the only lawyer in the Law Department who stays, year after year.

Lisa also stays in Harow for Christmas. The one year she went to Hawaii, she missed her home in the snow so much that she cried and swore to never again leave Harow for Christmas again.

On Christmas Eve, Lisa takes the trash out to the dumpster and pauses to breathe in the cold, clean air. Aside from the streetlights, the night sky is totally dark. She sees Larry Atkoot across the street, taking out his own trash, and waves.

"Merry Christmas!" she shouts out.

Larry nods and starts to go inside, but then turns and walks across the street to Lisa.

"Merry Christmas," he says quietly.

"Are you and your wife having Christmas dinner at your house tomorrow, or going to church?" Lisa asks. On Christmas Day, the churches distribute the leftover Thanksgiving whale to whoever is left in Harow.

Larry shrugs. "I think my wife is cooking something. My brother and his family were supposed to come, but he's been having trouble with his heart again, so they're down in Anchorage for his surgery."

"Ohhh," Lisa says softly. She wants to invite them to her apartment for dinner but it doesn't seem appropriate. She can't picture Larry there, in the din of the T.V. and the kids shouting, trying to step over the toys spread across the floor.

Larry and his wife would have been Lisa's parents-in-law if her first boyfriend had lived and they had gotten married. Lisa wonders if they've ever thought about that. Or if they even know that it was their son who got her pregnant. If she'd married their son, Britney and Jimmy would have been their grandchildren. The twins know nothing about Larry and his wife except that they're the people in the house across the street who are almost elders.

"You and your family should come by," Larry says, meaning it, but not wanting to impose the invitation on her.

"Oh, thank you!" Lisa says. "We'll stop by!"

On Christmas morning, Larry wakes up to the smell of his wife cooking duck soup. It's going to be a huge feast for two if Lisa and her family don't come.

Larry's grandfather told him that when he was growing up, the Iñupiat still celebrated the Messenger Feast in the month with no sun. A whaling captain from one village would go to the next village and invite its residents to come and feast and trade gifts. Everyone would gather at the *qargi*—meeting center—for the feast on the solstice.

Larry looks out the window. Every house around him, even those whose owners are on vacation, has a full set of Christmas lights that show through all 24 hours of winter darkness. He sees Lisa walking across the street, holding hands with her twins. He turns from the window and quickly gets dressed. It's so easy to sleep away the day this time of year.

Larry opens the door when Lisa knocks. "Merry Christmas," he says.

"My honey's at home," Lisa says. "He don't feel good. But, um, Jimmy's friend wanted to come, if that's okay."

Larry notices for the first time an Asian boy standing a few feet away from Jimmy.

Lisa continues, "He's Korean and his family don't celebrate Christmas."

Larry nods, and motions for them all to come in.

The two boys shuffle in, whispering to each other. Britney comes in next, glaring at the boys and her surroundings in general.

"Smells like duck," she says.

"We're having duck soup!" Mandy calls from the kitchen. "I didn't think you're gonna come so early. But it's good you're here."

"Oh," Lisa sighs. "My honey's kinda grouchy today, so I'm just leaving him alone." She turns to Jimmy and says hesitantly, "Tell them what you saw last night."

Jimmy sits on the couch and blushes. "We went out on the sea ice and I saw this light like I've been seeing this fall. Usually it starts off like this big glowing thing, and then it gets darker and moves around, especially whenever I'm walking."

Larry shifts uncomfortably. His grandfather told him that the UFOs belonged to the *imunarukit*—the little people. His grandfather hadn't actually seen the lights, but he had seen the little people on the shore when he was a kid. There were seven of them, and they spoke to Larry's grandfather. They said they only traveled at night. Larry's grandfather said that they didn't come around anymore, not since the *taniks* had come.

But the night before his son died, Larry had seen the bright lights that could only come from a UFO. He looks at Lisa, and wonders if she saw it then, too. He decides not to say anything. The world is complicated enough now, without having to worry about UFOs.

"What do you think it means?" Lisa asks.

Mandy comes in the living room, and says thoughtfully, looking at the Korean kid, "You know, when Jesus was born, the wise men saw a bright star in the sky and followed it to find the baby in the manger. Maybe that's what it's all about."

No one says anything else about UFOs after that, and the conversation devolves into community gossip and food. Larry says a long blessing in Iñupiaq, and everyone eats well except Britney, who gives her duck soup and pickled *maktak* to the Korean kid.

Chapter 20- One More Spring Whaling

There are three co-captains on the Whitehead whaling crew, but only one can inherit the title of captain that Gill's father left open when he died. Which one will depend a lot on who has an ice cellar big enough to hold the captain's share of the whale. So Gill is enlarging his ice cellar.

It's a brilliantly sunny March day, one of the coldest days of the year outside of the cellar. But the inside is warm. The deepest ice cellars don't begin to absorb any of the summer's heat until September, and they reach their warmest in March.

Out of voyeurism rather than kindness, Vik has offered to help Gill. The first item of business is to move aside the current contents of the cellar—500 pounds of frozen meat protected by bloody plastic garbage bags. Holding her breath, Vik heaves the bags into a row along the wall opposite from Gill. She'll probably smell like a whale for the next week. Gill is swinging his pickax at the wall with the same force he uses to clear a trail through the ice for spring whaling. After moving all the bags, Vik goes up into the house to attempt to wash some of the smell off her hands. Gill is so absorbed in the wall that he doesn't hear her say she's going up.

Gill's son and daughter are stretched out on couches in the living room, eating chips and watching TV.

"Don't you want to come and help your dad in the ice cellar?" Vik jokes.

No one answers. They're laughing at the TV or their text messages, or maybe at her.

Vik descends into the ice cellar again. Gill has succeeded in making a two foot hole in the wall. He's taken off his coat and is sweating through his T-shirt.

"I'll put this in the pulley bucket, okay?" Vik says. Gill has set up a pulley system to haul the permafrost-turned-mud out of the cellar.

Gill bangs away in response. Vik runs her fingers through the melting permafrost, noticing the roots from prehistoric tropical plants. It almost seems like something that should go in a museum instead of a dumpster. But she puts the mud and roots in the pulley bucket and sends the load to the waste pile on the surface.

"What are you going to do with all these plastic bags of whale?" she asks Gill, who's bringing his own mud load toward the pulley. "I thought all the fall whale got eaten by Christmas."

"Not all of it," Gill says. "Somebody's still going to eat it."

"Oh. Do you know who?"

"We'll share it with the people here. Or we'll send some down to the Bethel area—they love this stuff. I'm not going to waste it—it's whale!"

Vik frowns and nods. She's slowly understanding that no matter how popular TV and cell phones and potato chips may be, whale will always be sacred.

Chuck knows this. And he knows his own inability to hunt whale. It's a source of worry, what with the upcoming election for his assembly seat. His opponent is a 25-year-old kid who became a whaling captain after his grandfather died. The kid's crew has caught a whale four out of the last five hunts. Some captains can go years without catching a whale at all. If there's one thing this community still respects, it's a good whaler.

Chuck's been doing all right as far as leading the moral majority. Sure, there are rumors about him knocking up Gloria Whitehead, but no one can deny that he's the most vocal opponent against drugs and alcohol. When the mayor of Harow used the city credit card to bail himself out of jail for drunk driving, Chuck lead the campaign to have the mayor resign. Chuck was even asked to say the opening prayer at a few of the Assembly meetings.

But Chuck is not a whaler.

Chuck seeks out advice from his Uncle Luther, who's always felt sorry for his overly *tanik* nephew. Luther admits to being a quarter Norwegian, but that's different from the white Mississippi stock that produced Chuck's father.

"Well," Luther says. "You *are* the only man in our family who hasn't gone whaling."

"I did go to college for a year," Chuck insists. "I spent a lot of time in school, you know."

Not one to be impressed by school, Luther ignores Chuck's self-endorsement. "Yeah, you really ought to do something about this. I tell you what, why don't you join my crew this spring? I can give you all the equipment and training you need, and your aunt will make sure you get enough to eat. You come with us this spring, and you'll learn fast."

Chuck pictures himself trying to maneuver a skin boat—much less a harpoon—and shakes his head. "I don't think I can," he apologizes. "I don't have a clue what to do. Is there any way I could be, like, an honorary crew member without actually going out on the hunt?"

Luther shakes his head and looks at Chuck with tears in his eyes. "Do you know what it's like to catch a whale—a great big whale? This is the greatest feeling a man can ever get. When the whale starts to turn over, you say to yourself, 'This is my whale—I did it! It will feed many people for a long time.'"

Chuck feels himself getting choked up, and he knows he's got to try. Not just for his campaign, but also for Uncle Luther, to make him proud.

It's not going to be an easy job for Luther. Chuck has to be taken out in the *umiaq*—the whaling boat—and shown everything, as if he were a boy who just graduated from kitchen duty. Luther realizes that at best, Chuck would be able to sit in the boat and try to paddle without totally ruining the crew's chances of catching a whale.

"Don't ever touch the *umiaq* with your paddle—it will drum. The whale has very keen ears—he will hear it. Dig your paddle straight into the water so it don't gurgle. If it gurgles, the whale will hear it."

While Chuck's getting lessons, the rest of the crew is busy carving the trail over the shorefast ice to the open water. It isn't near the amount of work as usual, though, since the ice only extends out for a mile and a half now. In the past, it would be at least four miles at this time of year. Luther wonders if it even makes sense to camp out on the ice, when all the comforts of home are just a little more than a mile away. But Chuck needs to learn how to make camp, and it seems so contrary to tradition not to stay out on the ice for spring whaling.

Two weeks after Chuck first gets into an *umiaq*, the trail is cleared, the camp is set up, and spring whaling has officially started. On the crew's second day with Chuck, someone spots a whale a half-mile away.

The crew silently and swiftly launches the *umiaq* toward the whale. Luther takes his position at the bow as captain and harpooner. He's traded his eye patch for a pair of goggles he got in 1987 that have brought him luck on many hunts. Chuck sits on the starboard side, trying to contribute to the crew's paddling and feeling impotent.

The whale surfaces three times, each time a mile farther, shooting a geyser of steamy breath high up into the air. The crew keeps up with it, paddling one-two-three, in perfect rhythm, with Luther calculating the direction. After a while, Chuck decides his greatest contribution to the crew's efforts would be to pull his paddle out of the water and sit still.

The sun is close to setting when the whale surfaces seventy feet ahead. The crew sprints to catch up with it, and Luther sets the course about 25 feet parallel to that of the whale. The water swirls to the left, indicating the whale is about to surface. Luther turns the *umiaq* 45 degrees toward the whale, and then throws his paddle behind him. At this point, noise doesn't matter—it's time to harpoon. He takes hold of his weapon with both hands and raises it over his head, bracing himself for leverage. He strikes underwater, going for a thin bone on the whale's temple. He hits his mark, but no one knows it. The bomb has failed.

The crew feels a great force from below. Chuck is flattened onto the bottom of the *umiaq*, and then he's sailing through the air. The whale has caught them with its flukes, smashing the frame of the *umiaq* to bits.

Chuck hits the water hard, sinks, and then floats to the surface. The *umiaq* is no longer recognizable, just a wreck in the water.

"Is everyone okay?" Luther hollers, coughing. His voice is hoarse and strained. He's been thrown into an ice floe, which broke on impact.

"I'm okay!" Chuck shouts.

One by one, the other crew members shout that they're okay.

"I—I'm badly hurt," Luther says, wheezing and struggling to get up on a moving piece of ice. "I don't know if I'll make it."

"No way!" Chuck shouts. It's unthinkable that anyone could die in the water in this age of radios, phones, helicopters, and motors. But there aren't any other boats out here—Luther's crew was the only one to go after this whale. Chuck dogpaddles back to the wreck of the *umiaq* to look for his VHF radio and cell phone. It should be tied to the boat frame in a waterproof bag. But where is that part of the boat? Already the remains of the *umiaq* are drifting apart.

Luther shouts at Chuck, "You don't have time to waste, you got to get back to shorefast ice before you freeze."

One of the crew members knows this and is already swimming as best as he can back to shore. Chuck doesn't see the others. Nobody's wearing a life jacket.

"I'm going to call the search and rescue squad," Chuck says.

"Even if they come now ..." Uncle Luther's voice fades. The current is pushing him farther and farther away from Chuck. "You got to swim or there'll be no one left in the family to—" He breaks into a coughing fit.

Chuck hasn't swum since his time at the Indian school. His scrawny arms splash at the water. He somehow keeps floating even with the thick-haired caribou coat Luther gave him. When he reaches the landfast ice, he can no longer feel his limbs. He looks back at the wreck just before passing out. There's no sign of life—just a couple of paddles drifting out to sea.

When Chuck comes to, he's in the hospital. His mother is there along with her sister, Luther's wife.

"I tried to save him," Chuck whispers.

"I know," his mother says, squeezing his hand. "Don't talk."

Chuck's aunt bawls loudly when she sees that Chuck is awake.

"When's the funeral?" Chuck asks.

"Shhh," his mom says.

"His body's still missing!" wails Chuck's aunt.

"Maybe he became the whale," Chuck mumbles before drifting back into unconsciousness.

We all breathe a sigh of relief and sadness when we hear the radio announcement for Luther's funeral, after his body washes up a couple of weeks later.

Like almost every funeral in Harow, Luther's is held at the historic Presbyterian church. Most of the Iñupiat and many of the *taniks* crowd into the church to pay their final respects.

Lisa brings her twins, even though it means missing school. Luther was her honey's second cousin, and she thinks somebody ought to be at the funeral to represent her honey's branch of the family.

Lisa's honey will join in the Eskimo dances later that evening, and he figures that's enough participation on his part.

"It was a decent way to go, anyway," he tells Lisa when he drops her off. "I don't want to come to a funeral and hear people make a big fuss about it."

"Yeah, but it was two weeks before they found his body, and by then …"

"Well, it was nothing like what happened with my great-uncle Lenny from Point Latch. He was out by himself spearing belugas. Somehow he got tangled in the line that was hooked to his spear."

"Okay, okay," Lisa says, but her honey sees fit to continue.

"So when his speared beluga dove underwater, Lenny went with it. Nobody in the village knew what happened to his body for years until they hear some hunters killed a white beluga with a line coming out of it. The rest of Lenny is on the other end of the line. The hunters buried Lenny and the whale right there before we got a chance to see it."

"Ha, ha, ha," Lisa says. She doesn't understand her honey sometimes.

Mandy, Luther's youngest sister, sits in the front of the church with Larry, apart from her siblings. Years ago, she got in a fight with Luther over who would get their mother's *ulu*, the traditional knife that Eskimos use to cut whale and everything else. She kept the *ulu* in her house after their mother died, but Luther said he should get it because he was the oldest. Even though it was a stupid thing to get in a fight over, she ended up not speaking to Luther for years, and all the siblings took Luther's side. In the end, Mandy made peace with Luther, but not the others. Mandy looks around the church nervously. Seeing Lisa's squirmy twins, she gestures at them to come and sit by her. Britney marches to the front and plops down next to Larry before Lisa can say anything.

"Hello there," Larry says softly.

"Hi," Britney mumbles and pulls out her cell phone to text a friend. Larry pats her hand gently and says, "Now is not the time, sweetheart." He's never used the word "sweetheart" before and it sounds funny to him. He doesn't even know why he said anything to Britney. But the girl just shrugs and puts her phone back in her pocket. Red-faced, Lisa sits down next to Britney and motions for Jimmy to sit on her other side.

The slide show with pictures from Luther's life has already started. There's Luther with Evan Hooper, Luther standing on top of a whale,

Luther shaking hands with senators, Luther with his children and grandchildren, and Luther making a funny face, bringing a moment of comic relief to the funeral.

Larry seizes the moment to go outside for a cigarette. Funerals are hard on him—he's always afraid he might cry in public.

As he moves toward the exit, he notices Vik coming in. He's surprised—usually the transient *tanik* lawyers don't have the good sense to come to community funerals.

He feels his face flush when she smiles at him.

"Hey Larry!" she shout-whispers. "Do you know where I can put this?"

He notices then that she's carrying a garbage bag full of clothes. "What … what are you doing? What is that for?"

"I have these clothes I don't need anymore, and someone said I could donate them to the church. Is there a box or something where they go?"

Larry blinks and swallows. "This is the funeral for Luther Ericsen, my brother-in-law."

Now Vik turns red. "Oh. Oh, Jesus, I'm so sorry. I didn't know a funeral was going on. I'll just, ah, find the church office and leave this over there." She brushes past him without saying anything more.

Larry steps outside and smokes a cigarette, and then another one. He doesn't want to go back in, but he knows he should. He watches Vik come out of the church empty-handed. She sees him and approaches with a half-smile, the kind Larry usually has for her. Before he can move away, she throws her arms around him and mumbles that everything's going to be okay. Larry feels tears slipping out of his eyes and prays that Vik doesn't notice.

Lisa comes outside to make sure Larry hasn't left on account of Britney and her cell phone. She sees Larry and Vik caught in an embrace and decides to go back inside without saying anything. She's kind of glad she quit working with the *tanik* lawyers at the Borough's Law Department. It's so easy for the *taniks* to get themselves mixed up in things and then leave, clueless as to the upset they've caused the community.

At home after the funeral, Larry is even more quiet than usual.

"What's wrong with you?" Mandy asks. "It's like your brother died, instead of mine."

Larry sighs. "I don't know."

"Well, if it's not about Luther, what is it? Your crew?"

"I don't know."

The spring of 2009 is the fourth season in a row that Larry's crew didn't bring home a whale. The crew struck one on the day that Larry had to be in a meeting with the mayor and Shant, but the boat was a long way from shore and running out of gasoline. Larry's crew only rowed when close to the whale—the rest of the time they used a detachable outboard motor. The whalers decided to go to shore for gas rather than go out any further.

Larry and Luther's crews weren't the only ones with bad luck that season. The only crew that caught and successfully harvested a full-length whale was the Whitehead crew. Another crew pulled in a decent sized whale but couldn't get it up on the thin ice, even after cutting off the head. By then the most of the whale had cooked itself and gone bad, although the crew was able to salvage the fins and some of the *maktak*.

"It just seems like things are coming apart around here. I'm in meetings with oil companies when I should be out whaling, and then people like Chuck are out whaling and getting people like Luther killed. And then ..." he trails off, feeling like he's already said too much.

Larry's wife knows her husband's limits. She pulls him towards her and runs her fingers through his graying hair. There is nothing to keep Larry from weeping now.

Chapter 21- Values on Trial

When Chuck comes to again, his mother tells him that Luther's body washed up and that the funeral was already held. Chuck doesn't ask for details. He knows we hold it against him.

The Assembly election is just around the corner. Having struck out on whaling, Chuck figures he's going to have to do something really honorable if he wants to win—maybe even embrace family values.

He decides to own up to impregnating Gloria Whitehead. That is, if he's the one who did it. He hasn't talked to her since before the whaling accident. He texts her, and they agree to meet out on Gas Well Road, the same place where he might have gotten her pregnant.

She's a lot bigger than he thought she'd be, but her skin has a glow to it and her breasts are like two perfect globes.

"Hey," she says popping her gum and brushing an imaginary hair off his coat. He kisses her in spite of himself, then pulls back and whispers, "Is it mine?"

"Whose else's would it be?" she says, rolling her eyes. "A high school boy?"

"I don't know," Chuck mumbles, at a loss.

"So what're you going to do about it? Marry me?" she asks.

It hasn't occurred to Chuck that he might have to do anything at all about it, except make it go away. "I guess it's too late to, uh, have an, uh …"

"Abortion? No way." She pops her gum again. "I'm not going to Anchorage to have some creepy doctor stick a needle in me. Besides, I like babies. I took care of my sister's baby last summer." She pauses and looked at him more closely. He's gaping at her stomach.

"Snap out of it," she says, "I was just joking about the marriage. I don't wanna get married. But you can be my boyfriend in the meantime."

"Uh, okay," Chuck says. "I, uh, have to get ready for this election, but after that, we can …"

"Hmm," Gloria says knowingly. "Maybe I can help you, you know, come up with something really Iñupiaq for your campaign."

"Like what?"

"My grandpa's Ernie Whitehead, you know, and he used to be on the Iñupiaq Spirit Committee. I dunno whatever happened to it. Maybe you could make, like, the Committee for Iñupiaq Values."

Chuck's eyes come into focus. "That's not a bad idea."

"There's this little store I got a vibrator from last week, you could, like, go over there and try to shut it down."

"Not a bad idea at all," Chuck says.

"I mean, they don't have vibrators all over the place. For some of the, you know, heavier stuff, you have to go to the counter and ask the little Thai lady for it. She'll take you behind the back curtain and show you what she's got."

Chuck nods. "All right, let's do a sting operation."

Gloria pops her gum. "Awesome."

One week later, Chuck shows up at the only place within 500 miles that sells vibrators. He's equipped with a camera, a heavyweight bible, and a couple of witnesses from the newly formed Committee for Iñupiaq Values, with Gloria Whitehead serving as self-appointed secretary. Gill comes along in his official capacity as a Community Development Department inspector.

Gloria is the only one of the group who allows herself to pick up a porn magazine by the window display. The witnesses march tight-lipped to the back curtain and watch Chuck knock down the flimsy curtain rod with his bible. It crashes in two parts, the first falling at Chuck's feet, and the second teetering before smashing into a row of glass bongs.

Chuck is raising his bible to take another knock when the little Thai woman rushes over shrieking, "You break you buy!"

Gill lumbers between Chuck and the little Thai woman and pulls out his notebook.

"Uh, miss, do you have a permit to be selling the, uh ..."

"I have permit!" the woman shouts several times, not sure whether she should leave the bongs unattended to retrieve the permit.

"Yeah, but, I mean, you know, we just permitted this place as a gift shop. And you put on your permit application you were just gonna sell lamps and T-shirts and stuff like that."

"This very nice gift!" the woman shrieks, pointing at the smashed bongs. "Not made in China!" Turning to Chuck, she demands, "You pay for that or I call police!"

Chuck looks at the woman's usually olive face, which is a beet red. A horrible thought suddenly occurs to him—the police could come and he might be arrested by his half-brother Officer Shoak. No matter how much the community may admire Chuck's faith and family values, the arrest would ruin the election.

Gloria starts to laugh, and everyone turns to look at her. Then she clutches her ample belly and howls, and no one is sure whether she's still laughing or going into labor.

Chuck clears his throat. "We'll leave now, and uh, let you work out the permits." With his heavy bible, he waves the Committee for Iñupiaq

Values out of the shop. Then, retrieving Gloria from the porno display, he marches out of the store with as much dignity as he can muster.

A week later, the little Thai woman gets a letter from Gill saying she has to stop selling adult material and drug paraphernalia immediately, but that she can apply for a permit to sell these things. Since the Borough's permitting laws don't say anything about vibrators and bongs, the Borough's Development Planning Commission will have to hold a hearing to decide whether to issue the permit.

On the day of the hearing, the Borough's meeting hall is packed. The little Thai woman walks in nervously, clutching a 1963 report from the U.S. Surgeon General. When it's her turn to speak, she holds up the report. "This report say if you smoke tobacco from bongs, you smoke 50% less tobacco than smoking cigarettes."

One of the commissioners produces a different Surgeon General report saying that smoking through a bong actually doubles the amount of tobacco received from cigarettes.

"And my report's from 1981," he says.

The chairman of the commission doesn't see the relevance of either report. "This is assassination of our laws," he snaps. "She violated the permit, so there should be some discipline. But first we'll take comments from the audience."

Chuck stands up from the audience and takes his place behind the single working microphone. He unfolds a piece of paper and clears his throat.

"Once upon a time, I used to use those water pipes for marijuana. I smoked marijuana to run from myself to hide from the sexual abuse I was going through. I was ashamed of myself. Well, you should be ashamed of yourself for selling that stuff."

Someone from the audience starts clapping, and everyone joins in. Chuck continues, emboldened.

"There should be some kind of monitoring process to make sure people we don't really know are doing what they supposed to. We welcome Outsiders, but you need to respect our values. Get some cultural training. We're not individualistic, we think of others." He turns to face the little Thai woman and says, "We go to all the funerals in this community, but we don't see you there."

The clapping starts again. Chuck stands up, nods to the audience, and resumes his seat. The mayor of the city of Harow takes Chuck's place by the microphone.

"The City of Harow rejects without any reservation whatsoever to the sale of tobacco products," he says. The commission chairman scratches his chest and attempts to discretely push down into his pocket the pack of cigarettes he bought at the grocery store on his way to the meeting.

"The City of Harow will take all steps to have her license revoked," the city mayor finishes. No one refers to the little Thai woman by her name because no one can pronounce it.

Ernie Whitehead's wife is next. She gives a brief resume of her qualifications to assess the situation, and says that her family went to the little Thai woman's store just before Christmas. "My seven-year old grandson with disability problems got into the area and found these things she's selling. We're not here to judge her, but … I can tell you, as the wife of an *umialik,* a whaling captain, I'm very strict with the crew. When I find out they're drinking or on drugs, I won't let them participate with the crew. So the commission needs to look at every angle of the permit, think about our whalers, and give it due consideration."

The chairman nods. He's also a whaling captain, and he's been totally sober for eleven years now. Last year, after having to discipline five of his crew members for drinking, he ended up with only two good men on the crew. They ended the season early without even coming close to catching a whale.

Officer Shoak has the microphone now.

"I'm a police officer and I've been in law enforcement off and on for fifteen years. Bongs have been around for a long time. When we find them at a crime scene, we test them, and 99 times out of 100, they have illegal drugs. Same thing with glass pipes. I found a glass pipe being used for tobacco only once. And those soda cans that you can hide things in?" He holds up the store's best selling item, an empty soda can with a top that can be screwed on and off.

"They're not for your lunch, folks." He smiles slyly, opens and closes the can, and then puts it back in a bag he's carrying.

No one has dared to talk about the sex toys or even say the word sex, so the chairman bravely takes the microphone to share his thoughts on the subject.

"You know, we got people here in Harow who's on sex offenders lists, and this stuff is illegal for them."

Community Development Department Director Larry Atkoot shifts uncomfortably in his seat. He knows it's perfectly legal for people on the list to buy porn and pipes, but he isn't going to point this out.

Encouraged by the applause, the chairman continues, "Pornography is addictive and the addiction is progressive. It desensitizes the person and leads them to act out their fantasies on others." His voice cracks and he stops, gesturing to the female commissioner to say something else.

The female commissioner squints in the direction of the little Thai woman and says, "I got a thirteen-year-old grandson who likes to go to your store because he says you got cool things there." She looks around the room for support and continues hesitantly, "I seen what you sell—hip hop clothes with gang colors. There's nothing redeeming about that."

A number of people in the audience have started to whisper and stand up. The chairman debates on banging his gavel to close the hearing. Before he can, Chuck seizes the microphone for an impromptu speech.

"Our community is becoming deplorable. Our culture is under attack. I got victims in my family due to drug and alcohol and pornography addiction. Even crack. I used to be a victim, too. And my children had to see that. I don't want it to go to my grandchildren, or-or my next child." He pauses. "This is an embarrassing moment for me. I lost family, I lost children. I strongly, in the strongest sense of the word, deny this permit."

The audience bursts into applause, and Ernie Whitehead's wife leads a standing ovation.

The little Thai woman tiptoes to the microphone.

"I had no idea the community don't want this," she says tearfully. "I thought I help the community. So, I am very sorry, and I take back my application. I don't want to sell this no more."

The audience looks at each other, unsure whether to clap, until Ernie Whitehead's wife starts another standing ovation.

The chairman bangs his gavel for the heck of it and closes the hearing.

Three hundred miles to the southeast, in the village of Point Courage, another trial of Iñupiat values is about to take place—the trial of the eight men accused of causing the "Caribou Massacre." The trial, set for June 2009, will be the first one held in Point Courage since Alaska became a state.

The Alaska press has been flying reporters up to Point Courage for interviews with anyone willing to talk. An animal rights activist disguised as a reporter corners a resident and asks what the defendants were thinking at the time of the kill.

"Or were they thinking at all," the activist adds in a question-statement.

The confused resident responds, "The way we hunt was told to us from our forefathers. What was told to me was if the *tuttu* are sick to leave it alone, don't take nothing home unless you want to get sick or die. But always cut the head off the *tuttu*. I believe cutting the head off the *tuttu* or any animal is being respectful to them."

"So how did they know all those caribou were sick?" the activist presses. "Did they have a kit to test for radiation and lead, or could they just measure the radiation with your eyeballs?"

"It's not just radiation," the resident says slowly. "You know these days when I'm hunting *tuttu* and I'm skinning them, I sometimes notice the meat is yellow. 'Cause the mosquitoes are so bad, they got nests under the *tuttu* skin which turns the meat yellow. So I got to leave it there. It wasn't always like that."

Urbanites in Anchorage and Fairbanks have plenty to say about the case. They suggest that the defendants be banned from their village and forced to live off the land for a while. That was how it used to be done, they say. The case against the defendants is perfectly clear to them. Alaska law requires all hunters, whether white or native, trophy or subsistence, to take with them every scrap of edible meat, down to the gristle between the ribs. There's no exception allowing diseased meat to be left in the field.

The news reports don't mention that the law on diseased meat has never been enforced on the Arctic Slope until now. The Alaska Fish and Game Department agent who lives in Harow with an Iñupiaq wife and the only team of sled dogs on the Slope has never turned anyone in. He figures that the local caribou population is so high these days it can probably use a little thinning to avoid another starvation die-out.

The agent remembers well the 1992 Hagemeister Island disaster. Hagemeister was an uninhabited island off the western Alaska coast until 1965, when the Bureau of Indian Affairs decided to locate a herd of reindeer there. Within 25 years, the reindeer had eaten almost all of their lichen food supply, and would have to wait 75 years for it to grow back.

Federal law didn't allow the semi-domesticated herds to be moved to any region where they might mix with their wild caribou relatives. And federal law didn't allow alien vegetation, including hay, to be introduced to the island.

After 800 reindeer starved to death in one year, the U.S. Fish and Wildlife Service took over the herd. A team of marksmen was sent to the island to cull most of the surviving herd members. The marksmen brought some of the carcasses back from the island and distributed them to the native villages, but left the rest to decay.

Native groups and environmentalists joined forces to decry the waste. But nobody was prosecuted.

Times have apparently changed since 1992. The State of Alaska now seems to be a well greased engine, ready to prosecute any hunting violation brought to its attention. Or is it? State troopers failed to collect samples of the wasted caribou meat during their investigation. No one knows if the meat was really diseased or not. The case might derail on this point, much in the way the *Duck-in* case went awry a half-century ago for lack of specific evidence.

Aside from the evidence problem, there's the problem of trying the case in a town where almost every potential jury member is related to one of the defendants. The prosecutor tries to change the venue to Anchorage, but the judge won't allow it. In desperation, the prosecutor drops the charges that come with the right to a jury. The defendants are left with two charges, each carrying jail time.

The state prosecutor convinces seven of the defendants to accept plea bargains for lesser charges with no jail time. But the 73-year-old *tanik* lawyer, Friend of the Borough awardee and counsel for the eighth defendant, convinces his client to hold out. Maybe he thinks that if the case goes to trial, it'll be the pinnacle of his career.

Bertie sends Vik to Point Courage to observe the trial. Bertie figures that the Borough's already invested $40,000 in the hunters' defense, and there ought to be a Borough lawyer on hand in case the 73-year-old *tanik* lawyer goes off the deep end.

On the day of the trial, Vik sits in the back of the Point Courage community center with her laptop and ogles her surroundings. The place has been converted into a court room, with the bingo scoreboard moved aside to accommodate the judge's bench. Silent elders in their best parkas and thick glasses sit in folding chairs along the walls. The Borough's Wildlife and Subsistence Department director, who once tearfully testified to the Fish and Wildlife Service that she would never get a hunting license because it wasn't customary and traditional, sits in the back dabbing her nose with a tissue.

The proceeding starts with the 73-year-old *tanik* lawyer's opening statement.

"This case is not really about state or federal law, it is about something far more fundamental. It is about the right to life itself. The State would require my client to harvest diseased animals and then force him, as well as his relatives, including women and children, to eat those animals, or risk jail time."

"Counselor," the judge interrupts, "We're here on a misdemeanor trial. Let's try to keep this brief."

But neither lawyer wants things to be brief. The prosecutor has lined up a parade of witnesses, and she wants to get them all on the record.

A state wildlife veterinarian testifies that the bubbles one of the defendants claimed to see coming out of a caribou stomach were likely from a tapeworm that was harmless to humans.

"The substance may be smelly and have a foul taste, but the juices don't pose any risk to people," the veterinarian says.

A state biologist testifies that even if the carcasses were contaminated with the bacteria brucellosis, as one of the defendants claimed, the contamination wouldn't have been visible to the hunters. "Anyway," she says, "many people who contract the illness never know they've had it."

The 73-year-old lawyer is prepared for this. A cardiologist from Tennessee has been flown in to testify about his own battle with a brucellosis infection. The cardiologist says he and a fellow medical student contracted it in the 1950s, and the other medical student died from it.

Next come the state troopers, and the bootlegger who secretly recorded all the confessions. The white teacher who originally called in the troopers and Animal Planet is no longer available to testify. He had impregnated the daughter of Point Courage's Episcopal priest, and was persuaded not only to shut up, but to leave town.

The prosecutor thinks the teacher's abrupt departure is a real shame, since he had such good personal knowledge of the issues. He'd even made a video about proper hunting techniques to teach the Iñupiat value of "Respect for Nature." He'd been ready to testify about how every part of the caribou was supposed to be used, down to the botfly larvae in the caribou hide.

The judge asks the prosecutor if it would be considered waste if a hunter brought meat home from the field and immediately threw it into the trash. The prosecutor admits that this would be complying with the law.

"So it doesn't matter whether it's bad meat or not, it just has to wind up in a landfill rather than the field?" the judge asks.

The prosecutor sidesteps the question. "We can't leave it to hunters to make broad decisions as to whether meat is 'good' or 'bad.' If we did that, what would stop a hunter from just taking the antlers and claiming that everything else was 'bad'? As it stands now hunters always have the option to bring the meat out of the field and present it to, ah, the authorities for a determination on whether it is safe to eat."

After three days of testimony and arguments, the judge delivers his opinion from the bench. Vik thinks about how long judges usually take to put out opinions, and wonders if this judge had already written the opinion before the trial started.

The judge reads the brief opinion out loud in a tired voice. He says the defendants are not guilty of failing to salvage edible meat, since the State had no physical evidence against them, and the caribou found on the tundra couldn't be matched to the caribou the men admitted taking. Each defendant is held liable for not having a hunting license and fined $200.

Finished with his opinion, the judge stands up and walks out of the community center. No one realizes that the trial is over until the bailiff stands up, handcuffs the only defendant present, and leads him out of the room. The crowd begins to stand up and shout, and someone turns over the judge's bench. Things don't quiet down until the defendant's mother reminds the crowd that her son is serving a sentence in Nome for an unrelated matter and was allowed out of jail only for the Point Courage trial.

The bailiff comes back into the community center and hauls away the fallen judge's bench, and someone else returns the bingo scoreboard to its proper position at the front of the room. Things are almost back to the way they should be.

Chapter 22- Darkness in the Midst of Night

It's the summer equinox, with 42 days of uninterrupted sunlight down and 42 more to go. Or at least, 42 possible days of sunlight. Most of the time Harow is covered in a blanket of clouds. The endless day of summer is not enough to drive away the underlying darkness of living here. In fact, it's the light that really brings on the suicides. Almost every year, there's a suicide in early February just after the sun comes up. Usually there's at least one more before the sun comes up to stay in May. It's as if the smack of frozen sunlight gives the depressed just enough energy to do what they were wanting to do throughout all the months without sun.

Vik, who can leave Harow anytime she wants, has a morbid curiosity about those who decide they can't go on. She's never known any of the suicide victims personally or bothered to go to their funerals, but she does like to collect gossip about them.

Nineteen sixty-five was the first year that an Arctic Slope suicide was reported in the news. The story, written by a *tanik* reporter from Fairbanks, described a seventeen-year-old girl who was detoxing in the Harow jail. The guard had gone out of the building for a while, and when he came back she was hanging from the ceiling. She'd taken off her pants and used them in lieu of a rope.

Forty years later, the girl's great niece was taken down from a garage ceiling. She, too, was seventeen. Her fifteen-year-old sister tried it two weeks later, but they caught her before it was too late to do CPR.

Vik asks whether the suicide rate has changed since Harow found Jesus in the early 1900s, but no one has been able to give her a good answer. She wonders if a suicide prevention network might be more useful than Jesus in terms of preventing suicide. But people have told her that it usually happens with no notice, and no one wants to sit around with a counselor dwelling on it.

When Harow has its third suicide of the year just after the equinox, the new pastor at Fresh Start Church comes up with a way to combine Jesus and suicide prevention. He plans a series of Wednesday night public meetings that his flock can consider as their Wednesday night church service.

Only three people show up for the first Wednesday night meeting. One is a sixty-something Borough retiree, who sits quietly with crossed arms and a stern frown. After being asked to introduce himself, he says,

"In my day, people thought about survival, not suicide. That was when kids listened to their parents. And to the tribal council."

The pastor nods encouragingly and asks a middle-aged woman if she has anything to share.

"I lost two of my brothers," she mumbles. "One was a truck driver working in the oil patch. He couldn't take it no more, I guess, and killed himself. The other one ... he was still a teen. I don't know what he was thinking. He was out hunting with his friends and all the sudden he put the gun under his chin and said, 'Dare me to pull the trigger.' Nobody said nothing and he just did it."

The pastor takes a long breath in and lets it out slowly. "That must be a heavy cross for you to bear," he says.

"Well," she says, "I got kids. I can't afford to do myself in like that. But it's the same story in every village. There's not one family who didn't lose somebody like that."

The pastor nods and turned to the only other person in the room, saying, "I haven't seen you at church before—welcome!"

"Actually, I'm not a believer," Vik says. "But I did go to the Thanksgiving feast you had last year, just to check it out."

"Did you have something to share?" the pastor asks.

"Not really. I'm here to listen." She adopts the same pseudo-benevolent smirk as the pastor.

The pastor printed out some suicide prevention pamphlets he found on the web, but he decides his audience probably doesn't need them.

"Um, well, okay. Anyone else what to say anything?" he asks.

The two Eskimo attendees glare at Vik and remain silent.

"Well, let's pray on it. Heavenly Father ..."

Vik gets up before anyone can clasp her hand, and escapes out the back door before the others can finish the Lord's Prayer. She kicks at the gravel in the street as she walks back home, bummed that this is all she's going to hear about suicide in Harow.

Lisa told Vik when she first got here about the teenage suicide that happened in Vik's apartment. That explained why the apartment was vacant when Vik moved to Harow. Housing is so scarce in Harow that new Borough hires usually stay in a dorm.

All Lisa said was that the kid had been left behind when his mother went to the women's shelter. At fourteen, he was too old to be admitted with her. After that, things went downhill for him.

Vik googled the kid's name and found his Facebook page, which no one had ever taken down. It looked just like any other teenage boy's, with pictures of cars and talk about money, guns, and tools. He certainly didn't seem "mentally ill."

Most of the people in Harow who are truly mentally ill live unglamorous lives, outside the purview of Vik's voyeurism. The Borough funds an institution for them, right next door to the women's shelter, although it's staffed by only three people and the staff usually keeps the outside door locked. Those who manage to get in often find themselves sitting in the lobby until 5:00 p.m., when it's time to leave. The staff members lock themselves in the office and manage the paper work.

Gill's former Russian Internet bride volunteered at the institution for a while, since she couldn't get licensed in America as a doctor. She was one of the few who worked on treatment programs for the patients.

She put up quite a fuss about the lack of care the patients were given, but neither Gill nor anyone else at the Borough seemed to care. Her application for a paying position was denied. Shortly after that, she left Gill for the Lower 48, in search of the America she'd seen on T.V.

Chuck was one of a number of people to pass through the doors of the institution during his meth years. He's really come a long way since then. He reminds himself of this as he's lying in bed at 11 a.m. on a Tuesday. Normally at this time, he'd be sitting in the Assembly's monthly workshop. But not anymore. Chuck lost the election to his 25-year-old whaling captain opponent.

Chuck didn't really have a regular job when he was on the Assembly, and now his purposelessness seems painfully apparent. He turns over and looks at the window, which he's covered with aluminum foil to keep out the sun.

Chuck is alone now. Luther is gone and the rest of the family doesn't seem to want to have anything to do with Chuck. Even Gloria Whitehead is gone. She left to finish her pregnancy in Anchorage, and her parents made it very clear that Chuck would not be playing a daddy role in their grandchild's life. Gloria's father—Assembly President Ernie Whitehead's son—said that statutory rape charges would be pressed against Chuck if he came anywhere near Gloria or her child.

Chuck gets out of bed and shuffles to the toilet, then the refrigerator. He's still young, he reminds himself, and smart. Catching a whale isn't everything. In fact, catching a whale is only going to mean less as time goes on. Whether the whalers like it or not, oil and gas development is coming to Arctic waters. So far, the only people who seem to understand this besides Chuck are the former Mayor Ahgak, the Northern Slope Regional Co., and the native corporation in the village of Winters. The latter is providing Shant Oil with a supply base for its offshore drilling.

Chuck wonders why Harow isn't on board, when it has just as much waterfront land as the village of Winters and more services to offer. With its office in Anchorage and subsidiaries around the world, the Harow

Native Corporation is arguably more sophisticated than the Winters Native Corporation.

It hits Chuck as he's frying up some bacon—he should be the one to lead the Harow Native Corporation into the future. He pops a piece of glistening meat into his mouth and chews on it. He'll shave, put on some clean clothes, and go have a talk with the corporation president.

Chuck manages to catch the president on a day when all of his staff are out at their camps on subsistence leave, fishing or hunting for caribou. The president doesn't resent the absences—he just wishes he were at his camp, too. He's given up his place on a whaling crew to serve as the corporation's president, and at times he regrets it.

The president wades through a wad of paperwork on his desk, listening to Chuck's talk about the blessings of development with half an ear. When Chuck finally stops talking, the president asks if he wants a job as a project coordinator. Even if Chuck's slightly delusional, at least there's no worry that he'll take off on extended subsistence leave.

Chuck accepts and gets to work quickly. He books an appointment with the traveling psychiatrist that the Borough Health Department pays to pass through the villages every month.

We all know that the shrink gives out prescriptions like candy. He feels sorry for local residents and hopes the pills will help them avoid suicide. Chuck gets a prescription for an attention deficit disorder drug, which Gloria once described as "like meth, but way cleaner."

It turns out to be a wonder drug. Chuck is at the office by seven every morning, working through lunch, and not even stopping for coffee breaks.

At the corporation's next Board of Directors meeting, Chuck announces that he's applied for a federal grant for the corporation to develop a deep sea port in Harow.

"A *grant*?" one of the directors says skeptically. Chuck grins and tells the directors about all the federal grant programs out there that treat native corporations the same as tribes from the Lower 48.

"From the *feds*?" another director asks. He distrusts the federal government almost as much as distrusts Sarah Palin.

"What do you mean by a deep sea port?" another director asks. "Isn't that going to mess up whaling?"

Chuck waves his hand and smiles. "The port would just be right *here*, in Harow," he says. "The Coast Guard would keep it open with ice breakers, but it'd all be right along the coast, not out where the whales are."

The president frowns. "How can you possibly say that's not going to mess up whaling? All those ships will come through here like it's New York City."

Chuck sighs and looks at the president sympathetically. "You know, if they discover oil out there, the ships are going to be coming no matter what. We got a duty to our shareholders to make the most we can out of it."

The directors mumble to themselves. Chuck produces a sheet of paper showing his calculations on the revenue and jobs the port would create. And who can argue with anything that creates local jobs?

"Anyways, all I did was apply for the grant in the corporation's name," Chuck says. "Of course it'd be up to the Board to approve any kind of project if we do get a grant."

A couple of the Board members nod, but the president shakes his head in disbelief. Chuck hasn't said anything about the grant proposal until now. The president imagines that one day he'll look back at this meeting and remember it as the point his native corporation became indistinguishable from every other American corporation.

He doesn't hold it against Chuck, figuring that Chuck's just another white-washed Eskimo trying to walk the walk and talk the talk of the folks down in Anchorage. But he does submit his resignation letter just in time to join his sons for an inland caribou hunting trip.

At a special meeting, the Board appoints Chuck as Acting President. Chuck accepts the appointment with glee and an increased daily dosage of the wonder drug. In no time, he's running off to meetings in Anchorage and Seattle in search of more development funding.

With Chuck occupied, there's no one to serve as Master of Ceremonies for all the Harow events. The Borough mayor asks Bertie if she wouldn't mind doing the honors for this year's Fourth of July celebration.

"What do you mean?" Bertie asks politely. She remembers Chuck's performance behind the megaphone at last year's celebration, but it didn't seem significant enough to warrant finding a replacement.

"Well, you know our former assemblyman used to kind of gather the crowd together and announce the events as they're going on. I know usually there's not that much going on at Fourth of July, but this year we're planning to fly in all the village leaders and do some Eskimo Games."

"So you want me to be the Master of Ceremonies for the games?"

"Well, you have a normal voice—a good voice, I mean—and I thought it would be good for you to be calling out the events, you know, joining in our traditions."

Bertie blushes. She hasn't been to any Eskimo dances or games since the 1980s. She doesn't even remember the names of the Eskimo games. But the mayor said, "our traditions"—was he suggesting that she's been snubbing the Iñupiat? Has she missed any of the recent funerals where she should have made an appearance?

"It's just for *fun*, Bertie," the mayor smiles, "just to get out of the office for once! You and Nelson work too hard."

"I … I'd be honored," Bertie says nervously, wondering if her voice sounds normal enough.

Not only has Bertie missed all events involving Eskimo games since the 1980s, she's avoided any event that involves long periods of standing outside in bad weather. The day of the games is foggy and cool, with winds gusting up to 25 miles an hour. Bertie ventures out in front of a small crowd and mentally prepares herself for a day of misery.

Nelson is also there, with his standard vague smile that could be part of his public persona, or just an insulin high. He manages his diabetes with one of those control buttons that can be clicked for instant insulin.

"Isn't it nice that these kids can come outside for a change and enjoy themselves?" he asks Bertie. She looks at him warily. Nelson was her boss in the Law Department before he moved up to being lieutenant mayor. He made her nervous then and he makes her nervous now.

"So many kids are just inside these days playing video games and watching TV," he continues. Bertie checks to see if Nelson's pushing the button on the insulin pump that's eternally hitched to his side. He cut holes in the left hand pocket of all his coats so he can click on the button whenever he gets stressed. Bertie has watched him at Assembly meetings—whenever Chuck would speak, Nelson would reach for the button. Then he'd glaze over and leave it to Bertie to answer all the Assemblymen's questions.

But now, Nelson is reaching in his pocket for some sort of contraption. He holds it up for Bertie to admire.

"What is it?" she asks.

"I'm going to win this year's *nigliq*-calling contest," he announces. "I bought this *nigliq* whistle at the Christmas craft fest."

"I've never heard of anyone using a whistle for the geese-calling contest," Bertie says. "I thought the whole point was to use your vocal chords."

Nelson gives her a glazed over smile and walks over to the Samoan donut stand.

Bertie looks at her watch. It's a half-hour after the official starting time of the first contest, the four-wheeler race. A few contestants are revving up their engines and cheering.

The air is filled with four-wheeler fumes. Bertie coughs and clears her throat. She wishes she had Chuck's megaphone.

"Okay!" she shouts. "Good morning everyone, I'd like to welcome you all to the games and get the first contest going."

No one appears to have heard her. She clears her throat again. She's never been much of a screamer.

"Okay!" she shouts. "We're going to get started today with the ra—"

A kid on a four-wheeler roars past her, makes a sharp turn, and barely misses hitting her on his way back.

Bertie decides to view the antic humorously. She lets out a falsetto laugh and says, "I'm actually not the finish line of this race. But I think we're ready to get started now, everyone!"

"You're not the MC, either."

Bertie looks around to see who was talking.

The same voice says, "What are you doing here, anyway?"

The voice belongs to a light-skinned Eskimo with close-set eyes, likely one of Gill Whitehead's ten sisters. The man next to her takes an unsteady step toward Bertie and drawls, "Yeah, why don't you go back to—go back to Africa!!"

Bertie can smell the man's breath from five feet away. She opens her mouth to say, "Because I came from Colorado, and while I've been to fifteen countries in Europe and Asia, I haven't been to Africa."

But her mouth just stays open, silently. Another kid on a four-wheeler whirls behind her, and then in front of her. All around her are pale Eskimos and whites—she is the only spot of darkness in sight. She watches as one of the Eskimos produces a megaphone and announces the start of the four-wheeler race.

Bertie stands in her place for another minute, debating whether she's justified in feeling offended. She thinks that maybe this has just been a cultural misunderstanding. Perhaps the man lacks the benefit of an education—but now she's thinking like Nelson, pitying instead of empathizing. She throws up her hands and walks toward her car. At least she doesn't have to stand out in the wind all day with a fake smile.

Nelson is leaning on the back of the Samoan donut stand, trying unsuccessfully to produce a sound on his *nigliq* whistle.

"Want a ride home, Nelson? Or to the office?" Bertie asks. Nelson lives next door to Bertie, and she feels obliged to carpool with him.

"Sure," he says pocketing the whistle. "Looks like this was just for decoration, anyway." They both laugh awkwardly as they leave the games to take refuge at the office.

Chapter 23- Flying Away

After thirteen Steller's eiders were shot illegally in 2008, the U.S. Fish and Wildlife Service issued new regulations for bird hunting on the Arctic Slope. If any Steller's eiders were shot, they were not to be touched. And if they were shot on purpose, Fish and Wildlife could shut down bird hunting all together.

The elders' mouths trembled in anger when they learned that the *tanik* posse known as the Fish and Wildlife Service might shut down the hunt. The elders have told us many times that a successful *umialik*—whaling captain—is required to host a *nalukataq* for the community, with duck soup as the first course. What would *nalukataq* be without goose soup? Depriving the Iñupiat of their birds was like depriving Catholics of their Eucharist.

Steller's eiders always pass through Harow, but they only stop to build nests and lay eggs once every few years. With the population being so low, one would think that a nesting year would be welcome. But after the so-called "Eider Massacre," a nesting year is the last thing most people want. Harow hunters are worried that someone might accidentally kill a Steller's eider, leading Fish and Wildlife to shut down the whole bird hunt. The Iñupiat don't eat Steller's eiders anyway, so it doesn't matter if there aren't any of them around.

Fish and Wildlife agents—even the biologists concerned with low population numbers—don't really want to see the birds nest, either. Chances are that more of them will be shot. The agents will have to shut down the hunt, and then the Eskimos will start another *Duck-in*.

So when the Steller's eiders decline to nest in 2009, we all breathe a sigh of relief. We hope the Fish and Wildlife agents stationed in Harow will just go back to Anchorage. But it doesn't turn out this way.

On a Tuesday morning, the teary-eyed director of the Borough's Subsistence Department and a pair of local hunters march into Bertie's office to report on Fish and Wildlife's latest sin. Bertie recognizes the younger hunter as a Whitehead. She doesn't know the other one, who looks like he's never changed out of his hunting clothes.

Bertie closes her office door and passes the director a tissue. "Why don't you sit down and tell me what's going on?" she says encouragingly to the hunters.

The Whitehead kid begins, "Last week I got some number two shot shells for a twelve-gage at the store. The box didn't say anything about lead shot. So we—him and me—went out hunting last night. On our way home, at 10 p.m., three wildlife guys stopped us."

"He means the feds—the U.S. Fish and Wildlife Service," the director interjects. "Not the Borough Wildlife and Subsistence Department."

The Whitehead kid continues, "They asked us if we caught anything, what kind of shells we're using. They made us give them our name and address, and they're rude about it. They emptied our guns and took all the bullets because they're lead."

"We didn't even catch a duck," the other hunter adds.

"Then at 2 a.m. that night, I was rudely awoken up by the three wildlife guys," the Whitehead kid continued, "along with a cop from the Borough. And you know as well as I do that the Borough cops aren't supposed to help the feds."

"Mmmm," Bertie says. She's just finished working on a drug bust case where the Borough cops helped the federal cops set up a sting operation, but both sets of cops managed to bungle the evidence.

"Anyways," the Whitehead kid says, "They were very rude and tried to shove themselves into our home. They gave me a citation for using lead shot and did a background check, and then they called my parole officer and took it to a whole new level."

"He's not supposed to have a gun," the other hunter explains. "And me, I'm out on bail for a DWI. They didn't find me already but when they do, they're probably gonna make me go back to jail."

Bessie takes in a deep breath, and nods slowly.

"The thing is, lead shot is actually better to use in many cases than steel shot, because it goes into the animal clean. Steel shot can splatter around the animal and just leave it wounded," the director says.

"But, um, lead shot is against the law," Bertie says.

"Yeah, but the stores are still selling it. They're the ones who should get the citations, not hunters. These guys have families to support. They just need to put food on the table."

"Mm hmm," Bertie says. Sometimes it's easier just to leave the law out of these conversations.

"That's not the only thing the feds are doing," the director says. "There also looking into our boats when we come back from hunting and trying to see what we caught. They're even looking in our vehicles. In fact, one of them stopped me the other day and gave me a citation for not wearing a seatbelt."

Bertie looks at the hunters and says, "Well, unfortunately, I can't give you two legal advice. I represent the Borough, and you're probably going to want to get your own lawyer."

To the director, Bertie says, "Why don't you get someone from your department to go out with the, um, feds, and make a record of some of these incidents? There would need to be some proof if you wanted to, you know, bring a case against the feds."

The director shakes her head, as if Bertie just doesn't get it. "The thing is, I don't want any of my staff to be seen with Fish and Wildlife agents. People are already confusing us with the feds, and it's interfering with our ability to do our job, because people don't trust us."

"Well," Bertie says. "Thanks for stopping by." She stands up to open the door, hoping this will encourage the hunters to leave. No one's going to take her advice, and the hunters might say something else to incriminate themselves even further.

"Thanks Bertie," the director says hopelessly, and leaves with the hunters.

The police chief later explains to Bertie that Officer Shoak was going to the Whitehead house on Borough business, but happened to show up at the same time as the Fish and Wildlife officers and decided to assist them.

"And the Fish and Wildlife agents cooperate with the Police Department on issuing traffic tickets?" Bertie asks.

"Don't know about that," the chief says. "I'll check with Shoak, but I think he was just following protocol."

Bertie sighs. The Law Department has had to defend Officer Shoak on a number of occasions when he was "just following protocol."

Fish and Wildlife agents issue three more citations for lead shot use that summer, including one to the hunter with the DWI, who has to go back to jail. They also spend a lot of time watching hunters through binoculars, or hovering right behind the hunters when they're about to shoot. Some of the hunters assume that the bird hunt has been shut down. Some just stop hunting. At the Whiteheads' *nalukataq* that summer, there's no duck soup.

But as the summer goes on, the federal agents seem to get bored with their job or tired of the hatred radiating towards them from the hunters. By August, only one of the six agents that arrived in May is left. When the subsistence duck hunting season closes in September and the Steller's eiders fly away, the agent declares the season a success. No Steller's eiders were shot, and only four citations were issued. The Alaska director of the Fish and Wildlife Service invites the mayor, Bertie, and the director of the Borough's Wildlife and Subsistence Department to come down to Juneau, all expenses paid, and receive a certificate of appreciation.

The director refuses on the Borough's behalf. "Spend the money training your officers the basic tenets of decency and respect for our culture," she says.

Decency could be too much to ask for, though. The Borough would probably settle for more federal money instead.

In the late summer of 2009, a chance for federal money comes in the form of a Congressional bill allowing offshore drilling revenue to be shared with Alaska and its municipalities, the way it's done with the Gulf of Mexico states.

Nelson sits in his office pouring over the text of the bill. He's pretty sure that the Law Department—or at least Vik and Bertie—isn't going to like the bill. Vik is always lamenting what happened to her home state of Louisiana, "It's just a petro-chemical whore, bought off by oily money." Bertie will say that accepting revenue makes the Borough complicit in offshore drilling, which we all know is incompatible with a subsistence lifestyle.

Nelson is more realistic. Like the native corporations, he takes the view that development is going to happen no matter what, so the Borough might as well make a buck off of it. He decides to meet with the mayor and the Assembly president about how they might support the revenue-sharing bill.

Despite his 1989 conviction, Assembly president Ernie Whitehead has achieved a measure of respect by being a successful whaling captain and perfecting a certain measure of grouchiness that makes people think he's important. He agrees to meet with the mayor to talk politics, although he's worried that the mayor's *tanik* lieutenant is going to co-op the meeting.

Ernie sits in the mayor's chair, sipping his coffee and watching Nelson pour coffee for himself. Nelson adds four cubes of sugar, reluctantly pulls two out, and leaves them to melt on the side of the coffee machine.

The mayor comes in full of good mornings and smiles, ignoring the fact that Ernie has taken his chair. Ernie nods dismissively in the mayor's direction.

"Well, Nelson called us in for this meeting today," the mayor says. "Nelson, what do you have for us?"

Nelson clears his throat and hands them a copy of the revenue-sharing bill. "This bill has just been introduced in the Senate. It would allow the Borough to get 12.5% of the federal revenue from drilling in the Beaufort and Chukchi Seas."

The mayor looks confused. "Does that mean offshore drilling is a foregone conclusion?"

Nelson clears his throat. "Well, Mayor, you know that a number of oil companies just bought leases in the Chukchi, and then there's Shant in the Beaufort, who's just waiting on the federal government to approve its exploration plan and permits. As you know, I—we filed suit against the government last year for improperly approving Shant's exploration plan, but since then Shant has submitted a revised plan."

Ernie slurps his coffee and says, "The Assembly's passed six resolutions opposing offshore, already. What are you getting at, Nelson? You want a different resolution now?"

Nelson puts on his classic blank smile. "Of course, that's for the Assembly to consider. Alls I'm saying is that the stakes may be changing. Before, the Borough was being asked to take an unacceptable risk without any compensation whatsoever. Now, there at least seems to be some consideration for the Borough. The Assembly could, if it chooses, pass a resolution in support of the bill. Likewise, the Mayor's Office could come out with a policy paper expressing its position on the bill."

The mayor looks confused. "But we're supposed to be opposed to offshore drilling."

Nelson raises his eyebrows. "And you can still be opposed to it, in principle—this would just be a more nuanced position."

"I don't know," the mayor says.

"Well, no one's making you decide right now," Nelson assures him. "It's just something to keep on the radar."

Just then Chuck walks into the mayor's office, followed by the mayor's secretary. "He don't have an appointment with you," she says, "but he's here anyways and says he got to see you."

Glowering at Chuck, Ernie spits the coffee in his mouth back into his cup. He slams the cup down and storms out of the mayor's office.

"Well, I guess we're done with the meeting," Nelson says, following Ernie out the door. He doesn't want to stick around and deal with Chuck, the sole Assemblyman who voted against the mayor's appointment of Nelson as lieutenant mayor. As far as Nelson knows, no one else in the history of the Borough has ever voted against an appointment, and Chuck never voted against any appointment but Nelson's.

"Wait, Nelson, maybe you ought to stay for this," the mayor says.

Nelson goes over to the coffee machine, scrapes up the melted cubes of sugar he took out of his cup, and puts them back in. He reaches into his left pocket to give himself some more insulin and sits down at the table.

Chuck eyes the revenue sharing bill on the table. "Things are really about to heat up in the Arctic."

"They certainly are," Nelson says, wondering if Chuck has come to believe in global warming.

The mayor mumbles politely, "Congratulations on your success with the corporation, Chuck. I mean, being president and all." The Harow Native Corporation Board bumped Chuck up from Acting President to President last week.

"Thank you, Mayor," Chuck says, pleased with the mayor's acknowledgment. "But I'm actually here to talk about the corporation and the Borough leading the Arctic into the future."

"What do you mean?" the mayor asks.

"Well, we all know that offshore oil development is just around the corner. But that's only half the story. This place is turning into the Northwest Passage. Like it or not, you're going to have all kinds of Russians and Japs cruising through here on their way to Europe."

"Not much we can do about that," the mayor says despondently.

"But there is," Chuck says. "The corporation—me actually—got a grant from the feds to build a deep sea port right here off of Harow."

Nelson reaches in his left pocket again to push the insulin button.

"Doesn't the Assembly have to pass something to let that happen?" the mayor asks.

"Not unless the Borough owns the land where the port is or a rezoning is required," Nelson says distantly. "But your corporation will be responsible for getting all the permits ..."

"Yeah, our guys in Anchorage are working on that now. In fact I'm going down there today to meet with them."

"When is it going to happen?" the mayor asks.

"Well, we're a little behind the game. The grant is conditioned on having all the permits and contracts in place and coming up with matching funds, and we're not going to have all that until 2011. Shant plans to start drilling in 2010, you know."

"Well," the mayor says.

"Isn't 2010 when your term ends?" Chuck asks the mayor. "My corporation might have a spot for you, by the way, you never know."

Nelson is looking out the window. Chuck waits for someone to say something else, but no one does.

"So I'm just giving you the courtesy of letting you know about all this before I go to Anchorage today for a meeting on the permitting," Chuck says. "Anyway, I'm on the 11:00 flight, so I guess I'll see you later."

He shakes hands with the mayor and leaves Nelson to gaze out the window.

Once on the plane, Chuck eases himself into his first class seat and asks the stewardess for a shot of bourbon. He always takes the Tuesday 11 a.m. flight to Anchorage because it's the only flight with first class service. The rest of the flights are on "combis," planes with passenger seats in the back half and cargo in the front.

Tourist season is winding down, but there are still plenty of Outsiders getting on the plane. A flock of Asians in weird clothes and *taniks* in baseball caps shuffle in. Then comes Gloria Whitehead, holding her little baby. Chuck's little baby. Chuck gasps when he sees them. He hasn't seen Gloria since her pregnancy, and he's never seen the baby. Gloria is a little fatter, but it looks good on her. The baby is gorgeous.

"Gloria!" Chuck yells out as she walks by. Gloria keeps walking. "Gloria, where are you going?"

Gloria ducks into her seat, and Chuck runs down the aisle to her row. Only when he gets there does he notice Officer Shoak sitting next to Gloria, with his arm around her.

"What the ..." Chuck says.

Officer Shoak smiles. "Congratulate me," he says. "I've moved up to being a State Trooper. I go back and forth between Harow and Anchorage now. I was actually supposed to bring a prisoner down today, but they let him out on bail."

Gloria still hasn't looked at Chuck.

"What are you doing with her?" Chuck sputters.

Officer Shoak tightens his grip on Gloria. "I've been looking out for her while she's been in Anchorage. Ladies have to be careful with all those creeps out there." He leers at Chuck.

It occurs to Chuck that Gloria might have had no clue that Officer Shoak is his half-brother. If she did, would she be with him? Would she do that?

Chuck almost hollers out, "But you're my brother!" but stops himself. People are already turning to look at Chuck and Officer Shoak. He doesn't want to be associated with Officer Shoak any more than he has to.

Chuck turns and walks back to first class, excusing himself as he steps on tourists' feet. The stewardess has already brought his bourbon, and he takes a long drink. He can't fly away from everything.

Chapter- 24 Curses

The day before the twins' eleventh birthday, Jimmy gets beat up. Britney finds him cowering under their building, behind the bags of aluminum cans that Vik is saving to recycle.

"What the heck happened to you?" Britney asks. Jimmy's glasses are broken, and he looks at her with crossed eyes.

"I don't know," Jimmy whispers.

"What do you mean you don't know?" Britney roars, as worked up as Jimmy is spiritless. "Somebody beat you up. Who did it?"

Jimmy points toward the home of his perpetrator, the fourteen-year-old son of a police officer.

"Oh, God," Britney says. "Was it that guy who gets high on drugs and goes crazy?"

Jimmy nods.

"Why'd he beat you up?" Britney asks. Jimmy shrugs.

"You think he was high?" she presses.

Jimmy shrugs again.

"We got to go inside and tell Mom," Britney says. Jimmy shakes his head.

"Well you can't stay out here," Britney says. "Besides, everyone's gonna find out anyway, that's how it always is."

Jimmy shrugs, and Britney says, "Fine, stay here. I'm gonna go get Mom."

"No!" Jimmy shouts.

"Come on, just tell me what happened to you!" Britney pleads, noticing for the first time the tear in Jimmy's jeans and his bleeding knee.

"He pushed me off my bike," Jimmy says. "He said I couldn't tell anyone 'cause his dad is the police."

"And you believe him?" Britney asks. Jimmy just looks at her, cross-eyed. "Please don't tell Mom," he whispers. "Or just say I fell off my bike."

"You gotta at least come inside and wash off," Britney says.

"Later," Jimmy says.

After Britney goes inside, Jimmy lies on the ground beneath the building. It's the end of summer, but the sun is still setting around 10 p.m. He wishes it were dark, so no one could see him except for whoever might be watching from up above. He hasn't seen the flashing lights in the sky since before summer started. When he saw the lights then, he understood they weren't something to be scared of. They were from someone that he would meet one day, if he were patient.

Britney also wishes it were dark already. She knows what she's going to do after the sun sets. She's going to get the bones she left in the back of her closet—the ones she got from the Whiteheads' backyard—and … She's actually not quite sure what she'll do with the bones. But somehow, she's going to put a curse on the guy who beat up her brother.

At 6 p.m., tired of waiting for darkness, Britney pulls the bag of bones out of the closet shelf and opens it. The bones smell musty. She wrinkles her nose and wonders why she took them in the first place. She doesn't want to put them back in the closet—whatever she's going to do, she's got to do it now.

How did the Iñupiat put curses on people a long time ago? Britney doesn't know. No one ever talks about that kind of thing, except for some of the curious *taniks* who come to Harow and leave disappointed that it's just as Christian as Texas.

The sky is overcast as usual, and the streets are quiet aside from the barking dogs chained to their little houses and the sound of four-wheelers in the distance. Britney skulks over to the house where the officer and his son live and stands behind one of the storage connexes in the yard. She wonders if anyone's home. She waits a while, then looks into the windows. Everything inside is dark and quiet.

Suddenly Britney slings the bag of bones against the window, yelling "*Aarriga*—great!" It's not exactly what she planned to say, but it sounds right. The window and bones crack and fall in pieces on the dirt. Britney runs home, satisfied.

Larry Atkoot looks out the window when he hears the breaking glass, but he doesn't see anything and it's not worth going out to look. It's a Sunday afternoon, the first day Larry's had away from the office for a while. He's alone. His wife is at a church bazaar raising money to pay off the expenses of local families who sent their kids to bible camp in Anchorage during the summer. It seems a bit ridiculous to Larry—not because he's against Christianity of course, but because the kids would benefit more from staying here and going to some sort of subsistence camp. He's even thought of taking time off of work to lead a camp, but it's been so hard just to take the weekends off lately.

The oil and gas applications seem to be non-stop these days. It's looking more and more like offshore drilling is going to go forward in spite of all the law suits. The oil companies are gearing up to do seismic surveys all along the coast and out in the ocean.

Gill is supposed to be writing the permits, but he's got a broken arm from falling off the roof he was putting on his new house. He can only write with his left hand, and the permits he's been issuing are full of mistakes. It worries Larry enough that he's asked Vik if she can double-check them. But Vik has a tendency to completely rewrite all the permits, adding so many extra requirements that oil companies call Larry and complain. Larry has found himself in the strange position of having to tell Vik to go a little easier on the oil companies.

"If you put all those rules in the permits," he explained to Vik last week, "they'll either complain to the mayor or just totally ignore the permit and sue us if try to bring an enforcement action."

Vik suggested that Larry do the permits himself if he doesn't like her work. Instead of arguing, Larry, with some help from his secretary, has started writing permits.

The phone rings and Larry answers it. It's his secretary inviting him to dinner. He's had dinner with her twice in the last few weeks. The first time was with her husband, kids, and mother, who is Larry's first cousin. The second time, it was just the secretary and her kids. He wonders if this time she'll be alone.

Larry starts to head out the front door when he sees Nelson standing on the front steps.

"I was just about to knock," Nelson says. Larry stiffens. Nelson is Larry's back-door neighbor and the person Larry's supposed to report to. But Larry avoids Nelson as much as he can, mainly because it's hard to talk to Nelson without feeling uncomfortable or stupid. Not only is Nelson a lawyer with a degree in geology, he knows more about how the Borough works than anyone else, including the mayor. And Nelson has a way of tricking people into saying the wrong thing.

"Oh, come in, Nelson," Larry says dejectedly.

"Thanks, I will." Nelson tugs off his giant white tennis shoes and makes himself comfortable on Larry's couch.

Larry wishes his wife were here to say something nice and offer Nelson some of her junk food, since Larry has no idea how to handle the man.

Larry stares at the holes in Nelson's socks for a while before asking, "So, what's going on?"

"Oil," Nelson says with his queer little smile. "And offshore drilling."

Larry waits for Nelson to continue.

"Shant's about to submit an application to your department for a permit to use Borough waters for transit purposes and to construct a small supply base near Harow. It would add on to the base if oil is discovered, and if Harow ends up with a deep sea port."

"So did you want us to deny the permit?" Larry asks.

Nelson's queer little smile expands. "That would seem to be consistent with the six resolutions the Assembly's passed opposing any offshore activity. But then, we might want to take the opportunity to assert our jurisdiction to issue permits for passage through Borough waters. To my knowledge, no one else has applied for such a permit, and the Borough's never tried to control nautical traffic."

Larry nods.

"And then," Nelson continues, "There's the offshore revenue to think about, which might change the Assembly's opposition."

"I heard about that offshore revenue bill in Congress," Larry says. "Did it pass?"

"Not yet," Nelson says. "But it will. Especially if our lobbyists push for it."

"Is that what they're doing in Washington?" Larry asks. The Borough's lobbying activity is a big secret from everyone in the Borough except the mayor, Nelson, and Nelson's wife—the manager of the Borough's government affairs office in Anchorage.

"The mayor still doesn't know what to do about the bill," Nelson says. "He asked me to talk to each of the department directors and get an opinion. That's why I'm here."

"But once we support the bill for sharing offshore revenue, how can we oppose offshore drilling?" Larry asks.

"That's what the mayor wanted me to ask each of you," Nelson says, trying to sound empowering, but instead sounding patronizing.

"I don't think we can take the money," Larry says after thinking a minute. "We're already way too far in with onshore oil money. Every application for onshore drilling that comes in, we—I end up approving. And our subsistence—our subsistence foods are just moving farther and farther away. It's like we're cursed already." He's never acknowledged this out loud before, and the words have a kind of a sting to them.

Nelson nods absently and looks slowly around Larry's house, and then at the Atkoots' four boats outside the living room window. "I see," he says. "Nice house, by the way. Don't think I've ever been inside before."

Larry feels his face turning red and says nothing.

"Well, Larry, I'll take that back to the mayor," Nelson says. Larry's arms are crossed, and he's still looking at the holes in Nelson's socks. Nelson stands up and gives Larry a pat on the back. "See you later."

Larry waits until Nelson is out the door and out of site before getting up to go. He starts to get in the car, but then decides he's in no mood to have dinner with his secretary's family. He comes back inside, gets a beer, sits down on the couch, and texts her to come over to his place.

At the office the next day, Nelson tallies up the directors' opinions, for what they're worth. "No" from Wildlife and Subsistence ... "yes" from Public Works ... "no" from Health ... he didn't bother to ask Bertie the Law Department's opinion—he already knew she'd say "no."

Nelson almost feels sorry for the directors and the mayor, thinking they actually have a part in any decision regarding offshore oil development. Shant's going to start drilling in 2010, and there's nothing the Borough can do about it except try and get a little revenue to offset the impacts. He's already directed the lobbyists to work on getting support for the bill in Congress.

Normally Nelson would at least brief the mayor on decisions regarding lobbying and major policy issues. But now, the mayor's off at an International Whaling Commission meeting in Morocco, completely out of touch.

The annual International Whaling Commission meeting is almost always held an exotic country with no ties to whaling. Both pro-whaling and anti-whaling countries have done an impressive job of recruiting these countries to join the International Whaling Commission and vote on the quotas. The United States is caught in the middle, with a handful of indigenous whale hunters whose rights they must protect, and a much larger number of environmentalists that decry whaling of any kind. It's really up to the Borough and the Alaska Eskimo Whalers Council to attend the meeting and stand up for Iñupiat whaling.

The Iñupiat whaling quota is adjusted every five years, based on estimates of the bowhead whale population and the Iñupiat need for whales as a food source. The International Whaling Commission doesn't care that the entire Iñupiat culture is based on whaling—it wants to see reports documenting how many pounds of whale Eskimos must eat each day to avoid going hungry.

As the years have gone by, and people are eating more fast food and leaving more whale meat outside to rot, Borough mayors have been having a hard time making the necessary showing. To prepare for the Morocco meeting, the Borough has put together a 1,000-page report prepared by dieticians, anthropologists, and biologists from the Lower 48. The report breaks down the average number of calories of whale meat that each Borough resident consumes every day, and explains all the diseases that whale meat prevents.

But whether the report is enough to preserve the quota really depends on who has been recruited to vote in favor of the Iñupiat quota. Borough lobbyists invested heavily in getting Tanzania and Kyrgyzstan to join the International Whalers Council as pro-whaling countries, and the mayor will find out if these efforts have paid off.

While the mayor is on the edge of his seat in the Morocco meeting, Vik is slumped over and yawning through an all-day Iñupiat History, Language, and Culture Commission meeting in Harow. The meetings are supposed to be conducted entirely in Iñupiaq, and all the *taniks* are supposed to listen to a simultaneous translation through radio headsets.

But most of the headsets are broken, and the Commission chairwoman isn't really fluent in Iñupiaq anyway. She speaks in English with an Iñupiaq word thrown in every so often.

Vik is surprised that there isn't more pidgin on the Arctic Slope. There're just a few Iñupiaq words that get used in regular speech, mostly for family members and animal species. She wonders how much longer the language will last, and what'll happen to the culture after the language dies.

The chairwoman gives the floor to Harow's *tanik* elementary-school-teacher-cum-archeologist. The teacher-archeologist talks about a grant she got to create a computer map linking important sites to videos of elders talking about the sites. She projects the map on a screen and clicks on a point south of Harow. The screen turns into a video of one of the Whiteheads talking about a lake that has vanished from the site.

"The idea is to have this on a website where people can come and add more information, kinda like Wikipedia," the teacher-archeologist says.

"But how are you going to keep Outsiders from coming in and trampling our ancestors' graves?" the chairwoman asks. "You can't just take all our traditional knowledge and give it to people who don't share our values."

"Well, if you don't have something like this, how are you going to pass down your traditional knowledge to your kids?" the teacher-archeologist asks. "People aren't taking their kids camping these days. They're sitting at home on the Internet. If traditional knowledge doesn't change with the times, it'll be lost. The library here is full of dusty old videos with elders telling their stories in Iñupiaq. No one's watching them."

"Some of our knowledge isn't good no more," says an elderly commissioner who speaks through a trachea device. "Animals and lakes that used to be in one place, now they're not there no more."

The teacher-archeologist nods. "That's what these interviews I did are showing. They're filling in the spotty Western science of climate change."

She shows a video with Larry Atkoot's father talking about old military trails that filled with water and become like canals into the interior. Next is a video taken of Luther Ericsen before he died, talking about a site on the Chiliq River.

"The name of the site translates to 'Don't sleep there,' but it's a misnomer," the gravelly voice rumbles. "I used to camp there often on the way to my allotment, and I slept there just fine. Probably someone named it that to keep others away, 'cause it's such good hunting there." He lets out a throaty laugh that turns into a cough.

The commissioner with the trachea device says, "The problem is English. Our knowledge is getting mistranslated. We have names for each creek that non-natives can't pronounce, like Ikputnumiut, which people call 'Iko' now."

Luther Ericsen is still coughing on the video, and the teacher-archeologist turns it off.

"Thank you Commissioners," she says. "That concludes my presentation."

The next item on the agenda is the local museum. The chairwoman explains, "We've had the same stuff in the museum for the past fifteen years, and we really need to get some new stuff."

Vik can't contain herself and raises her hand to make a suggestion.

"You know, something I've never seen that has a lot to do with traditional knowledge, actually, would be an exhibit about pre-Christian Iñupiaq beliefs. Maybe something explaining the reasoning behind taboos or the origin of curses."

The commissioners shake their heads in disbelief, and the chairwoman glowers at Vik.

"We have to respect our elders," she said.

"I'm sorry," Vik said. "What do you mean?"

The teacher-archeologist shoots Vik a look of pity.

The chairwoman, amazed that she has to explain this, says emphatically, "Having an exhibit like that would be like saying that our elders went to hell, because they weren't saved."

"Jesus," Vik mutters.

Chapter 25- Work, Play and Sex

Bertie almost enjoys the absurdity of going to the grocery store. She stops by a display of twelve-pack sodas, "on sale" for only two-and-a-half times their cost in Anchorage, and wonders who would waste money on such a thing. She's then forced to move over, as two people swooping in from different directions simultaneously reach for a twelve-pack.

Bertie moves on to the frozen meat section and picks out a Styrofoam tray of reindeer, which is essentially the same thing as caribou, except that caribou is illegal to sell, and only Native people are supposed to sell reindeer. Whatever it is, Bertie thinks it tastes better than beef. And hopefully the purchase is going to support Alaska Natives instead of confined animal feeding operations in the Lower 48.

Going to the store is a diversion from the office. She's just learned that another lawyer is quitting, and he's only given her a week's notice. Few lawyers in the past decade have stayed more than year. Even the staff doesn't stay. The last secretary quit when she got too pregnant, and the current secretary just announced her own pregnancy.

Bertie looks up and sees Lisa, who held the position two secretaries ago.

Bertie waves, and Lisa comes over to envelope Bertie in a bear hug.

"How've you been?" Bertie asks. "How are the twins?"

"Oh, okay," Lisa says. "I was kinda mad at Britney because she failed math and reading last year. They coulda made her repeat the grade, but they gave her an honorable promotion so she don't fall behind the rest of her class. I don't know, she's always texting and playing video games, she don't seem to care about school. Somebody ought to take her hunting, but her dad don't pay no attention to her."

"Oh," Bertie says, having expected Lisa to just say "fine" and move on to the soda section. "What about Jimmy?"

Lisa sighs. "I don't know. He always did so good in school, and then towards the end of last year he was failing a lot of his tests. He passed only 'cause it all averaged out."

Bertie wonders if people like Lisa dump on her because she's black and an Outsider—someone who's never going to be part of the community and whose opinion doesn't really matter.

Lisa's still talking about Jimmy. "And then he got beat up by some kid who was calling him gay. Can you imagine? He's eleven years old!"

Bertie can't bring herself to inform Lisa that it's possible to be both eleven years old and gay, even in Harow.

"Well, Lisa, you've got a good head on your shoulders," Bertie says. "I guess you're doing the best you can ..."

Bertie doesn't go on. Lisa's looking at someone in the bakery section and doesn't seem to be paying attention.

"Well, nice seeing you, Bertie!" Lisa says, wheeling her overloaded basket away. The guy in the bakery section looks so much like the boyfriend Lisa lost at age sixteen, it's creepy. Lisa wonders if it could be Tommy, the son that her cousin had taken away to Anchorage and renamed—what was it—William. He would be twenty now, the same age as his father when the accident happened.

She starts to approach him but decides not to. She might be wrong. Or she might be right, but Tommy might not want to talk to her. She'll ask around to see if her cousin's come to town with her son.

When Lisa gets home, Jimmy's lying in bed watching T.V., and Britney's on the couch texting her friends.

"It's a beautiful day," Lisa says. "How come you guys don't take the four-wheeler out?"

"It's broken," Britney says, still texting. "And Jimmy won't go out anyway."

"Well, don't you have homework or something?" School started a few weeks ago, but the twins hadn't said much about their classes. "You're in middle school now."

"Duh," Britney says. "There's no homework until high school."

Lisa sighs, remembering the School Board's no-homework-for-kids policy, and goes to watch T.V. in her own room.

Back at her apartment, Bertie is logging onto her work email and trying, with little hope of success, to finish the day's work. She's stressed by the lack of stability at the Borough. There's the impending offshore drilling, the idea of revenue sharing, the mayor's term coming to an end next year, and then there's the constant turnover of employees. More than ever, Bertie feels the need to be involved in everything happening at the Borough. But she's getting left out of whatever's going on in the Mayor's Office. She can't talk to Nelson about it—he just has a way of making her feel inadequate. To add to her stress, she weighs 250 pounds and has high blood pressure and a bad back.

When Nelson's wife was in Harow, she and Nelson led the campaign to get Bertie to quit smoking. They made her feel guilty about it, like she was ruining the environment of the people she was supposed to be protecting. It worked.

Recently, Nelson's wife has been pushing the idea of a program she calls GOYFA, or "Get Off Your Fat Ass." It's designed to get employees to be healthier in the workplace, just by doing shoulder shrugs and leg lifts at their desks and using the bathroom on a different floor.

"It'll save the Borough a lot of money in insurance payouts," she says when she calls Bertie to sell her on the idea.

"Maybe the Borough should just stop sponsoring a Thanksgiving dinner," Bertie suggests. "It would save thousands of dollars and the people would save thousands of calories."

Nelson's wife dismisses the idea and says that Bertie is actually going to be in charge of GOYFA. "I can't do it from Anchorage, Nelson's too busy, and besides, it would benefit you."

Now, on top of all her other work, Bertie's supposed to organize health walks between Borough buildings and put out monthly newsletters with factoids on the number of calories burned by activities like gum-chewing.

Bertie looks up from her computer and out the window at the small patch of grass in the neighbor's yard. It's already turning red—Harow's only sign of autumn. Within a week it'll be brown, and the snow will start to stick.

Bertie gets a brief respite from work in September 2009, when she gets stuck as a juror in a rape trial. It takes weeks to put together a full twelve-member jury, in part because any woman who's been a rape victim herself can't serve.

Just before trial, the judge decides that Bertie will have too much influence on the other jurors, and Bertie is dismissed. Bertie thinks it's laughable that she'd be able to influence anyone around here, but it's just as well that she has to go back to the office.

The jurors argue on everything, and the only charge they can agree to stick the defendant with is second-degree sexual assault, which carries a maximum sentence of 10 years. The defendant probably wouldn't have even been convicted if the woman weren't in a wheelchair with lupus. The victim and the defendant grew up across the street from each other and partied together for years. Both were drunk when the rape happened. The woman passed out, and woke up to find the man having sex with her. She told him to get off, but he was still too drunk to realize that the woman wasn't enjoying it.

After the judge and the jury leave the courtroom, the defendant looks at the victim and says he's sorry. "I was just so drunk I didn't know what I was doing."

She nods her head in acceptance. It would surprise none of us if the whole thing happens all over again after the defendant gets out of jail. Maybe it has something to do with the Iñupiat culture that, for thousands of years, saw sex as an activity no different from sharing food. Or maybe it's because of the Christian gospel of sexual repression, introduced by the missionaries a hundred years ago. Maybe it's a combination of both. Whatever the reason, no one in Harow sees any reason to talk about sex, or to prevent or enhance it.

It takes Gill a week to work up the guts to call Vik for advice about "The sex problem."

"Um, what do you mean, 'the sex problem'?" she asks him.

"You know," Gill says, "That store with the little Thai woman who was selling the, uh, sex stuff."

"Oh, the one who was selling penis lighters without a permit?" Vik asks. "I thought that was over with. She said at the Development Planning Commission hearing that she wasn't going to sell that stuff."

"Well, I got a call that she's still selling it," Gill said.

"Have you done an inspection of the place?" Vik asks.

"Yeah, I sent one of our guys out there last week, but he didn't see anything," Gill says. "I don't know if she's got it hidden away somewhere or what."

"I don't know," Vik says. "I would think we have more important things to deal with, like revising our land use code to deal with offshore drilling and global warming."

"So should I send out a notice of violation?" Gill asks.

"I don't think you can take any action unless you have evidence of a violation," Vik says.

"Well, okay," Gill sighs. He knows it's not the end of the matter, and he's right.

At the next Development Planning Commission meeting, a Korean woman from a competing gift shop comes in with props to show the commission what the little Thai woman is selling.

"All this porn and drug supplies—it's criminal!" she shouts. Turning to Gill, she says, "And you're not doing anything about it! I told you one month ago. And look, you got suicide in your family because of drugs!"

Vik leans forward, wanting to hear more about the Whitehead suicide. No one ever tells her when suicides happen. Gill takes a deep breath and mumbles that the matter is under investigation.

The Korean woman gets up in a huff, saying that if Gill doesn't put an end to it, then she's going to start selling porn and drug supplies herself.

Gill sighs and looks around the room for Larry, but he isn't here. Larry would be able to say something wise in a situation like this.

Larry seems to be missing a lot of work lately. Vik wonders if he's put out by the mayor's increasing inability to stand up to offshore drilling. Or maybe Larry's just worn down by his office job and wants to be out at his camp. Or maybe ... the rumors that he's having an affair with his secretary really are true. She can imagine how awkward it would be to work with a lover and a wife in the same department.

Vik has a hard time believing the rumors, though. She doesn't see Larry as the type who'd take any kind of risk involving sex—not after having done jail time for his sexual assault conviction. And the secretary is Larry's cousin, twenty years younger than him. And she's got greasy hair.

Vik calls Larry that evening to find out what's going on. He sounds drunk.

"Maybe you could come over here and give me a ride?" he asks. "I'm too drunk to drive."

"Okay," Vik says. She's too curious to resist.

Larry lives just across the street from Vik. She walks over and finds him sitting in his truck with the engine running. "Uh, where do you need to go?" Vik asks.

"I don't care, anywhere," he says.

"Let's go out to the Point and look for polar bears," Vik says.

"There won't be any now, but okay," Larry says.

"What happened to you?" Vik asks, backing Larry's truck out of the driveway.

"I gotta quit this job," he says. "That's what my wife said before she went to Anchorage yesterday. 'Either she quits, you quit, or I quit, but the three of us can't work together no more.'"

"Who can't work together anymore?"

"So you don't know about the affair?" Larry asks.

"Oh," Vik says. "I heard rumors ..."

"It's true," Larry says, opening a beer. "I'm having an affair with my secretary-cousin."

"Oh," Vik says with some disappointment. "Well, I myself am inbred if it makes you feel any better."

"I don't know what to do," Larry says.

Vik knows from experience exactly what to do. "You're going to have to get rid of both women. Neither one is ever going to measure up to everything you want her to be."

Larry looks at Vik out of the corner of his eyes. "Then who's the right woman?" he asks.

"There's no such thing," Vik says decisively. She's brought along her own mixed drink and takes a quick slug of it.

"And I'm sick of my job, anyway," Larry says.

"Why don't you just quit and go live out at your camp? You ought to have enough to retire now—you've been working at the Borough for more than 20 years."

"I don't know if I can quit, though. Especially now, when there's all this talk about offshore drilling and a port in Harow—"

"A port in Harow?" Vik asks incredulously. "I haven't heard about that. I wonder if Bertie knows."

Larry shrugs. "That's what the mayor says Chuck is doing with the Harow Native Corporation."

"Really?" Vik says. She thinks of Chuck's rambling Assembly speeches and can't imagine him having the wherewithal to lead a development project.

"And, you know, there's some part of me that doesn't want to let the mayor down," Larry says.

Vik begins to psychoanalyze Larry. "Maybe you had the affair wanting to get caught, so you could have a good reason to quit your job?" stop here

Larry laughs. "No, I had the affair because I wanted a good piece of ass."

"Aha," Vik says. She's never heard Larry talk like that. She switches the subject back to Larry's camp. "Anyway, what's to stop you from going off and living at your camp? Not that we'd want to lose you as a director, but man, if I were into hunting and knew how to survive out there in the wild like you do, I'd love to just leave it all behind."

Larry is silent.

"Wouldn't you love to leave behind your job and this truck and all these petty little trinkets of American life?" Vik says, pointing to Larry's cell phone, VHF radio, and beer cans. She turns to look at Larry and sees that his eyes are closed.

She pulls the truck off the road, turns off the engine, and kisses him, long and hard.

Larry's cell phone goes off. Vik jumps, hitting her head on the window. Larry looks at the number and turns off the phone. He pulls Vik back to him and says, "Let's drive way out and fuck."

Vik laughs awkwardly. She only kissed him out of curiosity, and to lift his spirits a bit. Since she's turned thirty, her once-ranging hormones have become almost imperceptible—so much so that she's been able to stay faithful to her Filipino husband.

"I'll, uh, take you back to you house," she says.

"I mean it!" Larry says. "I never got with a *tanik* before."

For a minute, Vik wonders if Larry really had raped a woman in the 1980s and made up the story about the false accusation. But the hand on her shoulder is too tender for Vik to see Larry as anything but a drunk Eskimo with the blues. She squeezes his hand and gently removes it from her shoulder.

Larry closes his eyes again and leans back in his seat. Vik starts the engine and drives back to Larry's house. She kisses his forehead before leaving him to sit silently in the truck.

Chapter 26- Drilling, Dredging and Shooting

Bertie shifts uncomfortably in her plastic chair, bracing herself for a two-hour infomercial from Shant. Normally it would be Vik's job to sit through a public meeting like this one, but Vik is already at a meeting on Chuck's deep sea port. So it's up to Bertie to figure out what Shant is telling the people of Harow.

Shant has managed to get all the federal and state permits it needs to start drilling in 2010. The only thing standing in Shant's way now is a few Borough permits and the possibility that the Borough or someone else might sue the government for approving Shant's drilling plans.

Shant's trying to avoid a lawsuit by smothering the Arctic Slope with its public relations campaign. Last week, Shant sent well paid executives to have lunch with Borough officials, and Shant's Social Performance Coordinator gave out free hotdogs to the public. The whole thing makes Bertie sick, especially the antics of the Social Performance Coordinator. Bertie sees the skinny little bleached-blonde now, passing out door prize tickets. She's dressed in "Eskimo" fur and ivory that's just a little nicer than anything people in Harow would wear.

A few days ago, Bertie gave Nelson and the mayor a memo explaining that it would be consistent with the Borough's position in previous cases to file a lawsuit against Shant and the federal agencies that approved Shant's plans this time around. Neither Nelson nor the mayor has gotten back to her. Bertie wonders if the Mayor's Office is going to go the way of past administrations and ignore the Law Department.

The meeting room is full of people slurping sodas and wolfing down pizza. If everyone's going to get up and make a statement, the meeting will go on for hours.

"Hi Bertie," the Social Performance Coordinator says to her. It irritates Bertie the way all these oil people memorize everyone's name and make a point of individual greetings.

"Did you get your door prize ticket?"

"Mmm hmmm," Bertie mutters. She's too tired to explain that she's never been tricked into getting a door prize ticket and has no plans to get one now.

The lights are flicking on and off, which means that Shant's about to start up a big shiny slide show. Images of all five Iñupiat Eskimos employed by Shant flash up on the screen, followed by pictures of rigs in Norway.

When oil companies first started talking about offshore drilling, the Borough hired consultants to look into how Norway managed to drill in the offshore Arctic. As far as Bessie can make out from the memos and badly translated permits, Norway isn't doing all that much drilling in icy waters. The Norwegian rigs above the Arctic Circle have the benefit of the Gulf Stream, which leaves the region mostly ice-free even in the winter. Weather conditions are nothing like what oil companies will face in the Arctic waters above Alaska.

The mayor was quite taken with Norway's high standards, or at least what he understood them to be. Shant humored the mayor by arranging several all-expenses-paid trips to bring him and the Assembly members over to look at Norwegian rigs—in the summer. Shant never let the Borough representatives get out of the Shant hotel or off the Shant boat, but everyone was glad they got to see the Norwegian rigs with their own eyes.

No one asked Bertie if she wanted to go, but it didn't matter. If she weren't going to accept door prize tickets, she certainly wasn't going to accept a cruise around Norway.

When the slide show is over, the Social Performance Coordinator says there'll be a brief question-and-answer session before more refreshments are served. To ensure brevity, the Social Performance Coordinator refrains from handing her wireless microphone to anyone in the audience. The audience members shout out everything on their minds in no particular order, and the Social Performance Coordinator answers with as much patience as she can muster.

"What are you gonna do if there's an oil spill?"

"Oh, there won't be an oil spill, because Shant has state-of-the-art equipment and highly trained professionals."

"What if there is one?"

"Well, in the extremely unlikely event of a spill, Shant's contingency plan, which is fully approved by the state and federal government, would be put into action. And Shant would contract local whalers to go out in their *umi*—uh, traditional boats and make noise to scare the whales away from the oil."

"What's the drilling gonna do to whales?"

"Just so you know, Shant's spent millions of dollars changing its drilling plans in response to the Borough's concerns. As part of the new plans, Shant's agreed to avoid drilling when the whale hunt's going on."

Bertie shakes her head at the Social Performance Coordinator's gall. Shant changed its plans because a court required it to, not because of anything the Borough wanted.

"Are you gonna make sure that the smoke from your facility don't reach our houses?"

"The rig's going to use ultra low sulfur diesel—because the Borough mayor said to—and emissions are going to be monitored and modeled."

"Because the *court* said to," Bertie mutters to herself.

The man next to Bertie says, "We hear a lot about terrorists these days. What kind of security do you have in place to make sure nobody outside of Shant can get in and use your equipment?"

"Oh, Shant's going to have a great security system in place, for sure."

"If I test your security system and get in without you knowing, do I get a prize?"

The Social Performance Coordinator ignores the question, and starts to thank everyone for coming. But the audience is just warming up.

"We got a history of losing our people—of *taniks* taking our people away," an elder says. "Don't let this happen."

"Um," the Social Performance Coordinator says. "Shant's not going to let anyone get kidnapped, if that's what you mean."

"I heard in the news the world's gonna end in 2012. Is that in your schedule?"

The Social Performance Coordinator looks at the audience very seriously, and says, "The Lord will take us when he will, and there's nothing we can do about it except plan to drill in 2010."

Bertie feels nauseated. She looks around the room for like-minded Borough employees with whom she could share a knowing glance. Normally Larry would be at this kind of event, leaning against the back wall in his familiar stoic pose. But aside from the director of the Wildlife and Subsistence Department, Bertie doesn't see anyone from the Borough.

Bertie knows why Larry's not here. The Human Resources director called her this morning, asking with some confusion how to handle Larry's resignation letter, which the mayor refused to accept. Bertie was stunned. She's known Larry for decades. She feels left out that he never told her he was going to resign. Aside from that, losing Larry is bad for the Borough. For as long as he's been director, the Community Development Department has stayed out of trouble. If the mayor makes Gill the new director, the department could turn into a liability. Every permit application that comes through the door will get Gill's rubber stamp of approval.

Is Larry retiring so he can spend more time at his camp? Or does he know something about the Borough that Bertie doesn't know?

There is a lull in the questioning, and Bertie asks the Social Performance Coordinator where Shant is in the process of signing onto an oil spill mitigation agreement. To the audience, Bertie explains that the agreement requires an oil company to set aside $25 million in case there's a catastrophic oil spill. If there is a spill, the money will immediately be used to relocate subsistence hunters and/or subsistence foods, so subsistence needs can be satisfied.

"That's a legal matter," the Social Performance Coordinator says dismissively, "but I'd be glad to discuss it with you after the meeting."

Bertie waits with a numb butt while door prizes are announced and collected. At 10:30 p.m., the Social Performance Coordinator announces that since they didn't start the meeting with a prayer, they'll now end with one. She calls on an elder who's dozing in the front row to lead the prayer. The elder stands up, confused, and begins to call out to Jesus in a low Iñupiaq wail.

Bertie crosses her arms, deciding that the combination of door prizes and prayer makes the Social Performance Coordinator even more manipulative than the missionaries.

When the prayer finishes five minutes later, Bertie's at the edge of her sanity. She marches over to the Social Performance Coordinator and demands to know what happened to the oil spill mitigation agreement.

"Well, I wish I had a lawyer here to explain it to you," the Social Performance Coordinator says. "But the crux is, we don't think that's an enforceable requirement. It's not written anywhere in your code, and even if it was, I can't say that it'd be enforceable."

Bertie glowers. The Social Performance Coordinator is right, really. The drilling is taking place a few miles outside of the Borough's jurisdiction. The Borough's only power out there is the force of its goodwill, which isn't all that much. Bertie watches the audience pass by the food table and load up with leftovers before trickling out. Shant's clearly exercising its goodwill in the form of a few hundred dollars spent on pizza, instead of putting up a $25 million bond for an oil spill agreement.

Bertie mumbles something about talking to Shant's lawyers later, and wanders out the door empty-handed.

The next day, Gill starts sorting through the stacks of paper in Larry's office and bringing some of them to his own office. He's made himself the Acting Director until the mayor figures out what to do about Larry quitting. Gill doesn't know what exactly happened to Larry. He's heard a lot of gossip, and he's heard Larry's secretary yakking on the phone about the affair. He's not sure if he believes the secretary's version of it. But then, he doesn't really care. If Larry wants to have an affair with his cousin and screw up his career, that's his problem.

One of the stacks of paper consists entirely of Shant's applications for the 2010 offshore drilling season. Even though the Borough doesn't have any control over the actual site of the drilling, Gill has made it clear that a permit will be required for every trip Shant makes through Borough waters.

Gill remembers his conversation with Vik last week, when she asked him, "If you're going to make people apply for permits for every little thing they do within Borough boundaries, don't you think you should have some qualifications for issuing them?"

"What do you mean?" Gill asked.

"I mean, just because someone turns in an application doesn't mean you *have* to issue the permit. If it's a bad project, you should deny the application."

Gill frowned. "Well then they'd just do whatever they were going to do anyway without a permit."

"Well, wouldn't you take some enforcement action in that case?"

"I dunno. It'd be hard to do unless you want to sue them."

"So you're not taking any enforcement action now if someone violates the permits?" Vik asked.

"Sometimes we fine companies for leaving trash or ruts on the tundra."

"That's it? So what's the point of permitting?"

"It's revenue. And our Borough ordinances require permitting."

Gill heard Vik exhaling heavily into the phone and added, "You're the lawyer. You know what the ordinances say."

Vik hung up after that, and Gills considers the matter resolved. He prints out a batch of permits that Larry's secretary prepared, allowing Shant's vessels to dock on Borough land. If he'd thought about it earlier, he would have called the guys he knew at Shant and worked on some kind of impact fund requirement for the permits. He's done that before with some of the other projects, so the oil companies have to give local people a little money to make up for any impact they might have on subsistence. He feels pretty good about those projects.

But this stuff with Shant has come up so fast, there hasn't been enough time to get Shant to set up an impact fund or sign an oil spill mitigation agreement.

Gill flips through another stack of papers and finds some sort of preliminary assessment about a deep water port for Harow. He's heard a little bit about the project and thinks it might be a good idea, except for the fact that it came from Chuck. Gill's a Whitehead, after all, and the Whiteheads don't trust Chuck.

Gill doesn't consider himself much of a reading person. He skims through the 300-page assessment just to see if anything catches his eye. Towards the end, there's something about the Utilador, the utility corridor buried underground, which is now just twenty feet from the ocean. The assessment says that with the current erosion rate, Harow will have to pave the coastline or relocate the Utilidor if it wants a port.

Otherwise, all the dredging and shipping will expose the Utilidor, and ice scouring will probably destroy it.

Gill thinks that paving the coastline isn't such a bad idea. The Whiteheads have a lot of property right up along the coastline, and every year they lose a couple feet of shoreline. Some sort of concrete wall like what they have in Holland could be just what Harow needs.

There's a letter from the Army Corps along with the assessment, informing the Borough of the deadline for comments and for letting the Army Corps know if the Borough wants to cooperate with the Army Corps on more assessments for the port. Gill writes "no thanks" next to the part about cooperating and "looks good" at the top of the page, and asks Larry's secretary to fax it to the Army Corps.

When Vik learns a few weeks later that the Borough won't be considered a cooperating agency for the Army Corps' environmental impact statement on the proposed deep sea port, she calls Gill to find out what had happened.

"Oh," Gill says. "I told them we didn't need to be a cooperating agency."

"Why? The project is literally happening in your backyard, and you don't even want a chance to weigh in on it?"

"Well," Gill says. "It looks good enough to me, I mean, if they get a Borough permit and all. Besides, the Community Development Department doesn't really have the capacity to be a federal cooperating agency, especially with Larry gone."

"But you're not the only department in the Borough! Other people would have been involved, too!"

"Like you?" Gill asks.

Vik pauses. Ever since she concluded that the Borough would end up supporting offshore drilling, she hasn't done much at the office besides working on drafts of her latest novel.

"For-for example," she stammers.

"I'm pretty sure it'll work out anyway," Gill says, hanging up.

A minute later, Vik gets an email copy of a letter drafted by someone in the Mayor's Office—probably Nelson or his wife—on a different development project. It's an onshore drilling project proposed by Cacoco Oil, but rejected by federal permitting agencies. The email says "For your review," but the letter has already been signed and sent out. The letter says that denial of the federal permits would amount to denial of the Iñupiat culture. Vik rolls her eyes as she reads, "We Iñupiat won't be able to afford to maintain our traditions, or even live in our Arctic communities, if we are deprived of the cash portion of our economy."

She spends the rest of the day on the Internet looking for job openings with environmental non-profit organizations.

After work, Vik tells her husband that the Borough seems to have lost interest in preserving the land and the way of life of people who depend on the land.

"It's all about development and oil money now. They were living here for thousands of years without any money, and now they're saying they're going to get kicked off the land if the federal government puts any limits on oil drilling? I don't get it."

Vik's husband usually ignores her ranting or changes the subject. Today, he says, "We finally got another Eskimo working at the Iñupiat Housing Authority."

"Really?" Vik asks. "Who's the first one?"

"Our neighbor, the guy with the twins."

"Lisa's honey?"

"Yeah, but I think he's quitting again."

"So who's the new Eskimo?"

"I don't know. He's young, just moved to town. I worked with him today to make some repairs in the nine-plex."

"Good for you," Vik says absently. "Well, I hope you're not set on working there the rest of your life, I've about had it with this place."

On the other side of the wall from Vik and her husband, Jimmy is lying asleep in bed. The apartment is quiet except for the sounds of the T.V. Lisa's honey has gone to see friends, Lisa's writing out checks for overdue bills, and Britney's watching T.V. and texting.

Lisa's brother comes over to bring her a share of the whale his crew had caught. Before the fall whaling season started, he'd tried to get Jimmy involved again. But the kid wouldn't answer his cell phone, and each time he went over to the apartment, Jimmy was sleeping or gone. Lisa's brother gave up after a few tries, deciding he didn't have time to force whaling on someone who didn't want to do it. He's got his own son to teach. Stop here

"Why's he always sleeping?" Lisa's brother asks when he comes in. "It's 7:00 in the evening."

"I dunno," Lisa sighs. "I guess he's getting to be a teenager. We just gotta give him some room."

Britney looks up from texting and says, "He's sad 'cause his boyfriend moved away."

"What are you talking about, Britney?" Lisa asks.

"That Oriental kid. His family moved to California. And now Jimmy don't have any friends besides me."

"Are you calling your brother a faggot?" Lisa's brother asks angrily.

"He just don't like to do the things boys are supposed to do," Britney says. "I'm the only one who wants to go whaling and hunting."

Lisa's brother storms into the twins' room to wake Jimmy up.

"Leave him alone!" Lisa shouts, running to stand between her son and her brother.

Jimmy turns to the wall without waking up.

The twins' father comes in drunk, slams the door, and hollers that he's home.

"Oh for the love of God," Lisa's brother mutters. "I give up on you all."

"I said I'd go whaling with you and you never let me!" Britney shouts.

"Nobody better be shouting in this house!" her father bellows, waving his arms and knocking over a lamp. It crashes into the flimsy wall separating the living room from the master bedroom. The plasma T.V., which is bolted to the same wall, wavers, blinks, and releases itself with a thud onto the floor. The walrus skull hanging next to the T.V. quivers and crashes down alongside the T.V. The longer tusk snaps off and rolls toward the fallen lamp.

The family turns to look at the crumbling plaster and the holes left in the wall.

"I'm outta here," Lisa's brother says, slamming the door as he leaves. More plaster crumbles onto the living room floor, and Lisa can see inside her bedroom.

"You better get that fixed tomorrow," she says to her honey, choking back tears.

"I quit my job today," Lisa's honey grumbles. "One of the other guys'll fix it."

Jimmy hears the noise and shouting through his dream. The door slams again, and then everything is quiet.

Jimmy missed school all of last week. He told his mother he just didn't feel good. She didn't know what was wrong with him and decided it was best to leave him alone. He's been staying in bed most of the time, wondering how much longer he can stay like this. Occasionally he sees lights flash in his window, and though they're probably just snowmachines, he thinks of his lights in the sky.

When Jimmy gets up the next day, everyone is gone. The living room wall is bare, and the broken T.V., lamp, and walrus tusks are lying in a heap on the ground. Jimmy sees his parents' bedroom through the holes in the wall. The closet door is open, and the closet light has been left on. Jimmy wanders into the room. He looks at the clothes on the floor, the old cans of beer on the dresser, last year's calendar hanging on the wall, and the light in the closet. He hasn't gone in his parents' closet since he was a little kid. Back then, his dad had spanked him, saying "There's guns in there."

Now, Jimmy sees the rifles leaning against a broken tent frame in the corner of the closet. He picks one up, runs his hands along the barrel, and puts it back in the corner. He hasn't shot a gun since his uncle took him out for shooting practice before last year's fall whaling, and he's never shot a pistol before.

On the shelf above is a pistol and boxes of bullets. Jimmy reaches up and pulls the gun down. He wonders if it's loaded. Sitting down on the floor of the closet, he stares at the gun. What would it be like to go? Would it hurt? Would he stop hurting?

Jimmy sees the face of his only friend, as he saw it the last time. Jimmy's crying, but the face is laughing. Now he sees the face of the cop's kid, standing over Jimmy's beaten body and laughing. And then the faces of the kids at school, shouting at him and laughing.

Jimmy looks into the barrel of the gun.

"Holy Jesus!" someone yells. Jimmy drops the gun, startled. He didn't hear anyone coming into the house.

"Holy Jesus, what are you doing?" A man with a hat that says "IHA"—Iñupiat Housing Authority—pulls Jimmy to his feet and gawks at him. "I just came in to fix the holes in the wall and here you are about to blow a hole in your head!"

"I … I'm not," Jimmy says.

"Come out here in the living room, I better call your mom."

Jimmy closes his eyes and says nothing. The man leads him to the living room, sits him on the couch, and pulls out a cell phone. "Gimme your mom's cell number," he says.

But Lisa is already walking in the door with bags of groceries. She looks at Jimmy and then at the man with the cell phone.

"Tommy," she says, setting the groceries down. It's the same man she saw in the grocery store two months before, the one who looks so much like her old boyfriend. "I mean, William."

"Uh, yeah?" the man said.

"Oh, my son, my son," she whispers. She runs to him and takes him in her arms.

"Lady, I just came here to fix the wall," he says, pulling himself out of Lisa's clutches.

"You're the one that called me. That's your son right there. He was just about to blow himself away before I came in."

Lisa feels dizzy. "Oh," is all she can say, and she stands there with her mouth hanging open.

"Listen, I'll come back another time when there's no one here, okay?" The man steps gingerly around Lisa, over the walrus tusk, and out the door.

Chapter 27- Time to Get Out

Larry sits on the couch in the dark. He hasn't shown up at the office in months, but the mayor still hasn't accepted his resignation, and he's still getting a paycheck. It doesn't feel right. He wonders why the mayor hasn't just fired him. Maybe the mayor understands Larry's position—twenty years before, the mayor left his own wife for a while to live in Anchorage with another woman. Maybe the mayor thinks Larry will come to his senses, like the mayor finally did.

Larry picks up the phone and calls the mayor directly.

"Listen, you have to come back to work, Larry," the mayor says when he gets on the line. "You know, besides the Community Development Department and the Wildlife and Subsistence Department, every department here is run by a *tanik*. If you go, a *tanik* will replace you. I hate to say it, maybe Chuck was right that time he said there's too many *taniks* in my administration."

"You could appoint Gill Whitehead," Larry suggests.

"Uh, seriously, I don't think that would work too well," the mayor says. "You know how the Whiteheads are, everybody in town always has to clean up after them."

"You're not running for re-election, are you?" Larry asks. "You already did two back-to-back terms."

"No ..."

"What are you going to do, work for one of the native corporations?"

"No ..."

"Who, then?" Larry asks. "Or are you going to retire?"

"I'll be working for Shant, Larry."

Larry says nothing, and the mayor continues, "I'll be a consultant. I get to stay here in Harow, you know I'm getting too old to travel. And after I'm gone, there's got to be at least one person left in the Borough to look out for subsistence."

"I'm not coming back," Larry says.

"All right," the mayor says after a pause. "I guess we understand each other."

After they hang up, Larry leans his head back on the couch. He's run out of beer, and the person who usually sells it to him is out of town. He closes his eyes and thinks about what he should do. If he wants to stay here and make a decent salary, he's going to have to work for oil money. He doesn't want to do that. Nor does he want to move to Anchorage or the Lower 48, and start a totally new job. He's too old, like the mayor.

Larry remembers his grandfather telling him that one day, the *taniks* would take over the Arctic Slope, and towers of metal would cover the landscape like wildflowers. When oil was found at Prudhoe Bay, Larry thought about the rigs being the towers of metal. Now, the *taniks* really have taken over, and the towers of metal are creeping out into the ocean.

Larry believes the environmentalists when they say that an oil spill in Arctic waters can't be cleaned up. All the experiments the oil companies have done with a few gallons of oil in water took place in a laboratory, or on perfectly clear days on the Norwegian coast without waves, wind, or ice.

With ice, none of the cleanup equipment would really work. Neither would burning. If the spill happened towards the end of the summer, it would just go under the ice for the rest of the winter. No one was going to go out in the dark and try to dig it up. By the time the ice melted enough for the cleanup equipment, oil would have made its way into the food chain, and it would be only a matter of time before it got in the whales. Larry tries to stop thinking about all of this, but he can't.

Larry's wife comes home from work and finds him sitting alone in the dark. She turns on the lights and the heater.

"Still sitting here, huh?" she says. "Why don't you take your snowmachine out to the camp? If you're not working you could at least go hunting."

Larry hears his wife as if from a distance. He hasn't been back to his camp since the time he woke up next to the bear. Larry never told Mandy what happened. He starts to say something now, but Mandy's already in the kitchen and Larry can smell frying Spam.

He knows he's got to get out of here. But everything, everything is tied to oil and gas—his snowmachine, the plastic boxes he would cart the food in, the cabin's stove, his Borough paychecks, and even whaling.

Larry's whaling crew didn't go whaling this fall because there wasn't enough money. They needed at least $20,000 to get the food and supplies together, and then to serve whatever whale they caught. Larry's father had been sick, and Larry's brother was having heart troubles again. And then when Larry's wife found out about the affair, she went off to Anchorage for a month and spent all kinds of money.

Larry's wife stays in the kitchen to eat her Spam sandwich. Larry lies down on the couch, drifting between thought and dream. He remembers the story his grandfather told him about Sedna, the giant girl who was thrown off a kayak by her father. She clung to the side of the boat until her father chopped off her fingers. She sank into the spirit world and became immortal, and her huge fingers became the seals and walrus that would feed the Iñupiat forever after.

No one in Harow alive today has ever heard of Sedna, except for a few *tanik* scientists, who know that there's a planet-like object beyond Pluto named Sedna. It's funny to think that just two hundred years ago, no one had heard of Jesus Christ—they just followed the traditional rituals to make sure Sedna provided them with food from the sea.

Larry remembers the stories, but not any of the rituals his grandfather taught him. Larry's a Christian, after all. The idea of a compassionate man who shared fish and bread and died for the good of the community is much more comforting than the taboos and rituals of his ancestors. And if people don't go to Heaven when they die, what's the point of living? There has to be a point.

For Lisa, the point is her children. The day after she finds her son on the edge of death, she takes him to the Native Medical Center in Anchorage for mental treatment. She's never been to a counselor before, and the idea of a mental hospital terrifies her. She tells her honey and Jimmy over and over again that no matter what happens, nobody's going to take Jimmy away from her.

Jimmy's father doesn't need much assuring. He pities the boy—sees him as a lost cause—and is relieved that Lisa's taking him away.

Lisa's honey stays at home with Britney. He doesn't have a job now, and winter has set in. Except for ice fishing and seal hunting, there's not much to do. Britney wants him to show her how to ice fish, and she whines and begs so much that he finally has to smack her. Ice fishing is for old people and women, and he has no desire to go. And the best time for ice fishing—right after freeze-up—has already passed.

But then he starts to pity Britney for being a girl—someone who's never going to become a great hunter or whaler. In the early afternoon twilight, he takes her out to the sea ice to fish for *iqalugaq*, Arctic cod. He carries a jig—a metal fishing lure—that's been in the storage closet for God knows how long and a ladle for scooping slush from the holes.

He doesn't have an auger to make holes in the sea ice and isn't going to borrow one. If there aren't any large tide cracks or holes made by someone else, then they'll just come back home.

Lisa's honey steps outside and shivers—he wasn't expecting the cold to get to him this much. But it's been so long since he's gone out on the ice at this time of year. Hell, he hasn't gone jigging since he was a child, when going out in the dark to ice fish was sometimes a necessity.

The ocean is two blocks away from their apartment. As they cross Beach Road, they see an elder jigging for fish in a hole she's made. Feeling ridiculous to be out here doing the same thing as the old woman, Britney's father steers her in another direction.

He finds an opening in the ice and tells Britney to scoop it clean. She gets down on her knees and scoops the ice with relish, oblivious to the cold or the thinness of the ice. He shows her how to put the *niksik*—the hook—on the line attached to the jig, and then drop it in the hole. He's forgotten to bring something to sit on, so they squat, taking turns jiggling the line up and down, side to side. Occasionally Britney scoops more ice out of the hole.

The time passes slowly, and neither of them speaks. Britney's father remembers how his own father had known every kind of fish in the Ikpuq River where his family camped, and the best spot to catch them at any time of year. He realizes that he doesn't have any idea where the *iqalugaq* are supposed to be now. The chances of catching any are slim. Finally, he asks Britney, "Do you want to go in for now?"

She shakes her head stubbornly.

"You're not worried the *nanuq* will come out?" he jokes.

Britney shakes her head and laughs. The twilight is fading, but the ice all around them shines brilliantly. Everything is silent except for the omnipresent roar of snowmachines, which fills the long Arctic winter nights.

Neither one of them can think of anything else to say. More time passes—he can't tell how much—and then he sees the line pull from the bottom.

"Bring it up, quick!" he says. Britney jerks the line with too much force, bringing up a small fish that flies off the *niksik* and across the ice. They hear it bounce, already frozen, a few yards behind them. Britney laughs and runs to look for it.

"I can't find it, Dad!"

"Never mind! We gotta go inside now." He feels as frozen as the fish. He must be getting old. They walk back towards the house.

"Look," Britney says, pointing to the old woman who's still out by her fishing hole. Five large fish that she's pulled up are lying out on the ice. The woman sees Britney watching her and calls to her, "Come and take one!"

Britney leaves her embarrassed father standing by the shore and runs to the pile of fish. They stare up at Britney blindly through yellow irises. Britney's so used to frozen fish sticks, she finds the eyes surprising. "Go ahead, take one," the woman says again.

"Thanks," Britney says, picking up the one with the smallest eyes. She runs back to her father, who waves weakly at the elder. Gently putting his arm around Britney's shoulder, he leads her back to the apartment. It'll be just him and his daughter for a little while longer, since Lisa's going to stay with Jimmy for another week in Anchorage. That's what Lisa said when she called last night, but talking on the phone made her so homesick she could hardly stand it.

Each night, Lisa sits by Jimmy's bed in the mental hospital. She hasn't been able to speak since the doctors put him on "suicide watch." When Jimmy's with the counselors during the day, she sits out in the lobby, resting her head on the back of a couch. One morning, she sees a pair of counselors guiding former Assemblyman Chuck down the hall. She looks at him, confused, but Chuck pretends not to see her. A few minutes later, she sees her half-brother Gray in the lobby. He gives her his typical condescending smile.

Lisa's Athabascan mother had Gray before she married Lisa's father. But Gray grew up with the Shoaks on the *tanik* side of his family. Lisa doesn't talk to him much outside of family events. She knows he's got a violent side and she doesn't want him around her kids.

"Gray," she says with a tired smile, getting up to hug him. He's her half-brother, after all. "What's going on?"

He's wearing his State Troopers uniform, and Lisa remembers that he's moved to Anchorage. "Just business," he says. "How are we? What's happening with Lisa's little family?"

"My son," she says with a sigh. Officer Shoak, suspecting the worst, makes a clucking noise with his tongue and tries to look sympathetic. "We had a little scare," Lisa continues.

"So did we," Officer Shoak says. "Chuck came banging on my door after dinner last night—scared the piss out of my girlfriend and her little boy."

"Oh," Lisa says.

"He was hollering about how he's gonna take Gloria back or take her boy away if she don't go back to Harow with him. I think he lost it again, you know? So I say to him, 'You can either come with me and voluntarily check yourself into the hospital, or I can bring you down to the stationhouse in handcuffs.' He ran off after that, but this morning I found him at the corporation's office and brought him here."

"Oh," Lisa says again.

"That's what we gotta do sometimes, when we're family, you know," Officer Shoak says, patting Lisa on the back. "Anyway, we'll be seeing ya."

Lisa leans back on the couch and watches her half-brother jaunt out the door. She hardly feels like they're family. She wonders if her mother feels the same way about Gray, or if her mother regrets that Gray was taken away from her.

She suddenly remembers the shock of seeing Tommy, and her sinking feeling when she realized he didn't recognize her as his mother. But maybe now it's too late for her to intrude into his life. Maybe he'll never feel any more connected to her than she does to Gray. And she's got the twins to take care of. She knows they both need her. Even if Britney doesn't show it, Lisa heard it in Britney's voice when they talked on the phone last night.

A few days later, Jimmy is discharged with a bottle of medication and a bundle of warnings. They get a taxi to the airport and Lisa buys the last two seats on the plane, which are first class. Only then does she notice it's Christmas Eve.

On the plane, across the aisle from Lisa and Jimmy, Chuck sits huddled over a stack of his corporation papers. Lisa reaches over and taps him gently on the shoulder. "Are you okay? I mean—how did you get out?"

Chuck looks around to see if anyone's listening, and then whispers, "I'm the president of the corporation, for godssakes. We own a quarter interest in that hospital. If anyone should be in there, it's Gray."

Lisa looks sympathetic, and Chuck feels encouraged. "Talk about a guy with no Iñupiat values," he adds.

"Well, Merry Christmas," Lisa says, settling back into her seat.

"Merry Christmas," Chuck says absently, turning back to his papers. If everything works out his way, he'll have the deep sea port sooner rather than later, and Shant will quit its contract with the Winters Native Corporation and sign one with his corporation.

Chapter 28- Lonely Winter

The winter of 2009-2010 is the first that Vik spends in Harow without any vacation. She didn't notice before how much winter slows everything down. Sleep seems to be a better option than anything else. Most weekends she doesn't go outside, not even to take the garbage out. She wonders whether this dull sleepiness is better or worse than cabin fever.

Almost everyone is out of town at the end of the year, when Shant starts submitting permit applications to the Community Development Department. Shant doesn't really think it needs Borough permits for a project that's technically beyond the Borough's jurisdiction, but Shant's Social Performance Coordinator recommended that they humor Gill—the recently appointed Community Development Department director—by going through the motions of applying.

Gill comes back to Harow on January 12th and realizes that the decision on Shant's applications was due two days ago. He tells the secretary to go ahead and issue the permits.

The secretary managed to do very little work under Larry's watch, and she's not interested in doing any now.

"How am I supposed to write permits? I've only been trained to arrange people's travel."

"We-ell," Gill says. "All the permitting staff is gone now. You'll be doing the same thing they always do, which is to just copy and paste from other permits."

"But we haven't had permits for offshore drilling before."

"Actually, we do," Gill says. The Borough has always supported offshore drilling within the Borough's boundaries, which go out three nautical miles from the coastline. Two companies have already built offshore islands, and the Borough gets to tax the island, the equipment, and all the oil below.

Gill rummages through the stacks of papers in Larry's old office—now his—and produces a model permit for the secretary. "You'll want to finish by this afternoon, since everything's already late."

Vik hasn't heard anything about the Shant permits. She sits under a fluorescent marijuana grow lamp at her desk to fight Seasonal Affective Disorder and tries to focus on a draft environmental impact statement for the impending deep sea port. It's too late to be a cooperating agency, but the Borough can still comment on the draft.

The proposed plan is not all that different from Project Chariot, the government's 1958 plan to build a Chukchi Sea harbor by dropping a bomb near Point Courage. Except this time, the government wants to use dynamite instead of nukes.

The phone rings. It's Larry's wife, wondering if Vik knows where Larry might be.

"What do you mean?" Vik asks, hoping Larry never mentioned anything about their quasi-rendezvous on the side of the road last fall.

"He left on his snowmachine yesterday and didn't say where he's going. I checked with Alaska Airlines, and I even called his … his cousin, but no one knows where he is. I thought he mighta asked you for advice, maybe. He always respected lawyers, I don't know, he seemed like he kinda trusted you …"

"Jesus," Vik says. "Are you serious?"

"Yeah," Mandy says weakly.

"You don't think he went out to the camp?" Vik asks.

"The weather's so bad now, it don't make sense."

"We could, uh, call the search and rescue squad," Vik suggests. The Borough's search and rescue squad is so used to going out and rescuing people that it offers free emergency locator beacons to anyone going camping in the winter.

"Oh, that would just about kill him if he had to get rescued by the Borough. I'll give him another day, and then maybe I'll drive out there."

"Want me to come with you?" Vik asks, out of voyeurism. She's more curious than worried.

"Oh no," Mandy answers. It's hard enough bringing a *tanik* out to the camp in the summer—she can't imagine trying to deal with one in the winter.

Larry didn't think about what his wife would do if he left. He didn't think of anything, really. He just got in his snowmachine and headed east along the coast.

He passes by some of the places where he used to go hunting and fishing with his grandfather. *Siniktagnailaq*—Don't Sleep Here—the place where the dogs would wine and stay up all night, even though he'd always slept like a log. His grandfather told him an *anatquq*—a shaman—had died there. Western scientists say it's just a place where methane gas comes up.

Somewhere near *Tuungaqagvik,* the Place of Devils, Larry's snow machine runs out of gas. He gets off and decides to build an igloo for shelter.

He's heard people who still go camping in the winter say that *pukaq,* the dense bottom layer of snow required for igloo building, has become too thin and soft in recent years. They're right. He spends what seems like hours trying to force *aqilluqaq,* the recent snow coverage, into some semblance of an igloo before he gives up.

He lies down in the hollow he's dug out and embraces the land, just like he did as a child. He may not have an igloo, but he's finally in the middle of his people's land. A place where there are no oil rigs or *taniks* or any reminder of Western civilization.

Larry's hand touches something hard. He picks it up and realizes it's an empty plastic bottle of motor oil. The label is bleached, but the plastic is as strong as it had been the day it was dropped here. The cap was screwed back on—a little act of neatness that did nothing to rectify the littering. He stares at it for some time, wondering how far it came only to find itself resting here, permanently. He laughs and closes his eyes.

When he opens them again, he can see bright lights flashing from the sky, coming closer and closer to the land. In the past, they would have scared him. But not now. Now, he's ready. He gets up and walks forward.

For two days, Harow hardly moves. A storm has blown in from the west and is blanketing the Arctic Slope in white. Mandy stays home, waiting. On January 23rd, the snow stops and the sun comes up for the first time since November. Mandy borrows a snowmachine from a neighbor and drives off into the whiteness with a small bag of food and supplies.

She's made the trip between Harow and her family's allotment dozens of times since she was a child. Back then, it was by sled dog. It was her job to prepare the sled. She remembers the hours of trying to slip harnesses and attach lines to the howling, restless animals, each of whom weighed nearly twice as much as she did. She remembers the fights between the dogs and the times when one lost its footing and was dragged by the others across the tundra until it choked. Mandy is not one to reminisce about the old times. The dogs would have taken forever to make it across all this unpacked snow. It barely slows the snowmachine, and within an hour she's already at the halfway point. Snowmachines may be as loud as chainsaws, but they get the job done.

As she gets further inland, the cloud cover dissipates, and she can see the giant orange sun shining on the fresh snow. It's been so long since she made the trip at this time of year, when there are no animals out. The caribou and the birds went south in the fall, and the only food to be had is whatever *aanaakliq*—broad whitefish—could be brought up from under the ice. With the sun up, the coldest and most beautiful part of the winter starts.

The first day of sun only lasts an hour and fifteen minutes, and then the Arctic Slope sinks back into twilight. Mandy has GPS to find the cabin—she could have never found it on her own in the darkness. Finding the way to the camp and home was the one thing the dogs were good at.

She gets to the cabin just before total darkness sets in. The wooden planks that Larry usually keeps on the doorway have been removed, but Larry's snowmachine isn't there. She wonders if he might have gone out for a while—maybe he's ice fishing further upriver.

She turns on her flashlight and steps through the open doorway. If Larry was in the cabin, there's no sign of him now. She shines the flashlight around the room and gasps when she realizes that two brown bears are asleep on the floor. She's surprised the snowmachine didn't wake them up. But neither has heard her, and she backs out of the cabin cautiously. She didn't think to bring a gun with her.

Mandy drives across the river to her family's old cabin, where Luther used to stay. She hasn't been there since before Luther's death.

Everything is just as it was the last time she saw it, except with another layer of dust on the wood stove. Luther's old clothes hang from a hook in the corner, and a few poptart wrappers are piled under a chair.

She half-expects Luther to come bounding in from the ice cellar, carrying a rack of caribou. She goes to the ice cellar now. No one ever removed Luther's fish, and they're aging badly. Lots of ice cellars on the Slope can't make it through the summer anymore without ice being added to insulate the meat.

Mandy climbs out of the ice cellar and gets back on her snowmachine. Maybe Larry was waiting out the storm and is already on his way home. She heads home full of hope.

Chapter 29- Arrivals and Departures

As the head of the Law Department, Bertie has to suffer through twenty or so unplanned meetings every week. On an ordinary Wednesday in February, the manager of the Iñupiat History, Culture, and Language Commission comes in to ask if the Borough would pay for Bibles for a cultural seminar put on by the commission. An hour later, the deputy director of the Health Department stops by to ask if the Borough can euthanize the director's vicious dog. Ten minutes later, the Health Department director calls to see if the Borough can put a restraining order on her husband, who owns the vicious dog. Then, a man on a snowmachine bangs on Bertie's window and asks for tax advice. When Bertie gets up to shut her office door, two high school kids come selling raffle tickets for an iPod. Bertie buys two tickets out of sympathy and throws them away as soon as the kids leave.

Just as she's about to actually start working, someone else comes in. Bertie doesn't look up from her computer until she realizes that she's being subjected to a big bear hug from the side.

"Oh, hi Lisa, I didn't realize it was you," Bertie says. "I thought it was the woman who always comes around here to sell her artwork." Bertie nods over at a giant whalebone carving of what appears to be a polar bear, standing between her inbox and the rest of the world. "I don't think I need any more right now."

"Actually I was coming to ask if you have any job openings."

"Well, let's talk about it," Bertie says, not really wanting to talk about it at all. "So how are you?"

"Better than before. My honey quit his job, but he's been going out hunting. Last week he got a ringed seal and showed Britney how to butcher it. He says he wants to go whaling this spring with my brother's crew. So he's putting food on the table, but you know all that takes money."

Bertie nods and picks at a hangnail.

Lisa continues, "And Jimmy—he's back in school and he made an A on his last math test."

"Great," Bertie says, deciding not to ask why the boy had out of school in the middle of the school year. "So, you wanted to take the legal secretary job again?"

"It could just be temporary," Lisa says. "Just to get us through spring whaling, and maybe my honey will find a construction job in the summer."

"Actually, that could work, maybe. Our secretary's about to take her maternity leave, and we're probably going to need a temp for three months."

"Oh, thank you!" Lisa says, throwing another hug on Bertie. "I can start whenever, just call me."

Bertie swallows as Lisa leaves. She wasn't actually planning to hire a temp. But then, it would be good to hire an Iñupiaq to fill the position, even if only temporarily. It's embarrassing that the Law Department never manages to have more than one Iñupiaq working there at a time.

In her office down the hall, Vik's calling Mandy. There's no answer at work, so Vik tries Mandy's cell.

"Hello?" a tired voice answers.

"Hey! It's Vik. I hadn't heard from you in a while and just wanted to make sure everything's okay."

"It's not."

"What's going on?"

"Larry's still missing. It's been a month now. I don't even know if he's alive."

"Jesus," Vik says. She wants to offer to do something, but what? She doesn't have any food to offer that would be considered decent by Iñupiat standards. She can't go out in the snow and look for Larry. As much as she likes to use Jesus as a swear word, she couldn't imagine praying to him. And there's nothing worse than the catch-all American phrase for responding to grief—*If there's anything I can do, just let me know.*

"I could stop by later if you'll be home," Vik sputters.

"Oh, no thanks," Mandy sighs. "We've got church tonight."

"Well," Vik says, "Uh, if there's anything I can do, just let me know."

"Okay," Mandy says, hanging up.

Over at the Community Development Department, Gill thinks about how annoying it is that Larry just took off without leaving any instructions, and now Gill can't even get in touch with him. Gill heard about Larry disappearing into the snow, but he's not sure he believes it. If the secretary weren't still there, Gill would have guessed that they went to live in Anchorage together.

Gill likes being the director, but he didn't realize before how much work it involves. All of the stacks of paper that Larry kept in his office are still there, only now there are many more. The worst part of it is that he won't be able to go whaling in the spring. He's gone out whaling every season for forty years, since he was six years old. But this spring there'll be all kinds of meetings with Shant and the Harow Native Corporation and the state and the federal government. The mayor told Gill he'd need to be there for all of them.

When March comes, instead of cutting trail for his *umiaq*—his whaling boat, Gill is meeting with Nelson, the Public Works director, and Chuck to talk about whether the Borough should pay for the onshore infrastructure needed for the deep sea port.

"Right now, all of that land is owned by the corporation," Chuck explains. "And of course the corporation could build the docks all by itself, but then, you, the Borough, the stakeholder, wouldn't get to play a role. And I assume you'll want to enter into an agreement with us to make it a public port, subject to your taxing authority."

"Doesn't your federal grant require you to make it a public port?" Nelson asks skeptically.

"I'm not sure," Chuck says, doodling on a folder.

"Could we see the grant?" Nelson asks.

"Actually, I think it's private, sort of like a contract," Chuck says.

"Actually, I think it's subject to the Freedom of Information Act," Nelson says. "So if you don't show us, we can just get it from the federal government."

Nelson keeps his left hand in his pocket, as if he might pull out a pistol. Chuck's doodling gets bigger and more furious.

Gill doesn't know who's more difficult to deal with, Chuck or Nelson. At least Chuck's not going on anymore about Iñupiat values. If he starts that again, Gill's going to remind him of Value Number Seven, Conflict Avoidance.

"It seems like the port's a good idea for the Borough, isn't it?" Gill asks. "And you guys are going to apply for a permit at some point, right?"

Nelson smiles at Gill condescendingly. He advised the mayor not to make Gill the director of Community Development, but the mayor did it anyway. Now the mayor and the rest of the Borough are going to have to live with the mayor's failure to take Nelson's advice.

"That's not the question, Gill," Nelson says. "The question is the proper use of Borough money. You may be aware that in the past, the Borough's administration has had some problems with this." It's obvious to everyone in the room that Nelson is referring to Gill's cousin, Ernie Whitehead. Every person in that administration but Nelson went to jail for fraudulent capital improvement contracts and embezzlement.

"And the other question is whether this port is really just going to be a staging area for Shant's offshore drilling, in which case, perhaps Shant should be paying for some of the infrastructure," Nelson continues. "I don't suppose you have a contract with Shant to provide support services?"

Nelson heard that Shant was pulling out of its contract with the Winters Native Corporation for onshore support, and Nelson can only assume that Chuck and the Harow Native Corporation have something to do with it.

"Nelson," Chuck says, "our corporation's contracts are proprietary. You know quite well that Congress passed the Alaska Native Claims Settlement Act to empower our people to build a future using the American corporate system. That's exactly what our corporation is doing. And under that system, our contracts are proprietary."

"What are you hoping to get out of the Borough, Chuck?" Nelson asks.

"I'm just offering you an opportunity to invest in the Iñupiat future."

The *tanik* director of Public Works giggles and then covers his mouth. He's only been with the Borough for a year, and still finds its personalities funny.

"I'll take it back to the mayor for his consideration," Nelson says, effectively ending the conversation.

"Where is the mayor, anyway?" Chuck asks.

"He's out getting ready for whaling, Chuck," Gill says.

Nelson restrains from adding, "while he still can." With Shant drilling and the federal government dynamiting a port in the middle of the whales' path, he doesn't see how the Iñupiat can keep on whaling around here. He figures that all he can do now is help them manage their money. He's given up on trying to make them understand that they're now part of the United States, so that there's no escaping federal law.

The next battle with the federal government is going to be the federally controlled spring-summer migratory bird hunt, which officially starts on April 1st every year. Since the 2008 shooting of the endangered Steller's eiders, the feds have made it their business to patrol the bird hunt.

Vik suggests to the Borough's Wildlife and Subsistence Department director that some of her staff go out with the federal agents and be there to intervene in case of a conflict between an agent and a hunter.

"Oh no, no, we can't do that," the director says, remembering that Bertie said the same thing last year and thinking about how these Outsiders just don't get it. "If we did that, then everyone would think we were part of the same agency. It's bad enough as it is ... I had hunters calling me last year complaining about our agents bothering them out on the tundra!"

"If everyone's confused anyway, you might as well send your staff out with the agents," Vik says. "Your staff could wear their Borough jackets, so they'd look different."

"I think maybe the problem is that we both have 'Wildlife' as part of our names. I was thinking of asking the mayor to take the 'Wildlife' off of our name so we could just be the 'Subsistence Department.' That's what our mission really comes down to. And it would cut down on the applications we get from Greenpeace biologists."

"But if your department could work with the federal agents, maybe they would start to trust that you can enforce laws without the agents having to be there. And then maybe the agents would go away."

The director sighs. "The feds are never going to trust us, and we don't trust them. I think that's just the way it is."

"Well," Vik says, "maybe 2010 will be another year that the Steller's eiders decide not to nest here … maybe they'll move on and the agents' undies won't be in such a bundle."

"Actually, there's a good chance that they'll nest this year," the director says. "There's not much snow and there's been a lot of lemmings, which the owls and jaegers will eat instead of eider eggs."

Vik nods and waits for the director to finish up and go away.

Within a week, the Steller's eiders and all the other birds start flying in. Britney watches them fly across the sky from the vantage of the ice, where she's out making coffee and doing the grunt work for the Atkoot crew. Last week, Lisa asked Mandy if her honey and Britney could go out with the Atkoot crew for spring whaling, since her honey wasn't getting along with her family's crew, and since …

Lisa didn't say it, but they both knew that the other "since" was that Larry has never come home. Larry was the co-captain of his father's whaling crew for nineteen years. Since Larry's father turned eighty a few years ago, it was really Larry who was leading the crew.

Larry's father welcomed the help, even if it was from a man who hadn't gone whaling in years and a young girl who'd never gone at all. He said to Britney's father, "If you're willing to take the lead on cutting the trail through the ice, then you can have a seat on the boat, and your daughter can help out at the camp on the ice."

Britney is disappointed that she wasn't invited to sit in the boat. But being out on the ice is better than staying in the kitchen and making Eskimo donuts, and her mom is even letting her skip school. The work is easy, and she can hunt for eiders when she's not working.

"Just don't show up in town with a Steller's eider," someone warns her, "or the feds'll get ya."

Britney already knows that the Iñupiat don't really eat Steller's eiders—only the common and king eiders are good to eat. She doesn't know exactly how to tell the different kinds of eiders apart, but she's not worried about it. Even if she accidentally shoots a Steller's eider, they can cook it out on the ice and no one in town will ever know.

It's a bad year for spring whaling. There aren't many open spaces in the ice where the crew can see the whales passing, and sometimes the weather is so rough they have to move the camp closer to shore. In a week's time, the crew brings the boat out only twice.

Some of the whalers go home each night to take showers and sleep in their own beds. But Britney's willing to stay in a tent on the ice for as long as they'll let her. She loves not taking a shower, and she doesn't even miss her TV and cell phone. A couple of the whalers show her a better way to hold her rifle, and they point out which kinds of birds she should aim at. The only problem is getting the bird to land in a good place. Some of the birds she shoots fall in the open water, some on ice that's too thin to walk on. Others fall so far away they're not worth going after. Towards the end of the week, Britney finally manages to shoot an eider that falls along the trail her father helped carve.

She lets out a little cheer and runs down the trail to retrieve the bird. A man coming from the shore on a snowmachine beats her there. Britney waves, assuming it's one of the whalers coming back to the camp. "I finally got one!" she yells.

The man picks up the bird, looks at it carefully, and snaps a picture of it with his camera. Britney realizes that he's not a whaler.

"Did you just shoot that?" he asks.

"Yeah," Britney says.

"Are you aware that you just shot an endangered Steller's eider?"

Britney sees the patch on the man's jacket that says, "U.S. Fish and Wildlife Service agent." She doesn't answer him.

In the past, the agents never came out on the ice. But this year, with hardly anyone shooting at Duck Camp, this agent has decided that he better come out on the ice if he wants to catch anybody.

"I didn't hear you," the agent says.

"'Cause I didn't say anything," Britney says, frowning.

"Looks like you really don't know what you're doing. And I don't like the way you're holding that gun right now. I'm going to have to ask you to hand it over to me."

Britney looks back towards the camp, hoping one of the whalers will see them and come over. She feels the agent pulling the gun from her. She grabs it tighter, exclaiming, "It's mine!"

"Hand it over!" the agent barks.

Britney moves her hands to get a better grip. Inevitably, the gun releases its bullet into the agent's shoulder.

The agent and Britney both scream. Britney's father runs towards them.

"The gun just went off," Britney wails.

"Calm down," he says, radioing for help from the Borough's search and rescue squad.

"There's been an accident, can you send the chopper out here quick?"

"It's broke right now," the voice on the radio says.

"I thought the Borough has two helicopters."

"The other's broke, too, down in Houston waiting for spare parts. They can't get any parts now, you know, that stuff's all being sent to Afghanistan. What's the problem, anyway?"

"One of the feds just got shot."

"Serves him right," the voice on the radio says, and then there's just static.

Britney's father looks at the radio, then at the bleeding agent, then at Britney. "You go back to the camp and stay with the whalers," he says. "I'm gonna take this guy's snowmachine and drive him to the hospital."

He maneuvers the sagging body of the agent onto the snowmachine, sits behind him, and drives back to town as fast as the machine can go.

In a minute, the snowmachine is out of sight, and there's nothing left next to Britney except her gun and a pool of blood. Britney feels like she's the one bleeding. She knows this is much worse than shooting the polar bear, because it's going to screw things up for everyone. She runs the entire four miles back home.

Mandy has been at home all day, making Eskimo donuts to bring out to the Atkoot crew. The kitchen is quiet except for the radio, and the house is dark.

Two months have passed since Larry left. Two unbearable months. She can't think about the future without him, but she can't tell herself that he's coming home.

When Mandy's friends and family call her, they avoid mentioning his name. Some of them think it's for the better or even God's will. After all, he cheated on her with his cousin. And for a while, Mandy was actually thinking of leaving him. But she decided to come back from Anchorage and stay in the house Larry built until she died. If Larry wanted to leave, that was up to him.

Larry used to tell Mandy his grandfather's story about the brave men who would decide to leave their villages and wander out onto the tundra all on their own, never to come back. Mandy laughed when Larry talked about the "brave men." A man who wanted to wander out on the tundra these days would just be plain crazy. No one she knows has the skills to live in total wilderness, let alone by himself.

One night, feeling foolish but desperate, she tries the old method of stretching a line across the living room and hanging Larry's boots on it. The movement of the boots is supposed to tell whether her husband is dead or alive. In the morning, the boots are still in the same place. She can't remember what this is supposed to mean, but she knows in her heart that Larry's dead. Last night she saw him in her dream at a distance, running with a bear and then turning into a bear. He didn't stop to talk to her. He moved on, leaving her behind.

Mandy keeps the VHF radio on day and night, waiting for someone to report finding his body. Surely he would have wanted to be buried here in Harow next to his family, and have a Christian funeral. But there's no news about Larry, just an announcement that the Whitehead crew caught a whale. They always catch at least one, every season. Larry used to say it was because they don't stop to help any other crew that strikes a whale—they just keep on going after their own whale.

The next thing she hears on the VHF is someone calling for help because one of the feds has been shot out on the ice. She wonders what a federal agent was doing on the ice. *Taniks* never go out there except the Borough's biologists, who are in charge of measuring and assessing the whales after they're landed.

A day later, Mandy hears that the feds are shutting down the migratory bird hunt in Harow, and that anyone found in possession of a migratory bird will be arrested. She shakes her head, thinking that the people of Harow are going to have to have another *Duck-in*.

Vik sees the news about the shooting and the closure in the online Alaska news, which she scours daily in search of writing material.

"Jesus!" Vik says to Lisa, who's been working as a temporary secretary since March. "Did you hear that a Fish and Wildlife agent got shot and now they're closing down the hunt?"

Lisa sighs, ignoring Vik's use of the Lord's name in vain. She sits down in one of Vik's office chairs. "Yeah," she says. "Britney's the one who shot him."

"Shit!" Vik says. "On purpose?"

"Oh, no, no. It was an accident—the gun went off when he tried to jerk it away from her. She shot a Steller's eider, I think. Anyway, my honey drove him to the hospital, and they medevacked him to Anchorage. Last I heard he's out of the hospital, but I just feel awful about it."

Lisa looks like she might cry, and Vik feels obliged to indulge her in a bear hug.

"Is Britney okay?" Vik asks.

"She's shook up, all right, but she'll snap out of it. Better her than Jimmy."

"Was Jimmy there when it happened?"

"No, he's in school. He don't like hunting. I was letting Britney skip school for whaling season. She really need to, you know, get in touch with her culture. And now ..."

"Shit," Vik says again. The phone on her desk rings, and she picks it up. It's the director of the Wildlife and Subsistence Department.

"I just wanted to let you know," the director says tearfully, "that since the feds closed down the hunt I've advised my staff and the mayor to have another *Duck-in*. They can't come up here and do this to us!"

"Do you really want to advise people to do something that might get them put in jail?" Vik asks. "I mean, wouldn't it be better just to advise them to go to their camps out of town and shoot birds there?"

"You don't understand, Vik. You can just go to the grocery and buy your vegetables or whatever, but this is our food. And in the words of my great uncle, 'Hunger is not bound by law.'"

"Um, okay. Thanks for letting me know. I'll tell Bertie."

Bertie is already in a meeting with Nelson and the mayor about the hunting closure.

"If we have a *Duck-in,*" the mayor is asking, "can the Law Department defend anyone who's arrested in court?"

"Well," Bertie says, pulling nervously at her hangnails. "It's kind of like with the caribou case in Point Courage—there would have to be a finding that the defense is for a public purpose in the Borough's best interest."

"Is mass civil disobedience really in the Borough's interest?" Nelson asks, with a noise that might be a snort.

Bertie looks at him skeptically. "What do you think Martin Luther King and the lunch counter sit-ins were?"

Nelson raises an eyebrow. "So you're saying it's a civil right to shoot endangered birds."

"No one's saying we should shoot endangered birds, Nelson," the mayor says. "Our people never ate Steller's eiders. But we need the king and common eiders and the *nigliq* and yellow-billed loon. It think—I think this could be cultural genocide if we just accept the closure without doing anything. Alaska Natives really look to the Arctic Slope Borough for support on things like this, they know that our congressmen will never be willing to fight these battles for us."

"Well," Nelson says, "it sounds like the Law Department is going to be very busy."

Bertie swallows. She didn't mean to suggest that a *Duck-in* would be in the public interest, but Nelson's attitude pisses her off. Bertie had great-great-grandparents who were slaves. She can identify with the concept of cultural genocide. Nelson can't.

Over at the Harow Native Corporation, Chuck is getting worried about the idea of a *Duck-in*. What if the Fish and Wildlife Service decides to retaliate by designating Harow as some sort of critical habitat for birds, where no new development can take place? It could kill his deep sea port and maybe even Shant's drilling. Or what if—he doesn't know how much all these federal agencies are connected—what if the feds decide not to give the corporation the grant for the port after all? The first payment is supposed to come through this summer, but he doesn't really trust the feds enough to count on it.

Chuck decides that the best way to handle the situation is to declare a big fat corporate dividend right now, in the middle of the year, so all the shareholders—anyone in Harow who's at least a quarter Iñupiat—will go off to Anchorage on a shopping trip. That'll definitely distill the tension for a while, and by the time people get back to Harow, maybe they'll have forgotten about the whole thing.

The corporation's board is skeptical.

"You want to declare a dividend that's twice the normal amount, when we just gave out the annual dividends a few months ago?" the chairman asks him. "Why?"

"I guess by now you've all heard about the bird hunting closure," Chuck says.

"What does that have to do with it?"

"How are our people going to feed themselves if they can't go out hunting at Duck Camp or anywhere in Harow?" Chuck asks. "I mean, you and I are lucky, we have jobs, we can afford to buy food from the store, and we can afford gas and four-wheelers to, uh, get out to our camps and hunt there. But for a lot of folks around here, the Duck Camp is all they got. And now it's closed. If we don't help them out with some money for food and gas, what are they going to do? How are they going to be able to stay in Harow? It could be the start of cultural genocide ..."

Chuck stops. He didn't think he'd need to take it that far. Most of the board seats are up for election next month, and he thought that the directors would be more than willing to give out a dividend that would boost their chances of reelection.

In the end, the measure passes in a rare split vote—normally boards and commissions on the Arctic Slope like to vote unanimously. Chuck is relieved. The thought occurs to him that the dividends might boost his own popularity, in case he ever wants to run for mayor.

Within a week of the dividend announcement, about half the town has booked tickets for Anchorage and beyond. Chuck's plan seems to have worked—talk of a *Duck-in* is overtaken by talk of shopping trips and new snowmachines, four-wheelers, and guns. Every flight going out of Harow is full.

Officer Shoak comes up to Harow two weeks later on a flight packed with shopping bags. There was a complaint filed against him for police brutality, and the State Chief of Police told him last week that he was fired. He applied for a job with the Anchorage Police, but they wouldn't take him because of his record. If anyone would take him, it'd be the

Arctic Slope Borough Police Department. He figures it's worth a try, anyway.

Gloria left Officer Shoak around the time of the complaint. He promised to marry her if she would stay with him, even though they both knew he didn't really mean it. She laughed at him, and told him he was a loser like his brother. By the time Officer Shoak left Anchorage, she'd already found some schmuck from Arizona to move in with.

Officer Shoak has managed to take the whole thing in stride. After all, in Anchorage, he's an anonymous nobody. In Harow, he's somebody, even if not everybody there likes him. They all know him, and they know when to get out of his way.

The Borough police chief rolls his eyes when he sees Shoak coming through the door.

"Guess you want your job back," he says.

"I was thinking about it," Officer Shoak says.

"Well, get with the secretary and fill out the paperwork, 'cause I got a bunch of work for you. A federal agent got shot week before last, and the feds are on our ass to look into the case. Get the file from the secretary."

The next day, Officer Shoak puts on his Arctic Slope Borough police uniform and bullet-proof vest on with relish. He takes a car out to the Iñupiat Housing Authority apartments and finds Lisa at home on her lunch break. The kids are finished with the school year already and are bowling in the living room with their new wii.

"How are we?" Officer Shoak asks.

"Oh hi, Gray," Lisa says, giving him a stiff hug. "What are you doing here?"

"Got my old job back. My first assignment is to check out what happened with this, uh, shooting. Can I ask Britney some questions?"

"As long as I can be here with her."

"Where's your, uh, honey?"

"He got his old job back with the housing authority."

Britney pauses her game and comes to see what's going on.

"He just wants to ask you a few questions about … what happened when you went whaling."

Britney shrugs. "We didn't catch anything. I left early, anyway."

"Tell us what happened with the Fish and Wildlife agent, Britney," Officer Shoak says, taking out his pen and notebook.

"Oh that. This guy just showed up outta nowhere and said I shot an eider and he didn't like the way I was holding my gun. Then he tried to pull it outta my hands and it went off somehow and shot him in the shoulder. It was all bloody and he screamed like a baby. Then my dad came and took him to the hospital and I went home."

"Did you pull the trigger?" Officer Shoak asks.

"No," Britney says. "Not on purpose, anyway. I don't really remember."

"Were you trying to kill him?"

"No way!" Britney says. She turns to her mom, and asks, "Can I finish my game now?"

Officer Shoak closes the notebook and says, "I'll come back later with a few questions for your dad."

"Do you, uh, want to stay for lunch?" Lisa asks. "I got pickled *maktak*."

Officer Shoak smiles. "If you're going to bribe me, sis, come up with something better than pickled *maktak*."

He whistles as he jaunts out the door. It's June already, and a few patches of grass are starting to come up through the mud and remnants of snow.

Mandy is startled to see the grass. It reminds her that almost half a year has passed since Larry's been gone, even though everything in the house is just as it was on the day he left. She hasn't even emptied the ashtray with Larry's last cigarette butt.

She decides to hold a memorial service for Larry. Maybe after that she'll have the strength to clean out the house and put his things away. She can't remember the last time there was a memorial service in Harow, though. There's always just the funeral at the Presbyterian Church, followed by the burial at the old cemetery by the high school or the new one on the other side of the airport.

Mandy plans the service so it'll be just like a funeral, except without a body. The things Larry held dearest—a bow and arrow that belonged to his grandfather, his first mukluks, a bit of scrimshawed baleen, and some old photos—will be buried under a cross at the new cemetery. Then, she'll take all the other reminders of his existence, except for a few pictures, and give them away.

When the day comes, she's nervous that no one will show up. A lot of people are still in Anchorage, or out at their camps. She gets to the Presbyterian Church early and sits in the first row with her eyes closed.

It never occurred to her to pray to God for Larry to come back. Of course, she believes in Jesus, the same as Larry did, but praying is no comfort. She realizes that she hasn't prayed since their son died.

Mandy keeps her eyes closed as people trickle into the church. No one approaches her except Vik, who doesn't have enough sense to refrain from interrupting someone who appears to be praying. Vik might not have come at all, except she had made the PowerPoint slide show for the service.

"Hey," Vik says, touching Mandy's hand. "The church is really filling up! I think this is going to be a good, uh, service."

Mandy nods without saying anything. "I'll just go make sure the projector's warmed up," Vik says, tip-toeing away.

Lisa and the twins come up to Mandy after Vik is out of the way, and Lisa locks Mandy in a side-bear hug. Then she sits down with the twins, whispering to them to turn off their cell phones. Lisa's cousin is coming up to her with William. Lisa hasn't seen him since the day he came to the house and took the gun away from Jimmy. She feels dizzy, wondering if he'll say something to her and Jimmy.

Lisa's cousin is whispering to William, "It's time you met your real *aka*—your grandmother—Aka Mandy."

Mandy looks at them, confused.

Lisa's cousin explains, "Your son. This is his son, from ..." she looks at Lisa, who's looking at them with tears in her eyes. William is looking out the window, embarrassed.

Mandy looks at Lisa, amazed. "But what happened, then?"

Lisa's cousin says simply, "I adopted him. His name is William."

Lisa can't hold herself back anymore, and traps William in a giant hug. "I told you," she whispered.

"Oh thank God," Mandy blurts out, meaning it. "I got something left." She puts her arms around Lisa and William and bawls.

Outside the church, Chuck sees all the parked cars and wonders whose funeral it is. He hasn't heard about anyone dying, but he's been so out of touch lately, going to Anchorage and Seattle. The important thing is that he hasn't heard any talk around town of a *Duck-in*. As far as he knows, the federal grant for the port is still coming through.

No one has sued over the port so far. Chuck figures that the environmentalists are too focused on Shant's drilling this summer to think of anything else. And the Borough seems to have lost interest in suing anyone these days. Before, the mayor had joined the environmentalists in suing the feds about the Beaufort Sea oil and gas lease sales. But he didn't join in the recent suits brought over oil and gas in the Chukchi Sea, or over Shant's plan to drill in the Beaufort Sea this summer.

Chuck is still waiting to hear from the mayor as to whether the Borough will share the costs of building the port, although he's pretty sure that the mayor will play ball.

Chuck walks along the shore, imagining what the port and all the docks will look like. Most of the ice has melted for the summer, and the slush left behind is just starting to dry up. The shore is a mixture of slush, sand, and gravel, with the occasional piece of driftwood embedded in the sand. Bits of trash blow into the water and wash up onto the shore again.

Chuck hasn't walked along the shore since he was a child, when he used to look for washed up ivory. Sometimes he found pieces of mammoth tusks. Once he found an entire walrus skull that he sold to a tourist from the Lower 48. Back then, Beach Road was farther from the water and there was hardly any traffic on it. Walking along the beach was a solitary experience.

Now, so much of the beach has eroded that there's not much land between the water and the road. Four-wheelers speed over the sand to avoid the road traffic. At high tide, the water comes up almost to the road in some places.

Chuck hasn't read over all the details of the port construction, but he understands the basic idea. The dynamiting will start as soon as all the federal and state permits come through. Then they'll have to bolster the shore with sandbags and cement armoring. The docks will be a state-of-the-art design that can withstand fall storms, Arctic winters, and the slowly melting permafrost.

A woman on a four-wheeler with a baby hanging on her back breezes by Chuck. He thinks of Gloria and his kid—the kid he has yet to meet. He might never meet the kid now. He might never talk to Gloria again. The last he heard, she ditched Gray and moved to Arizona with her new boyfriend.

It shouldn't have been such a big deal to Chuck. He had two kids with the wife who left him. He doesn't see those kids, either. His wife got full custody and some sort of protection order to keep him from coming around. Not that he really misses those kids. The boy looks too much like Gray, and the girl was always the kind of kid who cried for anything and nothing at all. He never tried to get visitation rights.

Chuck sees the bloated, headless body of a walrus a little ways in front of him. It's cut into on the right side, and some of the intestines have come out. But all the meat is still there, slowly rotting on the beach. He stands over the walrus and grimaces. He can't imagine eating something like that. It's fine to eat a little *maktak* on the holidays, but he'd just as soon leave most of his ancestors' eating habits in the past.

Chuck walks on a little farther until he's standing at the exact center of where the port will meet the shore. Even if it turns out that there's no oil and gas out in the ocean, ships will still be coming through on their way to Europe and Asia. Chuck sees the port, more than anything else, as the future of his people. And he, Chuck, is the one who'll bring it to life.

The cars are starting to pull away from the church now. Many of us are headed to Larry's house, not really sure where to go after a memorial service. Vik goes back to the office. She's surprised when Lisa comes in an hour later, since most of the Iñupiat take at least a half-day off on funeral days.

"You're really putting in some hours!" Vik says to Lisa. "I thought you were only going to work here for a couple of months. I mean, not that I don't like having you work here."

Lisa exhales. "That federal agent who got shot said he's gonna sue us. I gotta hire a lawyer now, so I gotta keep working."

"Seriously? Geez, there's only one private lawyer in town. And he's an idiot. Are you going to hire him? You'd be better off representing yourself."

"Really?"

"Yeah, you wouldn't believe how dumb you can be and still be allowed to practice law in this state."

"I think I better hire a lawyer anyway …"

"Ask Bertie to represent you. She'll do it for free, just tell her it's all about civil rights. She'd be glad to stick it to The Man."

Lisa sighs, but then her eyes brighten and she says, "My son is home."

Vik heard they stuffed Jimmy in a mental hospital for a while. "Yeah? Is he back in school?"

"I mean my first son," Lisa says. "William."

"Ooohhhh," Vik says, thinking about how incredible the fertility rate on the Arctic Slope is. She doesn't know any local female over thirty who doesn't have at least two kids.

"He was in Anchorage—he got adopted," Lisa explains. "Now he's grown up but he came back to live in Harow. He got a job with the Housing Authority. He took the twins to the gym last night and showed them how to shoot hoops."

"Nice," Vik says. She doesn't know how to relate to people with kids, much less people whose kids were adopted by someone else and then came back.

"So, uh, what do you think about all this stuff with Shant and Harow Native Corporation losing their equipment?" Vik changes the subject. The oil company is getting set up to drill in the Beaufort Sea. Last week, a vessel came to the as-of-yet-non-existent Harow dock to unload some spill response equipment there. Workmen were supposed to haul the equipment to the Harow Native Corporation's hanger near the airport. But a little ways down the road, the trailer with the equipment detached from the truck. The trailer slid off Beach Road, down the short beach, and into the sea water. The workmen spent the rest of the day fishing for the equipment.

"It's crazy," Lisa says. "You know, before everything used to be so simple. I remember when I was a kid and the axle on our truck broke way out by Duck Camp, and my uncle just replaced it with caribou bones!"

"Hmmm," Vik says. "You know Shant's supposed to start drilling next week already? The Harow Corporation is supposed to be helping with the shore-based operations. Can you believe it?"

"Oh, I don't know," Lisa says. "I really don't know anything about drilling. We just gotta hope they know what they're doing, I guess."

"Hmmm," Vik says again. She has her doubts that anyone but the environmentalists and people like old Luther Ericsen know how much Shant doesn't know what it's doing.

Shant promised to drill two wells in only 75 days, so it wouldn't have to get a major air pollution permit, just a minor one. But the 75 days doesn't allow for any extra time in the event that something goes wrong with one of the wells. Shant's contingency plan says that the possibility of something going wrong with the wells is so remote as to not even be worth considering. The federal agency in charge of approving the plan agreed. It approved Shant's plan to bring a couple trailers full of boom and dispersant spray, one of which fell in the water, instead of the well capping equipment that would be needed if there were a well blowout. Apparently, this is okay by the Borough, or else it would have joined in the suit that the environmentalists brought against the government for approving Shant's plan.

Vik knows that Bertie shares her opinion about the stupidity of Shant's plan. But no one in the Mayor's Office seems to listen to Bertie these days. And certainly no one is going to listen to Vik. She was instructed her first day in the office to never contact the mayor, and to follow the chain of command at all times. Completely disempowered, Vik has been devoting more and more work time to her novel. She plans to have it finished in another month.

"I'm resigning in August," Vik says to Bertie the next day. "I'm giving you more than a month's notice, so you can get a head start on finding someone else."

"Okay," Bertie says, with a helpless laugh. Vik has already exceeded the average stay for Law Department employees by sixteen months. "That's the way it goes, I guess."

After Vik goes back to her office, Bertie sits at her desk and stares out the window. She's the only person in the Law Department who has a window by her desk, and she wonders if this is a factor in the high turnover rate. Bertie always feels a sense of gratitude when she looks out her window, knowing that she's safe inside the office no matter the weather.

Outside, the sky is overcast, and there's a light breeze. It could be 12:00 noon or 12:00 midnight—both look the same this time of year.

A week later on the Fourth of July, the sky is still the same, except there are people outside to appreciate it. Most of us are huddled in the muddy area between the sea and the lagoons, which is now covered with ethnic food booths. There are Eskimo donuts and Samoan donuts, Filipino noodles and Thai noodles, and a smattering of hamburgers of questionable quality. A table features entries in the Sailor Boy Pilot Bread cracker contest—trays of crackers smeared with people's favorite recipes. This year's most popular recipe is caribou-blueberry ice cream with Twinky bits in it.

There's no music or official games. Kids on bikes do wheelies around potholes in the street, and kids on four-wheelers zip up and down the beach. A little ways down the shore, workers are laying cement next to where the docks will be erected. It'll be the only cemented area in Harow besides the airport and the basketball court that the Coast Guard put in two years ago. The corporation isn't going to start building the docks themselves until after the dynamite blast that hollows out the port.

"I never thought they'd go ahead with putting those docks right here in Harow," Mandy says to Lisa and William.

"It'll change things for sure," Lisa says. "We'll be able to ship cars and things here much easier."

"But all that traffic will be coming through the Arctic," Mandy says.

"Harow's gotta do something for itself after all this oil and gas passes," William says. "I'm lucky I got a job now, plenty people don't and plenty more won't after they get all the oil out the ocean."

They've eaten their fill of everything that's for sale in the stands, and William is getting restless. He says goodbye to his mother and grandmother and goes back home to watch T.V.

"Do you think he's happy here?" Mandy asks Lisa after he's gone.

"Oh, I guess so," Lisa says. "I don't know, 'cause I can't imagine living anywhere else. But some of them who come back from Anchorage get really bored here."

Mandy was thinking about leaving but changed her mind when she learned she had a grandson in Harow. She wants William to know who he is and who his ancestors were. She's been making the effort to invite him and Lisa every time there's a holiday or some reason for eating a big meal. Lisa's honey and daughter never come, but Lisa's little boy usually does. He really looks up to his big brother.

Even if William weren't here, Mandy has to admit that she doesn't really have anywhere else to go. She's never been anywhere but Anchorage, and then only for a few days. Harow is home, no matter how hard life here can be at times.

Chapter 30- Blowout

For the last year, Gill has been building a new home on the lot where he'd ended up building his greenhouse. It's not that he really needs a bigger house. He only has partial custody of two of his kids—most of the time they live with their mothers. But he's decided he wants his own place away from the property with the ice cellar, which isn't entirely his. He has sixteen brothers and sisters, and ever since his dad died, there's been a lot of fighting over who would get what.

Gill has title to only part of where his old house is. The rest of the property is "restricted property" that was granted to Gill's father. "Restricted property" is held in trust for its Eskimo owner by the Bureau of Indian Affairs, and as long as the owner doesn't sell it, he doesn't have to pay property taxes. But when the owner dies, it takes the Bureau decades to handle the probate. Gill wanted to buy out the property and just pay whatever taxes he had to pay, but his brothers and sisters wouldn't allow it. They were sure the ice cellar would fall into the hands of a *tanik*, who would close it in.

So Gill gave up on the restricted property and let one of his brothers take over the house there. Gill's new house will be nicer than the old one, anyway, and it'll have its own ice cellar.

Now that the mayor's term is close to ending, Gill has lots time to work on the house. He hasn't had to go to any big meetings lately, and no one expects him to come in at a certain time. He's hired a couple of *tanik* planners based in Anchorage to do most of the office work, and once a week he just mails them whatever stacks of paper have accumulated on his desk.

In July, the house is finished. Gill is pretty impressed with the way it turned out. There's none of the old painted-over wooden paneling that most Harow houses have. All of the windows are big, and they open. The cabinets have actual handles on them, and the carpet is the only one in town that doesn't look like it's been ripped out of a Lower 48 dentist's office.

But it's too quiet. He really notices the absence of his last girlfriend, who left him for the brother that moved into Gill's old house. He almost misses her.

Gill gets high-speed internet and starts looking around online. He won't make the mistake of getting some Russian bride again ... no, he'll get an American.

He finds a girl in Arizona who seems to have some promise. Her name is Glory, and she says she's been to Harow before. Gill doesn't know if she's telling the truth or not, but at least she knows something about Harow. She even knows about the Whitehead family. She talks about how much she wants to come to Harow and be with Gill, if only he'll send her a ticket.

Glory hasn't sent Gill a picture of herself, and they've only talked once on the phone. But he figures he's got nothing to lose by getting her a ticket to come up and see him. On a Thursday afternoon, he transfers 30,000 of his Alaska Airline miles to the account of Glory Johnson. She says she'll be with him in a week.

Officer Shoak is likewise single and restless. He doesn't so much need a woman as he needs something to get his adrenaline pumping. The case with Lisa's kid and the shot federal agent has deteriorated into a run-of-the-mill gun accident. Officer Shoak hates to waste his time working on a case where there's no deliberate shooting or drug/booze bust involved.

He knows that the bootleggers in Harow get sloppy, and that's when he catches them. When he has the time, he'll wait at the airport or post office to see who's picking up packages. Chances are, a package will have been damaged during shipping, and the booze will be leaking out.

Officer Shoak is at his airport post on a Tuesday when the Thai owner of Harow's only massage parlor arrives to pick up a large cardboard box. It's not leaking, but something about the whole thing doesn't look right to Officer Shoak. He hovers over the nervous Thai man and scribbles down the return address. Back at the office, Officer Shoak runs a search on the address and comes up with a liquor store from the Lower 48.

He manages to track down the judge later that evening to get a search warrant. Then he drives over to the massage parlor around 10 p.m. to see what he can seize.

Just as he's driving up, a man walks out the door holding a grocery bag with two bottles of whiskey in it. Officer Shoak lets the man get in his car and make it halfway down the street. Then he turns on his siren, speeds down the street after the man, and arrests him. After handcuffing the arrestee to the grate in the police vehicle, Officer Shoak goes back to the massage parlor to arrest the Thai bootlegger.

No one answers the door when he knocks. Without bothering to turn the knob, Officer Shoak kicks the door in. He appreciates how reliably degenerate housing on the Arctic Slope is.

The large cardboard box Officer Shoak saw earlier is sitting right inside the *qanichaq*—the Arctic entry. He pulls out a switchblade knife and cuts into it. Inside are ten more bottles of whiskey.

"What else do we have in here?" Officer Shoak asks the quivering Thai bootlegger, who came to the door when he heard it being kicked in. "Marijuana? Meth?"

Officer Shoak looks up at the sign on the wall, which says, "Thai Message Parlour." "Prostitutes?" he adds.

"No, no, nothing," the Thai bootlegger says.

"It's a shame you're going to have to go to jail for twelve sorry bottles of cheap liquor," Officer Shoak says, handcuffing the Thai bootlegger and throwing him in the back of the police vehicle with the purchaser.

It's especially a shame that there was no violence involved, and that the street value of the contraband was so low. The week before, another officer intercepted a package containing three and a half pounds of marijuana worth nearly $24,000. Officer Shoak figures that a fresh bottle of whiskey could go for $100, but these bottles, which smell vaguely like Thai food, won't be worth more than $50 a piece.

In another hour Officer Shoak's shift is over, and the sun has just come out after being in the clouds for a solid week. It's August 1st, and the sun has one more day to circle the cloudy Arctic sky before it can set.

Officer Shoak isn't paying attention to the sun. Like almost all the windows in Harow, his are covered in aluminum foil to block out the light. He hangs up his weapons belt, turns off his police radio, and turns on the VHF radio. The Iñupiat have a general policy that no one's supposed to get on the radio while drunk, and no cursing is allowed, but the policy is often disregarded. Officer Shoak tunes his radio to Channel 53, which is sometimes used by whalers from Kusoq but more often used by drunk teenage girls looking for love.

The radio is quiet for now. He turns on the T.V. for background noise and falls asleep on the couch.

Sometime after 2 a.m., he hears screaming that doesn't sound like his familiar teenage girls. It's a man, in fact, screaming about an oil blowout. Officer Shoak stumbles across the room to turn off the radio and goes back to sleep.

Bertie hears the news on the AM radio the next morning—something about one of the wells in the Beaufort Sea blowing out. There aren't any details yet. Bertie swallows down the bile in her throat, hoping that it's just a small spill that can be cleaned up easily, like the hundreds of onshore spills in the past decade.

"They said on the radio that a well blew up in the Beaufort Sea!" Lisa says as Bertie walks into the Law Department. "I wonder if it's a terrorist attack."

"I don't know," Bertie says. "It seems more likely to be the result of poor planning by the oil industry."

"I think it might be a terrorist attack," Lisa says, sure that mass pollution and death are products of terrorism, not development.

Later on, the newscasters will rule out any external force. It was just an inglorious failure of some valves on one of Shant's wells. Shant's Social Performance Coordinator releases a soundbyte to let us know that nothing has "blown up." The drilling vessel is a little worse for wear—it might have to be replaced—but in the meantime Shant is sending its experts out to fix the broken valves.

No one says anything about whether any oil is leaking into the water.

Before Shant can get its experts to the well, the pressure drops and a storm comes barreling across the Chukchi Sea and into the Beaufort Sea. Another soundbyte from the Social Performance Coordinator says that the waters are too rough to go out and check on the well, and that the drilling vessel will have to come into shore. "Safety first, nobody gets hurt" is still Shant's motto.

The drilling vessel that pulls into Harow just after 2 a.m. on August 3rd is burned, but no one on board was hurt beyond the means of the ship's first aid kit. Shant sends a private plane from Anchorage to whisk the crew away before they can fall prey to reporters and environmentalists. Most of us never even see the drilling vessel, since it's moved down the coast a few miles to avoid attracting attention.

By morning, the swell from the storm pounds onto Beach Road, washing away the sandbags that were piled on the shore. Around noon, workmen from the Borough's Public Works Department put up barricades to keep people from using the road.

The Shant experts that flew in to fix the valves are stranded onshore. Most of them sit in the Harow Native Corporation building with Chuck, desperately checking their Blackberries and occasionally attempting to joke about the weather in Harow.

"Well, I have to agree with you all that it's not worth risking human life to go out and cap a gusher," Chuck says after waiting all day with no news on what's going on. The Shant experts look at each other and then at Chuck. "Who said there's any oil spilling out there?" someone asks him.

"Oh come on, if there wasn't a spill before the storm, there's bound to be something now," Chuck says. "Maybe I don't know nothing about whaling, but I can tell you that sea is rougher than you ever thought. Anyhow, the corporation's supposed to be your support services, you can't just not tell us what's going on, if you know. I mean, we're here to fix things. All of this stuff can be fixed."

The Shant experts look at each other again and say nothing. They have been instructed that Shant, and only Shant, will be in charge of any cleanup. No one else, including Harow Native Corporation and the government, needs to know any more about it than absolutely necessary.

Gill is up early the next morning. He takes his four-wheeler to the beach to see what the storm churned up, dreading the idea of seeing oil in the water. He's relieved to see that the water is still blue. Clean chunks of ice brought in by the storm are bouncing on the surface.

But both Beach Road and the barricades are gone, and the Chukchi Sea has moved twenty feet inward. Even now the waves are throwing themselves and the ice onto the shore, as if the twenty feet weren't enough.

Gill shivers. The Utilidor runs just under Beach Road, and God willing, it's still there. He goes back to his house and makes good use of the toilet, just in case this is going to be his last flush.

Chuck is up early, too, walking along the coast to assure himself that there's no cause for alarm.

The area that his workers cemented just weeks ago is covered by water. The waves are rolling across where the warehouses are supposed to go. Chuck sighs, deciding that they'll just have to pour some more cement.

At the Harow Native Corporation office later that morning, one of the Shant experts tells Chuck that they're taking a boat out later in the day if the water is calm enough. Chuck nods dismissively. The experts are just a bunch of awkward Outsiders, and he's tired of having them hang around the office. He doesn't ask to join them—not that they invited him—since he has plenty of work to deal with on the port project.

By mid-afternoon, the sky starts to clear, and the Shant experts leave on their mission. A half-hour later they see the oil slick, stretching out a couple miles around the well. Something is coming up from the bottom.

One of the experts radios the Harow Native Corporation and tells Chuck to get the cleanup equipment out, call the Coast Guard, and round up whomever's available to come out and start cleaning up. Shant has a contract with Alaska Clean Oceans for cleanup services. But Shant knows, as does everyone else who hires Alaska Clean Oceans for purposes of satisfying federal planning requirements, that the cleanup folks are hard to find when you really need them.

From the surface, it's not clear what had happened. The drilling vessel workers said they had tried to activate the blowout preventer, but it didn't work, and the automated backup system didn't kick in. With a little luck, the Shant experts will be able to figure out the problem before the Coast Guard comes in and starts calculating the leak rate.

The experts have a couple of remote controlled robots with cameras that Shant has used to snuff Gulf of Mexico spills before—sort of like performing arthroscopic surgery on a well. The robots haven't been tested in Arctic waters, but there's a first time for everything.

One of the robots dies as soon as it hits the water. The other lasts until it gets to the sea floor and then freezes up. It's not going to be a quick fix.

"We're going to have to get a Top Hat from Houston," one of the experts says. The Top Hat is a little five-ton shed that can be dropped over a blown-out well. As long as the pressure isn't too great and the stuff coming out of the well isn't too gassy, it ought to hold the oil in the well.

"I don't know if there's going to be any available right now ..." another expert says.

"They can build something—they got all the parts they need—and get it on a plane to Harow, then helicopter it out here."

"We don't even know the pressure down there or the rate of oil coming out ..."

"Look," the first expert says. "This ain't no Exxon Valdez. We're going to get this thing capped, and then we're going to go on with the drilling season."

The others nod. "In the mean time we got to start scooping this shit up."

The experts, who know everything about wells but not much about cleanup, head back to shore to look for the Alaska Clean Oceans cleanup crew. They find two men hauling skimmers and boom out of Harow Native Corporation's hanger at the airport.

"Uh, where's the rest of your crew?" one of the Shant experts asks.

"They'll be some more coming later," one of the crew members says, wiping sweat off his forehead with a greasy hand. "There was a little pipeline leak over at Prudhoe Bay yesterday that they're still looking at. How bad's the oil out there?"

The Shant experts look at each other. "It's pretty thin right now, mostly just a rainbow sheen," one of them says.

"Are you all gonna help with the skimming, or what?" the sweating crew member asks.

"I thought the Coast Guard was going to come up with their guys and direct the Unified Command with your guys," one of the Shant experts says.

"Yeah, they're all on their way," the other Clean Oceans crew member says. "They only got one Arctic class vessel, and they gotta bring it up all the way from Dillingham. You guys could help in the meantime."

The Shant experts realize they have a choice between appearing to be proactive or having to sit around in the corporation office with Chuck. They opt to go out with the Clean Oceans crew.

The crew and the experts load skimmers and boom onto an Alaska Clean Oceans vessel capable of storing up to 500 barrels of oil waste. They'll have to come back to shore and change out the storage tanks every so often, depending on how much they collect.

The sky is clear, but the waters are still rough. Chunks of ice knock into the vessel and each other.

"At least the ice'll help contain the oil," one of the Shant experts says.

The sweaty Clean Oceans crew member snorts. "Boy, wait 'til we put the boom down and try to corral the oil—you're gonna see chunks of ice slide right under the boom, and the oil's gonna follow." The crew member knows what he's talking about. He's cleaned up oil spills this way for years, circling over the same water again and again and managing to skim just a little bit of oil each time.

"We're still waiting for some expert to invent something better," he says.

The rainbow sheen of oil now stretches five miles from the well. Closer to the well, the oil has mixed with the water to form a mousse. Some of the mousse has broken into solid chunks that bob alongside the clean ice. "Well, here we go," one of the Clean Oceans crew members says, hooking up the boom to the back of the boat.

For the rest of the day, the vessel circles the well, grazing on whatever patches of oil are thick enough to remain in the boom and warm enough to be sucked up without clogging the hoses. The rest of the oil follows the chunks of ice further out in the ocean, or joins the mousse that can't be picked up with the skimmers.

"We're actually not doing too bad," the sweatier crew member assures the experts. They're all sweaty now.

"When there's more ice we only get like 20% of the oil. I'd say today we're getting at least 40%, although a lot of what we picked up is just water. It'd sure help if somebody else would get up here with another boat."

"The holding tank's full!" shouts the other crew member. "We gotta bring her back to shore."

It's just after 1 a.m. on August 5th, and the sun is beginning to set. The exhausted men bring the boat back to shore, put the oily water they collected into a massive tank in the corporation's hanger, and shuffle off to their hotels. Surely the Coast Guard will be here in the morning.

Chapter 31- Burning

The ocean is closer than it should be. It's gotten into the open part of the landfill and washed out some of the trash. But foremost on our minds is the water in the Utilidor. The structure is holding out for now, but it's not going to last without some serious repairs. The director of the Borough's Public Works Department decides to shut off all the utilities indefinitely so the repair work can start.

"No power. Just like before the *taniks* came," Nelson jokes to Bertie. Bertie is not in a joking mood. She stands in her office looking out the window, waiting for Nelson to go away. Nelson has a habit of wandering into the Law Department whenever he's bored and making Bertie feel inadequate.

After Nelson wanders into Vik's office, Bertie turns on her laptop to do some research. The mayor has asked her to figure out if there's any way the Iñupiat can claim sovereignty over the Arctic Ocean, even though the U.S. Supreme Court already ruled that the ocean belongs to the federal government.

Her other task to finish before the laptop battery runs out is to determine whether former Mayor Ahgak would be considered a Borough resident for purposes of an election. The Borough Clerk told Bertie that Ahgak is running again, even though we all know he lives in Anchorage. Ahgak says that having an allotment on the Arctic Slope ought to be enough. And since the *taniks* took so much of the Iñupiat land anyway, why should it matter where he ends up having to live?

The battery runs out at 3:00 p.m., and Bertie manages to spend the rest of the day shuffling through papers on her desk. At 5:30 she joins the huddle of people standing in the tiny dark airport. The airport has a generator to keep a couple of computers and the screening equipment running, but that's about it.

Bertie's aunt from Alabama is coming in on the evening flight. She's is the only person in Bertie's extended family to have made it past 60 without getting high blood pressure and becoming obese. Bertie was struck with both many years before.

Also, Bertie's aunt is the only one of her siblings that stayed in the Deep South—the rest are scattered from Colorado to Connecticut. Since she retired last year, she's been traveling around the U.S. and staying with any family member who'll have her.

Bertie hears her aunt before seeing her.

"Gawd all mighty, I done come all the way up here for this?"

Bertie runs over to silence her aunt with an embrace.

Across the room, Gill is looking around nervously for Glory, his Internet lady. It occurs to him that she never did send a picture—just a description that could have fit a third of the women in the airport.

While he waits, he watches the two black women open a Styrofoam ice chest to reveal what looks like a bunch of gray and white insects. Bertie has a disgusted look on her face. The older woman is saying, "I done hauled this ice chest all the way from the Gulf and you mean to tell me you don't eat shrimp?"

"Oh, no, no," Bertie says. "I mean I haven't eaten it since the last time I visited you in Mobile. We'll figure out something to do with it, though."

People from Shant who aren't important enough to have come in a corporate jet are filing through the airport, looking around in a state of disbelief. Gill wonders if they're here to clean up oil. He's seen some of the guys from the Harow Native Corporation taking the skimmers and boom out, but he hasn't heard anything about what's going on. With the excitement of the Utilidor breaking and Glory coming, he didn't think to call anyone in the Borough or the Corporation and ask for news.

By now, everyone's made it off the plane. Gill decided that carrying a sign saying "Glory Johnson" would attract way too much attention. So he waits. The airport clears out after a half hour, except for one of Gill's many Whitehead cousins standing by the bathroom. She's trying to shush a screaming toddler while making a call on a cell phone that has no reception.

"Hey," he says, walking up to her. "You didn't see a woman on the plane with long dark hair and dark eyes, you know, really young-looking?"

"Look, it's me, Gill," she says.

"What do you mean, it's you?"

"It's me, Gloria Whitehead Johnson. I married this guy Tim Johnson in Anchorage and went with him to Arizona before I realized he was an asshole. He said he'd take care of me and I wouldn't have to work, but then he wouldn't let me have any money and he wouldn't buy anything I need … and I'm pregnant again."

The toddler yowls. "And he hit me," she adds.

Gill's mouth hangs open. "So you got on Singles.com and lied to get someone to buy you a ticket home? Geez, why didn't you just call your parents?"

Gloria squeezes a few tears out of her eyes and whispers, "They said I had to live with what I did. They wouldn't help me."

"Well, I'm sure when they see you they'll be able to put all that behind them, you know … I'll just bring you there now."

"Oh God, please don't," she says.

"Well, what am I supposed to do with you, then?" Gill asked. "Take you to Chuck's? Or maybe Gray Shoak's?"

Gloria blushes. She's been out of Harow just long enough to forget what it's like to have everyone know your business.

"Let me just crash at your place for tonight, and I'll work this out tomorrow," she says.

"Well, okay. But you sure picked a bad time to come. Power's out, toilet won't flush, and it looks like there's an oil spill out there," he says, nodding toward the ocean.

By the next morning, the Coast Guard officials have arrived. They announce on the radio that they've got to start burning the spilled oil, since it's leaking 1,000 barrels a day, and it'll be a while before the well-capping equipment can be brought up from Houston. They're rounding up pools of oil and the occasional piece of trash as best as they can with fire-resistant boom, although the ice chunks in the water have made it difficult. It takes an hour just to get a pool of oil thick enough to ignite. The trash actually helps to get the fire going.

From the shore in Harow, we can see thick black smoke from the fires. The power is still out, and Gill decides that he and some of the men from the Community Development Department should take a boat out to the well for a closer look. They load Gill's new boat—he bought the biggest of Larry's boats from Mandy—onto a trailer and head out to the boat launch. Hardly any of the cleanup crew are on shore, and no one tries to stop Gill's boat.

The smell of burning oil is so acrid Gill can taste it. Fifteen miles out, he sees the rainbow sheen from the oil. Five miles later, he sees the orange-colored pools of oil. Everyone on the boat is coughing.

"You gotta turn around now!" one of the men shouts to Gill. "I can't hardly breathe!"

Gill turns the boat around slowly. "Darn," he says, stifling a cough, "I wanted to get out there and see what it's really like."

"You can't see what it's like from here?" the man who can't hardly breathe asks. "It's a disaster! You think the whales are gonna come through here this fall? No way they are!"

Gill feels sick to his stomach. It's the first time he's thought about what could happen to fall whaling.

"We-ell," he says, trying to reassure himself. "Now the Coast Guard's here and we have Alaska Clean Oceans and all these people working on cleanup, I'm sure they can clean this up before ..." He doesn't finish his sentence. The men are glaring at him, and he realizes he sounds ridiculous.

As they ride back to shore in silence, Gill thinks about the village of Kusoq, and how much people there complained when the Community

Development Department let Cacoco Oil put another rig right next to the village airport. They said they were already surrounded by rigs, and the rate of asthma was getting higher. Vik believed them, and she tried to get Gill to have a health impact assessment done before giving out any more permits. Nelson heard about Vik's idea and scoffed.

"The air quality problem in Kusoq has a lot more to do with people sitting around in their houses and smoking than it does with oil and gas development miles away," he said. Gill didn't know whether Nelson or Vik were right, but he figured Cacoco should be allowed to drill. It had applied for a permit, after all, and paid the application fee. Gill had signed off on the permit.

Gill remembers talking to the nurse from Kusoq after the approval. She told him he and his department were just as responsible for the cultural genocide that was going on now as the oil companies and the *taniks* were. Gill shrugged it off. He's not one to overreact about anything.

The next day, the power is back on. The Utilador has been patched up enough to make it at least until the next storm. But the winds have changed, sending the black smoke toward Harow. There's a Coast Guard announcement on the radio warning people to stay inside as much as possible.

It's Sunday, but Vik rushes off to work to read the news on the Internet. There's hardly any news on the local radio, and no one around town seems to know what's going on. She wears her winter burkha even though it's August. The smoke has blown in and mixed with fog, and the air is worse than anything she's ever been in, even Mexico City in the 1990s.

Vik is divided between feeling devastated over the environmental catastrophe and smug in her conviction that offshore Arctic oil development has failed. She wonders if the Borough will have the balls to sue Shant at some point. It won't happen under this mayor—we all know now that he's going to work for Shant in October when his term is over. If former Mayor Ahgak wins the election, he won't push for a law suit, either. For the last twenty years, his only job besides being the Borough mayor has been working for Shant.

Vik's nose is running and her eyes are tearing up with all the smoke. She thinks this must be the beginning of the end of Harow. It's a good thing she's leaving.

Vik's surprised not to see Bertie at work. A quiet Sunday morning is the best time to get work done in Harow. But this Sunday, Bertie's aunt insists on taking her to church.

"Back home I go to the Church of His Blessed Salvation," Bertie's aunt says. "Where do you go here?"

Bertie hasn't been to a church service since the last time she visited her aunt in Mobile. She dodges the question. "I guess the closest thing we have to the Church of His Blessed Salvation would be the Fresh Start Church."

"They got a drum set?" Bertie's aunt asks.

"Uh, maybe."

It's the first time Bertie has ever been inside a Harow church other than the Presbyterian church, and then just to make brief obligatory appearances at funerals. Not only is there a drum set, a piano, and six guitars, there's a giant screen showing the words to all the songs. There aren't any notes to go with the words, but this doesn't seem to bother anyone. The people in the front row are singing without the benefit of knowing the notes.

The service won't get started for another twenty minutes. Bertie sees Mayor Kitok standing by the side door, shaking hands with everybody there. For a minute she wonders if he's going to scrap the Shant job and run for mayor again. But he's talking about his sixtieth birthday party, at his house after the service.

"Well, I didn't expect to see you here," he says to Bertie with a smile when she comes to shake his hand.

"There's hope for the heathens," Bertie's aunt announces, giving the mayor a gratuitous hug and wishing him a happy birthday.

"This is my aunt from Alabama," Bertie says apologetically.

"Well, she's welcome to join us after the service today," the mayor says. "As are you, of course!"

Bertie nods. Bracing herself for one of the few events worse than a Shant Oil public meeting, she leads her aunt to the last row of folding chairs. Bertie's aunt pulls Bertie to the front and giddily joins in the tuneless singing.

Two hours later, Bertie and her aunt join the slow shuffle toward the mayor's house. Bertie's aunt coughs. "Somebody having a barbecue out here or burning something or what?"

Bertie adjusts her scarf over her nose. "It's the oil spill. They're burning it."

"Lawd have mercy," Bertie's aunt says. "That's awful. I don't know how these poor people can stand it. That happen a lot?"

"First time," Bertie says. "Hopefully the last after everyone realizes how much of the Arctic is going to be ruined. With the winds the way they are today, oil's going to be washing up on shore any time now. I still can't believe it."

They pass by a house with four junked cars and pieces of formerly functioning machinery out front. "Shoot, it's like I'm in Alabama again,"

Bertie's aunt says. "Look at that. And there's another one over there—and there too!"

"We can drive by the house with Santa and his reindeer on the way home if you want," Bertie says stiffly. "The reindeer are made from real caribou parts. They're up all year round."

"Lawd have mercy," Bertie's aunt says again.

The mayor's wife had to miss church to get together a giant spread of Western and traditional food. There's *miqiaq*—fermented whale meat cooked in blood, *quaq*—muscle meat, and *maktak*—the bottom layer of skin and the top layer of blubber, all left over from the last *nalukataq*, and caribou that had just been caught at someone's camp. Another table is crammed with Vienna sausages, potato salad, sandwiches, rice, spaghetti, and desserts.

"Looks like somebody tried to work up some soul food over here," Bertie's aunt says, hovering over the potato salad and apple pie.

"Try the traditional food," Bertie says. "It's really good for you."

"Good for you," Bertie's aunt mumbles, picking up a piece of *maktak*. She puts it in her mouth and chews. And chews. And finally swallows. "It's like a cross between catfish, pork rinds, and the bottom of somebody's shoe," she pronounces.

They squeeze into the kitchen to get something to drink, and Bertie pauses to listen to the radio broadcast. The local radio announcer cuts into the all-afternoon Sing-spiration to announce that oil has washed up by the Colville River delta north of Kusoq. "According to the Associated Press, the rate of the leak is now 2,000 barrels a day," the announcer says.

Bertie feels sick. She sits down in a chair and closes her eyes.

The mayor's wife touched Bertie's shoulder. "You okay?"

"I'm ... I'm fine," Bertie says, embarrassed. "Just listening to the news. It's hard to listen to that."

The mayor's wife nods.

"I hope it doesn't spoil the celebration," Bertie says.

The mayor's wife shrugs. "Whatever happened to us, for thousands of years, we've always overcome. This isn't any different." She walks over to the traditional foods table and consumes the last slice of *maktak* with minimal chewing.

From across the room, Gill sees that the *maktak* has run out. He knows that the mayor's crew didn't catch anything in the spring, and that there's no more *maktak* in the mayor's ice cellar. He decides that the decent thing to do would be to bring over the *maktak* from his family's cellar. He gets in his truck and heads over.

Gill hasn't been in the ice cellar since before the storm. As soon as he opens the door, he knows something's wrong. Everything smells like seawater and rotting meat. Acid rises in his throat as he climbs down the ladder. Sea water from the storm has washed in and turned the contents of the cellar into a foul soup. The walls of the cellar, which are already softer and warmer than in previous years, are dripping.

He wants to cry, but knows he won't let himself. Gill is a man of action—he always has been. He goes in the garage and finds the pulley he used to haul dirt out when he was expanding the walls two years before. Now, he's going to pull up meat and water.

Except for a couple buckets of *maktak* that were sealed off from the water, everything is ruined. Gill loads the wasted meat into the back of his truck and drives out where the boat launch was before it, too, was washed away. He unloads the meat into the ocean that was the whale's home before it gave itself to Gill's crew. The whale floats up and out with the blocks of ice.

Gill drives slowly back home. The smog is so thick he can barely see more than twenty feet ahead. His eyes burn with tears. He reaches over to the passenger's side to touch the sealed buckets of *maktak*, to make sure they're still there.

Gloria is cleaning the kitchen when he gets home. Gill drops the buckets on the kitchen floor and rummages through the fridge for a beer.

"*Maktak*?" Gloria asks, inhaling the smell that the buckets can't hold in.

"Can you pickle it?" Gill asks.

"I don't really know how," Gloria says, "but I'll put it in the freezer for you."

"The ice cellar washed out," Gill says.

Gloria nods sympathetically but doesn't know what to say. She's only been in an ice cellar once, and it stank. She opens one of the buckets and starts wrapping up the *maktak* in aluminum foil. Gill shakes his head and goes off to shower.

It's Gloria's third night at Gill's house. We all know she's back, but no one—not her parents, Chuck, or Gray—has called her. She hasn't called anyone, either. She's going to stay right here, cooking and cleaning, trying to keep her toddler out of trouble, and staving off morning sickness, until something better comes along.

Chapter 32- Homecoming

Chuck gets up on the sixth day of the spill and stands by the window in his underwear, looking out at the ocean. It's too smoggy to see the trash or the rising smoke anymore. He can barely see down the street. He's going to have to put an end to this burning, or sooner or later, somebody will blame him for it.

He calls up the CEO of Alaska Clean Oceans and explains that the burning is putting the cleanup crew in mortal danger. "The Coast Guard and Shant are killing off your crew with this burning, because so many of them are Eskimo, you know, and the Coast Guard thinks we're all just replaceable."

"What are you saying?"

"I'm saying Shant isn't even giving them face masks. You, uh, better tell the Coast Guard and Shant to cut out this burning or your crew guys are going to end up with big workman's comp claims." Chuck doesn't actually know whether the men have face masks or not, but then, neither does the CEO. As long as the CEO believes it, then maybe he'll take on the task of doing something about the burning.

"I hadn't heard anything like that," the CEO says.

"You know, all it takes is one worker law suit against you, and none of the oil companies will contract with you again," Chuck assures him.

"Why don't you tell Shant yourself? Or get the Borough mayor to say something?"

Chuck hangs up. Assuming this oil spill blows over, and the deep sea port goes forward, he wants to be sure he stays on good terms with Shant. Contracts with Shant could be the corporation's biggest source of revenue yet.

On its own initiative, the Coast Guard calls off the burning. It doesn't want a repeat of what happened after the Exxon-Valdez spill, when village residents were clamoring for an all-expense-paid relocation until the burning finished.

By now it's clear that a relief well is going to have to be drilled to shut off the well at the top of the oil reservoir, in case the Top Hat plan doesn't work. The question is where to get an available rig. The Coast Guard doesn't have any rigs, and it barely has enough vessels to send to the spill site. Shant doesn't have any rigs nearby. It'll have to get one from the Gulf of Mexico, which might take a couple of weeks. And drilling the relief well could take months.

Until the Top Hat arrives, the only response method other than burning is to get some chemical dispersants and spray the hell out of the oily, icy water. The environmentalists will moan like they always do, particularly since there aren't any long-term studies on dispersants in Arctic waters. But Chuck figures that a little dispersant would at least result in the appearance of clean water. Anyway, something has to be done, before people start calling Chuck and taking out their pain on him.

Gill is the one who gets the call from Kusoq village residents who've been fishing at the mouth of the Colville River. "The oil—it's here. I'm looking at it now. Bright orange globs of it, like paint."

Gill rummages helplessly through the stacks of paper on his desk, looking for the most recent Borough permit issued to Shant.

"You heard me?" the voice on the line says. "This shit is covering the coast. We're not gonna catch nothing today, nothing tomorrow. You gotta do something!"

"I'm looking for their permits," Gill says.

"Forget about the permits! They're supposed to have put up a multimillion bond to pay for this kinda shit! The Borough's supposed to get the money from it and bring us somewhere we can get food."

"The oil spill mitigation agreement" Gill mumbles. "I'll ... I'll find it," He hangs up and calls Vik.

"Um, do you have a copy of the oil spill mitigation agreement that Shant signed?" he asks.

"No," Vik says flatly.

"No?"

"Shant didn't sign an oil spill mitigation agreement. None of the Borough permits required it."

"But the oil's on the shore already!" Gill says. "Somebody from Kusoq just called me about it."

"Well, one of the whaling captains just called me to tell me Shant had offered him $1,000 in full compensation for all of his damages," Vik says. "He said Shant's got its Social Performance Coordinator up here, going door to door, giving out cash and getting people to sign releases."

"We-ell," Gill sighs. "A thousand bucks is something."

"It's shit," Vik says. "One thousand dollars for ruining someone's way of life is shit."

"We-ell," Gill says. "Lotta shit going on today."

Vik hangs up and tells Bertie that oil has reached the Colville River. Bertie's mouth quivers with anger. "Somebody should stuff the Shant executives into that well," she says.

"And the Social Performance Coordinator, too," Vik says.

"I, uh, hate to be dramatic about this, but I wanted to ask if you'd be willing to stay on a little longer—just a couple months until the worst of this is over," Bertie says. "I'm going to have a hell of a time trying to get somebody new to come up here now."

Vik wrinkles her forehead. "If they can't get a relief well drilled before it gets dark and everything freezes up, oil's going to be flowing all winter. It'll just keep getting worse."

Lisa is listening to them and says, "My term's not much longer, either. I'm just a temp, even though I been here six months already."

"You could apply for your full-time position again," Bertie says nervously. It'll be almost as hard to find a decent secretary as it will be to find another lawyer.

"I was actually staying on because I thought that Fish and Wildlife agent was going to sue us," Lisa says. "Because of the shooting accident with Britney, you know. But we haven't heard anything for months. I guess he forgot about it."

"Maybe he's waiting until the end of the two-year statute of limitations to see if he develops post traumatic stress syndrome," Vik suggests.

"You don't have to decide this minute," Bertie says to Vik. "Anyway, I have to go back home and pick up my aunt. She changed her ticket so she could leave on this afternoon's flight."

"Yeah, I guess she couldn't get out any earlier with all that smog," Vik says.

"She was supposed to stay a whole month," Bertie says. "It hasn't even been a week since she got here."

An hour later, Bertie and her aunt are sitting in the little airport waiting for the plane.

"I hate to leave you in this mess," Bertie's aunt says.

"I'm the Borough Attorney," Bertie says, trying to sound stable. "I clean up messes."

"You know, you oughtta stop fooling around with that lawyer stuff and run for mayor of this place. No doubt you could do the job."

Bertie looks around to make sure no one is listening, and says, "Hello, I'm black."

Bertie's aunt chuckles. "This ain't the 1950s. We gotta black mayor in Mobile."

"Yeah, but you have a majority black population there. The black population up here doubled when you came to town." She knows she's exaggerating. She's met five African-Americans in Harow and has heard of one out in Point Courage.

"Girl, you got nothing to lose," Bertie's aunt says, surveying the little airport and its inhabitants for the last time.

Bertie kisses her aunt and heads home. She doesn't like long emotional goodbyes.

Up in the air, Bertie sees a helicopter flying in. It's weighted down with what could well be the famous "Top Hat" that's supposed to close off the well. But Bertie has no faith in its success. She can't help feeling like she's a character in a badly written novel with an apocalyptic ending.

Fish and Wildlife agents are also coming in to make sure no endangered or threatened species are hurt by the spill, and that the Eskimos don't go on some crazy bird shooting rampage, as if the world's going to end.

Gill doesn't know if the world's ending or not, but he knows he's got to do something before all the subsistence food out there gets covered in oil. The next day he picks up a few guys from his whaling crew and drives over to the search and rescue squad's office.

"In light of the oil spill, we're going to need a helicopter to get out to the Colville River," Gill tells the office receptionist.

"Uh, did the Mayor's Office approve the helicopter request?" the receptionist asks nervously, looking at Gill and the pack of gun-toting Whiteheads he brought with him.

"It's an emergency," Gill explains. "So we don't need a permit or anything. And I'm the Director of Community Development now, anyway."

The receptionist calls the Mayor's Office but can't get an answer. "Uh, could you guys come back in a few hours, maybe? Or tomorrow? We just got the helicopter back from being repaired and our own guys haven't even had a chance to use it."

"Look, we got to get out to where the spill's washing up before all the animals out there are killed. If you can just get one of the pilots to take us and our boat out there, that's all we need. He can just leave us there and we'll get back on our own."

"Um, I guess that'd be okay," the receptionist says. "If you think it's really an emergency." She radios one of the pilots to get a helicopter ready.

When the helicopter lands at the mouth of the Colville River, Gill sees that someone's already there. A group of Greenpeace volunteers has four-wheeled over from the village of Kusoq. It didn't occur to them that non-subsistence tundra travel is closed for the season, and that the tracks they leave behind will survive for as long as the effects of the spilled oil.

The Rainbow Warriors are squatting on the beach in ripped up jeans, rounding up oily birds in nets. They're going to haze them to get the oil off, and then find a way to four-wheel them somewhere else for release.

Gill looks at the helpless birds tangled in the Greenpeace net and pulls out his gun.

"Um, if you guys don't mind, we're going to go ahead and harvest these animals and then test them for toxicity ..."

A man carrying a caribou calf coated in oil marches over to Gill.

"And if we clean them and there's nothing wrong with them?" he asks.

"Then we can eat them before they go back into the ocean and get covered in the oil again," Gill says.

"But we're going to release them somewhere else!"

"The oil has already spread 100 miles. These animals aren't going to survive being transported and released in a new environment. And," he adds, looking at the mud encrusted wheels of the four-wheelers, "I don't think you got a tundra travel permit from the Arctic Slope Borough. Or a wildlife-handling permit."

The oil-coated man snorts. "The Rainbow Warrior Ship is on its way. It doesn't need a tundra travel permit."

"You know," Gill explains, "you're supposed to get a permit to travel through Borough waters."

The oil-coated man is quiet. He doesn't actually know if the Rainbow Warrior Ship is really coming. Last he heard, it was going after Japanese whalers near Australia. "Well," he says.

"I'll have some people from our Community Development Department come out here with boats to collect the bird harvest," Gill says. "We're going to go out in the water and look for seals, and then we can take you back to Harow with us."

The Greenpeace volunteers look at their feet. The oil-coated man puts down the oil-coated calf and starts crying.

"Geez," Gill says, "I guess you never tried seals?"

The Greenpeace volunteers abandon their nets, get back on their four-wheelers, and make another permanent trail back to Kusoq. Gill waits until they're gone to start shooting.

The hunters gather up the birds and a couple of caribou calves and put them in the boat. They ride through the oily water in the direction of Cross Island, looking for seals. But there's nothing swimming through the oil, and the motor's starting to make funny noises.

"Let's hug the shoreline where it's not so oily and head back towards Harow," one of the hunters suggests.

"We should stop at *Tuungaqagvik*—the Place of Devils—on the way," Gill says. "Just to see if we could get a few more caribou." He sighs. "I used to hunt there with my dad when I was a kid. Nobody else wanted to go there, and it was always the best place for caribou."

About five miles before *Tuungaqagvik*, the motor breaks down completely. Gill stops the boat, pulls the motor off, and opens it up with his knife.

"I don't think the oil is the problem," Gill says. "It's missing some screws and washers." He looks around the boat for inspiration, and seizes upon a caribou leg. The sinew from the ankle is the thread that holds his and every other whaling captain's *umiaq* together. He cuts some of it off and ties together various parts of the motor.

After fifteen minutes, Gill has the motor running. The other hunters grunt with approval and share stories of using guns and all kinds of animal parts to fix broken vehicles.

Gill stops the boat at *Tuungaqagvik*. "Maybe I'll leave the motor running, just in case," he says. "We got enough gas. I'm just going to go in a bit and see if there's anything there."

He surveys the landscape and smiles for the first time since the oil spill started. It's been twenty years since he last walked on this land.

Something up on the bluff catches his eye, and he heads over for a closer look. At first he can just see the navy color, then the navy coat and jeans, and then the body of a man.

He runs toward the body and turns it over. It's Larry.

The temperatures haven't gone above forty degree this summer, and the body is mostly intact. Gill picks Larry up and stumbles down the bluff with him.

"Holy Jesus," one of the hunters says when they see what Gill's bringing back to the boat.

"Forget about the caribou," Gill mutters. "Let's take him home."

One of the other hunters helps Gill get Larry into the boat, alongside the oily birds and caribou calves. No one says anything until the boat reaches the launching spot in Harow. One of the hunters notices that Fish and Wildlife agents are there, checking boats. "We better pull up somewhere else," he says.

"We're already here," Gill says. "They'll probably come after us if we turn around now."

The hunter looks back at Larry and mumbles, "This is going to be fun to explain to the feds."

An agent tromps through the water and jumps into the boat before Gill has a chance to turn off the motor. The agent flashes a badge and announces that he's looking for Steller's eiders and anything else the Eskimos are hiding.

Gill ignores the agent. Pulling out his cell phone, he calls Gloria and tells her to come out to the launching spot with the trailer.

"What the hell is this?" barks the agent, pointing at Larry.

"That's my cousin Larry," Gill says. "He's been missing from Harow since the winter."

The hunters start to get out of the boat, but the agent says, "Nobody's going anywhere until we get to the bottom of this." He turns to Gill and says, "Shut off that phone, *now*."

"Look, I'm calling my cousin to come and get us, and we're going to take the body to the hospital," Gill says. "We don't have any Steller's eiders or untagged marine mammals, so I dunno what you want." He dials Gloria's number.

Panicking, the agent fires his gun up in the air and calls for back-up on his radio. Then he calls the Borough police.

Gloria pulls up in Gill's truck with the trailer a few minutes after Officer Shoak arrives in the Borough police SUV.

"Don't get out, Gloria, we'll just get the boat up on the trailer and then drop these guys off," Gill says to her through the window. The agent has finished taking photographs of Larry, the oily birds, and each of the hunters, and is allowing the hunters to get out of the boat.

Officer Shoak sees Gloria and saunters over to the truck, trying to think of something snide to say. Gloria's son begins to scream from the backseat. She picks him up, rests his head on her shoulder, and coos at him.

Officer Shoak swallows. The baby's grown so much, it's incredible. There's no way the little tike would recognize him now. He remembers how he said he would marry Gloria and adopt the baby, back when they were all in Anchorage. He looks away from Gloria, and instead of saying anything, turns toward the boat.

"I'll take care of the body," he says gruffly to Gill. "You guys are free to go." He lays Larry's body in the back of his SUV and heads for the morgue.

Autopsies are rare on the Arctic Slope. Death usually isn't questioned. But Officer Shoak orders an autopsy, given the circumstances. The report says it's a heart attack, the same kind that nearly killed Larry's brother in church two years ago.

Mandy comes with William to take the body from the morgue. She isn't planning to have a funeral—the memorial service was more emotion than she ever wants to feel again. William and some of Larry's nephews have dug a grave in the new graveyard by the airport, next to where William's father is buried. They'll go straight from the morgue to the graveyard.

Larry's coffin is simple and wooden, not all that different from the one he made for his son. They load the coffin into the back of Larry's old truck and drive in silence to the graveyard.

Mandy didn't tell anyone to come to the graveyard except Larry's nephews, who will put the earth back in place after the coffin is lowered. But when they get there, the graveyard is full of Harow residents who've come out for support. Bertie nods at Mandy with a sad smile, and Vik comes over and hugs her. It's a surprise funeral.

After the coffin is lowered, an elder begins to pray in long, low tones. Everyone else stands in silence, heads bowed. The elder prays. And prays. Drops of rain begin to fall, and then the skies burst into a rare downpour. The crowd slowly makes its way toward the parking lot, and Larry's nephews began shoveling. William drives his *aka* home, where she lies in bed alone and listens to the rain.

Chapter 33- Onward

Shant tries three times to lower the Top Hat over the blown-out well. Each time it fails. The icy slush created by frozen gas welling up through the ruptured pipeline makes it impossible to get the Top Hat in the right place.

It's one thing for oil to wash up at the mouth of the Colville River, where no one lives. It's quite another when oil begins washing up in Harow, coating chunks of ice and the gray shoreline with red-brown stains.

Crews imported from Anchorage and the Lower 48 are deployed on the shore to clean up the mixture of oil, sand and tar balls. The beach that was ravaged by the storm just last week is now being shoveled up and put it into trash bags. It will be barged off to Seattle and laid to rest in a secure landfill.

The estimated leak rate has doubled, then doubled again, then again. At the current rate of 20,000 barrels a day, the amount of oil spilled will surpass the Exxon Valdez spill in a week.

Shant's plan now is to try a slightly smaller Top Hat, a design that will allow robots to pump methanol into the well to stop the icy slush from forming. But it'll take weeks for the Houston employees to build it. And no one knows for sure whether it will work. Shant's also going to start drilling a relief well next week, since it found an available drilling rig in Thailand.

Federal scientists whose glory days were during the Cold War weigh in, suggesting that a nuclear bomb be detonated to melt and seal the well immediately. As much as he distrusts the feds, Chuck's inclined to go with the idea. If all of the whales are going to die anyway, why not just nuke the place and pave the way for a big harbor?

The beach shoveling comes to a pause when someone hits the Utilidor, opening it up to a spray of oily water. Harow's power has to be turned off again for repairs. The lights dim and blink out just as a fresh flock of Fish and Wildlife agents walk into the Harow airport.

The kids in the airport whoop and holler, and one of them, taking advantage of the dark, runs over and whacks a federal agent in the knee with a water gun. The agent clutches his own gun, steps on the kid's foot, and looks around for a local authority figure. He sees Officer Shoak waiting by the shelf for incoming luggage and bootleggers.

"What's going on around here?" the agent asks.

"Must be something wrong with the Utilador again," Officer Shoak says. "Last time they shut it down for two days."

"Aren't you going to declare martial law or something?" the agent asks. "You can't trust these people to ... to—"

Officer Shoak shrugs and ignores the agent. He's taking advantage of the dark to open up luggage and look around for booze. The first bag he opens has two bottles of Crown King whiskey. He picks them up and discretely tucks them under his bullet proof vest.

Deciding the local police are useless, the federal agent rounds up his flock and announces that they'll patrol the beaches while it's still light outside.

It's late August, and the endangered eiders are gone. Seagulls, migratory birds that the agents are charged with protecting, are in full throttle. We consider seagulls a nuisance. After all, they're the predators that eat the eggs of the endangered eiders. And they aren't edible themselves. Local hunters would shoot them like ravens and foxes if it weren't for the Fish and Wildlife agents.

Two years ago, the agents were terrified to discover sea gulls out on Point Harow, swimming around in dumpsters filled with rainwater and whale remnants. The agents decided that the whale oil in the water would get into the seagulls' coats and cause the birds to freeze to death. It was late at night, but the agents called every biologist in the Borough's Wildlife and Subsistence Department to come over and help haze the seagulls. The Borough's biologists laughed. They knew whale oil was different from crude oil. The seagulls could swim in the dumpsters all they wanted, and unfortunately still come out clean.

There are still seagulls flying around Harow with no signs of oil in their feathers. But on the beach, where cleanup crews are hauling away bags of contaminated sand, oily birds have begun to wash up in throngs. The cleanup crew piles the dead ones next to the bags of contaminated sand.

"Excuse me," an agent says to one of the cleanup guys. "What are you planning to do with these birds?"

"Take 'em to the dump with the sand, I guess."

"Are you aware that you could be found in violation of the Migratory Bird Treaty Act for possessing this bird?" the agent asks.

"If you want 'em, take 'em, but for godssakes get out of the way."

The agent starts to pick up the birds, but then realizes there are piles of birds just like this one, down the beach as far as he can see.

"Are you with the Greenpeace Warriors or something?" the cleanup guy asks.

The agent clutches at his gun for assurance, and then tells the other agents they'll go back to the hotel and wait for orders from the Fairbanks office.

While the agents worry about seagulls, we worry about whales. Whaling in the Beaufort Sea this fall will be out of the question. A fair number of whales will be able to make their journey unscathed, but these whales won't be passing anywhere near the coastal villages. They'll be way too far out for the whalers to safely reach them.

"Couldn't you, like, all go down to Point Courage and go whaling there?" Gloria asks Gill one day after he comes home from work. "I mean, it's 300 miles west from Harow so it's not like the oil's gonna get there any time soon. You could get all the whalers from the Harow and the Beaufort Sea villages and go down there to catch all the whales in case ..."

Gill thinks about this. There are still 27 whales left in the year's whaling quota. Normally, leftover whales from one year's quota carry over to the next year. But this oil spill could kill off enough whales so that the quota could be reduced or even eliminated. Subsistence hunters are always the ones punished for species destruction caused by others.

"Who's gonna pay for us to go down there?" Gill asks.

"Isn't Shant supposed to be paying for this stuff?"

"So far, they aren't giving anybody more than $1,000," Gill says.

"Couldn't the Borough, like, go ahead and pay, and then sue Shant?"

"Well, you know, not under this mayor. He's gonna leave the Borough to work for Shant. And he only spent forty grand on that Point Courage caribou trial. Even if he's willing to give us money, the state and all the Outside people are gonna put up a big fuss. You wouldn't believe how big-baby-ish the State and everybody back in Anchorage and Juneau was about the Point Courage caribou trial. They almost sued the Borough just for helping the people who got sued."

"I dunno," Gloria says. "But if you guys don't figure out how to go whaling this fall, and it turns out to be the last chance ..."

When Gill gets to work the next day, the power is still off and the phones aren't working. He uses his cell phone to call Shant's Social Performance Coordinator and every other Shant representative whose number he has. Maybe somehow, he can convince Shant to help the whalers. But every call ends in a transfer to a voicemail.

Gill goes to see the mayor, but he's in Anchorage meeting with Shant. Nelson's in Anchorage, too, in the hospital after an insulin overdose. Most of the Mayor's Office staff is out on account of the power being off.

At a loss, Gill goes to the Law Department for advice. He bypasses Vik's office and goes straight to Bertie. "What are the chances of the

Borough paying to send whalers to Point Courage to harvest the whales before they hit the oil?" he asks.

"Not great," Bertie says. "Why isn't Shant paying for it?"

"Well, you know, they didn't sign that agreement, the oil spill mitigation thing, and now I can't even get anyone on the phone. Time's running out—the whales'll probably be there in two days."

Bertie sighs. "It's a public purpose if ever there was one. The last chance for the Iñupiat to whale for who knows how long. Maybe the knowledge will be lost altogether by the time the ecosystem rehabilitates. Who knows what'll become of the whole whaling culture."

She looks at Gill, who seems near tears.

"I think," Bertie says carefully, "That I would advise the Borough to go ahead and cover the expenses, and then try to recover the costs from Shant."

"You mean, sue 'em?" Gill asks. "That's what Gloria said."

"If this mayor can't ..." Bertie starts to say, and then says, "Just go ahead and make the arrangements with purchase orders. It'll have to come out of the mayor's special project fund, and if that gets used up, then we'll have to make an appropriation from the permanent fund."

Gill nods silently. He almost feels like hugging Bertie, but he restrains himself.

Two days later, the power is back on, and Bertie is at the airport. Eight planes have been chartered to carry the whalers and their gear to Point Courage, and the airport is packed with whalers, wives, children, and elders. It's as if a legion of men is going off to war.

In the corner of the airport, the Fish and Wildlife agents stand silently studying their boarding passes. The Fairbanks office has told them to forget about enforcing the Migratory Bird Treaty Act for now. They can either stay and help haze the oiled animals, or come back to the office. Most of them have opted for the office.

Lisa stands next to her honey and Britney, who are going with Larry's crew. "This time I'm gonna get in the boat, Mom," Britney says. Lisa nods. She knows it might be Britney's first and last time.

Gloria stands with Gill, assuring him she'll take care of everything at the house while he's gone. She'll be alone for the first time in more than a year, and she feels relieved and guilty at the same time. Gill scoops up Gloria's toddler to kiss him goodbye. He shrieks and giggles and then cries when he's put down.

Mandy makes her way over to Bertie. "Hey there," she says.

"Oh, hi Mandy," Bertie says. "I haven't seen you since ..."

"The burial," Mandy says.

"I'm sorry," Bertie says.

Mandy sighs. "Well, it's all over now. I got to go on and do something with my life. I always been in his shadow."

"You're not leaving Harow, are you?" Bertie asked.

"Oh, no, no, I'm gonna keep working for the Borough until I retire. But not just as an office specialist. I went to college once, if you can believe it," she smiles.

"Why wouldn't I believe it?" Bertie asks.

"Maybe I'll apply to be the Borough Clerk. Or work in the Mayor's Office. We'll see."

Lisa sees Mandy and comes over to give her a hug. To escape the hugging, Bertie makes her rounds among the whalers, shaking hands and wishing them good luck. Many of them heard about her help with organizing this trip, and they're glad to shake her hand. This makes things a little easier for Bertie, since meeting and greeting sure isn't her forte. But she's going to have to get used to it. An hour ago, she went to the clerk's office and filed to run for mayor of the Arctic Slope Borough.

Bertie drives home from the airport, wondering whether her chances of success are any higher than the chance of Shant getting control over the blowout any time soon. The downsized Top Hat hasn't been able to seal off the blownout well, and the relief well drilling has only just begun. In an apparent act of desperation, Shant has hired experts from Norway to come over and assess the problem. The experts have advised Shant to forget about capping the well for now, and just focus on just capturing as much of the leak as possible.

Shant experts decide to use the original Top Hat as a battering ram to break the ruptured pipeline still attached to the well and get it out of the way. The plan is to install a riser, cobbled together out of spare pipes from Prudhoe Bay, to channel oil from the well to a tank on the surface.

At first the operation causes even more oil to gush out of the well. After two days, Shant is capturing 20,000 barrels a day through the riser, leaving only 10,000 barrels to flow into the sea. All day long, vessels carrying the oil make their way back to shore. But the vessels can't keep up with the rate of oil being collected, and Shant is forced to let some of it slide back into the sea.

In September, the Arctic begins to return to its familiar frozen state. The oil is weathering and freezing, the recovery equipment keeps choking up ice and stalling, and even the dispersants aren't doing much to make the oil go away. Recovery of the oil comes to a standstill. Whatever can't be recovered from the water now is just going to have to wait until next summer.

The oil mess means that Chuck's days as the Harow Native Corporation president are numbered. The infrastructure the company invested in for the port is either underwater or covered in oil, dead birds, and cleanup equipment. The corporation wasn't ready to deal with the oil spill, and the buck stopped with Chuck.

Chuck would love to say that he's resigning to spend more time with his family. He saw Gloria in the grocery store the other day, looking just as pregnant and pretty as she was on the day she left him. Except now she's walking around with a little boy—*his* boy.

The day after the whaling heroes go off to Point Courage, Chuck gives the corporation's board his letter of resignation. The letter explains that he's running for Borough mayor. Even if he's a recovering alcoholic dead-beat dad who's screwed things up at the corporation, Chuck is not an employee of the company that just caused the biggest oil spill since Exxon-Valdez. That would be former Mayor Ahgak, who's now running for a sixth term.

Ahgak's chances of getting elected are still pretty good. We know that Mayor Kitok's opposition to offshore drilling wasn't the only reason he beat Ahgak in the last election. Ahgak's father-in-law—Gill Whitehead's father—one of our most respected elders, went missing two days before the election. Everyone related to the Whiteheads, which is almost a third of Harow, was busy looking for or fretting about the old man. Gill and his brothers found the body a day later. In the meantime, none of the Whiteheads went to vote for Ahgak.

In previous campaigns, Ahgak plastered Harow with posters featuring him and Evan Hooper standing on the first whale caught after the quota was put in place. This year, neither Ahgak nor anyone else has put up signs.

"Guess he's running on his own recognizance this time," Chuck says to the Borough Clerk, when he sees Ahgak's name on the list of contenders.

The clerk ignores him. She's a Whitehead, and she instinctively dislikes Chuck.

"What's this—Bertie's running for mayor? Bertie? The Borough Attorney?"

"She don't have any dirt on her, that's one thing," the clerk says.

Chuck shrugs. The Iñupiat don't care about dirt.

Chuck isn't the only one surprised by Bertie's run. After recovering from his insulin crisis, Nelson comes down to the Law Department to offer the long shot candidate a little encouragement.

Bertie regards him nervously. "Feeling better, Nelson?" she asks.

"Well, I guess you're feeling lucky!" he says. "Running for mayor!"

"Yes I am," Bertie says tersely.

"I came to offer my services as Lieutenant Mayor, just in case you win."

"I appreciate that, Nelson."

"Your people must be proud of you."

Bertie turns back to her computer without responding and waits for Nelson to go away.

"On another subject," Nelson continues, "I hear you sent the whalers off to Point Courage to hunt while they still can. Sounds like a big bill's going to be coming the Borough's way."

"I guess the next mayor will have to deal with that, Nelson."

Nelson clears his throat. "So who would be your Borough Attorney, Vik?"

"She's been trying to resign since July," Bertie says. "I'd asked her if she wanted the position, but yesterday she told me she had to leave by next week, or Greenpeace would rescind its job offer to her."

Nelson guffaws. "Greenpeace?"

"It's actually a newly created attorney position in Greenpeace's Juneau office to deal with offshore drilling," Bertie says, feeling defensive on Vik's behalf.

"I see," Nelson says, with a vague smile. He wanders out of the Law Department without stopping in Vik's office.

Vik's already quit thinking about Nelson or Bertie or anything related to the Borough. She's ready to go. She leaves work early on her last day, hoping to escape one of Lisa's hugs or anything else that reeks of a dramatic goodbye. When she gets to her apartment, she decides to keep on going for one last walk along Beach Road.

The snow has begun to stick enough for snowmachines, and a couple roar past her as she walks. She sure isn't going to miss that noise. Or the sight of yards filled with junked cars, chained-up barking dogs, and the occasional large animal carcass.

The street ends in a lagoon, covered with a layer of ice that Vik doesn't trust enough to walk on. She turns right toward the tundra and makes her way around the lagoon. She's hardly ever walked out on the tundra in almost three years of living in Harow. It suddenly seems sad and beautiful—romantic, even—to be walking out on the tundra for the last time.

Some distance ahead, she sees what might be a polar bear. She walks toward it for a closer look, thinking about all the white people who go out with binoculars every weekend in the hopes of seeing a polar bear. As she gets closer, she sees that there are two bears, not fully grown, play-fighting with each other. She stands still and watches.

Snow begins to fall. The bears continue their tussle and another bear, maybe their mother, approaches. Vik hears a snowmachine behind her and hopes it won't scare the bears away. It doesn't seem to. The mother bear looks up, sees Vik, and lopes toward her.

Vik can't remember whether she's supposed to make a lot of noise, or just play dead. She feels a little silly doing either one. For all she knows, the bear is going after the snowmachine. Just to be safe, Vik decides to lie down in the snow and wait. She doesn't wait long. The blow comes a minute later, leaving her unconscious.

When she wakes up in a hospital, the nurse tells her she was medevacked there after the accident.

"What accident?" Vik asks. "The polar bear?"

The nurse snorts. "More like a Polaris 550." She hums "Grandma Got Run Over by a Reindeer" to herself as she sticks a thermometer under Vik's tongue. Vik wants to ask more, but she falls asleep before the nurse takes the thermometer out of her mouth.

When Vik opens her eyes next, Larry is sitting on the chair by her bed.

"Did the *imunarukit* get you?" Larry asks.

"What?" Vik asks.

"The mischief makers, the little people. They didn't get me. I left before anything worse could happen."

"What do you mean?"

"It's not just the *tanik's* fault," Larry says softly. "Or even the *imunaruk*. I guess there's a little destructive part of all of us that questions why we go on living the way we do."

Vik looks around the room, annoyed, and bellows, "I don't understand. First it was a polar bear, then a snow machine, and then the *imun*-little people? And now you—what are doing here?"

Larry reaches for Vik's hand and holds it. She calms down.

"I missed you," she says suddenly.

"Why are you leaving now?" Larry asks.

"You mean, going to Juneau?" Vik asks. "I got a job there. I think I did all I could in Harow—wrote a few permits, made some code changes, almost finished a novel ..."

Larry laughs. "Turning us into a story, are you?"

"Oh, no, no, we're all part of this story, it's not just a '*tanik* visits the Iñupiat' kind of thing."

"Who's 'we'?"

"I mean, everyone in Harow."

"You mean 'you.' You're the one telling the story. You should say, 'I,' not 'we.'"

Vik is quiet.

"Why don't you go back?" Larry asks. "Bertie's going to end up being mayor, I can tell you that much. And she's going to ask my wife to be lieutenant mayor."

"Wouldn't that be something," Vik says noncommittally.

"You'll see," Larry says. "Why don't you go back and head the Law Department? *We* need you."

"'You can make a *tanik* Iñupiaq if you let him work with you,' huh?" Vik says, quoting what Larry told her years before. "Then would it be okay for me to say, 'we'?"

Larry just squeezes her hand and holds it until Vik falls asleep.

Epilogue- All the Pieces

By the time Shant finally stops the blowout with a relief well, the oil has traveled far beneath the ice. A dead zone stretches across much of the Arctic Slope's 2000 miles of coastline. The plan is to resume cleanup in June 2011.

When the spring ice-break-up comes along, the oil is spread so thin that not much can be done other than to let it keep weathering. Still, Shant makes a pretext of continuing the cleanup. A couple of vessels cruise around the Beaufort and Chukchi Seas, sprinkling dispersants and taking samples in the hopes of demonstrating that something in the water is still alive.

All together, Shant has spent a little more than $2 billion on the cleanup. It's budgeted the same amount for the next federal lease sale of Beaufort and Chukchi Sea parcels, set for the spring of 2012.

The Arctic Slope Borough triumvirate—Mayor Bertie Bowman, Lieutenant Mayor Mandy Atkoot, and Borough Attorney Vik Alcazar, who recovered after being run over by a snowmachine—are filing a lawsuit against the federal government for approving the lease sale without taking the spill into account. They've also filed a lawsuit against Shant, hoping to force the company to take responsibility for ruining marine subsistence for the foreseeable future.

Winning a suit against Shant will not be easy. The Exxon Valdez litigation took twenty years. This case might take even longer. And even if the Borough wins, the whales might never come back.

One thing that will be coming is the deep sea port. The Army Corps took over the project as soon as the Harow Native Corporation abandoned it. All of the contaminated sand and gravel, along and whatever relics they might have held, have been excavated and hauled to the Lower 48. In its place is cement.

Bertie and Vik consider filing suit against the Army Corps for dynamiting the port without doing a complete Environmental Impact Statement, but decide that the suit would get nowhere. Honestly, there's not much more environmental damage to be done at this point. And they have to admit that, without the jobs created by the port construction, most of Harow would have packed up and left.

As it stands, a third of Harow's residents have moved to Anchorage or Fairbanks since the blowout. Some have gone even further. Nelson retired in obscurity in Washington State. Chuck moved to Jones Country, Mississippi, where he reconnected with his white family and started working for the Bok Homa Casino, run by what's left of the Choctaw Indians. After he was fired from the Borough for what could be the last time, Officer Shoak followed Chuck to Jones County and got a job as a traffic cop.

Gill stayed behind, and after being relieved of his job as Community Development Director, was appointed president of the Harow Native Corporation. Bertie and Vik blame him for dropping the ball on Shant's permits and the oil spill mitigation agreement. But the Iñupiat herald him as a hero for leading the only crew to catch any whales at Point Courage in the fall of 2010. He held a giant *nalukataq* out of season to distribute the meat, and all the families in Harow have little memorial pieces tucked away in their freezers.

Gloria had her baby around Thanksgiving and kept on living with Gill. Rumor has it that she's pregnant again.

More tourists have come to Harow since the spill than ever before.

"It's just like the post-Hurricane Katrina tourists," Vik says. "People coming to ogle at somebody else's trouble."

Locals with no money and high hopes for getting out sell the tourists any old knick-knack from the pre-blowout days. And the tourists will buy anything, even a dusty piece of baleen with a single line of scrimshaw, knowing that it'll be their last chance for the foreseeable future. Even though the whaling quota hasn't been officially reduced yet, the feds have put a freeze on all marine mammal hunting until the populations can recover.

On a Saturday, Lisa sits at a table just inside the grocery store with the walrus skull that her honey broke two years ago. The price tag she made for it says, "2900 dolars." A Texas woman who saw it yesterday has promised to come back today with all the money.

At lunch, Lisa goes over to the food court and gets a pizza. She'll be glad when the McDonald's franchise finally gets here, if it ever does. Most of the stuff from the food court gives her heartburn. She still has a jar of pickled *maktak* from two years ago, but she's saving it for something big, like the twin's graduation from high school.

The Texas woman comes back just as Lisa's biting into the pizza. She pulls out 29 hundred-dollar bills and counts them in front of Lisa. "I guess lots of Eskimos are moving away, huh?" she asks.

"Some people," Lisa says, looking at the walrus skull for the last time before wrapping it up. "I'm gonna stay as long as I can, though. My honey's outta work but I got trained to be a paralegal and we're working on all these lawsuits now."

The Texas woman sighs with pity. "Don't it just break your heart?"

"Yeah, but the pieces are all here."

Entities with Authority in Harow

Federal Government Agencies

Including the Fish and Wildlife Service, the Bureau of Indian Affairs, and the Army Corps of Engineers, the Federal Aviation Administration, and the Coast Guard

State Government Agencies

Including Alaska Troopers, Alaska Fish and Game Department, and the Alaska Labor Department

Arctic Slope Borough

Including the Mayor's Office, the Development Planning Commission, and the Departments of Law, Subsistence and Wildlife, Community Development, and Public Works

City of Harow

Including the City Council and Mayor

Tribal Entities

Iñupiat Community of the Arctic—regional tribal government
Alaska Eskimo Whalers Council—formed to regulate whaling
Native Village of Harow—village tribal government

Corporations

Northern Slope Regional Co.—regional native corporation
Harow Native Corporation—village native corporation

Other villages within the Borough include Winters, Kusoq, Ankvut, Point Courage, Point Latch, Atkuq, and Tovak. Each has its own mayor and city council, village tribal government, and village native corporation.

About the Author

Elizaveta Ristrova, author of *Small Fish in a Small Pond, Something Short of Salvation,* and *Taking Off My Sweater,* never tires of sticking her large nose into other people's cultures and lives. She is now pulling her nose out of Arctic Alaska and moving back to the tropics—this time the Philippines. Eventually she will return to her native Louisiana or another Third World setting with the delusion of getting a job as a tree-hugging lawyer.

ALL THINGS THAT MATTER PRESS ™

FOR MORE INFORMATION ON TITLES AVAILABLE FROM
ALL THINGS THAT MATTER PRESS, GO TO
http://allthingsthatmatterpress.com
or contact us at
allthingsthatmatterpress@gmail.com

www.ingramcontent.com/pod-product-compliance
Lightning Source LLC
LaVergne TN
LVHW020707110826
845149LV00012B/2137

* 9 7 8 0 9 8 4 6 5 1 7 5 7 *